Elizabeth Young started writing after a variety of jobs that included being part of an airline cabin crew, modelling for TV commercials in Cyprus and working for the Sultan's Armed Forces in Oman. She lives in Surrey. Her first novel, *Asking for Trouble*, was also published by Arrow to great acclaim.

*Praise for Elizabeth Young*

'Perfect comic timing and wickedly funny moments' *Cosmopolitan*

'Feel-good romance' *Marie Claire*

'A lively Lisa Jewell-esque debut novel with a bit more bite than you might imagine' *Mirror*

'A warm, sunny read that is as astute as it is humorous' *Good Housekeeping*

# FAIR GAME

## Elizabeth Young

ARROW

Published by Arrow Books in 2002

3 5 7 9 10 8 6 4

First published in the United Kingdom in 2001
by William Heinemann

Arrow Books Limited
Random House Group Ltd
20 Vauxhall Bridge Road, London, SW1V 2SA

Random House Australia (Pty) Ltd
18 Poland Road, Glenfield
Auckland 10, New Zealand

Random House (Pty) Limited
Endulini, 5a Jubilee Road, Parktown 2193, South Africa

The Random House Group Limited Reg. No. 954009
www.randomhouse.co.uk

A CIP catalogue record for this book is available from the
British Library

Papers used by Random House are natural, recyclable products made
from wood grown in sustainable forests. The manufacturing processes
conform to the environmental regulations of the country of origin

ISBN 0 09 941507 0

Typeset by Palimpsest Book Production Limited,
Polmont, Stirlingshire
Printed and bound in Germany by
Elsnerdruck, Berlin

# ACKNOWLEDGEMENTS

With special thanks to: the RNA, because I missed them out before; Lynne Drew and Anna Dalton-Knott at Heinemann, for cushioning the sharp end with kind words; Sarah Molloy at A. M. Heath, for her humour and for taking me on in the first place.

And with much love, as always, to A, P and W, for being my rocks, and to the O.W., for everything and for offering to come and hoover when deadlines were looming and my printer was playing up.

For my mother, with lots of love always, X.

# PROLOGUE

My sins caught up with me outside the deli, on one of those January afternoons we hardly ever get in London. It was arctic, ear-biting cold; the air smelt of coming snow.

Not that I cared; my personal central heating was on Dangerously High. Next door to the deli the travel agent's window was offering long-weekend cheapies to the Gambia, but even they couldn't tempt me. I was popping in for some fresh pasta when I almost collided with Rosie, coming out. 'Harriet! I was just on my way to see you! I hope you weren't after any of that tomatoey salady stuff, because I've just had the last of it.'

'No – why were you coming to see me?'

I don't know why I asked. Rosie was a lovely person but if she'd had a website the address would have been *don'ttellanyoneItoldyoubut.com*. She had round brown eyes, full of what I can only describe as guilty relish. 'I just *had* to tell you the latest in the Nina/Helicopter saga.'

Rosie, Nina and I had all been at school together. 'Helicopter' was what Rosie called Nina's ex, and since he *was* ex, and had been for about a week, I didn't quite follow. 'What do you mean, the latest? He dumped her!'

'Yes, but she was just a teensy bit put out, remember?'

I hadn't witnessed the scene but Rosie had heard about it and passed on every gruesome detail. Nina had ranted and screamed and demanded to know if there was someone else, and he'd said no, there wasn't, and she'd shrieked that he was a lying bastard, she knew he'd been seeing someone else, and who was she, the bitch?

'Of course, she never believed there *was*n't anybody else,' Rosie went on. 'So no prizes for guessing what she's been up to now.'

I have special sensory equipment for occasions like this: antennae finely tuned to pick up 'oh shit' situations. 'What?'

'She's put a private dick on to him!'

'*What*?'

'Yes, that's what I thought. Bit OTT, isn't it? It's not as if they were engaged or anything.'

Maybe the Gambia wasn't a bad idea, after all. 'Since when? Since when did she put the dick on him, I mean?'

'Since right after he dumped her. I mean, what's the use now? Except that she'll know who to make wax images of and stick pins into.'

Forget the Gambia – maybe a cheapie to Ulan Bator?

'It's costing a bomb but she said she had to know,' Rosie went on. 'The bloke said it might take a while to catch him at it – well, not exactly *at* it, perhaps, but *with* whoever she is.'

'They'll see him. Some furtive bloke in a grubby raincoat . . .'

'Oh, come on! He's a *pro*! Mega-zoom paparazzi lenses, you name it. I hope they keep their curtains drawn, that's all.'

They most certainly would.

'She's got a fair idea who it is, you know,' she went on. 'Some dopey blonde she sacked a few weeks back – mind you, Nina'd call any blonde dopey – she had to introduce them at some do and Dopey was eyeing him up even then. She's done it to get her own back, Nina says.'

I moistened my lips. 'How would she know? The girl's no dopier than the average, either.'

Rosie's eyes popped wide. 'Are you telling me you actually know her?'

'I do, actually,' I said. 'Intimately.'

'You're kidding!'

'I'm not. I've known her for as long as I can remember.'

'You're *kidd*ing! Why the hell didn't you tell me before?'

Actually, Rosie's not that thick. As she gaped at me I saw her brain furiously working back, going whirr whiz bang, and so on. When it finally went 'click' her eyes popped wider still, if such a thing were possible.

Just across the road was the Drunken Dragon. 'Fancy a drink?' I asked. 'You look as if you could do with it.'

Rosie found her voice. '*Me*? What about you? You do realize she's going to kill you?'

# ONE

I don't quite know why I said 'sins' back there. I never set out to pinch anyone's bloke, let alone Nina's. The day it all started, picking up a bloke was the last thing on my mind. Even I don't go out on the pull in manky old combats, a sweater that's seen better days, and hair sorely in need of Frizz-Ease.

All I was thinking of, that drizzly afternoon, was calling it a day and finding a cab home. Since it was early December I was laden with what was supposed to be highly organized Christmas shopping. I'd made a methodical list saying *Mum, Bill, Sally, Tom, Jacko . . .* so I could go round the shops briskly and efficiently ticking them all off.

With customary efficiency I'd only ticked off Tom. My bags were full of impulse buys for the house; having come late to the nesting bit I was making up for lost time. There were also two bottles of ready-mulled wine. I buy stuff like that when Christmas is coming and I need something to put me in the mood – the weather certainly wasn't. Mild and damp, it felt more like October.

Having started off in mist-like fashion, the drizzle had moved up a gear, as if it were thinking about turning to proper rain, instead. At this point I was just up the road from Covent Garden, with drizzled-on hair, arms coming out of their sockets, and a jumper starting to smell of wet Shetland sheep. That was when I saw Nina, coming out of some smart little restaurant, with a bloke on her arm.

If I can misquote Jane Austen here, it is a truth universally acknowledged that if you are fated to bump into someone like Nina when you haven't seen her for four years and don't particularly want to ever again, you'll be looking like a pig's break-fast.

While she'll be looking like, well, like Nina.

Like a *Sunday Times* fashion shoot of some taupey thing in silk and cashmere, a snip at only £799. That dark-haired bob as sleek and glossy as ever. A face like an airbrushed L'Oréal ad.

Only about six paces away, she was talking and laughing in her silver-tinkle way to the bloke, who was holding her umbrella up to stop her getting drizzled on.

If she'd seen me, and recognized me, she'd have been over before you could say 'sick as a pig', with a delighted smile (delighted to make me sick as a pig, I mean) and a '*Harry*! How *are* you!' Then there'd be a couple of *mwah-mwah* kisses, and a 'This is Gorgeous Bloke – Gorgeous Bloke, this is Harriet – we were at school together and I used to be terribly nice to her on the surface but laugh behind her back

6

because she had size eight feet and looked like a scarecrow.'

So before any such daymare actually occurred, I turned around and pretended to be riveted by a shop window. For maybe half a minute longer I heard tinkly laughter with stuff like, '. . . and don't you *dare* be late – tinkle tinkle,' a kissy noise, and the sound of a car door slamming.

Of course I'd never intended to lurk there, eavesdropping. I'd have been fifty yards back down the road by then, telling myself I was pathetic, when was I going to grow up, etc., if something in that window hadn't detained me. To be frank, it had given me a bit of a jolt. When you're hiding from the Ninas of this world you don't expect to find yourself gaping at a massive wooden willy.

No, it wasn't a sex shop; the window was full of ethnic art. And the pride of the display was a six-foot-ish twisty chunk of tree, carved into a misshapen man with a crown thing on his head and an outstretched hand with what looked like an egg in it. The carved whopper wasn't half as riveting as his face, though. It was such a powerful mix of noble suffering and raw masculinity, he looked like a primitive Jesus and fertility god combined. I was just searching for a price tag when someone beside me said, 'Different, isn't it?'

And lo, there he was. Standing quite casually about three feet away, hands shoved in his trouser pockets.

7

They were grey trousers, if you're interested: the bottom half of a quietly pricey suit. There was a black polo shirt, I think, only I wasn't really looking at his clothes.

It took me a second to get over the shock, but I said, casually enough, 'That's one way of putting it. I suppose you can't see a price tag?'

He peered a bit closer, straightened up, and turned to me. 'Fifteen hundred quid.'

And I took my first, proper, full-face look.

My first thought was: well, might have known, just the sort of bloke I'd expect to see attached to Nina, followed swiftly by: on the other hand, maybe not.

The last time I'd seen her (at a wedding four years back) she'd had some tall, dark specimen in tow, of the type generally described as classically good-looking, with an eligibility rating of eleven and a half out of ten. I say 'generally' because although everything about him was theoretically perfect, personally I hadn't been particularly impressed. OK, maybe it was sour grapes, but to me he'd seemed just a bit *plastic*, somehow. It had been quite a boost to my ego to realize I didn't actually fancy him, especially when everybody else was saying, 'Trust Nina to get a bloke like that.'

I don't quite know what it was with this one – he wasn't classically good-looking, exactly, but there was definitely no plastic and the spark hit me at once. His eyes were greeny-blue, his hair the colour of old, polished oak. He was taller than me by half a head (and I'm five foot nine) and marginally heftier than is currently fashionable.

I said, 'Oh, well, I suppose it's a bit steep for a cat-scratching post,' and he laughed.

Well.

His spark had practically turned into a fire hazard, most of it coming from those greeny-blue eyes. For some reason I thought of those corny old films in which the hapless Lady Arabella's carriage is held up on the Great North Road. '*I will never part with my jewels!*' she says hotly to the horrid, rough-looking fellow in the mask. '*I would sooner part with my virtue!*' And the rough-looking fellow drawls, '*Then I will have your virtue, my lady,*' and she suddenly sees the wicked glint in the eyes behind the mask, and thinks, '*Well, actually . . .*'

Thinking, trust bloody Nina to get a bloke like this, I said hastily, 'Well, better hit the road, if I can find a cab,' and readjusted my shopping. In addition to five carrier bags, my bag was slung over my shoulder, and I suddenly realized the zip was open and my purse wasn't in it.

If you've never done anything so stupid as to leave your bag open when you've just been shoving your way through Christmas-shopping crushes you won't know the feeling, so I'll tell you. I went all cold and frozen and gaped at my bag. I said, 'My purse has gone,' like an idiot, and he said, 'Christ – are you sure?' and I hunted through my bag again, as you do, but I knew it wasn't there.

I said, 'Yes, God, what a *fool* – there wasn't much cash, but all the other stuff . . .'

He said, 'When did you last have it?' and I thought back, and realized it was twenty minutes ago, in some shop called Expensive Useless Stuff That Seems Like A Good Idea At The Time.

Twenty minutes! The thieving scum could have bought himself three Paul Smith suits by now. In a frozen panic I said, 'My credit cards – I must ring and cancel them . . . God, I didn't even bring my mobile . . .'

'Use mine, then. And let's get out of this weather.' In the relative shelter of the shop doorway, he handed me his mobile.

Of course I hadn't a clue what numbers to ring, so I phoned Sally at home, asked her to dig out credit-card statements and cancel for me. Then I said, 'If Jacko's in, ask him how much cash he's got. I'm laden with shopping – I want to bum a cab fare.'

'He's just gone out, wouldn't you know it. And I've only got about six quid.'

'Never mind. See you later.'

I handed the phone back. 'Thanks so much. If I had any money, I'd buy you a drink.' I only said this as a throwaway line because I'd just noticed a little wine bar two doors away. I certainly wasn't expecting the reply I got.

10

'Look, I can let you have a cab fare.'

I was appalled. If he thought I'd been dropping hints . . . 'No, really, I don't need a cab.' From the thigh pocket of my tatty old combats, I dug out my One-Day Travelcard. 'See? I'll take the tube.'

He glanced down at all my bags. 'With that lot? How far have you got to go?'

'Putney, but it won't kill me.'

'Christ, that's miles!' Almost before I'd blinked he'd whipped his wallet out and extracted a couple of notes.

I gaped at the proffered thirty quid. 'Look, it's very kind of you, but I really couldn't.'

'Why not?' He sort of smiled and added, 'It's Christmas.'

And I sort of looked at him, and he looked back at me, and I thought: God, it's not *fair* – I could fancy you rotten. But since I hadn't fancied anyone even half rotten for months, I decided I might as well make the most of it. Waste not, want not, as my Great-Aunt Dorothy used to say when she was saving the oval tops off Kleenex boxes. (Handy for shopping lists, you see.)

Besides which, a cab beat the tube any day, especially with four tons of shopping and a ten-minute walk the other end. 'I'll only take it if you let me pay you back. Give me your address and I'll send you a cheque.'

'It's really not necessary.'

Great. I could see I'd put the wind up him. If you

dished out your address to drizzled-on messes, they might turn up on your doorstep.

'But you could maybe buy me that drink some-time.'

*Er, sorry?* I waited for him to grin, 'Only kidding – my girlfriend would kill me,' but there was just a raised eyebrow and a little half-smile.

Well, I can be as cool as the next drizzled-on mess. 'Do you actually know anywhere that does thirty-quid drinks?'

'A couple of drinks, then.' The smile turned into three-quarters. 'And a packet of pork scratchings?'

I have to say, a wicked little *frisson* went through me. All I could think was: God, if Nina could see this, she'd go ape. 'Give me your number, then, and I'll give you a call.' I scrabbled in my bag for my organizer, only I was so organized I'd left it at home. All I could find was a Tesco's receipt, so I gave him that.

It was while he was scribbling that I went all frozen again. In fact, I felt as if I'd just been nicked for criminal deception. Because in a sudden flash I knew exactly where my purse was.

I'd bought a cast-iron warthog in that Expensive Useless shop (because he looked cute and it seemed like a good idea at the time) but after paying I'd ended up with my hands full of shopping and my purse tucked under my arm. And because I couldn't be bothered to put all those bags down again and put

12

my purse away properly, I'd let it drop in a carefully aimed manner into the Expensive Useless carrier bag, with the warthog.

Only just as he'd stopped scribbling, and I was about to open my mouth to tell him, he opened his first.

'Right, let's find you a cab – before this rain really gets going.' And sod's law being what it is, one hove into view even as he uttered this, while I was still trying to work up to telling him my purse was cuddling up to a warthog.

Two seconds later he'd not only grabbed the cab but put that thirty quid and the receipt into my hand, and I just didn't know how to come clean. I'll admit I didn't altogether want to, either. He might have put me down as a worrying case of pre-senile dementia.

In any case, there wasn't time. The taxi driver was saying, 'Where to, love?' the rain was beginning to show downpour ambitions, and my saviour was getting wetter by the minute. All I said was, 'Thanks again – bye bye.'

'Bye.'

I waved, and once he was out of sight peered sheepishly into the Expensive Useless carrier bag. There it was, battered brown calf, saying, are you mad, or what? Credit cards cancelled all for nothing, all that hassle, just for a ride home and a drink with a bloke of Nina's?

Sally said much the same, moments after I was in

the door. 'You dope! After I'd gone mad unearthing Visa numbers, too.'

However, I hadn't got to the best bit. Once we were in the kitchen I tipped one of those bottles of mulled wine into a pan. 'Remember Rosie? Ex-school Rosie who came round the other week?'

'Yes, she was nice. She had two helpings of my gone-wrong veggie lasagne and pretended it was lovely.'

'Well, she was talking about someone called Nina, remember?'

'You were both talking about her. She always had everything, except spots and bad-hair days, and you both loved her to bits.'

OK, I'll admit we were having a little bitch.

'What about her, anyway?' she went on.

I turned just enough to see her face. It was almost an act of charity to drop such morsels in Sally's lap. She got so few lately, except courtesy of TV soaps. 'Her bloke just gave me his phone number.'

A couple of minutes later, after I'd related every juicy detail, she said, 'So what's his name?'

I realized I hadn't a clue.

'Had a good day, dear?' said Sally, when I made it home two days later after my nightly game of District Line Sardines. 'It's been so exciting here, I can't tell you. The milkman said would we like a free bottle of apple juice to try and there were terrible ructions on

*Home and Away* – I needed a good strong cup of PG to settle my nerves.'

Sally was 'unwaged', as they like to put it, and had been for months. She didn't feel any more brain-dead or useless than the rest of us, but was sensitive about other people thinking she was brain-dead and useless.

While spooning coffee into the filter I started telling her about my day, to perk her up. I left out anything to do with work, however, especially the bit about making a fat commission on an IT placement, as it would only make her feel more financially challenged than she already was. 'I gave Rosie a call this morning and we met for a sandwich. I told her about Mr Cab Fare and she's met him.'

Sally's green eyes widened instantly. 'And?'

'At least, I suppose it's him,' I went on. 'Nina's been seeing him for a couple of months and thinks he's the *cojones del perro.*' This had a more sophisticated ring than 'the dog's bollocks'; we'd used it almost since we'd met, which was eight years ago now, on a bus from Malaga airport.

Having clicked immediately, Sally and I had never seriously unclicked since. She could be unbelievably pig-headed but so could I, so I didn't hold that against her. We'd had masses in common. Both heading for English-teaching jobs in Granada, we were also both recent graduates with no idea what we wanted to do, except that we didn't want to do it in England, and

15

both thought teaching English would be a brilliant way to travel and get paid at the same time.

We'd soon discovered even more similarities. Both only children, we had the kind of parents who'd made tutting noises about offspring who were putting off getting 'proper' jobs. Why hadn't we applied for a graduate traineeship with Price Waterhouse, like Louise Bradshaw down the road (*'That girl'll go right to the top, you see if she doesn't'*) who'd always kept her bedroom tidy, too.

Actually it was my mother who'd said stuff like this. Dad had said, 'Do what you want – I wish I had,' and slipped me a cheque, bless him.

I'd done the TEFL bit for five years, since when I'd had more jobs than you could shake a P45 at. Frequently I'd had two at once, while frantically saving for six weeks' scuba-diving in Sulawesi or whatever.

Back to Nina and Mr Cab Fare, though. Rosie had met him at Nina's flat-warming only last week, having been dragged there by Suzanne, another old contemporary from school. Having only recently moved to London, Rosie was staying with her on a temporary basis while Suzanne's co-sharer was 'doing' India.

Rosie had talked about Nina's do all through our lunch. 'She was up to here with Nina even before they went,' I told Sally. 'Even Suzanne was, and she's supposed to be best buddies with Nina. Nina had been swanking on about this bloke's five-star gorgeousness, his corporate high-flying-ness and all that. She'd even chucked in a snippet about some flight the other week being forty minutes late, which would have been a disaster had it not been for his personal helicopter waiting to whisk him off to an urgent meeting with God.'

'Well, I suppose God gets a bit hacked off if people are late.'

'Sally, you've missed the *point*,' I said patiently. 'God was about to get a right old bollocking about getting his act together and running a more cost-efficient universe.'

'Oh, right.' Sally poured two coffees and came to join me at the battered pine table. It was antique and might have been worth a bit if not riddled with squillions of worm holes.

'Even Suzanne was browned off with all this helicopter swank,' I went on. 'So by the time they left for Nina's do, Rosie was hoping this Helicopter'd turn out to be a pompous prat, at least.'

'Can't blame her.' Sally rubbed at what looked like dried sick down the front of a grey sweatshirt. It was one of Jacko's cast-offs and already manky, quite apart from having LIVERPOOL FC emblazoned on the front. She had exhausted circles under her eyes and her chin-length, natural blonde hair had that mind-of-its-own look, telling me she'd let it dry itself again.

'But she had to admit that he was at least four-star

17

gorgeous and seemed really nice, too,' I continued. 'Not only that, but the flat was a state-of-the-art loft conversion with acres of blond wood floors, and the goats' cheese tartlets were ambrosial. In short, there was nothing to pick even a minor, bitchy little hole in. Rosie said it was enough to take away all your faith in natural justice. She had to have two helpings of tiramisu to cheer herself up.'

'And this helicopter bloke's the one who gave you his phone number?'

'Looks like it, doesn't it?'

'So what's his name?'

'John,' I said, tasting it on the way out. 'I rather like "John". Conjures up a sort of what-you-see-is-what-you-get nice-bloke-ish-ness.'

'Harriet, nice-bloke-ish-ness doesn't exactly tie in with kissing your girlfriend goodbye and chatting up someone else the minute she's gone.'

'You could hardly call it a chat-up. I've got a horrible feeling he *was* just being a nice bloke. Sort of humouring me. He wasn't bothered about the money, but he didn't want me feeling bad about taking it. Anyway, I was looking like a pig's breakfast.'

'OK, but if she's always that perfect, maybe he's sick of perfection.'

This was a gratifying notion and I won't pretend it hadn't occurred to me already.

'Or maybe he just likes pigs' breakfasts,' she added.

18

Great. She'd be saying maybe he fancied a bit of rough, next.

'Especially if they've got legs up to their tonsils,' she went on. 'But are you sure your bloke *is* Helicopter? Maybe he and Nina are just old mates.'

Before talking to Rosie, I'd been exploring this minute possibility, too. And not only 'old mates' but 'old exes', fourteenth cousins twice removed – anything that would mean he was potentially available.

But even without the evidence of my own eyes, everything Rosie had told me fitted. 'Sally, I think I know "old mate" behaviour when I see it. She was all tinkly and flirty like she always was, and Rosie said she's obviously obsessed with him. When she wasn't hanging onto him at that do she was watching him like a hawk, in case anyone else got ideas.'

Sally fetched the jug and poured me another coffee. 'So when are you going to phone him? You are *going* to phone him?'

'Of course! There's the little matter of that thirty quid, isn't there?' There was also a weird little flutter in my stomach. It was a cocktail of guilt and that *frisson* you get when you're even thinking about a brand new object of prime fanciability. Which explains the guilt, of course, because he was Nina's object of PF, damn it.

'I wish someone'd give me thirty quid,' she grumbled. 'There's some mail for you, by the way.' From the debris at the end of the table she retrieved a small pile.

There were two credit-card statements, which I didn't open, and five Christmas cards, which I did. The first four were from Mum and an assortment of my widely scattered friends. It was the fifth that gave me a jolt.

I gaped at Sally. 'Nina's sent me a Christmas card! Rosie must have got pissed enough to give her my address.'

The card was a glossy, fine-art thing. Inside was written, in arty, flamboyant script, 'Much love, Nina.'

I was seriously spooked, I don't mind admitting it. The last card I'd had from her, about four years back, had included one of those round-robin photocopies that ought to be banned on the grounds that they arouse unseasonal feelings of loathing for the sender. You know the kind of thing: *'Hi, fans! Yes, it's me – I'm far too busy to write to you individually, but I'm sure you'll all be thrilled to know my life is even more stunningly successful and deliriously happy than it was a year ago.'* I mean, you absolutely never get one of these that says the sender's been made redundant, her bloke's been banged up for GBH, and she's lost all her hair from the stress. A letter like that might just cheer you up a bit, if it was from Nina.

This time, however, she'd added a paragraph. 'I saw Rosie the other week at my flat-warming. I gather you're only a couple of miles up the road – maybe I'll pop in sometime!'

I thought, God, I hope not, she'd be sure to pop in on a Sunday morning when the place was a complete tip.

I showed Sally. '"Much love"! It's a bit weird, when we were never even third-best friends.'

'Some people send much gushy love to everybody,' Sally yawned. 'It's a good old Christmas tradition, like rowing with your entire family and pretending you like Brussels sprouts.'

Talking of family . . . I re-read the card from my mother, who was no longer married to my father. Under 'Lots of love, Mum and Bill,' she'd written, 'I do understand about Christmas, but I'm sure Sally's parents will be very hurt if she doesn't go home, even if they don't show it. If you change your mind we'll be very pleased to see you, of course.'

I handed this to Sally too.

'Why does everybody have to make me feel guilty?' she groaned. 'OK, they might be a bit hurt but they'll be relieved, too, even if they won't admit it. All their loathsome friends'll be popping in and out non-stop for drinks; I'll just be rubbing their noses in it.'

Sally's relationship with her folks had been a mite strained since the minor bombshell she'd dropped in May. I should explain here that Sally's parents are somewhat 'proper'; having married late they'd produced Sally when they'd just about given up.

In fact a much less 'proper' aunt had once confided to Sally that she thought they'd never quite got to grips with that messy conjugal stuff in the first place. She'd said something like, 'If you ask me, they were on the point of saying, "Well, we tried," and ordering single beds. They met through bridge and married for bridge – Penelope always said if you find a good bridge partner, you hang onto him.'

Back to that bombshell, though. Unlike me, Sally had continued to capitalize on the global English explosion and was by then working in Muscat on the Arabian Gulf. Home on leave for a couple of weeks, she'd been staying with me, trawling the London shops for new summer stuff to take back and trying it all on in my bedroom.

It was the black bikini that did it.

With a frown she'd said, 'Maybe I should get a couple of one-pieces. I know I've never exactly had a wasp waist, but I'm getting positively lumpy around the middle. Look at this!'

I'd seen only a marginally thickened version of the usual Sally. She had one of those figures they call apple-shaped – lovely slim legs, but a bit of a tummy she was endlessly wittering on about. I was about to make my usual soothing noises when she'd added, 'Anyone would think I was pregnant!'

'I almost wish you were,' I'd retorted. 'Then at least you'd really have a massive gut to bitch about.'

'It's not funny! I could hardly do my jeans up yesterday! My tits have got bigger, too!'

'I wish mine would,' I'd grumbled, until I'd seen her face. It had gone all weird and frozen.

And suddenly, so had mine.

In a weird, frozen voice she'd said, 'They were tingling the other day, too – is that a sign?' Putting her hands to her stomach, she'd said in a panic 'I *can't* be. Please, let me wake up . . .'

She'd gone on hoping to wake up until four and a half months later, when eight-pound Tom put in an appearance. The clinic had said it was nothing unusual to overlook the signs, especially when your usual signs were highly erratic anyway, but if she was going for a coil again added precautions might be a good idea.

She'd known at once who the proud daddy was: a certain Steve she'd met at an overnight beach party on Bandar Khayam, a little island half an hour by speedboat from Muscat Yacht Club. I know this because I'd been a reveller at that party, too. My feet had been itching badly at the time, so I'd got a cheap ticket and invited myself to stay with Sally for a fortnight.

There had been around twenty of us at that beach party, and the lethal setting had nothing to do with the bar some joker had erected on the beach out of a few bits of plywood and his kitchen curtains. The stars were like diamonds on black velvet, the sea lit with silvery phosphorescence. As Sally had said, when you've just met someone you fancy rotten it certainly beat Bognor, and who could sleep anyway, on a beach towel with hermit crabs crawling over you half the night? The thought of sharks had only increased the buzz as they'd swum round the rocks to a secluded little beach in the small hours.

This Steve had not been one of her usual crowd. Working in Singapore, he'd been on an en route visit to friends of Sally's. Barely twelve hours after their little twosome (once in the sand, once in the sea) he'd carried on to Singapore and the wife he'd somehow forgotten to tell her about. Sally had only given her folks the blunt details a couple of months ago, when they'd demanded for the thirty-eighth time that she contact the father and make him 'face up to his responsibilities'.

Catatonic shock had ensued. 'You'd known him *how* long?'

Going back to Muscat had been out of the question, as expat single mothers in Muslim countries can be a mite embarrassing to the institution that arranged their visas. After spinning them some line about 'family problems' she'd stayed with me from then on. Nobody in Muscat even knew about the baby, let alone who the father was.

Tom was now six months old, with Father Christmas scheduled to make his first visit down a London chimney, rather than his grandparents' one in Chester.

Apart from Sally and Tom, the other residents of our house these days were Frida, a Swedish girl who was hardly ever in, Jacko, who usually was, and Widdles, a geriatric cat of dubious personal hygiene.

'Where's Jacko?' I asked.

'God knows. He had a physio appointment at three, so he's probably crawling home via half a dozen pubs.'

Just as she said it a faraway bang announced the front door. Seconds later the kitchen door opened and Jacko hobbled in.

Sally said, 'Shut the door, Ape-Face, it's blowing a gale from the hall.'

He gave the door a whack-bang with his crutch and flopped noisily into a chair at the kitchen table. He had short, sandy-brown hair, non-designer stubble to match, and a Scouse accent that had been thicker than Cilla's when I'd first met him, although he'd toned it down now. We'd both been nineteen then, sharing a grotty student house with five others. At the time he'd been the most outrageous, foul-mouthed and instantly likeable boy I'd ever met. He'd inhabited one of my best soft spots ever since.

'How's the itching?' I asked, looking at his right leg which was in plaster.

'Murder,' he said pathetically, turning hazel eyes on me. They were quite nice when he'd had a full complement of sleep. 'I'm dehydrated from drinking myself to death last night, to get some sleep.

Harry, my angel, for fuck's sake stick that kettle on, would you?'

I obliged, if only because of said plaster and an arm that was similarly recovering from a fair old mashing. Jacko was still based in Liverpool but since I'd been in London he'd come down often, usually for some football match. On the last occasion, ten minutes after leaving, he'd collided with a joyrider. It had been the umpteenth accident of his driving life and by far the worst, but one of the few that wasn't his fault. He'd been in hospital for three weeks; his mother had stayed with me much of the time and been constantly frantic. Once he'd been discharged she'd been desperate to get him home. Not to his own place but back to the nest, so she could fuss him to death.

Still too weak and wobbly to manage alone, Jacko had nevertheless amazed me by putting his foot down. He told her he wanted to stay if I'd have him, and would go for his follow-up to the hospital that had sorted him out. Sorry, Mum, but her fussing would do his head in.

While I made him a cup of tea, Jacko was inspecting my mail. 'Who's Nina, then?'

'An old friend she can't stand,' Sally said. 'Her bloke tried to pick Harry up on Saturday – even gave her his phone number.'

He put on his hurt-puppy look. 'You never told me!'

'I was looking like nothing on earth! It wasn't *exactly* a pick-up, either.' I explained briefly, playing it right down.

'Why can't you stand this Nina, then?'

'She was a little cow,' Sally said.

You will gather that I'd been having another quiet bitch about Nina. 'That's a slight exaggeration. She just used to make me feel like one of those *Blue Peter* things built from bog-roll tubes that's supposed to be a dinosaur, but just looks like bog-roll tubes falling apart.'

'Why?' he asked.

Well, if he really wanted to know . . . 'Because she was five foot five and perfect, with silk-curtain hair and size three feet. And I was all awkward and gangly, with a mouth full of braces and feet I hadn't grown into, tripping over everything and blushing like the Revenge of the Killer Tomato and feeling a prat. And even when I was past the killer-tomato stage, she *still* made me feel like a bog-roll dinosaur, OK?'

'Plus she was a little cow,' Sally said. 'One of those little cows who pretend they're not, which is even worse.'

'How can you tell, then?' he demanded.

I was wishing Sally had kept her mouth shut. Blokes never understood these things – at that age they simply thump each other. 'You just can. They give you sweetly patronizing smiles and say, "Oh, your hair looks really nice," but the second your back's turned you know they're saying, "My God, her *hair*!" and cracking up.'

'What's wrong with your hair?' he asked, as if he'd only just noticed it after ten years, which wouldn't have surprised me.

'Nothing,' I said. 'I've come to terms with it.' It was just fine if you liked bunny-coloured clouds, but it'd never, ever shine, no matter how much I spent on hot-oil conditioners.

Apparently satisfied, he went back to inspecting my mail. 'So are you two off home for your turkey after all?' he added, scanning Mum's card.

'No way – I'm staying put,' Sally said. 'But I wish Harriet would. Her mother's going to blame me for depriving her.'

'She won't,' I said. 'She'll be too busy to miss me and I'm not sure I can face those kids again, anyway.' I got on fine with Mum now, though all had not invariably been pink and cosy in earlier years. Bill was great, too, and the picture-postcard Devon longhouse was lovely, but it would also be full of Bill's son, plus son's wife and three kids, two of whom were whiny little pains. After a couple of weekends in their company I wasn't sure I could stand a repeat without Prozac.

'Maybe I'll stay too, then,' he said. 'The mistletoe between two prickly bits of holly, scattering little baby sunbeams when you're fighting over what crappy Christmas telly to watch.'

'God help us,' said Sally.

As Frida had already booked her ticket home, I'd been hoping he'd stay. He'd be gone for good soon enough, and more was always merrier. 'Won't your folks be put out if you don't go home?'

'Probably, but you don't know Christmas in our house – Auntie X bitching about what Auntie Y said thirty years ago, Granddad snoring with his mouth open, and Uncle Dick putting a grape in it for a laugh and nearly choking him to death, and Mum wishing she and Dad could just piss off to Barbados for once.'

'Then why don't they?' Sally asked. 'They're not exactly skint.'

'They're going in February,' he said. 'So they have to suffer first. It's the rules.'

Just as he said it, a faint whimpering came from the baby alarm on the sideboard. 'Oh, God, not *again*,' Sally groaned, heaving herself to the door.

'She's knackered,' Jacko said, as she departed.

'She's been knackered for a week.' Tom wasn't usually so exhausting but he was teething on top of a bad cold; poor Sally had hardly slept for several nights.

Jacko was rereading Nina's card. 'So you're going to see this bloke of hers?'

'It's not exactly "seeing", is it? Just a little thank-you drink.'

'Sounds like "seeing" to me. Speaking from the

enemy camp, I can tell you that dishing out emergency dosh is one thing. Dishing out phone numbers is something else.'

'Jacko, he was just being nice.' I said this largely to fool Fate, who was bound to be listening. Privately I was wallowing in the piquant possibility that he wasn't just being 'nice'. Even more piquant was the off-chance that he was also, after all, a fourteenth cousin of Nina's who had a phobia about silk-curtain hair.

I started tidying up, though the kitchen never looked tidy even when it was. The house was one of those six-bedroomed Edwardian jobs that fetch bombs when done up, and lesser bombs even when they're not. This still possessed 'a wealth of original features', including prehistoric chain-pull loo and built-in, wall-to-wall draughts. It had been the family home of my father's old Auntie Dorothy, who'd spent virtually nothing on it since circa 1937, unless you counted a brief mad impulse circa 1962, courtesy of the kind of builders who love old ladies on toast for breakfast. Besides what passed for central heating, they'd knocked an old-fashioned pantry and scullery into the breakfast room to make a big kitchen, and added a few 'modern' units. These had been falling to bits ever since, which was why three of the cupboards had possessed no doors for fifteen years.

Poor old Dorothy was still there, tucked up in an urn on the dining-room mantelpiece. I felt bad leaving her there, especially as she'd left half the house to me, but she was waiting to be scattered off a particular cliff in Dorset. Only Dad knew where it was and he was in Turkey, according to the latest phone call.

Sally came back, with Tom on her hip. He was pale, poor little sausage, but he gave us a dribbly grin. 'Hi, stinker,' I said. 'Keep Mummy at it, there's a good boy.'

Jacko said, 'Start the way you mean to go on, mate. Treat 'em mean. And when you've got it sussed, give your Uncle Jacko a few pointers.'

Sally shifted a pile of washing, flopped onto the sofa, and yanked up her sweatshirt to give Tom his comfort food. I'd made the kitchen into a living room with a Tulley's sofa (it's amazing what you can find in charity shops) and a 14″ all-in-one TV and video on the sideboard. Since October we'd hardly used the sitting room, because although it would soon be described by estate agents as an 'elegant and well-proportioned drawing room', it was perhaps best suited to de-frosting a chicken over six weeks or so. It contained the only truly modern item Dorothy had ever lashed out on: a massive Sony television, as her main pleasure in life had been the racing and her eyesight had been getting dodgy.

As always when Sally was feeding Tom, Jacko watched in unashamed fascination. If any other bloke had been gawping like that, Sally would have uttered a tart 'Have you never seen boobs before?' or at least felt uncomfortable. With Jacko it was impossible to feel uncomfortable; even in his worst excesses there'd always been a certain disarming innocence about him.

Tom soon drifted off, and Sally crept away to put him down.

'It's enough to make you wish you were six months old again,' Jacko sighed, after the door had shut behind her. 'Trouble is, at that age you don't appreciate what you're getting. Life's so sodding perverse.'

As this was normal rambling, rather than new and original thought, I made no comment.

He then picked up Nina's card again. 'My bog-roll dinosaurs always fell to bits, too. Or was it egg boxes? I once made a really great stegosaurus out of egg boxes.'

My mind was elsewhere.

'So when are you going to phone this bloke?' he went on.

This was where my mind had been, of course. Saying, 'Just get on and *do* it, Harriet. Nice bloke, fourteenth cousin or even wrong number on purpose, there's only one way to find out.'

# Two

'Now,' I said. 'Might as well get it out of the way.' Which sounded nicely casual, I thought, as I delved in my bag for mobile and receipt. Not even Fate would realize I suddenly had a stomach full of baby pterodactyls.

My call was answered almost at once with a crisp 'Hello?'

'Oh, hello – I do hope I'm talking to the right person – did you give me a cab fare on Saturday?'

He laughed. 'Yes. And I don't even know your name.'

Phew. 'It's Harriet – hideous, isn't it? Most of my friends call me Harry. Or Aitch.'

'I don't think it's hideous.'

'Well, neither do I any more, though I used to think it akin to child abuse.'

'At least it's not boring. Mine's the most boring name in the book.'

'I'm sure I couldn't guess,' I lied.

'I bet you could. It's John.'

Shit.

It was sod's law, wasn't it? Sod's law Section V, sub-section iii(a):

'When you haven't particularly fancied anyone in ages it follows that when you do, the object of fanciability will not only be involved with someone else, but that someone else will be the person who always had everything you previously coveted, inc. one of those leather skirts you begged your mother to buy, but she said certainly not, they were tarty. (See also sub-section iii (c): "People who get new Suzuki Jeeps for their 17th birthdays.")'

But I just said, 'John's hardly common any more. After all the Dans and Lukes, it's supposed to be an endangered species.'

'I'll take your word for it.'

Even his voice sent a buzzy little tingle through me. Now it was disembodied, so to speak, it made me think of that melted dark chocolate you pour over profiteroles, and lick off the plate when nobody's looking.

Not that I let it show. 'It's payback time, remember? Drinks and pork scratchings, if you're still up for them. Or I'll send you that cheque after all – I promise it won't bounce.'

'I think I'll go for the drinks.'

Just like that? Was Fate taking a sickie or something?

'Unless you're tied up and it's going to be a pain,' he went on.

Well, yes, it was going to be a colossal pain, fitting a bloke like him into my hectic social round. 'Hang on, I'll just check my diary . . .' For authentic sound effects

I actually flicked through a few organizer pages, dotted with rivcting stuff like 'Vet – 6.15'. 'IIow about Thursday evening?'

'Sorry, I can't do Thursday.'

Dammit. Already I was imagining three more regretful 'sorrys', whereupon I'd offer that cheque again and he'd say, 'No, have it on me, take care.' And then he'd say to Nina, 'I think I wriggled out of that one with commendable skill, darling.'

Might as well make it easy for him. 'Pre-Christmas is a nightmare, isn't it? One do after another. I could manage an hour on Friday, seven-thirty-ish.'

'Yes, I can do Friday.'

This surely couldn't be right, either. Even my *Evening Standard* stars had been crappier than usual.

'Where would suit you?' he went on.

I hadn't even thought that far. 'Er, how about that little wine bar? The one near old Wooden Wally?'

'Fine. See you there, then.'

I hung up feeling nonplussed, in a guiltily chuffed sort of way. 'Well, that's a turn-up,' I said to Jacko, in a beautifully casual manner. 'I never thought he really meant it. I was looking like something Widdles dragged in.'

'Yes, my angel, but beneath the old tat he saw this vision of ineffable gorgeousness.'

Much more of this and I'd make him another cup of tea and a fried-egg sandwich, too. It wasn't often that Jacko got all poetic.

'Plus he could tell a mile off you fancied him,' he grinned.

'Who said I fancied him?'

'Oh, come on, Harry. I could see it in your face. It went all pink and girly.'

'My face never goes pink and girly!'

'OK, but I could see it. I could hear it in your *voice*, for fuck's sake. You'd never have taken the money in the first place if you didn't fancy him.'

Unfortunately there was no arguing with this.

'Sounds like he's a bit of a naughty boy,' he went on, in his stand-up-comic-innuendo voice. 'Because if he's seeing this non-mate of yours, and he's trying to get *you* out on the side –'

'It's just a drink, for God's sake.'

'Yeah, well, he sounds like a right smootharse to me.'

'He gave me thirty quid!'

'He's planning on giving you another little something, if you ask me.'

'Oh, grow *up*!'

Now, I really liked Jacko. I'd almost go so far as to say he was the brother I'd never had. We'd shared more than grotty student houses, like a trip to India, and when you've been through terminal Delhi belly together and stood guard for each other in the bushes, levels of intimacy don't get much greater. However, like real brothers, Jacko frequently made me want to

36

thump him, and there was no denying he had some deplorably laddish tendencies.

'Every bloke isn't like you,' I added acidly.

'No,' said Sally, who'd just come back. 'Some of them are possibly even marginally worse.' With a massive yawn she flopped back onto the sofa. 'If I don't get a good night's sleep soon, I'll die. I'm beginning to see distinct advantages in being dead. At least you're not woken up as soon as you've nodded off.'

'I'd get up and see to him, if you'd let me,' I said.

'It wouldn't be any use – the only thing that sends him off is me. I wish to God he'd take a dummy but he just spits it out.'

'Can't blame him,' said Jacko. 'That little lad's got taste.'

'Oh, give it a rest,' Sally said.

Then I filled her in on John.

'Maybe he's just going off Nina,' she yawned, which made me realize how infinitely more perspicacious and high-minded your average female friend could be than your average male ditto, even when half asleep. 'Which would serve her right for being a two-faced little cow,' she added.

'God, you girls can be so nasty,' Jacko tutted. 'Just look at this card: "Much love", she says. Maybe she's feeling bad now.'

In the circumstances, the thought of Nina feeling bad might have been custom-built to make me feel bad.

'She's even talking of popping round,' he went on.

If she ever did, I foresaw that she'd have him eating out of her little hand in no time. 'She'll have heard I've inherited half an expensive house,' I said. 'She's preparing the ground for a good old nose. And a swank about her perfect lifestyle while she's at it. Yes, I know it doesn't sound very nice,' I added, seeing Jacko's face, 'but it's probably spot on.'

With another yawn, Sally announced that she was going to have a bath but if she wasn't down in half an hour would someone please come and check that she hadn't fallen asleep and drowned.

Once she'd gone, Widdles decided to wake up and stretch himself. Then he jumped down from the sofa he now considered his personal throne, waddled fatly over to me and jumped onto my lap.

Widdles was another of Dorothy's goods and chattels. He'd actually been christened Tiddles, but as he watered his litter tray every hour the change had seemed apt. Jan, Dorothy's cleaner, had looked after him in the immediate aftermath, but at the funeral she'd said, 'I suppose he'll have to go to the rescue, poor old thing, but I don't suppose anyone'll want him at his age. I do hope they won't put him down.'

My mind was not on Widdles, however. Having psyched myself up for a 'nice' fob-off, I wasn't sure

38

what to think about John. He certainly didn't strike me as Jacko's in-with-a-chance-there type, looking for a pig's breakfast on the side. On the other hand, Sally's going-off-Nina bit was surely overoptimistic. Which left me with the hyperoptimistic fourteenth cousin.

It was all very unsettling, in a *frisson*-y kind of way.

Evidently sensing this, Jacko was fixing me with an uncharacteristically penetrating eye. 'You know your trouble?'

'I'm hungry,' I said, playing dumb.

'So am I, but I'm not talking food. All you've thought about in months is non-drip emulsion, Sally and the baby.'

I'd only emulsioned the kitchen, my room and Sally's. I almost wished I hadn't afterwards, as it made the rest of the house look fifty-seven times mankier by comparison, but there hadn't been much point doing rooms we hardly used.

Jacko hadn't finished. 'When did you last go out with a bloke you really fancied?'

'What the hell's that got to do with anything?' I asked, stroking Widdles' tabby old fur.

'Everything. You hardly even go out any more. All you and Sal talk about are Tom's poor ickle toofies and did that curry the other night go into the milk and give him funny-colour poohs.'

This was a monstrous lie. Sally and I had animated discussions about whether we could get a passable high chair from a car boot sale, and the relative merits of Tesco's versus Sainsbury's lasagne. We debated long and hard about whether to get *Pride and Prejudice* from Blockbusters for the fourteenth time, and if so, whether we were entirely sad or merely intellectually superior to those people who got *Ace Ventura – Pet Detective* for the fourteenth time. (We'd only had it six times.)

Having got *P&P* we then had long discussions about whether Mr Darcy was too noble and proper to have had any practice before his wedding night, and if not, whether poor Lizzie would be thinking, forsooth, is that it? Furthermore, we debated the merits of living in the early nineteenth century versus now: on the one hand you had no Tampax or deodorant, you had to sing sweetly and embroider cushions. On the other, you had blokes saying, 'You must allow me to tell you how ardently I admire and love you,' instead of 'Fancy a shag, then?'

'You used to be a right live wire,' Jacko went on. 'You just haven't got a life any more. Not what I'd call a life. You're starved of the buzz.'

'I had enough buzz last time. I practically needed a rest cure afterwards.'

'Sleep cure, more like,' he said. 'Hibernation. You've been hibernating ever since Shark-Arse took off.'

'It wasn't his arse,' I pointed out. 'And his name was Dirk.'

Dirk had taken off just after Sally had turned up, but the two were unconnected; he'd have taken off anyway. I'd met him in a riverside pub where he'd been pulling pints, and been immediately mesmerized by a) his blond, laid-back good looks, b) his accent (South African) and c) a fearsome scar on his arm. I'd done my best not to look but couldn't help it, and eventually he'd winked and said, 'Ragged-tooth shark – I was surfing. Had to hit the little bastard on the nose.'

As he'd told me afterwards, that shark had given him a chat-up line to die for, as long as he was in short sleeves. It had been a heady three months and then he'd moved on, but I hadn't missed him as painfully as I'd expected to, for which I can thank Sally. For general anaesthetic I thoroughly recommend the dramas of a bombshell pregnancy.

'Well, that's your trouble, if you ask me,' Jacko went on. 'The most exciting things to have happened in your life lately are finding a second-hand dishwasher for forty quid and murdering those poor little wood-worms in the chairs.'

'It's mercy killing, before they die in agony from overeating. I'm only trying to make the place habitable, anyway. We can't all have brand new warehouse conversions on the Liverpool docks.'

It had been a godsend that I *had* somewhere to make habitable. Although I still wondered what I'd done to deserve it, half a house could hardly have

41

come at a better time. Never married, Dorothy had been what they call 'a bit of a character', which roughly translates as forthright and crotchety. Apart from a few small legacies, everything was to be divided between her nephew David (my father) and her great-niece Harriet, who'd put up with a cantankerous old woman far better than she would have herself. And if anyone spent good money on flowers for her funeral, she'd come and haunt them.

I'd been almost appalled, at first. It was Dad who'd gone to see her every fortnight, attacked the garden and taken her out for Sunday lunches. I'd called in now and then, but not as often as I might have. I'd fetched her gin from the offie, put her bets on the horses, and done my best not to cringe when she'd asked me to cut her toenails.

Even if she'd left him everything, however, Dad would not have been cracking open the Bolly and ordering a new Merc. Comfortably off by his own standards, he'd recently retired and was about to go abroad to indulge a long-cherished dream. The prospect of sorting out mountains of junk and putting the house on the market had filled him with the sort of helpless dismay that had prompted Mum to leave him for no-nonsense, hands-on Bill.

When he'd suggested I live in it for now my first thought had been *no way*. The house had been so big, so chill, so full of that musty-fusty smell you only get in really old people's houses when they haven't thrown anything away for fifty years. The kitchen still had one of those pulley-operated clothes-airers, and on the wall was a glass-cased thing saying drawing room, bedroom one, etc., so the skivvy knew who was ringing for tea. The actual bells were still intact all over the house.

However, at the time I'd been living in a grotty flat in one of the few untarted areas of London, sharing with people who wrote Chris on their eggs to stop people nicking them, and said halfway through *Sex and the City* that they felt their old bisexual twinges coming back – would I fancy a threesome with their boyfriend?

And that was just the blokes.

So I'd moved in, fully intending to find a nice home for Widdles, sort out cubic miles of junk, and finalize plans for a trip to Oz and the Pacific. I should have been off by November at the latest.

Famous last intentions.

Jacko said, 'It won't be woodworms getting murdered if Sal ever finds out what you've been up to.'

'She won't unless you tell her, and if you do you're dead.'

What he meant was this. After that Clear Blue test, when Sally had still been in shock, I'd urged her to stay. I'd said probate would take forever, it would take me months to sort out Dorothy's junk and I wanted the company, which was true. However, since probate had come through two months ago the house could

43

have been on the market already, maybe even sold. If Sally had known this, though, she'd have gone into prime pig-headed mode and insisted on moving out, so I could get my half of the loot and zoom off on my trip. And since even the grottiest of flats would stretch her precarious finances, I'd told her there were problems with probate, some dozy idiot had lost half the papers, if I got the house on the market by March I'd be lucky. By that time she'd be back on her feet and earning – she already had something lined up for January. In fact she'd fully intended to go back to work when Tom was a month old, but that was before I'd seen for myself just how maternal instincts could kick in, even in a girl who'd often said she'd rather have a garden gnome.

Jacko's stomach let out a rumble even I could hear. 'Right, I'm going to phone the takeaway,' he said. 'What do you fancy?'

'We're always having takeaways! I'll throw something together – there should be some fresh pasta if you and Sally haven't pigged it all.'

I didn't object to takeaways on any purist grounds, but as Jacko sent out so often and usually insisted on paying as well, I felt guilty. Whatever else, Jacko was no freeloader. The fact that he could afford it was rather beside the point.

Jacko had been a bit like me, without a clue what he wanted to do except that it had to include plenty of laughs. After grasshoppering from job to job, he'd

44

eventually done what he'd said he'd never do: gone to work for his old man, who had sundry businesses on Merseyside. Having startled everyone, especially himself, by discovering a feel for it, Jacko had been his old man's number two for eighteen months now. The shock of finding out that Jacko wasn't just a terminally chilled-out waste of space had precipitated a heart attack in the previous number two, who'd subsequently retired.

Jacko should have gone home by now, but he was dragging it out till after Christmas. As he'd so unfilially put it, if his old man was hacked off with spending only two days a week on the golf course it was just tough. He'd been working his bollocks off for months – he was overdue for some slobbing.

As I was checking the fridge for that pasta, the doorbell rang. Like just about everything else in the house it was antique, and also deafening. I was half expecting one of those kids with bags of overpriced tea towels and pots of Wunda-Stain, but found Helen on the step.

'Sorry, but I was feeling a bit low,' she said. (Helen always preceded her opening remarks with 'sorry'.) 'You're not eating, are you?'

'Not yet, and even if we were it wouldn't matter. Come in.'

Helen lived next door, in a house much like Dorothy's, except that it had been done up with a colossally expensive vengeance. Over the months I'd got friendly with her. She'd been placidly soothing during Sally's first, panicky weeks with Tom, when I was about as clued-up as Widdles.

Helen's husband was a solicitor with a lucrative practice in Wimbledon. Four months previously he'd left her for his accountant, who was eight years younger than Helen and had a doll's-house cottage in Wimbledon Village.

'Hi, pet,' said Jacko, when I took her through. 'Found a nice bloke yet to get your own back with?'

She produced a wan little smile. 'At the moment I'm so fed up I'd have a fling with the first man who asked me.'

'Well, I get my plaster off next week,' he grinned. 'Might be a bit out of practice but I'll do my best.'

I swear she almost looked grateful for the offer.

'Have a glass of wine,' I said.

'I can't.' With a glance at her watch, she sighed. 'I've got to pick Matthew up soon – he went home with Sam after school.'

Helen was thirty-nine, but could have passed for twenty-eight. She had smooth, fairish hair, lovely pearly skin, and one of those faces that look mousy and ordinary until a particular expression makes you realize that it's almost beautiful, in a quiet, diffident way. Having married very young, she had three boys. Eighteen-year-old Oliver had just started at Exeter University and she missed him desperately. Toby and Matthew were twelve-year-old twins, and by now I was familiar with their friends and habits, including their custom of treating their mother like a doormat.

'Why can't he walk home?' I asked. 'Sam only lives about a mile away, doesn't he?'

'Yes, but I said I'd pick him up. He's going to ring when he's ready.'

While I was making her a coffee instead, Helen said, 'I'm so fed up – Lawrence is having the boys again this weekend. Of *course* he's not taking them to Francesca's – he's booked some adventure weekend thing with mud and dirt bikes and they're over the moon. It's barely a month since he took them to EuroDisney, for heaven's sake! And it was wretched Francesca who suggested the adventure weekend, so now they think she's the bee's knees.'

'Is she going with them?' I asked.

'Into *mud*? Of course not!'

Francesca had suffered the twins for a couple of weekends, on her own terms. She'd made them take their trainers off, and there was no telly or Play Station in the titchy spare room where Lawrence had installed bunk beds, and she'd made them eat 'horrible veggie stuff with no ketchup'. So what Helen was feeling, but not saying, was that she wanted them to go to Francesca's again, so they'd hate it and long for home and Mum, instead of which they were thinking she was cool, because she'd suggested the adventure weekend so she wouldn't get boy-muck over her cream carpets.

'You should tell Lawrence he can have custody of the twins,' I said. 'That'd sort Francesca out. Imagine if she had to cope with them on a daily basis!'

Jacko hooted, but Helen looked as if I'd just suggested running a couple of old ladies over, for a laugh.

'Well?' I went on, regardless. 'He never asked whether you wanted custody, did he? He just assumed!'

Jacko hooted again. 'She'd be off like a shot, I bet. Kicking him out like a shot, anyway.'

I was warming to this theme nicely. 'They're his kids just as much as yours. She'd screech, "*Kids*? Who said anything about kids?"'

'She'd have them, I bet,' Helen said wanly. 'She'd never give Lawrence up that easily.'

Her mobile rang just as she was finishing her coffee, and for once a furrow of irritation creased her brow. 'Toby, you've *had* your tea!' (Pause.) 'I don't know! Look in the fridge! Put some chips in the microwave!'

She hung up so abruptly, I was startled. 'I'm sick of it! Phoning me from next door because he's still *hun*gry! He's twelve, for heaven's sake!'

'Good on you, pet,' Jacko grinned. 'You sort the lazy little tyke out.'

On Friday night I left work bang on time for once and charged home for a panic shower and change. While I was throwing on my best grey suit and a pale pink

48

sweater, Sally came in with Tom and flopped onto my bed. 'I just had to get out of the kitchen – Frida's making her Swedish meatballs again.'

'Her meatballs are lovely!' I was trying to find the eyeshadow that was supposed to make my eyes all smoky and alluring, rather than that all-purpose grey which can also look vaguely blue or green according to what you're wearing.

'I know, but Jacko's making me want to puke. He's saying stuff like, "Oh, Freeds, Viking princess of my dreams, will you marry me and make me meatballs every night?" And Frida's trying not to laugh, but she *is*, and saying stuff like, "I don't think I'm quite your type, Jacko – I have tits like fried eggs," and Jacko's saying stuff like, "You've got *gorgeous* little tits! I love fried eggs, anyway." I mean, he just never *stops*.'

Whether it was the stitches, hormones or Steve (probably all three), ever since Tom Sally was about as interested in men and sex as Jacko was in needlepoint. She was almost getting like one of those old biddies who constantly moan about all the smut on the television. 'It's just the way he is,' I said, trying not to get exasperated. 'If Frida didn't like it, she'd soon tell him.'

Frida wasn't quite your stereotypical Swede, in that she wasn't blonde. She was typical in having virtually perfect English, however, and in being incredibly tall and gorgeous: two inches taller than me, which made a nice change. She said it was all the herrings.

I found the eyeshadow, made a mess of applying it, and cursed.

Sally said, 'I made a baby chicken casserole for Tom this afternoon, bought a fresh chicken breast specially, puréed it in the blender and everything, and he just spat it out.' Her tone altered considerably as she turned to Tom, propped beside her on my pillows and eating a rattle. 'Yes, oo *did*, oo naughty ickle bubba! Mummy had to give it to Widdles and he didn't like it either, did he, the great fat fleabag?'

In the dressing-table mirror I saw Tom beaming at her and Sally beaming back, in that mutual-adoration-society fashion. 'I think he's got another tooth on the way,' she went on. 'He's been chewing on that rattle all day and dribbling like mad. It's starting to give him a rash on his chin.'

'It'll go, once it's through,' I said, like Auntie Spock.

'Why don't you put something a bit flasher on?' she asked, getting her mind off Tom at last. 'That looks rather work-ish.'

'It's *supposed* to look work-ish, dopey. I don't want him thinking I've charged home to change, on purpose.'

Propping herself on her elbows, she said, 'Poor old Helicopter's going to get a bit of a shock after last time.'

'That was the general idea.' The suit was beautifully cut and short enough to show off my best feature, but it was also elegant and the pale pink lambswool sweater made my skin look delicately creamy. I'd hot-brushed my hair into something resembling controlled waves and my face was looking quite reasonable. I have a wide, slightly lopsided mouth, which I'd hated at the gangly stage, but someone I would now love for ever had recently asked whether it was the product of plastic surgery, it was so quirkily attractive.

Sally said, 'What if he wants to see you again?'

'I haven't even thought that far.' This, of course, was a massive lie. I'd thought endlessly about what I'd do if he did (still out on that one), whether I'd really care if he didn't (yes), and just how sick I'd feel if he told me about his wonderful girlfriend, who was making him think commitment was actually a pretty cool concept. 'Anyway, he won't,' I added, in case Fate was lurking at the keyhole.

'He might. I bet Jacko a packet of giant Smarties he's going off Nina. So I'd better be right.'

'How am I supposed to find out?' I demanded. '"Excuse me, but are you going off that woman I saw you with on Saturday, who just happens to be a non-friend of mine?"'

'Bit awkward,' she conceded. 'Jacko still thinks he's a potentially two-timing arsehole. Which is a bit bloody rich, the way he's carrying on with Frida lately. You should have heard him ten minutes ago, begging her to scratch his itch. I know he technically meant with one of Dorothy's knitting needles down his plaster, but the double entendre was so bloody puerile, it made me cringe. It'd serve him right if Erik Bloodaxe came over and duffed him up.' (This was Frida's boyfriend, back home in Stockholm, who was apparently about six foot five and built like a tank.)

'It's just Jacko! He's always been like that!' I thought of a couple of way-back friends who'd slept with him, having both said they'd die first. 'He made me laugh till I nearly wet myself,' one of them had told me helplessly, 'and then he said, "Aah, go on, give us a shag – I'm desperate . . ." and I just sort of, well, *melted*.'

I misted myself with CK1 and grabbed my bag. 'I've got to dash – enjoy your meatballs.' I charged downstairs, yanked the front door open, and found Helen on the step. 'Are you going out?' she asked, as if such a thing had never been heard of.

'Well, yes.' I peered at her in the half-light. 'Are you OK?'

'Fine.'

She didn't exactly look fine, but then she never did look very bushy-tailed lately. 'The others are here – come and have a drink.'

'No, it's OK, honestly. I was just going to ask you something, but it'll keep.' With a bright 'Have a nice time,' she departed.

En route to the station, I felt a bit bad about Helen. Ever since Lawrence had left, she'd come to rely on us as a sort of support system. Most of her friends were also his friends and she hated forcing anyone to take sides. However, once on the train I almost felt as if I were escaping, zooming down a runway to a world where baby casseroles and other people's problems just didn't exist. It was close to that exhilarating sensation you get when the plane breaks through the murk and suddenly you're in a world of brilliant blue and cotton-wool clouds, like some celestial bouncy castle.

Jacko was right. I'd hardly thought about men in ages, or even getting tarted up and having a wild night out. While queuing at supermarket checkouts I never picked up *Cosmo* any more, to speed-read 'Fifty ways to multiply your orgasms!' I'd started picking up *Mumsy World* instead, to speed-read 'Fifty ways to zap that nasty rash on baby's little botty!' If I were anyone else, I'd be getting seriously worried about me.

I'd planned to arrive at around twenty to eight , so I wouldn't have to sit on my own if he was late and get into a state, thinking he wasn't coming. But the wretched underground was playing up, so I half ran from the station. It was nearly ten to eight by the time I reached the bar and I'd got in a state anyway, thinking he might have come and gone already.

The bar was very busy. The decor was dark green and gold, making you think of 1920s Paris cafés and intellectuals expounding on existentialism as they knocked back pastis. The tables were small and round, and looked like dark green onyx.

He was there, all right, sitting in the far corner, with a blonde woman who was laughing up at him as if he were the best thing since takeaway sushi.

I know I said I was an only child, but I lied. I have a prissy elder sister who comes visiting now and again, but only in my head. When I was younger she used to say smug, bossy stuff like 'You'll get found out,' and 'It's no use hiding your school report under your bed.' I hadn't heard from her for ages, but suddenly the irritating girl was back.

'I knew this was a bad idea,' she said triumphantly. 'I *told* you.'

'No, you didn't. I thought you were dead. I wish you *were* dead.'

'Well, I'm not, so there. You're only fifteen minutes late and he's picked up someone else already. Just look at him.'

I was.

'Silk-curtain hair, too, only blonde,' she went on smugly. 'He's obviously got a thing about silk curtains. Push off quick before he sees you and you look a complete prat.'

I would have, once. But I'd have stood there gaping and dithering long enough for him to see me first, and then I'd have done the killer-tomato bit and blundered out, tripping over something en route, and gone home wishing I was dead. However, I was

54

grown-up now. I had instant bottled cool. Applied with care, like instant tan, I defied even a Helicopter to tell it from the real thing.

It was the blonde who saw me first, when I was still three tables away.

She gave him a little nudge and he looked up instantly. He stood up, too, which made me hear another voice in my head, my mother's this time: 'I do like to see nice manners. Nice manners do go a long way in a man.'

'Harriet!' he said. 'I'd just about given you up.'

Evidently. Wearing my best unfazed smile, I said, 'So sorry – it's been one of those days.'

'Don't tell me.' He turned to his companion, who was giving me the once-over with faintly amused interest. 'This is Amanda,' he said. 'Amanda, Harriet.'

She gave me a friendly enough smile. 'But I'm on my way. I was just going when John came in, but as I hadn't seen him for ages I thought I'd keep him company.' She gave him a peck on the cheek. 'I'll give you a call – you *must* come for supper. I'm dying for you to meet Miles; I just know you'll hit it off.'

'I'll look forward to it,' he said.

'Just come, that's all.' To me she added, 'John's getting as elusive as the Scarlet Pimpernel lately. We seek him here, we phone him there – and when we get him he's still tied up for the next three weeks.'

With a glance at me, John raised an eyebrow. 'Amanda always did exaggerate.'

'I'm not.' She gave him another peck. 'Be good.' With another smile she departed and I sat down, feeling a prat after all and remembering what else my mother had said about a million times: 'Do sit up *straight*, Harriet. It's so unflattering to slump like that.'

'Amanda got married three months ago,' he explained. 'I was away and missed the wedding, and I haven't seen her since.'

Well, it was just typical of my prissy elder sister to jump to nasty, suspicious conclusions.

Belatedly he was giving me an appraisal that told me my panic tart-up had been worth it. It was hardly 'Wow!' stuff, but his expression said, 'Well, I hadn't expected her to scrub up like this.' 'Let me get you a drink,' he said.

'No, this is my shout, remember?' I glanced down at a nearly empty glass of what looked depressingly like mineral water. 'Are you ready for another?'

'Yes, I'll have a gin and tonic.'

Thank God for that. I'm not exactly a piss-head, but I just can't relate to total abstainers. I ordered a large glass of red burgundy too, and some nuts, since I'd had nothing since lunchtime.

Until then I suppose I'd been wondering whether I'd worked him up in my head into a bigger 'thing' than he merited. Well, I hadn't. I liked the wrappings, too. I liked the dark grey suit. I liked the navy and white striped shirt and the gold cufflink peeping out. This meant sod all, though, as I'd probably have liked him in an orange woolly jumper and I hate orange, except on oranges. In fact my trusty inbuilt bloke register was quivering instantly into life, saying *Action stations! Promising stuff, and about time too.*

'I hope there wasn't anything vital in that purse,' he said. 'Like a winning lottery ticket with your perennial lucky numbers on it.'

Feeling guilty, I was almost tempted to confess, but what was the point now? 'Only a dry-cleaning ticket and I always lose those anyway. It was really very kind of you,' I added quickly.

For some reason he seemed to find this funny. He gave me an amused facial appraisal that allowed me a good chance to return the favour. And since we were fairly crammed together, this was a *frisson-y* sort of exercise. I still couldn't work out whether his eyes were blue or green, but I had a damn good try.

'I was feeling mellow,' he said, as our drinks arrived.

After lunch with Nina? This was not a good sign. In fact it was so depressing I needed a good swig of Jacob's Creek to wash it down. 'Everybody at work thinks I made you up. They said I must have been hallucinating on account of Christmas shopping on an empty stomach – men just don't dish out cab fares to strange women.'

His mouth gave a minute quiver. 'I wouldn't say "strange". Weary and bedraggled, OK.'

Great. I couldn't think of a witty, alluring reply, either. I couldn't even think of a boring one, not

that he was looking at me any more. He was cracking pistachios and putting them away like a squirrel
expecting nut blight for the next couple of seasons.
I was beginning to imagine conversations with Nina,
on the lines of, 'Sorry, sweetheart, but I've got to go
and have a drink with that idiot woman who lost her
purse on Saturday.'

'Oh, my poor love, what a *pain*. I hope she won't
think you fancy her.'

'*Fancy* her?' (Shock horror.) 'Christ, I hope not.'

Just as I located my tongue at last, he beat me to
it. 'The fertility god's still in the window – I took a
quick look on the way. He's looking a bit down in the
mouth.'

I wasn't surprised. Passers-by were probably making
coarse remarks about his equipment. 'He'll be homesick,' I said. 'I wonder where he's from?'

'Some remote area of Brazil. I called in the other
day – they told me he's a mix. Part Yoruba tribal reli-
gion the African slaves brought in, part Catholicism
from the Portuguese.'

It was satisfying to have my inklings confirmed.
'Really?'

'At least, that's the line they gave me,' he went on
wryly. 'For all I know he could have been knocked out
in some workshop in Wood Green.'

I laughed and tutted at the same time. 'Don't be
so cynical. If he was from Wood Green, he wouldn't
look so miserable at being uprooted. If you ask me,

it should be against the law to uproot fertility gods from their ethnic origins. Maybe we should start a campaign to send him home.' I nearly added, 'You know, like *Free Willy*', but bit it back as too puerile.

'Yes, maybe he could do with a change of residence,' he mused.

'Are you thinking of giving him one?'

'If I can work out a foolproof ram-raid strategy. As you said, fifteen hundred's a bit steep for a cat-scratching post, especially when you haven't got a cat.'

I laughed. 'I have.' I found myself telling him about Dorothy and the house, and poor Widdles.

Two minutes later it dawned on me that this didn't quite fit with the strategy I'd worked out in advance. I was supposed to go for the Tantalizingly Elusive bit, with a morsel of Sophisticatedly Intelligent and Alluring thrown in. Thanks to a *Times* Arts section someone had left on the train I'd even thought of openers, e.g. 'Have you seen that marvellously thought-provoking exhibition of avant-garde Slovenian art at the Tate Modern?' However, I'd discarded this as dangerous, in case he said, 'Yes, what did you think of the Resnik bronzes?'

'And then an old friend moved in and I'm still there,' I went on. 'I was supposed to be off to Oz and the Pacific for three months, but that's on the back burner.'

'Three *months*?' He raised an eyebrow. 'You must have a chilled-out boss.'

'I'd have given in my notice. That's what I used to do – work for a few months and take off.'

'Permanently itchy feet?' he asked.

'And restlessness. After three months anywhere I was bored.' Suddenly I felt I'd talked about myself quite enough. I thought of asking about his job, but it seemed over-nosy and I already knew from Rosie that it was something vaguely financial. Since a woman had just come in, laden with what looked like Christmas shopping, I found a safe topic. 'What are you doing for Christmas?'

'Sailing in the Grenadines.'

'God, you lucky devil,' I said, thinking, if you're taking Nina, I'll really hate her for ever. In fact I needed another hefty swig, in case he added, 'With my girlfriend.'

'Actually, I'm not,' he went on. 'That's what I'd like to do, but I have tribal rituals to attend.'

That was one way of putting it. 'Or the tribal elders'll be offended if you don't?'

'No, but they need a referee. Our tribal rituals have a tendency to turn into tribal warfare.'

'Sounds about normal for family Christmases.'

'That's what you think. Blood could be spilt,' he added, in mock-doom tones.

I burst out laughing. 'If you go ahead with ram-raiding old Wooden Wally, you might get banged up in time to get out of it.'

'Now there's a thought.' He started talking about

trawling East End pubs for ex-cons with relevant experience, and I said he might not have to go that far, there was usually a bloke in the Drunken Dragon flogging dodgy fags and watches, who'd almost certainly say, 'No problem, love,' even if you asked for a hit man. Then he asked whether I had any old tights they could use for disguise purposes, and I said no, but they wouldn't want manky old tights anyway, the holes might reveal identifying features. It went on like this, light, silly stuff, with lots of laughs and eye contact (plus another couple of drinks) but I still didn't feel I was getting anywhere, one way or the other.

Amanda had been spot on with that 'elusive'. Nothing in his demeanour said categorically either 'spoken for' or 'available', let alone 'up for a bit on the side'. Once or twice I thought I caught a hint of undercurrents, but they were so fleeting I decided I'd imagined them. I mean, you can usually tell straight off. You get that, 'Are you thinking what I'm thinking?' stuff that makes you go all pink and wriggly when you *are* thinking what he's thinking, and shudder when you're not. As for 'accidental' brushings of fingers, or thighs under the table, no such luck.

And I could have done with a morsel of such stuff, I can tell you. Close up, he was exerting the kind of pull you learn about in physics lessons, involving magnets and irresistible forces. It was unbelievably frustrating, especially as I was feeling on top form: witty, sparkling and desirable. I usually do, though, after one glass of anything on an empty stomach.

With time moving fast, I was getting desperate for some sort of signal, whether red or green. I thought for a moment of doing something really obviously suggestive, e.g. running the tip of my tongue over my lower lip in a supposedly casual fashion, while looking him right in the eye. Some man had once told me it got his loins stirring in a positively dangerous fashion. But I drew the line here. Some people are funny about tongues (including me) so maybe it would turn him right off, instead.

Beginning to see merely a 'Bye, then, take care,' looming at the end of the evening, I thought I might as well contrive some 'accidental' brushings myself. After all, such pathetic little crumbs were probably all I was going to get.

The bar was getting busier and noisier, so it was perfectly acceptable to lean slightly closer, as if to hear him better. In fact I managed this so cunningly that my hair fleetingly brushed his cheek. Even better, someone pushed past me rather roughly and I could shrink closer without it looking obvious. This made me go so warm and fluttery I almost wished some semi-drunk would bash right into me, send me slithering gracefully off my stool half into his lap, and really send my flutters into orbit.

Seconds later, it very nearly happened.

I had my right elbow on the table at this point, my

chin resting flatteringly on my hand as I gave him my full, rapt attention. The conversation had become positively intellectual by now. After we'd somehow got onto Poems on the Underground, he'd said the best poetry invariably contained some profound philosophical truth. So I put on my best intelligently riveted look, which was a bit difficult while I was having a wriggly mini-fantasy about what it'd be like to kiss him. 'Like what?' I said, wishing to God I'd paid attention when Miss Hardcastle was droning on about Sylvia Plath at school.

'If I give you the first line, you give me the poet.'

Shit. Still, if he turned out to be one of those prats who like making you feel stupid, at least I'd go off him instantly. 'Go on, then.'

With a dead straight face, he said, ' "It's very very funny how a bear likes honey".'

How I turned an almighty cackle into a sparkly little laugh on the way out, I'll never know. 'Yes, Pooh was quite a philosopher in his portly little way, and certainly more digestible than Nietzsche.' I was just congratulating myself on this sophisticated, intelligent reply, when some semi-drunk's elbow jabbed into my shoulder blade. He jabbed so hard that I jumped and jerked, my hand jerked from under my chin, and my arm jerked sideways and knocked my glass over.

And half a mega-glass of red went flying into John's lap.

# THREE

Who says time travel doesn't exist? In half a second I was fifteen again, all legs and elbows, wishing I could die and evaporate, in that order.

Semi-drunk was mumbling apologies, but I wasn't listening. I was too busy saying, 'God, I'm so sorry – how stupid – quick, get a cloth –'

A cloth was procured and he mopped up the worst, but any fool could see that no amount of Wunda-Stain would ever save that suit from the bin.

We had to stand aside while someone cleaned up the mess. 'I'm so sorry,' I said. 'That suit's going to be a write-off.'

'It couldn't be helped.' With a wry little smile, he dumped the cloth on the table and glanced down at the massive red stain in the worst possible place. 'Just as well it was red – white would look as if I'd peed myself.' Nodding at a table that had just been vacated, he added, 'Let's shift over there.'

I felt more like shifting out of the door, but he still had half a gin and tonic left.

I ordered an espresso. After all that Jacob's Creek, I needed it. I must have been half pissed already, trying to get up close and personal like that. Chucking in Nietzsche, too, as if I'd ever read more than two paragraphs, and that was only because I'd once really fancied a politics student and thought he'd be impressed.

And now he was making hideously polite conversation while he finished his drink. 'So what are you doing, while your trip's on hold?'

'I work for a high-street recruitment agency.'

'But only until you're restless enough to take off again?'

'It's fine for now. I started as a temp, but they offered me something more permanent. I'd temped so much myself, it was a change to see the sharp end. It suited me to be settled until Sally's back on her feet.' I'd already told him she had a baby. 'How about you?' Now he'd opened the subject, it didn't seem over-nosy.

'I work for a development bank. It funds capital projects in the Eastern bloc countries, or doesn't fund them, as the case may be.'

'So you get some travel chucked in?'

'Now and then.' After a pause he added, 'You said your old man was abroad – is he working overseas?'

'No, he's wallowing in antiquities. He always wanted to be an archaeologist.'

'Then why wasn't he one?'

'His father was a solicitor. He was expected to go into the practice, but his heart was never in it.' Not so long ago it had been a sleepy, market-town practice where even Dad had moaned that the old partners still had quill-pen mentalities. It had woken up now, though it was still nothing like Helen's husband's slick, bottom-line outfit. 'So now he's poking round the ruins of Troy and so on, hoping to find a stone tablet saying "Helen's diary, 1256 BC. Dear diary . . ."'

He chuckled politely. 'Go on – what would she tell it?'

Not about feeling an arse because she'd spilt wine over her fancy man, I bet. 'What any woman might say when she's run off with another man and her husband's sent a thousand ships to bring her back: "Might have known, the prat always did go right over the top . . ."'

As he chuckled again in that polite fashion, I thought how sickening it was that I could find absolutely nothing wrong with him. According to sod's law this meant that even if he wasn't Nina's, he'd be somebody else's.

But I made a polite effort in return. 'Why are you expecting tribal warfare over your Christmas dinner?'

He raised his eyebrows in a God help us fashion. 'My old man has an elderly aunt who's going gently demented and has been staying for the past year. My mother has an elderly ditto who is what they politely call "eccentric" and traditionally comes every Christmas. Between them these two work my old man into the kind of state where he threatens to shoot one or both of them with an illegal ex-service revolver he keeps in his sock drawer. Added to that, my younger sister winds him up at every possible opportunity, and between all these my mother goes quietly crazy and threatens to run off with the dog.'

'You were right,' he went on, as I laughed. 'Getting banged up looks like an increasingly attractive alternative. If I get this ram raid going, how do you fancy yourself as a gangster's moll?'

'Brilliant,' I said, perking up a bit. 'I could drive the van. I once knocked a brick wall down without even trying, so plate glass'd be a doddle. I was trying to move Dad's car so I could get my bike out of the garage, but I'd only had one driving lesson and I forgot where the brake was.'

Having just taken a mouthful of G&T, he practically choked. 'Jesus. What did he say?'

'"Never mind, dear,"' I had to confess.

'My old man would have had my guts on a plate. He used to bristle and bark like some wire-haired hound from hell. Still does,' he added.

'My father never barked in his life. He wouldn't know where to start.' Poor old Dad had been just like me, only he'd never quite grown out of the gangly, adolescent stage.

'So what are you doing for Christmas?' he asked.

I told him briefly, adding the Devon rituals I was getting out of. 'So I'm going to be cooking my first turkey. I dare say it'll end up like Mr Bean's, but nobody'll care. Mind you, I might have minor warfare on my hands, too. If the fourteenth rerun of *E.T.* clashes with the fourteenth rerun of *Top Gun*, Sally and Jacko'll be at it like a pair of kids.'

'*The Great Escape*'s the only film I'll be thinking of.' With that, he drained his glass and glanced at his watch. 'It's five to nine – don't you have to go?'

'My God – is it?'

'I should be off, too.'

More immediate Escapes were evidently in his mind, and I couldn't blame him.

'If only to change out of these trousers,' he added, as we headed for the door. 'On second thoughts, it does look as if I've peed myself. Looks like a nasty case of blackwater fever at the terminally incontinent stage.'

He shot me a little wink as he said it, as if he knew how bad I felt and was trying to make me feel better. Which was nice-bloke-ish, I dare say, but I didn't want nice-bloke-ish-ness, not unless it came with fancying-Harriet-ness and (more particularly) with not-fancying-Nina-ness. 'I'm really terribly sorry. I'd offer to pay for the dry cleaning if I thought it'd do any good.'

'It wasn't your fault. The trousers were getting tight anyway.' He gave himself a little pat where his gut would have been if he'd had one.

68

It was still unseasonally mild; the fresh, damp air was sobering me up fast.

He nodded along the road, where cab hunters were hugging the kerb. 'If you need a taxi, we'll have a better chance further down.'

I'd intended to take the tube, but what the hell. He was almost brushing me as we walked, and as we crossed the road he touched my arm in that protective-sheepdog fashion that's so intensely irritating from blokes you couldn't fancy in a million years, and so intensely delicious from those you could.

'Where are you off to?' he asked, as we reached a likely corner. 'You've got something else on, I take it?'

I'd prepared a lie earlier, but if I stuck to it and he suggested cab-sharing it might be awkward. 'I was going to a do in Battersea but I don't suppose they'll miss me – I might just go home.'

Two cabs went past in quick succession, both occupied.

He stopped suddenly. 'Look, if you're really going to duck out of this Battersea thing . . .' He paused. 'Have you eaten?'

If I hadn't written him off by then, my first reaction would have been *Yes! Yes! Yes!* As it was, I realized just how thick I'd been. We were standing right by a street lamp, and I saw in a flash that I hadn't imagined those undercurrents; he'd merely been playing it super-cool. That was why there had been no finger-brushing or anything else, because the devious devil had known I'd want it all the more.

And I did, I can tell you. 'Well, no . . .'

'Neither have I. So if you'd like to come back to my place and wait while I change, we'll go and eat.'

I was horribly tempted. The trouble was, I knew I'd never enjoy it properly unless credentials were on the table, which would be a terrible waste of the best flutters I'd had in ages.

'You're looking dubious,' he added, with an utterly disarming little smile that very nearly worked.

But I had to know. On an impulse I said more or less what was in my head. 'Dinner's fine with me. Only I saw you before you saw me the other day, you see, and I can't help wondering whether dinner with me would be fine with, well, whoever she was.'

His reaction was exactly what I'd been hoping not to see. Momentary, caught-in-the-act shock, which disappeared almost before I'd blinked.

I was beginning to wish I'd never asked. 'Look, I'm sorry, it's really none of my business,' I said quickly.

'No, it's OK. But since you ask, yes, I have seen her a couple of times.'

I didn't want to hear this. Not when it was standard bloke-speak for three times a week for the past couple of months. I could have sworn there was even a whisper of amusement at my quaint little scruples.

'But it's no big thing,' he added. 'It's really not going anywhere.'

70

He said it with such convincing candour I'd have believed him like a shot if I hadn't known the background.

'So how about that dinner?' he went on.

Half of me was saying sod it, just go. The other half was telling me here was a smootharse *extraordinaire* and I wasn't that desperate. Still, I like to give people the benefit of the doubt, especially when I fancy them rotten. If he was about to dump Nina, or already had, Rosie would be full of it ere another sun had set o'er the ructions. There was no harm in playing it cool, however, especially after the way I'd been carrying on before.

So I produced an apologetic expresion. 'I'd love to, but I really should be getting home. A friend next door was in a bit of a state when I left – I ought to go and see her. I was only going to put in an appearance at the Battersea do anyway.'

He raised his eyebrows minutely, but it could have meant anything.

'Were *you* ducking out of something?' I asked.

'Yes, but it's no big deal. I'll have to go home anyway and change – I might just stay there and sling something in the microwave. If there's anything to sling. I might have to settle for a sandwich.' He added another little smile that might have been designed to weaken the susceptible.

It was working, too. 'Is that supposed to make me feel bad and change my mind?'

'Not this time. Your friend's need sounds greater than mine.'

Bugger it. Just as I was thinking sod it, live dangerously . . .

'But maybe another time?' he went on. 'Buy me another drink. A pre-dinner drink, this time, and I'll get the dinner.'

*Yes!* 'No, I'll get the dinner. I still owe you most of that thirty quid, never mind that suit. I hope to God it's not Armani or anything.'

He smiled. 'No, it's not Armani.'

Well, maybe not. If pushed I might have said Savile Row.

'If you give me your number, I'll give you a call,' he went on.

As he wrote it on the back of a business card, I told myself matches could always be found later, if boats needed burning.

Then an unoccupied cab appeared, the first we'd seen. We hailed it both together. 'You grab it,' I said. 'If you stand here any longer in those trousers you might get arrested.'

'I'll take a chance.'

Just as I was about to get in, John caught my wrist. 'Take care,' he said. 'And thanks for coming.'

'I enjoyed it.' I enjoyed the next bit even more. As if he did it every day, he put a finger very lightly under my chin in a manner they should teach at evening classes in How To Make Women Go All

Fluttery, tilted my face up, and kissed me very lightly.

On the cheek, damn him.

He stood on the pavement as the cab pulled out, and waved, and I waved back. Once he was out of sight I sat back, put my finger to my cheek where he'd kissed me, and thought, what the hell am I getting myself into?

Not that I was exactly into anything yet.

Half a mile down the road, the buzz was already fading. In fact, I felt a bit like a seven-year-old who's just opened a present and been cruelly disappointed. You're dying for Barbie's Wonder Horse with his saddle and things for brushing his mane; you've been dropping colossal hints about Wonder Horse, and your target grown-up's made tutting noises and said it was terribly expensive for a bit of plastic, you'd get bored with a plastic horse in five minutes. But you think target grown-up might have got it anyway, especially when you see a present just the right size for Wonder Horse. So your heart goes *boing, yippee*! And you open it to find a sensible, educational kit on Discovering Nature.

Ten per cent of me, of course, had still been hoping he'd say, 'Oh, *Nina*!' with a little laugh. 'Oh, she's just an old friend/a pain in the arse second cousin I felt obliged to catch up with.'

Still, it served me right for hoping for Wonder Horse, when I'd known all along it was going to be Discovering Nature. Who wanted to brush his mane anyway, if Nina was going to be playing with him tomorrow, stroking his fetlocks and everything? These metaphors were unfortunate, as they led to images I could have done without, e.g. Nina stroking his tail, never mind sitting astride and practising her rising trot . . .

It would be just typical of Jacko to be right. And if he'd seen the way I was carrying on in that bar, I knew exactly what he'd have said: 'Harry, you were giving off more signals than Clapham Junction in the rush hour.'

So much for the Tantalizingly Elusive bit.

On the other hand, if he'd given a 'correct' reply, would I have believed him? After all, 'pain in the arse second cousin' was exactly the sort of thing an on-the-ball smootharse would say, especially if he was in the habit of smooth-arsing and had seventeen assorted excuses at his disposal.

Maybe it really wasn't going anywhere. Maybe he'd wanted to say, 'Actually, she's a bit of a pain and I'm going to dump her,' but had thought it would sound callously ungallant and put me off. This gratifying notion perked me up all the way home, where my mind was soon taken off Wonder Horse.

The instant I was inside, Sally came from the kitchen, shutting the door behind her. 'Thank God you're back,' she whispered. 'Helen's here – you'll never believe what she's done.'

Helen was sitting at the kitchen table with a nearly empty bottle of wine.

She looked up at me. 'I did what you said.'

I gaped at her, uncomprehending.

'What you said,' she repeated. 'I told Lawrence he could have custody of the twins.'

'*What*?'

'Well, I didn't tell him to his *face*.' She spoke with the careful enunciation of someone who's had a few, and is trying to sound as if they haven't. 'When he came to pick the boys up I said I wouldn't be here on the Monday night, so he'd have to have them after school. He was having them till Monday morning anyway.'

'So you haven't actually said it?'

'I have.' She took another mouthful of supersave Lambrusco. 'I wrote him a letter. I was going to ask what you thought of the wording, but you were on your way out so I just went and posted it before I changed my mind.'

'Helen, I didn't mean you to take me literally!'

'Maybe not, but once you said it, it seemed so unbelievably rational. I suppose I'd thought of it before, but not really seriously.'

I felt sick. All right, in theory I should have been applauding her all the way, but this was Helen we were talking about. 'You said yourself Francesca'd never give Lawrence up that easily!'

'I'm not doing it to get him back. He doesn't

love me any more – what's the point?' she went on, with the same semi-drunk control. 'Why the hell should I get the short straw? He's planning to sell the house, so the boys and I can move into something smaller and *he* can get something better than a doll's house with bloody Francesca. Why should I move downmarket and run round after the boys while he's living in civilized style with her?' She knocked back another mouthful. 'If she wants Lawrence that much, let her have the downside, too. Let her pick up the bloody football kit and run round after them.'

'Helen, those kids are your life! You'll miss them like mad!'

'Yes, but not like I miss Olly. They're just like Lawrence – *me, me, me . . .*'

However much I agreed with her, I wasn't going to admit it now. 'They're *kids*!'

'I know, but Olly was never like that. If I thought for a minute they'd care I'd never do it, but they won't. They've never once said, "Poor Mum, are you all right?" It's always just the same old "I'm starving," and "Where are my swimming things?" and moans because I was no use with their maths homework and they had to fax it to Lawrence.'

What could you say to that?

'So he'll get my letter on Monday morning,' she went on. 'When he'll be thinking he's done his fun-father bit until Francesca can either spare him for another "quality time" weekend, or suffer them messing up her doll's house. Well, hc's got another think. I had to present him with a *fait accompli* – if I'd told him to his face he'd have gone mad and worn me down.'

I'd just found out what shell shock feels like. 'Where will you go?'

'To an old friend in Muswell Hill. Felicity never liked Lawrence anyway and he'll never think of her. I'll take most of my stuff – he'll probably be so mad he'll have the locks changed.'

'He can't!' Sally said.

'He can. He'll be furious. He'll probably have the credit cards stopped, too, but I thought of that earlier. I took the maximum amount of cash out on each of them. He'll go mad, but I don't care. And then I'll get a job. I'd have got one years ago, but he always said I'd only earn peanuts so it wouldn't be worth it. He doesn't think I'm good for anything but cooking and shopping, and taking his suits to the cleaners, and buying birthday presents for his bloody mother, and managing just about everything in his life apart from his practice. And his fucking sex life,' she added bitterly.

I was shattered. Not once had I heard her say 'fucking' before.

It was well over an hour later that an echoey bang announced the front door. 'Oh, God,' Sally groaned. 'That's all we need – post-match arguments about club X's wanker of a goalie being more rubbish than club Y's useless twat of a striker.'

'Sorry?' I said.

'Jacko and Frida! There was a match on Sky at the pub – some Swedish club versus some English club – so of course Jacko had to go and help Frida yell rude things at the opposition.'

They clattered in moments later, well-oiled and merry, holding each other up. Jacko wore a baseball cap advertising some Swedish beer and a scarf of Swedish blue and yellow was wound around his crutch.

'We thrashed them,' Jacko chortled. 'It's great being Swedish – I think I might emigrate. Freeds says her mum does a great roast elk with cloudberry sauce – only trouble is the booze costs a bomb. Hi, pet,' he added to Helen. 'All right?'

'Brilliant,' she said. 'I just told Lawrence he could have custody of the twins.'

That cut the post-match euphoria; even Jacko was dumbfounded. After a five-minute rehash Frida said, 'I would have told him face to face. I would like to see his smelly-arse face. I would like to see *her* smelly-arse face and have a good laugh.'

'I really don't know where she gets this language from,' Jacko said, with his best mock-shock. 'It's not very ladylike, Freeds.'

She stuck her tongue out at him. 'On yer bike, Jimmy. Away and bile yer heed.'

'Frida works with a Scottish bloke,' Sally explained to Helen. 'He's teaching her the A to Z of quaint Caledonian insults. She picks up the pathetic English ones from Jacko.'

Helen knocked back about another third of a pint of Lambrusco. 'I'd like to boil Lawrence's head,' she said, slurring her words slightly. 'Like they used to boil pigs' heads in a pan, for brawn. That'd wipe the grin off his face.' She looked down at her empty glass as if she'd only just noticed it. 'I think I'm getting a bit drunk.'

'I'll put coffee on,' Frida said. 'I'm a bit drunk, also.'

Jacko eyed her as she glided over to the coffee-maker. In slinky black trousers and boots she was at least as tall as him, which was around six foot one. Despite her 'fried egg' remark she had a near-perfect figure – cupcakes might have been more accurate. If anyone had fried eggs in this house it was me, but Sally's blooming maternity in that department was enough to make anyone feel underendowed.

Frida was twenty-three, utterly good-natured and one of the easiest sharers I'd ever encountered. Jacko had met her at a club, on his last pre-crash visit. In London to improve her English, she was working in some fast-food place and constantly falling asleep on the job, because she never got much sleep at night. She was sleeping on someone's sofa, Jacko had told me, which might have been OK if it hadn't been 40 cms shorter than she was, but it was all she could afford and still go clubbing. Why didn't he bring her to look at one of the spare bedrooms? OK, they were on the grotty side but at least it was a bed and she'd pay something.

She'd moved in two days later.

It was nearly midnight before Helen left. Once the door had shut behind her, Sally said, 'God, what a turn-up! Talk about the meek little worm turning.'

'Yes, but has it?' I demanded. 'What if it's just a desperate, last-ditch attempt to get him back and that bastard Lawrence calls her bluff? What if *Francesca* does?' I put my head in my hands. 'God, why did I ever say it? Why the hell didn't I wait and find out what she was up to?'

'You'd have been late for Helicopter,' Sally pointed out. 'And if you'd tried to talk her out of it you'd probably have missed him altogether. What happened, anyway?'

Even if Helen hadn't put John right out of my head, I couldn't do with this just now. 'Nothing happened, for God's sake!' I said irritably. 'How can you be thinking of him, anyway? Helen's going to feel sick once she realizes what she's done, and I bet Lawrence'll turn nasty just to spite her . . . Why ever did I open my big mouth?'

'Maybe you did her a favour,' Frida pointed out. 'She's still young – she can make a life. But not alone.

80

I think women like Helen are not so good alone. She needs someone.'

'I know the feeling,' Jacko said pathetically. 'I need someone, too. It's been bloody months.'

'I mean to *love* her, not for planting cucumbers,' Frida said severely.

'God, this is getting right depressing,' he said. 'Anyone fancy a cheese toastie? I'm starving.'

'I'm going to bed,' I said.

Sally joined me five minutes later, while I was wondering whether I could be bothered to take my eye make-up off.

She shut the door behind her. 'Did nothing really happen?'

'Of course not.'

After I'd told her every last detail she said, 'So why didn't you tell Jacko?'

'I don't know,' I shrugged. 'Well, I do. He's already made up his mind John's a two-timing smootharse – he'd only be even more convinced he's right. Even if he is, I almost feel like having a little fling anyway, but I know I'd feel bad afterwards. Probably before and during, too. OK, I never liked Nina, but –'

'You'd hate anyone doing it to you. It's super-bitch stuff.'

'Hyper-bitch. Plus I couldn't face being a side order to Nina.'

'If she's still the main course, and not leftovers. You never know, you might even hear from Rosie that he's slung her in the bin. She phoned earlier, by the way, asking whether you'd seen him yet. Said, "Ooh, really?" when I told her – said she'd pop round tomorrow, to get all the dirt.' She paused. With a wincey face she went on, 'She'd told Suzanne you were seeing him.'

'*What*? Suzanne's best buddies with Nina! Even if Rosie's staying with her, I'd have thought she'd have more sense.'

'Yes, but it probably sounded reasonably innocent. Just a little drink to say thanks for charging to the rescue . . .'

'And that's how it's going to stay, as far as she's concerned,' I said, with feeling. 'I really like Rosie, but she never did know how to spell discretion.'

'Well, you'll find out soon enough.' Stifling a yawn, Sally got up but paused at the door. 'What if there's still no sign of leftovers when he phones?'

'I'll say I'm tied up, I suppose. I'm more worried about Helen at the moment. I bet you anything she'll be in tears tomorrow, asking how the hell she can get that letter back before he sees it.'

'Well, she can't, so don't lose any sleep over it.'

I lost quite a bit of sleep that night, and when I did get off it wasn't much better.

Widdles came scratching at the door at three o'clock, having graciously decided to favour my duvet. Then I dreamt I'd gone back to John's place, where he told me to help myself to a glass of Vimto while he went to slip into something more comfortable. He came back clad only in a mango-flavoured condom, asking whether I'd prefer pistachio, only unfortunately he'd turned into Lawrence and Nina was screaming blue murder because I'd been at her Vimto.

When I went downstairs at a quarter to ten next morning, the first thing Sally said was, 'Helen's gone already. She left a note.'

It said only, 'I'll call you. I won't give an address – Lawrence'll probably try to bully it out of you. If he asks you can tell him you don't know with a clear conscience. Love, Helen.'

'At least she's not in tears on the step,' I said.

'Not on our step, anyway.' She dumped Tom on my lap. 'Do your auntie bit while I shove some washing in.'

So we played bouncy babies, and blowing raspberries on tummies, which was Tom's favourite game. He laughed a lot, showing his perky little tooth, and I finished his breakfast, as he didn't want it. It was baby rice with apple, and a lot yummier than it looked.

Rosie popped in around eleven, ten minutes after I'd got out of the shower. Dating from roughly the Jurassic period, it burnt you when anyone turned a tap on, subsequently froze you, and dribbled lukewarm in between.

'So what happened?' she asked, wide-eyed, the instant she was in the door. This was one reason why you couldn't help liking Rosie. Anyone else would have pretended they'd just come to see you, and said, 'Oh, by the way . . .' ten minutes later, as if they'd only just thought of it.

So I dished out my 'innocent' lie, adding, 'Well, it was too much to hope that it'd be anything else,' in a suitably wry, jokey manner.

'Might have known,' she sighed. 'Anyone else's bloke would have been up to no good, I bet.'

I did feel a bit bad here, but by now we were in the kitchen and she was making a fuss of Tom. 'Ooh, he's just so yummy and squashy – I think I might be going a bit broody.'

'You can have him,' Sally yawned. 'The little bugger's only given me about six hours' sleep in the past ten days.' This was a cover for her real feelings, i.e. instant best-buddiness with anyone who found Tom yummy and squashy.

'Why on earth did you tell Suzanne I was seeing him, anyway?' I asked.

Having just plonked herself in a woodwormy chair, Rosie looked a bit sheepish. 'I never would have, honestly, only she was really browned off the other day, because she'd just been at Nina's, and Nina had just bought her fourteenth pair of Jimmy Choos and Suzanne had to say, "Ooh, how *gor*geous," and not get pissed off because she can't afford them herself.

84

And then Nina was planning a nice little trip to the Maldives with you know who. Or maybe it was Mauritius. Somewhere that costs three grand each with no meals, anyway.'

A nasty little green snake had suddenly appeared in my stomach. Called *serpentus jealousissimus*, it was closely related to *serpentus sick-as-a-pigus*, but more poisonous. 'Only three grand?' I said lightly, catching Sally's eye. 'Slumming it a bit, isn't she?'

'Mind you, she hasn't asked him yet,' Rosie went on. 'But it still made Suzanne sick. All she had with her bloke was a rainy weekend in the Lake District and he dumped her on the way home. She said she wished, just once, Nina would bite into a peach and find she'd eaten half a maggot, only she never would, because it was a law of nature that Nina never got maggots. So I felt a bit sorry for her, and I said, well, you never know, Helicopter might just turn out to have a little maggot. It's OK, she'd never *tell* her,' she added defensively. 'Nina's your archetypal Scorpio, you know. Jealous and possessive. Suzanne said she once went absolutely ape when some bloke tried to dump her. Shoved his mobile in the freezer, parked his car in a towaway zone, you name it.'

'That was a maggot, then,' I said, putting a packet of blueberry muffins on the table. 'Have a nibble, Rosie.'

'No, I mustn't. Are they low-fat?'

'No, but high-yum.'

'Oh, go on, then.'

Rosie was what Jacko would call 'cuddly', with brown curly hair and round brown eyes to match. She was permanently on the kind of diet that features no breakfast, two Twixes on the way to work (on account of no breakfast), salad for lunch, half a skinned chicken breast and three mangetout for dinner (on account of the Twixes) and a massive pepperoni pizza at ten to midnight (on account of the dinner). This then accounted for no breakfast, and so it went on.

'I'll tell you something, though,' she went on, 'if old Helicopter did have a maggot, I wouldn't mind luring it out. Mind you, I'd lure just about anybody's maggot out lately. I almost fancied that bloke of Suzanne's and he was like limp macaroni.'

Sally made a face. 'Listening to this lot makes me thank God I'm right off sex.'

'I wish I was,' said Rosie.

'Give me a baby any day. They never turn out to be married, and if they wake you up in the night at least you don't have to fake anything.'

How long was it since anyone had woken me up in the night, I wondered. Apart from Widdles, of course, and Sally trying not to make a noise with Tom, and Jacko thumping down the landing to the loo . . . Feeling suddenly confined and restless I went and peered out of the window. As the house dated from an era when it had not been thought advisable for skivvies to have a garden view, it only looked out onto next door's brick wall. However, the sun was shining on a window box of snowdrops that had amazed me by actually coming up and showing a few buds already. 'It's a gorgeous day – why don't we get out of here? Anyone fancy Richmond Park?'

'Brilliant,' Sally said. 'We could take Tom to feed the ducks.'

Just as Rosie was saying she would too, she needed the exercise, Jacko came in, saying hi, everybody, God, he felt rough. Sally said, yes, we could see that. Unshaven, unshowered and unbrushed, he was clad in the jog bottoms and sweatshirt which did pyjama duty.

Having put the kettle on, Jacko hobbled to a pinboard on the wall where an Advent calendar hung. Sally had officially bought this for Tom, but if you ask me she secretly still loved snowy-glitter woods with elves and bunnies and lots of exciting little windows. So did Jacko, but he didn't care who knew.

'I've already opened it, you ginger ape,' Sally said. 'And if you dare open any more of my little windows, I'll put itching powder down your plaster.'

'It's not fair,' Jacko grumbled, hobbling back to the kettle. 'Nobody buys me glittery Advent calendars any more. You're a right mean old hag, grudging me a couple of poxy little windows – I've got a good mind to take your Christmas present back to the Oxfam shop.'

'Sibling-substitute stuff,' I said to Rosie. 'They're worse than a pair of kids lately.'

'*I'll* buy you an Advent calendar, Jacko,' she soothed, giggling. 'With chocolates.'

Eventually we made it to my car, a nine-year-old Escort bearing various battle scars from arguments at lights, etc. Inside wasn't exactly pristine, either, what with assorted crisp packets and one of Dorothy's old vests, which I used for demisting the windscreen. Cars had never been my number one priority, not when there was the Great Barrier Reef to save up for.

'I wish I'd moved in with you lot,' Rosie said, as we stowed Tom, all his paraphernalia and ourselves.

I had offered, only Suzanne had offered first, when Rosie had bumped into her at one of those nightmare school reunions. And, as I'd pointed out, at least Suzanne's flat probably had post-Jurassic heating and a shower that understood its job description.

'I mean, Suzanne's really nice but she's permanently stressed,' Rosie went on as I pulled out. 'And half of it's Nina, still expecting her to drop everything and come over every time *she's* stressed. They were like that at school, remember?'

All too well. Nina had only ever been really intimate with Suzanne, and that had been a sort of princess/slave relationship. Suzanne had thought nothing of cancelling her lucrative babysitting because Nina had just chucked her boyfriend and wanted to go clubbing and pick up someone else.

'Every time someone rem*otely* hacks her off at work she's on the phone,' Rosie went on, as we headed for the A3 in milky, pale blue sunshine. 'And then Suzanne has to listen to Nina's battle plan for hacking *them* off.'

Nina had a plum job on one of the glossies, and by all accounts the first thing everyone did there every morning was sharpen their knives.

'I feel really sorry for Suzanne sometimes,' Rosie added, 'but I can't think why she puts up with it.'

'She's a masochist,' I said, as we approached Tibbet's Corner and the wrought-iron Tibbet brandishing his pistol in the middle of the grassy roundabout. A highwayman who'd come to a bad end, he'd surely be tickled to know his name was regularly mentioned on Capital Radio's traffic report.

As we crawled into the Robin Hood Gate with everyone else who thought the park'd be lovely on a day like this, Rosie said, 'By the way, Nina's having a girly lunch thing soon – Suzanne said she's going to send you an invitation.'

'Oh, shit,' I said.

'I knew you'd say that. I don't want to go, either – I hate girly parties – but she apparently said you can natter better without blokes. All right for her – she's *got* a bloke. Will you come?'

'I think I'm going to be horribly busy. Or dead, or something.'

'Yes, I told Suzanne I thought you'd run a mile.'

'You didn't!' Like all the best hypocrites, I was appalled. 'If she passes it on to Nina I'll feel really bad!'

'I don't see why.'

'She sent me a bloody Christmas card! *Idiot!*' This last was not at Rosie, but at a car coming in the other direction. On the left of the narrow road that ran around two thousand acres of parkland was a herd of grazing fallow deer. On the right a hesitant straggler was trying to cross the road to join them, and some cretin driving way over the speed limit had just missed hitting it by a whisker. Frightened, it ran off.

'Suzanne said she wouldn't be a bit surprised if you didn't want to go,' Rosie said. 'Actually, she started saying quite a few things. Don't for God's sake ever tell her I told you, but she said *she* felt bad sometimes because she and Nina used to joke about you behind your back.'

That was a turn-up. 'I know they did, but I couldn't give a stuff now.'

I parked at the Isabella car park. It was virtually packed, which was not surprising as it was more like spring than December. Along with the world and his wife and dog we pushed Tom's buggy down the path to the Isabella Plantation, licking cones. We stopped to admire a huge stag with a massive head of antlers, sitting placidly on a bed of dead bracken. He should have looked like The Monarch of the Glen, but he'd been poking his weapons in the bracken and bits were

90

festooned on them. They hung over his face and eyes, giving him a raffish but dopey air.

'Looks like he's recovering after a really wild night,' Sally said. 'Pity we haven't got a camera. He'd make a lovely card, saying *Boy, that was some party!*'

'Talking of parties . . .' Rosie started giggling help- lessly. 'I forget to tell you something I said at Nina's flat-warming – she was *livid.*'

As we carried on down the path she continued, 'I made some daft crack to Helicopter about his helicopter being dead handy for nipping to Tesco's when the roads were gridlocked, and he looked a bit taken aback, and Nina shot me a Look – you know – but then he just sort of laughed and said he'd only got a lift in the helicopter because his chairman was on the same plane.'

Here she paused for breath. 'But Nina felt a fool, I could tell, because he knew she'd been swanking about him.'

I enjoyed the thought of Nina feeling a fool, but I felt entitled to. If she'd only had the consideration to get involved with some pompous, arrogant prat, I wouldn't be feeling sick already, thinking of the polite excuses I'd have to make when he phoned.

There were no calls on the Monday night, but Helen's friend Felicity phoned on the Tuesday evening. 'She's gone for a walk – I'm afraid I got your number from her mobile memory,' she said. 'I'm a bit worried about her, actually. She had a really curt, furious text message from Lawrence, saying it was typical of her not to have the guts to tell him to his face, but if that's what she wants, fine. I know she's regretting it already, but she won't admit it. I can see why she did it, but I'm sure she's only going to be even more bereft without those boys.'

My heart sank.

'I was wondering if you might talk to her,' she went on.

I tried, half an hour later. Helen sounded on the brink of tears, but she was adamant. If she gave in now, Lawrence would only think she was more pathetic than he already did, and what little self-esteem she had left would be down the pan with the rest of it.

I slept really well that night, as you can imagine.

At half past ten on the Wednesday night, Sally said, irritably, 'Harriet, you're really getting on my nerves. Every time the phone goes you say, "Oh, God, *now* who?" as if you weren't dying for it to be Helicopter, and then try not to look disappointed when it's only your mother.'

It had just been my mother, saying would I please give her *some* idea what to get me for Christmas, and by the way had I heard from Dad lately? She was getting a bit worried in case he'd fallen off a Turkish cliff or something. (They were still friends and kept in touch.)

'If you ask me, he's doing it on purpose,' Sally went on. 'He's priming the plum.'

'Sorry?'

'Getting you all in a state, thinking he's not going to phone, so that by the time he does you'll be a ripe plum, all ready to go plop into his mouth.'

'I am not in a state,' I said testily. 'And I'm not about to do any plopping, all right?'

On the Thursday night I came home to find Sally in a state of her own.

She'd had a Christmas card from Tamsin, the girl she'd shared a flat with for her last few months in Muscat. On the left Tamsin had written, 'Remember Steve? He passed through again ten days ago, staying with Jan and Mark again, and guess what? He was asking after you. And guess what again? He's left his wife!! Jan said she was a bit of a boring cow anyway, she didn't blame him. He's heading for the UK around Christmas, and since I know there were vibes between you two (heh heh!) I gave him your address – well, you said to forward any *mail*, ha ha. Any chance of an e-mail or something? It's been yonks.'

Sally was as churned up as I'd ever seen her. 'I just can't cope with this. I don't *want* him turning up.'

Not so long ago, I'd have thought it was exactly what she did want, in theoretical fantasy. Not only would he have left his wife, he'd say he'd never stopped thinking about her. What's more, he'd be cracking champagne instantly over Tom's head, because his wife had been telling him for x years it wasn't *her* fault she couldn't get pregnant, he must be shooting blanks.

Theoretical fantasy was one thing. Practice was invariably less rosy. 'You're afraid he'll take fright once he sees Tom, you mean.'

'Harriet, I don't want him coming at all! OK, I liked him, but it was just a fling. How would I tell him now? It's been fifteen months! He'd never believe he was his, anyway.'

'I don't see why not. If you'd just wanted maintenance, you'd have told him before.'

'I don't want *any*thing out of him! He probably won't come anyway.'

'He might. And you liked him a lot more than you let on at the time. You were devastated when Jan said he was married.'

'It was shock! I couldn't believe what a bastard he was.'

'Maybe it was on the rocks already.'

'He still should have told me.'

'Sally, you'd only just met him! I don't suppose he actually set out to have a fling.'

As she sat silent, with Tom in her arms, I debated how to play it. 'Whether you want to see him or not, he has a right to know about Tom. And sooner or later, Tom's going to want to know who his daddy is.'

'Some daddy,' she said, looking down at Tom's downy little head. 'Some mummy, come to that.' In a baby, cootchy-coo voice she said to Tom, 'Naughty bad Mummy was a bit of an old slapper, wasn't she? A pint of sandy sangria and she was anybody's.'

I only laughed because she expected me to. Typically, she was trying to shrug it off, pretend she wasn't in a state at all.

I woke up that night at ten past two and heard her creaking round her room. Minutes later, I heard her creaking along the landing and down the stairs.

I found her in the kitchen with Tom, saying she couldn't sleep and cursing because there wasn't enough milk for hot chocolate. She looked as if she'd been having a little weep, but said irritably that she was fine, would I please not start all that soap-opera, do-you-want-to-talk-about-it stuff, because she didn't. Would I please just go back to bed, she was going to watch a corny old film.

Since there was nothing corny on, however, I drove in my pyjamas to the video machine at the petrol station (I got some funny looks) and came back with *Chicken Run* and a litre of milk. I finally went back to bed at four thirty, got up at seven and went to work to find that some virulent bug had descended overnight on the capital. Half our temps were suddenly sick, it was chaos, and then Lesley, our manager, hacked me right off.

Solutions Software, which was staffed almost entirely by *Loaded*-reading blokes, had thought it acceptable to specify 'Bubbly under twenty-five with long legs' when asking for a receptionist. I said to Lesley, 'They can't do this!' but Lesley just shrugged and said if we didn't find one they'd only go elsewhere. If I didn't want to handle it she'd do it herself.

Just as I'd made my twenty-seventh fruitless phone call, Jess said, 'You know that little paper-clip man?'

Jess was my number two equal. She was thirty-six and sweet as they come, but if she'd been married she'd have been the kind of person my mother calls a 'married spinster', if you know what I mean.

I sensed a Jess-ism coming on. 'What little paper-clip man?'

'You know, when you start writing a letter. On my PC at home there's this little paper-clip man who pops up and asks if you want any help with your letter. Anyway, I was doing a Christmas letter last night to my Auntie Hazel, and up he popped, just as I'd put "Dear Auntie Hazel", saying, "Do you want any help?"'

Where was this going, I wondered.

'So I clicked "cancel",' she went on. 'And I know it's really stupid, but afterwards I felt a bit mean.'

Sandie, our junior, gave an explosive snort.

'I mean, I always click "cancel",' Jess went on, 'but he's got such a cute little face I think I'll click "yes please" next time.'

Sandie gave another snort. Now, in normal circumstances I love Jess-isms, too, they can perk up grey days no end, but I was too tired and stressed to be in the mood. 'It's too late,' I said, trying to sound amused. 'Your computer's probably on the blink already. He'll have curled up in the circuits crying buckets because you've rejected him, and computers don't like wet.'

The instant it was out I knew it had sounded sarcastic, instead. I felt awful, especially when Sandie exploded into fits. Sounding hurt, Jess said, 'All right, I know it sounds really stupid . . .'

I said, 'Jess, I really didn't mean—'

'It's all right. Honestly!' With a closed-up face she got back to whatever she'd been doing before, and I felt dreadful because I'd hurt her feelings. If it had been earlier I could have nipped out and got her a making-up cream cake to have with her coffee, but it was already ten to five and there was no time for nipping out for anything, because of this bug-induced chaos.

So I arrived home exhausted and thoroughly ratty to find Sally equally exhausted and ratty, because she was exhausted anyway, Tom had been exhausted and whingey all day, and Widdles had sicked up half a mouse on her bed. Jacko was also ratty (for Jacko) because Sally had been a right ratty old hag all day, his itches were driving him mad, and Frida had gone to some fancy-dress hen night and refused to take him along.

'He offered to dress up as a guardian eunuch,' Sally said scathingly. 'I ask you.'

'I might as well be a bloody eunuch lately,' he grumbled.

'If Erik Bloodaxe ever gets to hear half the things you say to Frida, you will be a bloody eunuch,' she said. To me she added, '*And* he nicked the last bit of my squirty cream to have on his Weetabix.'

'You nicked all my Smarties!'

'Only because you nicked my M&Ms!'

That was when I exploded. 'Shut – *up*!'

They looked at each other. 'Now see what you've done,' Sally said to him.

'Me?' he said, all hurt. 'You started it!'

'Oh, grow up, the pair of you!' I banged out, but the door rebounded instead of slamming shut and Jacko's summing-up wafted after me.

'She needs a bloke,' he said to Sally. 'A bloke and a life, in that order.'

'I – do – not – need – a bloody – bloke! OK?' Having yelled this from the fourth stair, I then ran up to my room and banged the door. 'Up to here' was not the precise term I'd have used just then. Wherever 'here' was, I was way over it.

So when John phoned twenty seconds later, I was ready for him. In fact I'd never been readier for any plum-priming smootharse in my life.

# FOUR

I answered like snappy bullets. 'Hello?'

'Harriet?'

*My God, it's him. Shit, if he wants to see me tonight have I got anything clean to wear?* 'Oh, *John!* Hi, how's it going?'

'Is it a bad time? You sound a bit stressed.'

'Oh, no, not really. Well, maybe just a bit. I'd literally just charged upstairs after a day from hell.'

'Sounds as if you could do with a dinner out, then,' he said, in those melted-chocolate tones.

*Too right I could, and that pink top might do.*

'Could you make Sunday night?'

Damn it. Still, just as well he hadn't said Saturday, as I had something on, for once. 'Er, yes, I think so.'

'What nationality do you like to eat?'

I suddenly thought of a new place I'd just heard of – someone had described it as 'exotic'. 'There's some new Middle Eastern place not far from my office in Fulham – I can't remember the name but I can soon find out.'

'Let me know, then, and I'll book it. Eight-ish?'

'No, I'll book it. And this is on me – I owe you for that suit, never mind the remains of the thirty quid.'

He didn't argue. 'If you insist. Shall I pick you up?'

With Jacko and Sally nosing? 'No, I'll see you there. I'll ring and give you the details, all right?'

I hung up feeling as if I'd had a shot of some wild, intravenous drug.

Suddenly it all seemed so simple. I didn't care if he was Nina's or anyone else's. I didn't care if he was two-timing or three-timing, or even if he had more maggots than a case of tequila. Buried for months in *Mumsy World* and non-drip emulsion, in Pampers and Blockbusters, in Jess-isms and squabbling friends and other people's problems, I was desperate for some excitement.

Just one night of it. One night with vibes swirling like hot mist (because I knew they would be) and no faffing or dithering, or wondering whether I should be doing this because it wasn't very nice . . .

What would it matter? Nobody was going to find out, because I wasn't going to tell them. Jacko would only grunt about smootharses. Sally would tut, and remind me what I'd said about side orders, don't come running to her if I felt yuck afterwards.

But I had to tell them something; you couldn't just say 'going out' in this house. Plotting my alibi would only add to the buzz, but I didn't have to look very far. On the Saturday night I was going to a do thrown by an old friend from my Athens era. If I 'met' someone there, he'd do very nicely.

I went through the rest of the evening feeling as if I were planning a bank robbery and absolutely knowing I was going to get away with it. If it turned out to be reasonably legal after all, i.e. if I heard afterwards that Nina had got the elbow, all well and good. In the meantime, I was tingling with a better cocktail than Tom Cruise ever came up with.

Hiding it wasn't so easy. Later that evening Sally gave me a suspicious look. 'What's up with you? Helicopter hasn't phoned, has he?'

'No such luck. If you must know, I was just having a little fantasy about Nina going down with chickenpox and him taking me to the Maldives, instead.'

Devious, but it seemed to work.

I don't know whether it was that cocktail, but two quite passable blokes made considerable efforts on the Saturday night. Maybe I was giving off an aura of Tantalizing Hidden Depths. At any rate, I came home feeling as tantalizing as you like, with a perfect alibi, too. Only as everyone had gone to bed, he had to wait.

'Andy what?' Sally said, in the morning.

'Travers. He was nice.'

'And where are you going?'

One little white truth wouldn't hurt. 'That new Middle Eastern place near the office. How was your evening, anyway?'

'Not bad. Rosie phoned just after you left. Said she was at a loose end and a bit fed up, so I said join the

101

club, come round. And later on Jacko rolled in with a massive pizza and that Czech au pair.'

'What Czech au pair?'

'From number fifty-three. He met her the other day in the corner shop. She's homesick, poor girl, and hardly speaks any English, so he took her for a cappuccino and some preparatory softening-up. Another to add to his list of "in with a chance, once I get my plaster off".'

Some of her digs at Jacko were beginning to get to me lately. 'He probably just felt sorry for her!'

'OK, I didn't *mean* it!' she huffed, as if I was supposed to know.

She was vaguely huffy for most of the day, but it didn't stop her coming and flopping on my bed with Tom while I was getting ready for take-off. She always liked to supervise the operation.

'So what does he do?' she asked, as I wriggled into a silvery top that did wonders for my fried eggs.

'He's a journalist on the *Independent*.' It was actually *DVD Choice* or something, but the *Indie* sounded better.

For a minute or two she kept quiet, as I sat at Dorothy's Victorian dressing table, hot-brushing my haystack into something passably attractive.

Then she said, 'It's Helicopter, isn't it? He's phoned and you haven't told me.'

'Don't be stupid.'

'It is. I knew he'd got to you. You're like a fish on a

line, just begging to be reeled in. You'll be jumping into his frying pan next, saying, "Eat me! Eat me!"'

Possibly stripping my own scales off, too. But I half turned on my stool. 'It is not – bloody – Helicopter! All right?'

'OK, OK!' Other things were already on her mind. Her brow creased with anxiety as she gazed at Tom, who was restless and fretful in her arms. 'I think he's starting another cold – he hardly ate any tea and he's a bit hot. Come and feel, will you?'

I put a hand to his forehead. He might have been marginally warmer than usual, but I couldn't be sure. 'Where's that thermometer thing you put on his forehead?'

'I can't find it. Do *you* think he feels hot?'

'Well, a bit, maybe, but babies can get temperatures even from teething, can't they?'

'Yes, I suppose . . . I don't like to keep giving him Calpol, he's had gallons of it lately.'

'See how he is in an hour.'

'Yes, but what if he's still hot?'

'Then give him some Calpol.'

'Yes, but do you think I should phone the doctor?'

'Well, yes, if he *seems* ill, but it's probably just another tooth.'

'Well, thanks a lot, you're a great help!' Getting huffily off my bed she gathered up her angel and dropped a kiss on his head. 'Come on, darling – *Mummy* cares if you're not a very well bubba.'

I could have shaken her. 'I *do* care! But it's no use getting all worked up if he's just being normally whingey.'

This was entirely the wrong thing to say. 'He's not normally whingey!' she said, incensed. 'Are you implying that he's whingey and miserable non-stop?'

'Of course not! I just meant—'

'Oh, forget it. I don't expect you to give a toss.'

'Sally, for God's sake—'

'Forget it!'

And she banged out, leaving me torn between guilt and exasperation. Mostly exasperation, actually. She was getting so bloody ratty lately. All right, part of it was down to Steve, but I also had a feeling she was vaguely resentful because I was having two nights out on the trot.

It was grossly unfair. I'd been there for her ever since that ClearBlue test, held her hand in the delivery room and put her first ever since. It was even more grossly unfair to say I didn't care about Tom. She knew very well that the only person who loved him more than me was her, even if I didn't gush it every five minutes.

More than ever, I was dying to escape. I felt as if I was back on that runway, tingling with anticipation as the engines revved to screaming pitch . . .

I'd ordered a minicab, so I could drink and not have to spend twenty minutes looking for a parking space. Outwardly cool, I arrived at one minute to eight. Someone from the estate agents next to our office had told me about this place. He'd said anything straight out of *Harems and Gardens* had to be good for a laugh, the food was above average, and you didn't have to brace yourself for the bill.

He was right about the *Harems* bit. As the waiters were busy I stood at the little desk, taking in honey-coloured marble, silk cushions and hangings, exotic plants and a fountain going tinkle-splash. I was half expecting Aladdin to appear when someone tweaked my waist and whispered, 'Come wiz me to ze kasbah.'

Whatever drug I was on, this gave it a massive top-up, and made me laugh, too.

'I think we've strayed into *The Thousand and One Nights*,' he said. 'Are you sure you're not Scheherazade?'

'I hope not. Wasn't she in nightly fear of getting chucked into the Bosporus in a sack?'

'Or getting her head chopped off. Here comes Ali Baba,' he added *sotto voce*, as the head waiter came scurrying up.

I managed to say, 'Harriet Grey – table for two,' without erupting into fizzy giggles. He showed us to an intimate little corner with silk-cushiony seating, soft lamps, and a mini-fountain within tinkling distance. 'You have to admit it's different,' I said, after the waiter had gone. 'I wonder if they bring hubble-bubbles with the coffee?'

'Probably. And rose-water finger bowls offered by Circassian slaves from Shepherd's Bush.'

For escape purposes, I could hardly have picked anywhere better. The air was delicately scented with incense and jasmine, and evocative, Middle Eastern music was playing quietly in the background. If someone had wanted to create an oasis in west London they'd certainly succeeded.

It was a square table for two or four, but since there were just two of us we sat on two sides of a right angle, on a luxuriously padded corner seat. It was just made for hungry lovers; kneesie under the table would have been a doddle, and even significantly naughty stuff could have been accomplished with ease, as long as you could keep a straight face.

He looked even better than last time, which was saying something. Fresh from shave and shower, his hair was still slightly damp and the scent of shaving things and clean shirt were combining with incense and spices into a lethally seductive concoction.

After ordering two gin and tonics I said, on impulse, 'I have a confession to make.'

'Go on, then. But bear in mind that I'm very easily shocked.'

His mouth quivered as he said it, in a way that made me think, stuff dinner, I'll just eat you. 'I lied,' I said, with mock penitence. 'I hadn't lost my purse after all. I thought I had, but I remembered almost at once that I'd put it into one of my carrier bags.'

'So why didn't you say so?'

'You'd have thought I was a complete idiot.'

'No, I wouldn't.'

'Wouldn't you?'

'No, I'd have thought you were only half an idiot. I already thought you were a complete idiot for leaving your bag open in the first place.'

Who needed starters when you had this? Deliciously teasing banter, with more quivery stuff and eye contact to kill for. 'Then why didn't you say so?'

'Because I was very well brought up. And I thought you might hit me with your handbag.'

I stifled a volcanic giggle. 'I wouldn't have had the energy. Are we going to look at these menus or not?'

Once we'd ordered (mezze, hamoor and lamb with plum sauce), I said, 'How are the ram-raid plans going?'

'I'm not telling a shocking liar like you. How do I know you won't phone Crimestoppers and grass me up?'

'How could I possibly grass you up?' I asked, all innocent. 'I don't know your surname or where you live or anything. The Old Bill wouldn't be very impressed with "A tall, darkish bloke called John", would they?'

'You've got my phone number.'

'Well, yes, but you might have given a false address for your phone bills.'

'And it's Mackenzie.'

Well, it was a vast improvement on Helicopter. 'Scottish roots, then?'

'My old man was, originally. I'm still expected to put on a dress kilt occasionally and pretend I'm not a Sassenach.'

This was just another plus. I'd had a bit of a thing about dress kilts ever since a Burns Night in Granada when I'd got really drunk and danced the Dashing White Sergeant with a gorgeous bloke from Inverness.

From then on vibes swirled nicely. They were subtle, grown-up vibes, behaving themselves under a veneer of civilized conversation. That was how I liked my vibes. Discreet but potent, with spicy undertones, as one of those daft wine buffs might say. At any rate I was enjoying them like nobody's business until I nearly suffered cardiac arrest.

From where we were sitting I couldn't quite see the entrance but some woman in a cream jacket had just come from that direction. All I saw, in the first sick instant, was a swinging silk curtain of hair as she turned, obviously looking for someone. 'Magda! There you are!' I heard, as she swung around – and I saw her face.

Phew. As if it could have been Nina. It was ludicrous.

Or was it? What if Rosie had popped round again? Or phoned? She and Sally had obviously clicked – it wouldn't surprise me. What if Sally had said something? And Rosie, unable to contain this hot, tasty morsel . . .

What had she said about Nina? *'Jealous and pos-sessive . . . she went absolutely ape . . .'* No, surely even for Rosie this would be a mouth-opening too far. Surely Sally wouldn't open her mouth, either, even if we'd just had a row and she was still seriously hacked off with me . . .

*'She said Tom was always whingeing!'*

*'She didn't!'*

*'She did – I was livid. Poor little bubba – how would she like it if her teeth were tearing her little gums to bits? Not that she gave a toss, she was getting herself all tarted up for what's-his-face. If it* is *what's-his-face. If you ask me . . .'*

My mouth went dry. Why ever had I told Sally where I was going? What if a venom-spitting Nina was even now heading our way in the back of a cab? For some reason I suddenly had a vision of that evil, sledge-travelling witch in *The Lion, the Witch and the Wardrobe,* the one who made it always winter and never Christmas. I saw her cracking a whip, screaming, 'Faster, faster, fool!'

This was where prissy big sister came back. 'It'd serve you right if she did catch you,' she said smugly. 'What sort of cow are you turning into?'

I really hated that girl sometimes. 'I owe him a dinner, don't I? After I wrecked his suit? I still haven't paid off that thirty quid, either.'

'Oh, very convenient.'

'It's just one night! I'm not trying to pinch him!'

I'm afraid to say that twenty minutes later any guilt

I felt had been drowned by another glass of wine, increasingly potent vibes, and 'sweetmeats' straight from the Perfumed Garden. Honey and rose water, incense and John: it would have taken a saint to withstand that lot, and halos never did suit me. As I dithered between sliced fresh mango and baklava, John said, 'Why don't we get one of each and share?'

Lovely. There's something deliciously intimate about forking delicate morsels from someone else's plate.

By then we'd got onto how I'd bumped into Sally and my TEFL era.

'If you've got the travel bug, why didn't you stick with that?' he asked, as I forked a morsel of baklava from his plate. It was like Shredded Wheat, soaked in rose-watery syrup. 'You can go virtually anywhere and teach English.'

'Yes, but it was the same thing, over and over. One day, when I was teaching the third conditional for the four-hundredth time, I thought it was about time I did something else.'

He forked up a bit of my mango. I was beginning to wish I'd stuck with that, as the baklava was seriously sticky. 'What the hell's the third conditional?'

'You really don't want to know.'

'I wouldn't have asked if I didn't want to know.'

Well, he'd asked for it. For want of any other model, I said, 'If I *tell* you the truth about my purse, *you'll think* I'm an idiot – that's the first conditional. If I *told* you the truth, *you'd think* I was an idiot – that's the second.

110

If I *had told* you the truth, you'd *have thought* I was an idiot – that's the third.'

For a quivery moment he took this in. 'If I tell *you* a barefaced little truth, will you promise not to hit me?'

*My God*, I thought. *He's going to come clean about Nina.*

But his eyes dropped to my mouth, and I changed my mind. He was going to say something gorgeously corny like, 'Can we just get the hell out of here? If I don't kiss you soon I'm going to blow a fuse.'

I went like hot, melting jelly, just at the thought. 'Go on, then.'

'You've got a bit of baklava on your lip.'

Talk about confusion. 'Have I?' I said unsteadily. 'Where?'

'Hold still . . .' Touching a fingertip to the corner of my mouth he removed a morsel, which then stuck to his own finger. 'Lick,' he said, like a velvet-clad command.

As if hypnotized, I opened my mouth, touched the tip of my tongue to his finger and licked the crumb off. And during the entire operation, his eyes never left my face.

For tantalizing starters I defy anyone to beat it. In fact I was half expecting one of the staff to come and tell me that melting jellies were not allowed, they'd mess up the silk cushions.

But we got back to grown-up conversation. And five

minutes later, as little cups of Turkish coffee arrived, he glanced at his watch. 'It's still relatively early. Do you fancy doing something else afterwards?'

I'd been expecting it, but that weird, unnamed little organ still gave a wild involuntary lurch. 'Like what?' I asked, casually.

'We could maybe catch a late-night film?'

This wasn't quite what I'd had in mind. If anything, I'd been thinking of some intimate little place where they played 'Help Me Make it through the Night', and your fuses smouldered on a smoochy scrap of a dance floor, until you fell into a taxi and ate each other on the way to wherever they were going to blow.

However, cinemas had their pluses. 'Yes, lovely,' I said, thinking of sitting close to him in a cosy little art-house place, pretending to be engrossed in something deep and sexily subtitled, while vibes built up like that electric tension you get before a really spectacular storm. Except that it was Sunday night, which meant we'd probably be restricted to stuff like *Blair Witch II*, rather than *Le Plot Noir avec Soupçons de Hanky-Panky Dangereusement Erotiques*. On the other hand, Blair Witches would provide brilliant opportunities for pretending to be scared out of my poor little wits, having to hold his hand tight and cuddle even closer. 'Anything particular in mind?'

'Our options'll be limited on a Sunday night. What have you seen?'

That was easy. 'Nothing for months, unless it's in Blockbusters. How about you?'

'Ditto. Our best bet's probably one of the West End multi-screens.'

'How about the Trocadero?' The idea of scary Blair Witches was really growing on me, and I knew it was on at the Trocadero because Frida had just seen it there.

'Just off Piccadilly Circus?'

'That's it.' I tried to catch a waiter's eye for the bill, but they all seemed to be deliberately avoiding me. Feeling the effects of a high fluid intake I headed for the ladies, instead. Even the steamiest vibes can go right off the boil when all you want is the loo.

Naturally I gave myself a quick check in the mirror. My reflection was very slightly flushed in a purely flattering way, which matched how I felt exactly. Marginally pissed, full of sod-it recklessness, and loving it.

Suddenly remembering Sally, I felt a bit bad for thinking she'd have blabbed to Rosie. I felt even worse for rowing with her. She had a lot on her mind; I should have been more patient. Feeling a quick 'sorry' was called for, I gave her a call.

I let it ring for ages, but there was no reply. She'd hardly be in bed yet, but she could be in the bath. After the loo I adjusted my hair and sprayed a whisper of Jean-Paul Gaultier where my cleavage would be if I had one. I then reapplied my lipstick and blotted it so effectively it almost looked as if I hadn't bothered. Having done all that, I tried Sally again.

I let it ring even longer. Again there was no reply, but if she was in the bath, she'd hardly get out and go all the way downstairs in a towel. On a cold day the stairs and landing could be positively hypothermic.

On the way back I stopped at the head waiter's station. It was conveniently just out of sight of our table, and paying now would save any of those tedious 'No, please, let me . . .' arguments. Despite our agreement I had a feeling he might be awkward when it came to the crunch.

'May I have my bill please?' I said, proffering a credit card. 'Table fourteen.'

The waiter looked at me uncertainly, as if I'd committed some weird breach of etiquette. 'If Madame will please go to her table . . .'

'I'd rather pay it here, if you don't mind.'

From the way he was looking at me, I was wondering whether it was a sackable offence to dish out bills at the desk. Suddenly appearing relieved, however, he looked over my shoulder and said something in what was presumably Arabic to the approaching head waiter, who produced a professional beam. 'Is not necessary, madame.' He spread his hands in a gesture of expansive generosity. 'Is free, today!'

'Free?' I gaped. 'Since when does any London restaurant dish out free dinners? Are we your five-thousandth customers since opening, or something?'

114

'Is a special, madame,' he beamed. 'Just for you.'

The penny dropped. 'Are you telling me he's already paid?'

From my face or tone, or both, they could evidently tell I wasn't tickled pink. The head waiter gave a deprecating little smile and an almost Gallic shrug, as if to say, 'What could I do?'

Well, it was hardly his fault, poor man. 'Not much I can do then, is there?'

Except that there was. If he thought he could put one over on me, I was well up to playing him at his own game. I was just in the mood for piquant little games; at a time like this they only added an edge. Besides, it would serve him right.

With a brilliant game plan up my sleeve, I headed for our table.

'Sorry I've been so long,' I said brightly. 'I was trying to ring Sally. We had a bit of a row just before I came out, so I thought I'd say sorry. Only she's not answering.'

'Gone out?' he suggested.

'Hardly, with the baby. She might be in the bath.'

But I put Sally aside for now. 'I'll try again on the way to the cinema.' I added a bright, expectant smile. 'Shall we go?'

A momentary start didn't escape me. 'Well, if you're ready . . .'

'I am if you are. Oh, the *bill.*' I pretended to have suddenly caught on. 'I paid it just now, at the desk.'

With a confiding smile I went on, 'I thought I'd get it out of the way. I'm sure you're not like that, but some men can be boringly prehistoric about these things.'

For about a millisecond I saw it going through his head: *Just what the fuck is going on?'* But he said, 'Give me two minutes – I need to check the plumbing . . .'

I gave him precisely half a minute before following; I didn't want anyone outraged by accusations of dishonesty. At the desk he was already sounding heated in an even, controlled way. 'Yes, I *know* I paid it, but one of your staff must have been half asleep –'

This was quite enough. I tapped him on the shoulder. 'Funny place for a pee.'

It was barely a nanosecond before he twigged. His eyes closed briefly in an 'Oh, shit' fashion.

However, I wasn't looking at him. To the harassed-looking head waiter I shot my nicest smile. 'I'm so sorry – we got our wires crossed. Goodnight.'

John, meanwhile, was wearing the gratifying expression of a bloke who's just realized he's been had.

'*Now* shall we go?' I said sweetly.

He said nothing till the door had closed behind us.

'All right, I'm sorry,' he said, holding up his hands as if to ward off a frenzied bashing with a handbag.

Until then, I'd have left it there. I just wasn't the

116

type to throw a principled fit if a bloke who could afford it insisted on paying; I'd be more likely to pass out with shock. However, since he was obviously expecting a principled fit, it seemed a shame to disappoint him. 'Do you realize how stupid I felt? Was it your idea to tell me it was "free today"?'

'Is that what he said?' His grin was almost enough to provoke a frenzied bashing after all. 'All right, I'm sorry!' he added, seeing my face.

'We agreed!' Well, we had.

A passing couple gave us nosily interested looks as they went by, but we ignored them. 'All right, so I'm one of those prehistoric bastards who likes to pay,' he said. 'If it really bothers you that much, you can pay me back.'

'I don't carry that kind of cash!'

'A cheque, then. Look, can we continue this argument in a cab? It's brass monkey stuff out here.'

It was, too, with one of those winds that have only recently emigrated from Siberia. My coat was designed more for looks than thermals but it was a good deal better than his, which he'd evidently left at home. 'I haven't got my chequebook. I hardly ever carry it.'

'Then you pay next time. I swear I'll play ball.'

'Who said there's going to be a next time?' To tell the truth, I was enjoying this little game. I even thought I'd take it a bit further. After all, a brief chase would make it all the sweeter when I eventually let him catch me. I don't watch *Animal Earth* for nothing: all those stroppy female kangaroos cunningly repelling Mr Roo's advances to see whether he's got the requisite guts and stamina.

Accordingly I started a fast walk towards the underground, which was a good five minutes away, even the way I walk when I'm pretending to be mad and it's freezing. I will fully admit that I knew he'd follow. I can spot a wimpy Mr Roo at fifty paces.

He kept up manfully. 'It's starting to rain, in case you hadn't noticed.'

'It's not rain. It's sleet.' Already a few fat, wet splodges were decorating my black, fifteen per cent cashmere mix.

'So it is,' he said, in determinedly cheerful tones. 'Thank God I didn't bring a coat – I haven't felt this close to the elements in weeks.'

We carried on past shop windows full of Christmas displays and twinkly lights. 'Where are you off to, just out of interest?' he asked.

'The underground – where do you think?'

'All the way to Piccadilly Circus? Wouldn't you prefer to be stroppy in a cab?'

'You call this stroppy? Wait till I really get going. And who said I'm going to Piccadilly Circus?'

'You did. Before you decided I was a sexist bastard who needed sorting out.'

'Well, you said it.' He was doing brilliantly in the Mr Roo stakes – Mother Nature would have been proud

118

of him. The sleet was rapidly getting both heavier and sleetier. It was precisely the sort of weather that made me wonder why I wasn't still teaching third conditionals in the sun.

'Aren't you getting this just a bit out of proportion?' he asked, as I strode on like something out of *Soldier, Soldier*.

'That depends entirely on your perception of "proportion".' I was rather pleased with this: superficially intelligent and impressive while scoring zero on the Plain English scale.

'I'm too cold to cope with big words,' he said. 'Two syllables are about my limit in polar-bear weather. I could just about cope with "Sod off, will you?"'

I wasn't going that far, in case he actually sodded. 'Those are all one syllable.' I stepped off the pavement to avoid a crowd of thirty-somethings blocking the way. Having just spilled out of an Italian restaurant, they looked and sounded as if they'd been enjoying a riotous Christmas party. I stepped in a freezing puddle in the gutter and uttered a one-syllable curse.

'That feel nice, does it?' he asked, five yards further on.

'What?' My breath was coming out like clouds of dry ice.

'Water in your shoes. I can hear it squelching.'

It was, too. Apart from the fact that even I was getting cold, it was time to let him catch me. I wanted to try Sally again, anyway. Diving into the shelter of a shop doorway, I got my mobile out.

'If you're trying your friend again,' he said, 'it's a little-known fact that mobiles work far better from inside cabs, especially when the person you're trying to ring is in the bath.'

I bit my lip. Just as I was about to say, 'John, I was winding you up,' he said, 'Look, can we start again?'

*I thought you'd never ask.*

'Give me a good slap, if you like.' Inclining his head, he tapped his left cheek invitingly. 'Go on, before I chicken out.'

I did laugh then. 'It'll hurt.'

'I thought that was the general idea.'

'Hurt *me*, I mean. I did it once before and it hurt like hell.'

His mouth flickered in a lethally wooze-making fashion. Added to which, it isn't often a bloke can look down on me when I've got two-and-half-inch heels on. I was hoping he'd move in for starters there and then, but he just said, 'Stay there while I hijack a cab.'

Well, it'd be all the better for waiting. Watching him get wetter and colder on the kerb, I wondered whether I should join him, rather than waiting out of the wet like the classic girly type I'd never been.

Stuff it. You could take equality too far, especially

in weather like this. I was just about to try Sally again when he called, 'Harriet!'

Funny how a black cab can look like heaven; in these conditions I'd have expected to wait ten minutes. Once he was in beside me I shot a guilty glance at his trousers, where splodges of sleet were still melting. 'I'm sorry, I didn't intend you to get quite that wet.'

'Yes, you did. You're a merciless, cold-hearted woman.'

His mock-sorrowful tones made me laugh. 'That'll teach you to renege on an agreement.'

He brushed a splodge from a substantial-looking thigh. 'If you hadn't been so long in the little girls' room, I mightn't have done it.'

'If Sally had been answering, I wouldn't have *been* so long.'

He was giving me another of those deliciously lingering appraisals. 'You wouldn't have lasted long as Scheherazade. You'd have been slung in the Bosporus in ten minutes, in a sack labelled "Stroppy concubine – handle with care, she bites".'

'Well, concubinery was never one of my preferred career options.'

He ignored this. 'Even when I called the other day, you sounded as if you were about to bite someone's head off.'

'I told you, I'd had a day from hell. And I *had* bitten someone's head off, in a manner of speaking.' I told him about Jess's paper-clip man.

Predictably enough, he laughed.

'It's not funny,' I said wryly. 'I felt really bad afterwards.'

'Sorry.' As gently as he'd said it, he took my hand and gave it a little squeeze.

It's one of the great mysteries of life how, at twenty-nine, something like this can still make you go as gooey as a fourteen-year-old who's never been kissed. He didn't let go, either.

'Your hand's cold,' he said.

'Yours isn't.'

'It takes more than a half-hearted bit of sleet to mess up my thermostat.'

Even in the semi-dark, I could see his eyes. 'Just as well,' I said unsteadily. 'I wouldn't want you going down with a nasty chill.'

'I don't think there's much chance of that.'

Added to his eyes, and a minute caress with his thumb on the back of my hand, this was quite enough to get vibes swirling wildly. In fact, we could possibly have made *The Guinness Book of Records* just then, for the greatest amount of them ever found in the back of a London cab. Fleeting fantasies I would prefer not to describe shot through my head like a video on fast forward.

And when he spoke, his voice was subtly different. Rough and soft at once, like an old Shetland sweater. 'If you're going to try your friend again, why don't you do it now?'

*Clear the decks for action. Get it out of the way.*

'God, yes, I'd almost forgotten . . .' Wondering whether my thumping heartbeat could be heard in the Mile End Road, I fumbled in my bag for my mobile. 'She surely can't still be wallowing in Tesco's economy bubbles.'

I let it ring for ages, but again there was no reply.

'Gone to bed?' he suggested.

'Sally hardly ever goes to bed early. She's usually too shattered to drag herself upstairs. She falls asleep in front of the television.'

'Then that'll be why she can't hear the phone.'

In theory, perhaps. In practice, she'd almost certainly hear it. Because she was economizing, Sally had no mobile so it had to be the house phone, and the house phone was on the wall in the kitchen, and the kitchen sofa was where she invariably fell asleep. In any case, she always had an ear open for the baby alarm.

But I didn't say so. Suddenly I was becoming uneasy. She was alone in the house. What if she'd done something really stupid, like touching a light switch with wet hands when too tired to think? The wiring was hardly Health and Safety stuff in the first place. The last electrician had told me it was probably wildly overloaded, love, they hadn't had tellies and washers and microwaves all going at once during the Boer War.

And then there was that loose bit of carpet on the

stairs. The stair carpet practically dated back to the Bronze Age, too. Why the hell hadn't I fixed it?

On an impulse I tried Jacko. He might well be in a pub just round the corner – he could check on her.

His bloody mobile was off.

Telling myself I was getting as bad as my mother, imagining all sorts at the drop of an unanswered call, I looked out of the window. We'd just hit the river, on the Chelsea Embankment. The Albert Bridge lights were reflected in the Thames, but the night looked so black and icy cold, the sleet still falling, you couldn't imagine summer ever coming. 'Just look at it,' I said. 'I should have been diving off the Great Barrier Reef by now, saying hi to a few sharks.'

'Don't you mind the sharks?'

'Of course I do. I was petrified the first time, but they're an occupational hazard. Just when you're thinking this is the most beautiful coral you've ever seen, and you're looking at brilliant blue starfish, and fish like rainbows are swimming right past your mask, something comes looming out of the depths.'

'As they say, every Eden has its serpent.'

'Yes, unless it's a Disneyland Eden.'

I wished he hadn't said it, though. Not when I was already uneasy about Sally. Whatever drug I'd been on was rapidly wearing off. I wasn't sure I wanted this buzzy little Eden any more, not with maggots and Nina-serpents lurking under rocks. If he was going to evict that particular serpent, OK, but he hadn't.

And what about me? What sort of rock-lurker was I turning into? I was a Nice Girl, dammit. I just didn't *do* things like this.

Still, surely the Trocadero wouldn't hurt. Where was the harm in Blair Witches and a box of Maltesers? It would be easy enough to put the lid on anything else. After all, lids had barely been taken off yet. I might allow myself just one really toe-curling kiss, though. God knew I needed a little treat.

I tried Sally again as we were coming up to Parliament Square.

Still no reply.

I heard her voice, though. Like an accusation, it was suddenly ringing in my head.

*'Forget it! I don't expect you to give a toss!'*

Oh God, I thought. Tom.

# FIVE

The unease I'd felt before was nothing to this. It crawled over me like iced spiders. I'd read all Sally's baby books, you see. So that I wouldn't look blank when she was on about three months colic.

It wasn't colic on my mind now. '. . . *respiratory infections . . . the danger of pneumonia . . . small babies can succumb within hours . . .*'

'The baby wasn't well,' I said, my mouth suddenly desiccated. 'She said he wasn't well, but I thought it was just his teeth. What if he's got worse? What if she's taken him to hospital?'

'Surely she'd have phoned you?'

'My phone was off!'

Why hadn't I left it on? Why the hell had I gone out at all when she was worried? 'She takes him on buses, with people coughing and spluttering, and there's a really nasty flu bug doing the rounds. Half our temps have got it.'

Twenty yards further on I came to a decision. 'Look, I'm sorry but I've got to go home.' Without waiting for a reply I rapped on the driver's partition. 'Forget Piccadilly Circus – could you make it Putney, instead?'

126

'I'm sorry,' I added to John, 'but there's no way I can sit watching films at the moment.'

'Harriet, it's fine.'

It wasn't fine at all. While the driver did a U-turn I replayed everything Sally had said, feeling sick with guilt. I'd hardly even listened. My head had been too full of other things.

Tom had been under the weather for ages. If he'd picked up full-blown flu on top of all that . . . I'd never really watched hospital dramas, but scenes still flashed through my mind. Incubators. Ventilators. After these came recent news bulletins about hospitals being overstretched, the elderly and babies being especially vulnerable. '. . . *a particularly virulent strain* . . .'

As the cab crawled in heavy traffic I sat stiffly, sick with apprehension, eyes fixed on the road ahead. Evidently sensing my tension, John sat silent, which was just as well. Soothing platitudes would have made me want to thump him.

At the fourth set of red lights, I said, 'Look, don't you want to get out and pick up another cab?'

'I'll stick with this and turn it around.'

Of course. He wouldn't want to hang about on another freezing pavement.

For several miles, neither of us spoke. Perversely, though, as my tension grew, I almost wished he *would* say something. I almost wished he'd come out with something irritatingly soothing, like 'Look, I'm sure he'll be all right,' so I could snap at him.

Then he said, 'If she has taken him to hospital, would you have any idea which one?'

Even more perversely, I didn't want this, either. 'It'll be the big one where she had him, won't it?'

I didn't snap, but I felt like it. Hearing him say it only intensified those images of oxygen masks, scurrying nurses and Sally sitting white-faced in a corridor. It was all his fault anyway, damn him. If it hadn't been for him, I wouldn't have been too drugged to listen to Sally in the first place. Why hadn't he got drunk that first evening, leered and leched and groped me with sweaty hands, so I could just have felt sick?

I tried Sally again, but I knew there'd be no reply and there wasn't.

With a hideous feeling of foreboding, I fixed tense eyes on the road. We were only about half a mile from home. I saw a hastily scrawled note on the kitchen table, saying *'Gone to St Mary's – Tom suddenly went a funny colour . . .'*

Then I saw the meter, clocking up by the second. God, I couldn't let him pay this, too, and the rest of it, by the time he'd got home, wherever that was. Scrabbling in my purse, I dug out twenty-five pounds, which was all I had in notes, and thrust it at him. 'That's for the fare.'

'Harriet, it's really not—'

'Take it! I was supposed to pay for the dinner, wasn't I? Have you got some big macho thing about having to pay for everything?'

128

He looked at me a moment, before putting the cash in his pocket. 'I haven't analysed my motives, but I expect that's it.'

His dry, controlled tones cut me down far worse than overt sarcasm. 'Look, I'm sorry.'

'So am I.'

For what? I thought. For paying? Or for finding yourself with a snapping turtle?

But we were nearly there. Leaning forward, I rapped on the driver's partition and he slid it back. Dry-mouthed, I said, 'Next right and second left.'

Thirty seconds later, perched on the edge of my seat, I added, 'Number forty-seven, just past the lamppost.'

As the cab pulled into the kerb and I was hunting for my key, John broke his silence. 'Do you want me to wait? In case you need to go on?'

'No, I've got wheels. Thanks for the dinner.' Already I was opening the door. 'Goodnight.'

Slamming it behind me, I ran up the path, key in hand. As I pushed the door open, the house felt cold and silent. 'Sally?' I called, racing to the kitchen.

The light was off. Only Widdles was there, curled up on the sofa.

I raced upstairs. The room Sally shared with Tom was at the back of the house, next to mine. I flung the door open.

Tom's cot was empty. I felt sick.

In fact I could have thrown up, but only with relief.

Sally sat up with a startled jerk. 'For God's sake, Harriet!' she said, in a hissy whisper. 'You'll wake him!'

Tom was cuddled up beside her, the cot pushed against the side of the bed to stop him falling out. Sally's bedside light was on, a book lying on the duvet. The ancient gas fire was on low, the radio likewise, one of Chopin's Nocturnes drifting softly out.

'I was trying to ring you!' I whispered back. 'I thought maybe he was really ill!'

'No, but he was being such a miserable little whinge-bag I got sick of running up and down stairs – thought I might as well come to bed, too. Hope I've not started Bad Habits here,' she added, looking down at the small head beside her. 'Mind you, Classic FM might have had something to do with it, or maybe he was just knackered, but he's been flat out for a couple of hours.'

It seemed crazy now, but all the way home I'd been having visions of that empty cot. We'd bought it at a charity shop for next to nothing and spent hours cleaning it up. A mobile hung over it, a musical one with six teddies. I'd bought him that. It played 'Twinkle, twinkle little star' and 'Baa baa black sheep'. 'Why on earth didn't you answer the phone? I was getting frantic, thinking you'd rushed him off to hospital!'

'I was in the loo! At least I was the first time, and by the time I was out it had stopped ringing. When it went again, I just couldn't be bothered to get out of bed.'

'I phoned four times!'

'I didn't *hear* any more! I expect I was asleep by then.'

Well, she probably wouldn't hear, up here with the door shut and the radio on. These houses were built like Norman castles; you could have a multiple murder downstairs and be none the wiser.

'Until you had to bloody well crash in and wake me up. Honestly, the one night I go to bed early . . .' Suddenly her expression changed. 'You didn't charge home just because of Tom?'

'Of course I did! I was worried!'

'I hope Andy wasn't browned off.'

I had to tell her now. 'It wasn't Andy.'

She made a *God, I knew it* face. 'God, I knew it. Why the hell didn't you tell me?'

'You'd only have had a go at me. I never intended to go, but I was so up to here, and once he was on the phone . . .' I sat on her bed and related the whole farcical saga.

If nothing else, it brought back a ghost of the old, pre-Tom Sally. 'Harriet, I'm appalled,' she said, with mock-shock. 'Planning to throw yourself at him like some brazen old slapper – you're getting as bad as me.'

She meant Steve. 'You didn't plan it,' I pointed out.

'Same difference. Look on the bright side, though – he might have been crap at it. Lethally attractive blokes often feel they don't have to make an effort.'

'And he might not have been crap, so it's just as well. I think I'd have got addicted after one shot, like heroin. If it had gone that far. I've got a feeling he might be one of those types who like to get you into a fever of anticipation for a couple of nights first.'

'Did he say he'd call again?'

'Are you kidding? After I snapped at him like some hormonal nutter? But it's just as well. I'm not cut out for hole-and-corner intrigues. As for being a side order to Nina, I don't know how I could ever have contemplated it.'

'At least you'd have known you were a side order,' she pointed out. 'It's finding out you're the side order when you thought you were the main course that really makes you sick. Anyway, she might be leftovers soon.'

'Look, can we change the subject?' In some perverse way, those electric vibes had changed the way I felt. Although nothing had really happened, we'd been within a heartbeat of fuses blowing. In my head they already had, and I knew he hadn't been thinking about the Six Nations, or whether it was high time his car went for a service either. To me it felt as if we'd shared a certain intimacy already, so the thought of him blowing fuses with Nina, or anyone else, was increasingly difficult to stomach. Even if she was going to be leftovers by next Wednesday, the mere thought of interim electrics got my green snakes going again.

So I asked Sally what she was going to buy Jacko for Christmas, and we talked related rubbish until a quarter past eleven, when I said, 'I suppose I'd better let you get back to sleep.'

'Yes, but since you woke me up in the first place I wouldn't mind a hot chocolate first.'

'You're getting addicted to that stuff.'

'With squirty cream,' she called, as I left the room.

I came back with two hot, overfull mugs, but just as I'd kicked the door shut my mobile rang. It was in my bag, which was still where I'd dumped it on Sally's bed, but as my hands were full she pulled it out and answered it.

'Hello?' she said, as I was trying to find room on her bedside table for the mugs. There was a pause. 'No, it's Sally – Harriet's got her hands full.'

I was making space between *The Contented Little Baby Book* and a pot of Nivea Visage when I realized she was making frantic faces at me.

'IT'S HIM!' she mouthed.

Needless to say I slopped a bit of hot chocolate, but she was talking again. 'No, he's fine, thank you.' (Pause.) 'Well, yes, he had been a bit whingey, but that was all it was, thank heaven.' (Pause.) 'Yes, Harriet said. She'd got herself in a bit of a state.' (Pause.) 'Well, it was really kind of you to call – I'm sorry if I messed up your evening. Shall I pass you to Harriet?' (Pause.) 'You too. Goodnight.'

I felt relatively calm as I took the phone. I even sounded calm. 'Hi, John. You'll have gathered that it was a panic in a teacup, thank God.'

'I'm glad it was only a teacup. I guess it's a bit late to call, but I thought I'd check.'

'Well, it was very kind of you. I'm sorry I had to dash off like that, but I wasn't in any fit state for sharing a box of Maltesers in the Trocadero.'

He chuckled quietly. 'We can do the Maltesers another time. Shall I call you back in a couple of days?'

This was it, then. 'Actually, it's probably better if I call you. The thing is, I'm going to be really tied up for the next few weeks and I don't just mean socially. I've got to put the house on the market soon and it's a terrible tip – I need to slap some emulsion on the walls and tart it up a bit, never mind sorting out mountains of junk. You just wouldn't believe how much junk there is and I've hardly started.'

In the minute pause before he replied, I knew he hadn't been expecting this. I knew he was wondering why the hell hot vibes had suddenly gone lukewarm, but it was just tough.

'Sooner you than me,' he said, pleasantly enough. 'Have a good Christmas then, if I don't see you.'

'You too. Enjoy your tribal warfare. And thanks for the dinner.'

134

'My pleasure. Goodnight.'

'Goodnight.'

As I shoved the phone back in my bag, Sally was wide-eyed. 'Harriet, I never knew you could lie so convincingly.'

'It wasn't lies! At least, the junk wasn't.'

'It was bloody good lies at short notice. You haven't even burnt your boats to bits. Mind you, after a pretty categorical "sod off" like that I should think he'll pass out with shock if you *do* ever call him. I almost feel sorry for him,' she added, reaching for her mug.

'What do you want me to do? What if he's just a smooth, philandering bugger, anyway? He didn't even say, "Oh, come on, the odd night out won't hurt."'

'Well, would you?' She licked some squirty cream off the top of her chocolate. '*I* thought he sounded really nice, anyway.'

'He does. That's just the trouble, and you haven't seen him. You don't know what I've been up against. It's no use, if it's not on the level I just don't want to know.'

'Ask Father Christmas, then. "A no-strings Helicopter, please, because I've been a very good girl except for tonight, when I was planning to be a very bad girl."'

'He'd better bring me a Bad Girls' manual, too. It's been so long, I've probably forgotten how you do it.'

'You've been cooped up with me too long. I've

even forgotten how to *want* to do it. Not sure I want to remember, either.' Rather awkwardly she went on, 'Look, I'm sorry if I've been a miserable cow lately, but what with one thing and another . . .'

Steve, for starters. And the prospect of leaving Tom with a childminder when she went back to work, and all the other preoccupations of single mothers who aren't earning ninety grand with a live-in nanny.

'It's all getting on top of me,' she went on, in mock-woeful tones. 'There was a programme the other day about artistically colour-theming your Christmas presents, and now I'm in a terrible state about whether to go for midnight blue paper with silver ribbon, or forest green with gold.'

For once, I wasn't going to be fobbed off. 'Try sky-blue pink with purple. As for really trivial things, like where you're going to live once I get rid of this place, I've more or less made up my mind to buy a flat before prices shoot up any more. I'd be mad not to. At least a two-bedroomed one. So while I'm off on my trip you can keep it warm for me and dish out cod'n'mouse for Widdles.'

I'd mentioned this before, but I hadn't got very far.

'Harriet, I've told you often enough, I'm not having it.'

Not sponging off me, she meant.

'And I'm not living with you, either,' she went on. 'Not after you sell this place, anyway. You don't put enough chocolate in the hot chocolate, you're too skinny for me to borrow your clothes, and you lust after illicit Helicopters and wake me up.' She stuck her tongue out. 'So push off and let me get some sleep.'

Flu-chaos still reigned on Monday and Tuesday was worse, if anything. Jess said worriedly that she'd got a bit of a tickly cough, she hoped to goodness she wasn't coming down with it, as her mother was coming up from Dorchester on Thursday – they were going to see *The King and I.*

It was even colder that evening. I came home to find Jacko in the sitting room with the useless little fan heater on, watching some European League game on Dorothy's mega-TV. 'Why don't you watch it in the kitchen?' I asked. 'It's freezing in here.'

'It'd get on Sal's nerves. This picture's better, anyway.'

Sally was in the kitchen, folding some washing neatly, which was a pretty ominous sign. 'How did it go with that woman?' I asked. She'd had an appointment to see a childminder: about the sixth so far. With five mornings a week of classes lined up, something had to be sorted out soon.

'She seemed all right,' she shrugged. 'They all *seem* all right . . .'

'But you didn't take to her?'

'I don't know!' She started folding a pair of knickers as if some bossy official was about to come and check how perfectly she'd done it. 'Tom was upset when she picked him up, but he's been like that with all of them, the awkward little devil . . .'

Now, Sally was dying to get back to work. She was dying to have something other than puréed carrots to think about. On the other hand, she hated the thought of leaving Tom. Sally seemed convinced that however pleasant, however council-approved the woman might appear, the instant Sally was gone she'd turn into a vicious, baby-shaking schizo.

But since she knew it sounded ridiculous, she'd never say it. 'I expect they all get a bit upset at first,' I pointed out.

'It's all right for you! You won't have to go off and leave a baby who can't understand that you're coming back! He'll think I've abandoned him!'

It was no use telling her that his brain wouldn't be up to formulating such concepts. He'd feel lost and anchorless, at least at first. I'd hate leaving him too.

Having done with folding, she flopped onto the sofa and pointed the remote at the television. 'Oh, God, not *again* . . .' She said this because whatever she'd wanted to escape into had been shelved for that football match.

Zapping the TV off again, she gave an up-to-here sigh. 'And everything else on is crap, as usual . . .'

She'd quite liked football once, but all she wanted lately was the comforting anaesthesia of soaps. Or *Who Wants To Be A Millionaire?*, so she could beat the contestants and tell herself she wasn't brain-dead after all. And get cross, of course, if Jacko beat *her*.

On an impulse I said, 'Look, why don't we go out?'

'*Out?*' she said, as if I'd suggested we nip to King's Cross to pick up a couple of punters. 'Out where?'

'I don't know – just for a quick drink? You haven't been out in ages.'

'How can I?' she demanded. 'Frida's out and if you think I'm leaving Tom with Jacko, you've got another think. Bombs could drop and he'd still carry on watching that sodding football.'

'I'll get him to turn the volume down.'

'No, thanks,' she said flatly. 'I might as well go and have a bath. Admire the pearly opalescence of my stretch marks and really cheer myself up.'

She was still in the bath when Rosie came round.

'Thought I'd just show you this,' she said, unfolding one of those free local papers kids leave on your mat once a week. 'Unless you've seen it already.'

I hadn't. It wasn't our local paper, it was from Suzanne's area.

'Get a load of this!' she said, pointing at a half-page article. 'Suzanne and I were gobsmacked!'

After a cursory glance, I couldn't see what they were gobsmacked about. It was publicizing the opening of a new gym called Scott's, why not pop along for the opening night and get one month's membership absolutely *free*, plus organic juice cocktails and a free assessment of your personal fitness requirements?

'They all dish out "free" months,' I said. 'And then just charge more for the other eleven.'

'Not *that*, dopey! Look!' She pointed at a rather fuzzy black and white photo, showing the proprietor with one of his assistants: Melissa James and Stuart Scott.

I couldn't believe it. *'Stuart?'*

'Exactly,' Rosie said, with satisfaction. 'Done pretty well for himself, hasn't he? This is his third Scott's, but his first in London.'

*Stuart!* I was still trying to take it in.

Stuart and I had been an item in my last year at school. I'd found him just at the point when I'd finally left the awkward age behind and started to think it wasn't so bad being five foot nine, after all. Decidedly nice-looking but on the shy side, he'd been the first boyfriend I'd really been keen on, and not merely grateful for, because I had to have one like everyone else.

'Didn't he do sports studies?' Rosie asked.

I nodded. 'He was always sporty. Football, athletics, you name it.'

It was weird, seeing that photo. I hadn't seen him since that last summer; his folks had moved to Hereford or somewhere. He'd been tall, like me: long-limbed and on the gangly side, but in a lithely athletic fashion. He just hadn't outgrown the stripling stage.

He had now. He'd filled out, as boys like that do

140

when they're heavily into sports. But that wasn't the only change in him. Even in fuzzy focus he looked fifty times more confident. A nostalgic little pang washed over me. 'Well, I'm glad he's doing well, even after our non-happy ending. I really liked him, you know.'

'I know,' Rosie said. 'You nearly didn't come on holiday, you were so upset.'

With half a dozen others, Rosie and I had booked a September fortnight in Skiathos. It was to be a last fun fling together, before we all went off to various institutions of higher education, to learn more about sex and drugs than we'd managed so far. Most of our mothers had been the type who, if you said you were staying over at Laura's, actually phoned Laura's house to check that you *were* there, and not up to no good with that dreadful Mick.

So the holiday package wasn't going to be quite the girly thing our fond parents imagined. Four of us (including Rosie) had arranged, on the quiet, for our assorted boyfriends to get cheap flights and join us. The others were going to make do with local talent.

Three weeks before we were due to go, Stuart had phoned me and mumbled that he was terribly sorry, he didn't think he could afford it after all; he was going to Stockton-on-Tees, to work in some friend's uncle's print shop.

I'd said not to worry, he didn't have to afford it. I'd give him some money, I'd have enough by then, I was going to take some out of my Post Office account anyway.

He'd mumbled that no, he couldn't – he was really sorry – and hung up.

Our phone had been in the hall at the time. I'd sat on the stairs, unable to believe it, and my mother had come past, asking irritably what I was doing blocking up the stairs. If I hadn't got anything better to do I could help her sort out the airing cupboard.

I wasn't stupid. I knew it was nothing to do with money; he was giving me the elbow. After ten minutes I'd phoned him back. I'd said, 'If this is your way of telling me you've had enough of this relationship, you could have just said so. I was going off you too, you know.'

And he'd mumbled something about being sorry, he hoped I'd have a nice time in Skiathos, and hung up.

I'd run upstairs, thrown myself on the bed, and cried a fair-sized river into my pillow. My mother had knocked on the door and asked what was wrong, and I'd said, nothing, just leave me alone, can't you, but she'd come in anyway. With the dreaded maternal intuition she'd said if it was that Stuart she was very sorry, but she couldn't pretend she wasn't relieved. That car of his was a death trap and he was friends with Mandy's dreadful Mick, who'd been cautioned for possessing cannabis; her mother was worried sick. And Mandy's mother had found out from Laura's mother, who'd smelt it out by sheer mother-instinct, that shenanigans were planned for Skiathos – they weren't born yesterday, you know, we needn't think they didn't know what Went On – and while she was on that particular subject she'd found my pills in my pencil case.

I'd jerked furiously upright from the bed. How *dared* she go prying? – and don't give me that 'worried sick' stuff – she was a nosy, interfering old hag – if she'd lived a few hundred years back she'd probably have been burnt as a witch. (When I'm livid on top of heartbroken I do tend to get carried away.)

Of course, there had followed appalled 'How-*dare*-you-speak-to-me-like-that, I'm-your-*mother*' stuff, she was going to talk to my father, though goodness knew he'd never exerted any discipline in his life, and if he didn't put those wretched shelves up soon she was going to find a man who would. (I didn't know it then, but Bill was already on the scene.)

As I gazed at fuzzy Stuart, it seemed like another age. In another way, though, it seemed like last month.

Rosie said, 'Suzanne thought you might have seen it. Thought you might pop along and see him, for old times' sake. He's going to be there, at the opening night.'

'Maybe I will. I'll ask him for a free sub, on the grounds that he made me tell my mother she should be burnt as a witch and we didn't speak for ten days.'

Rosie gave an explosive giggly snort. 'You didn't!'

After I'd explained she said hesitantly, 'You're not really going to see him, are you?'

'Are you kidding? I'll leave him to his glory; he'd only be embarrassed. Especially if I asked him why he just went off me like that. At least, that's how it seemed. Maybe he'd been going off me for ages and I was just too thick to see it.'

'I don't think so,' Rosie said.

'How would you know?'

She hesitated in an awkward, most un-Rosie-ish way that alerted my antennae instantly. 'Rosie, what?'

'Oh, nothing.'

'What d'you mean, *nothing*?'

She made a wincey sort of face. 'The thing is, he didn't go off you, exactly. He thought you'd gone off *him*.'

I gaped at her. 'Rosie, what are you on about?'

'Suzanne told me,' she said. 'Last night, just after she'd seen the paper.'

'How the hell would Suzanne know anything about it? I knew he was trying to dump me, so I dumped him first!'

'I know what *you* thought!' Again she hesitated, but I knew it was only for the sake of form. 'Look, Suzanne'd kill me if she knew I'd told you, but he did think you were going off him.'

I stared at her. 'Why the hell would he think that?'

'Someone told him.'

'Who?'

After another wincey pause she said, 'Someone who fancied him.'

I could have strangled her. 'Rosie, *who*?'

It gushed out like one of Thames Water's best leaks. 'For God's sake, Harriet, who the hell d'you *think*?'

'Not Suzanne?' I gaped.

'Of course not Suzanne! Do you really think she'd have told me if it was her? It was *Nina*! She engineered the whole thing, because she fancied him herself!'

I don't know what my face looked like, but it can't have been a pretty sight.

'God, I knew I should never have told you,' Rosie said fearfully. 'You're not going to charge round and trim her tits with the garden shears or anything?'

I suppose something of the kind had occurred to me. Far more, though, I wished with monumental passion that she *had* found out about my dinner with John. How sweet it would have been to have her storm into the Arabian Nights, hissing, 'Just what the fuck is going on here?' like spat-out icicles. Then I'd have said sweetly, 'We haven't quite got to the fuck bit yet, but give us half an hour.' Whereupon she'd have gone white-hot with rage and I'd have risen to my feet, looked down at her (it's great being tall sometimes) and said witheringly, 'I don't *want* him, Nina. I can do better than two-timing reptiles. I only took him to pay you back for Stuart.'

And walked out.

'I mean, how could I not tell you?' Rosie went on anxiously. 'After you were feeling bad about not going to her lunch and everything?'

I suppose it was about fifteen minutes later that Sally came down, with a towel round her hair and a nice pink glow. She was wearing a pair of paisley flannelette pyjamas Jacko's mother had bought him for hospital, not realizing they'd be tight and awkward with his plaster. 'Oh, hi, Rosie,' she said. 'Anyone mind if I watch *Peak Practice*?'

I said, 'If you want dramas, how about *The Tale of the Scheming Witch*?'

Needless to say, Nina hadn't been part of the Skiathos party. She hadn't been in my immediate circle, besides which she'd had something swankier lined up than a self-catering cheapie, flying on the kind of airline that keeps you hanging around Gatwick for fourteen hours because their only other plane's taking a sickie in Ibiza. Some relative had a flash villa on the Italian Riviera; she was going for a whole month with some cousins, Rob (her then boyfriend), and Suzanne. But Rob was playing hard to get, thought he'd rather go surfing in Cornwall with his mates instead, so Nina was piqued and decided it would just serve him right if she took someone else.

So one day, while she was filling her jeep at the

146

petrol station where Stuart had a summer job, it occurred to her there was something wrong here. Although Stuart was decidedly nice-looking, for some weird reason he'd never made a move on her. So she'd set about correcting this glitch in the universe. She'd started chatting, fluttering her eyelashes. She'd somehow implied, very casually and subtly, that she'd heard I was going off him, I didn't really want him coming to Skiathos as he'd cramp my style with the beach bums.

'Suzanne thinks she almost believed it, at the time,' Rosie had said. 'She can convince herself black is shocking pink if it suits her.'

And poor Stuart had looked shocked, hurt, and so on, and she'd pretended to be horrified and terribly sorry, she should never have said anything, she'd thought he'd had an idea anyway, so please would he not mention to anyone that she'd said one word. In fact, she thought she'd heard that he was going off *me*.

'She actually told Suzanne she thought she *had* heard it,' Rosie had said. 'Did the injured-innocence bit really well.'

Having stuck her poisoned arrow right in she'd waited a day or two before going to fill her jeep up again, and Stuart had said he'd saved me the bother of dumping him. So Nina had fluttered her eyelashes again, and said what a shame about Skiathos, but as it happened . . .

Of course poor wounded Stuart had been unbelievably flattered that someone like Nina would invite him to a flash Italian villa. He'd hitched all the way there and after five days Rob had phoned to say he was coming after all, and Nina had told Stuart that Rob could get terribly jealous and might start smashing things, including Stuart, so maybe he'd better just slip off and pretend he'd never been there at all.

And I, poor mug that I was, had seen him briefly after I got back from Skiathos (I had a pretty good time, actually, there was a beach bum called Andreas) and said he had a good tan for Stockton-on-Tees, and he'd mumbled something about it being a brilliant summer, even up north.

Oh, and I nearly forgot the best bit. Nina had felt *bad*, afterwards. And Suzanne, to her eternal credit, had said, 'Oh, come off it – you just wanted to get him to prove you could do it.'

I was warming to Suzanne considerably.

'So it makes me a bit sick that Helicopter never made a move,' Rosie said plaintively, once Sally had been genned up. 'Lovely poetic justice, or what?'

I almost felt like filling her in anyway, but already she was going on, 'Suzanne said that even at the time she thought it was awful. She says Nina can't help it. She's got this psychological thing – she just *has* to have what she wants.'

'Psychological thing?' Sally snorted. 'It's called being a manipulative bitch.'

'Why didn't he just *ask* me if I was going off him?' I demanded.

'Because he thought you'd say yes,' Rosie said. 'Or he thought you'd say no, because you didn't want to hurt his feelings.'

I thought back to my tart 'I was going off you too, you know.' I couldn't have played into Nina's hands better if I'd tried. 'Yes, but he must have fancied her, or he'd never have gone to Italy.'

'They nearly all fancied Nina,' Rosie pointed out. 'Maybe he'd thought she was out of his league.'

Rosie could do wonders for your self-esteem. 'If you still go to her girly lunch and pretend to like her after all this, I'll kill you,' I said.

'I'm not!' she said, all hurt. 'I made an excuse about having to go home and help my mum do her Christmas shopping because she always buys the wrong things for everybody. So I'll *have* to go home now,' she added crossly. 'And traipse round the shops with her saying how about this for so-and-so?'

She stopped and looked from me to Sally and back again. 'Sorry,' she added, a mite sheepishly. 'I know we're in the middle of a major drama here; that was the commercial break.'

'I wish you'd said,' Sally tutted. 'I'd have put the kettle on and dashed off for a pee before part two and the really exciting bit. Where Harriet's eyes go all scary and glittery as she plans her fiendish revenge.'

She shot me a conspiratorial little look, but I

ignored it. 'How the hell can Suzanne still be friends with her, when she knows what she's like?'

'They go back a long way,' Rosie said. 'And in a funny sort of way I think she feels sorry for her.'

'*What*?'

'Well, she says Nina hasn't really got any proper friends except her. OK, masses of acquaintances, but not real friends. She says she's so intensely competitive, she puts everyone off.'

'Nothing to do with being a cow, then,' I said.

'Yes, but Suzanne says it's like having piggy eyes or mousy hair – she can't help being a cow. She was born like it. I mean, who'd choose to be a cow if they could be nice?'

A moment later she added, 'Anyway, the latest Nina bulletin might cheer you up. She's a bit upset with Helicopter at the moment.'

My antennae pricked right up. 'Why?'

'She was hoping he'd invite her to his folks for Christmas. They've got a nice little country place, apparently, but he said other people's families are a pain and she'd be bored. Which *she* takes to mean that he's not sufficiently serious to want to take her home.'

I shot Sally a Look, but she was already shooting me one. I'd told her all about his Great Escape Christmas, of course.

'So she's booked a week's skiing in Aspen with somebody from work,' Rosie went on. 'Which is

150

supposed to make *him* jealous in case she picks up some Silicon Valley billionaire on the chairlift.'

'Knowing Nina, she probably will,' I said.

When Rosie finally left, Sally said the one thing she'd been dying to say for the past hour and a half. 'For God's sake. *Now* she tells you.'

'Sod's law,' I said. 'Plus she only found out last night.'

'It makes me sick. You'd have had *carte blanche*, on a plate with parsley on top. Why the hell didn't you tell her?'

'She'd pass it on to Suzanne, after swearing blind she wouldn't.'

'I'd *want* her to pass it on! Talk about fair game – you should tell him you've found half a dozen slots in your diary, after all.'

It was hideously tempting, but for one minor thing. 'Don't you think I'd love to? But being a side order would really make me sick after this. It's main course or nothing.'

'OK, I can see that. You wouldn't fancy being a side order to a snake.'

I wouldn't even call her a snake. They got a bad enough press anyway. The Witch of Narnia was far more appropriate. She'd pretended to be nice, too, and before you knew it, she was turning all the little squirrels and bunnies into stone, just because Father Christmas had brought them some goodies.

'What about this not-taking-her-home business,

though?' Sally said. 'Smells of impending leftovers to me.'

'Sally, it could mean anything. If someone's not a big thing, you don't take them home because your family will start thinking it must be serious. And if they *are* a big thing, you still don't want to, because your family might put them off for life.'

This discussion got no further, though, as the football was over and Jacko had just joined us. I didn't want him in on this. Knowing him, he'd only say OK, but what if this Suzanne had got her wires crossed? Shouldn't we get Nina's side of it before slagging her off?

Besides, he had a gripe of his own. His mother had been on the phone, doing his head in.

'She wants *me* to talk to her!' he said. 'As if she's going to listen to me! They should just let her get on with it.'

All this referred to Jacko's much younger sister, Tara, who was giving her parents grief with a highly unsuitable boyfriend. While Jacko was in hospital, I'd heard every detail from his mother. Not only was Lee far too old (twenty-four), he played in an unsuccessful rock band ('so she's mixing with all sorts of nasty, druggy types') and was distracting her from her A levels.

'That's another prime reason for staying here for Christmas,' Jacko grunted. 'Tara can be a right arsey little madam – she and the old lady'll be at it like a bag of cats.'

Two days later Jacko got his plaster off at last and celebrated by trying to burn the house down. To be strictly accurate, he announced that it was bloody freezing in the sitting room and he was going to make a fire. Accordingly he went off in the Audi his old man had sent down for the son and heir to use, and called at the petrol station for wood, coal, and so on.

Sally and I watched as he set about his task like a man pretending he'd got something down to a fine art. First he rolled sheets of newspaper into sausages, twisted them into zigzags. Then he arranged sticks on the newspaper, lumps of coal on top of those, and applied a match.

It burned beautifully for twenty seconds, whereupon it went out. After he'd repeated the process Sally said, 'For God's sake let me do it, you ginger ape.'

'Fires are boys' stuff,' he scoffed. 'It's a law of nature. Get back in the kitchen and iron your baking tins or something.'

'You'll burn the house down,' she retorted. 'You haven't a clue.'

'I'll have you know I've got my Boy Scouts Pyromaniacs badge,' he said. 'So toddle off and polish your stretch marks.'

'If you two don't pack it in, I'll tell Father Christmas not to bring you anything,' I said. They were at it worse than ever lately.

'At least I haven't got ginger pubes,' she retorted.

'I've dyed them,' he said. 'Did them Burnished Brown with that stuff that colours and conditions all in one.' Looking over his shoulder, he gave a fatuous simper. 'Because I'm worth it.'

'Oh, for God's *sake* . . .' Sally stomped out crossly, probably because she couldn't think of anything to cap his last remark with.

'That's it,' he said, once she'd gone. 'I'm definitely taking her present back to the Oxfam shop. Pubes is hitting below the belt.'

'So is stretch marks! You know she's sensitive about them. And if you dare say "She started it", I'll thump you. She's still in a tizz about bloody Steve, if you ask me.'

'She's in a tizz about bloody something. What was he like?' he added, putting a match to a news-paper zigzag.

'I told you!' I said. 'Didn't I?'

'Don't think I ever asked.' He sat back, watching a few hopeful flames. 'Didn't want to be a nosy bastard.'

'Well, I didn't particularly fancy him, but Sally and I never fancied the same people. I suppose you'd say he was good-looking, confident, a bit full of himself. To be quite fair, though, before we found out he was married I might have said good-looking, confident, quite a laugh.'

Jacko's mind was back on pyromania, however. 'Get a load of that,' he grinned, as the flames began to take. 'A bit more practice and I'd be a great arsonist.'

I then went after Sally. 'He'll be gone for good after Christmas – can't you stop having a go at him?'

'I don't know why you're having a go at me – he's always winding *me* up,' she said irritably, picking up toys and junk.

'It doesn't mean anything! And I don't think it's very funny making fun of his pubes. They're not ginger, anyway. They're sort of reddy-brown.'

She raised her eyes to the ceiling. 'Don't tell me, he used to get pissed and get his kit off like a dickhead.'

'Of course. Plus once I had to strip him off after he'd gone for a dip in the fountain in the shopping centre and passed out.'

'Typical.'

'In November,' I added.

'Even more typical.' She was half laughing, though, which gave me an opening.

'Come on, we're going out. No excuses will be accepted.'

'Are you kidding? With Jacko burning the house down?'

'Oh, come on, he's not that much of a dickhead.

Frida's in for the next couple of hours; she'll keep an ear out for Tom and I'll take my mobile.'

For once she barely argued and we headed for the Drunken Dragon, the nearest walking-distance pub. It was unsmart and naff as you like, with coloured tinsel, an overdressed artificial Christmas tree, a proper fire, and a barman who said, 'All right, love?' To be honest, I was rather fond of it.

We stayed an hour and a half and Sally actually seemed to relax, which was partly due to two glasses of mulled wine. On the way home the air was sharp and frosty, tingling our cheeks and making puddles glitter icily under street lamps. It was so unusually cold we stopped for bags of chips with salt and vinegar and ate them walking along, giggling like a pair of sixteen-year-olds.

When we finally made it to the gate, she said, 'Whose is that?'

There was a shiny BMW sports parked outside. 'Maybe it's Helicopter's,' she giggled. 'Maybe Father Christmas sent him early, with your Bad Girls' manual.'

My stomach gave a massive drunken lurch. Suddenly I was back in that cab, with vibes swirling like hot mist and my fantasies going into orbit. I'd seen us in a lift, alone at last, like a couple of tightly lidded pans about to boil over. I'd seen the lift shoot up to penthouse level, the pans falling out and into his flat, tossing lids aside with frenzied abandon en route.

And just as my brain was re-running all this on fast forward, Sally jabbed the off button.

'But it's probably Francesca's,' she said.

'Probably,' I said, wondering how on earth I could get so steamed up in two seconds, on my own freezing doorstep.

As soon as I'd opened the door Sally charged upstairs to check on Tom. As I slung my coat over the banisters Frida came from the kitchen bearing mugs of coffee on a tray. 'Your friend's here – I was about to give you a phone.'

My stomach gave another drunken lurch.

She nodded towards the sitting-room door. 'Could you open it?'

I opened. Widdles lay flaked out fatly in front of the fire, which was burning so merrily it would have got an A plus in inviting glows. On the sofa sat Jacko, and on his lap sat Tom, happily eating a rattle.

And next to Jacko sat the Witch of Narnia.

# SIX

My first thought was that she'd found out and come to kill me, but murderers don't smile at you like that, all honey-sweet and wide-eyed. This was followed instantly by furious disbelief. How dared she sit there like a welcomed friend?

'You've got a nerve,' I said. 'And by the way, your BMW just turned back into a broomstick, so your cover's blown.'

I said it in my head, at least. What I actually said was, 'Nina! Goodness me, what a surprise! Long time no see, and all that . . .' I even smiled.

Yes, I can be as loathsomely hypocritical as the best of them.

Her voice was just as I remembered: the faintly patronizing, kind-to-lesser-mortals tone that had always irked me. 'Well, I'm only a couple of miles up the road – I expect Rosie told you – and I thought I'd pop round and give you an invitation to my little lunch. Did Rosie mention it?'

Before I could answer, Sally burst in. 'You might have told me!' she expostulated. 'I nearly had a fit, seeing an empty cot!'

From Jacko's lap, Tom gave his usual Mummy-greeting beam.

'You didn't give us a chance!' Jacko retorted, as she snatched him up.

'If he was screaming, you should have phoned me!'

If you ask me, she was a mite put out that Tom could survive for half an hour without her.

'He wasn't screaming,' Jacko scoffed. 'Just grizzling a bit. I turned his musical teddies on but he said bollocks to that, he wanted to party.'

The niceties were long overdue, but I shot Sally a private Look first. 'Sally, this is Nina. We were at school together – I might have mentioned her.'

Sally's taken-aback flash was only momentary, and it was Nina who spoke first. 'I've heard all about you,' she said, in tones so saccharine, I suddenly wondered whether she was making a pre-emptive strike. Suzanne might have shown her that Stuart article. She might have said, 'What if Harriet goes to that opening night? What if she talks to him and it somehow comes out?'

'I've heard all about you, too,' Sally replied, in tones so dangerously demure, they spelt incipient wickedness.

But Nina had turned back to me. 'How are you, anyway? It's been positively yonks – I don't think I've seen you since Tina Sinclair's wedding. They split up, by the way, but it was hardly surprising; they'd been going out practically since the fifth form.'

159

'I dare say it had turned into something of a habit,'
I said, wondering how the hell she could be sitting
there all honey-sweet, and why I wasn't spitting a few
poisoned knives.

'That's exactly what I said. Like one of those comfy
old jumpers you hang onto for ever.'

Whether Nina had ever hung onto an old jumper
for ever was an interesting question. She was wearing dark grey trousers, a pristine white shirt, and a
lacy little cardie draped over her shoulders. If any
of them had been out of the shop more than six
weeks, I'd have been surprised. On her feet were
pristine little black boots, of leather that looked glove-
like. As always, everything about her was immaculate,
including that hair, which still hung like a black silk
curtain around her perfect, neat-featured little face.
I'd forgotten how big and navy blue her eyes were,
how thickly lashed, and what a striking contrast they
made with that hair. I thought of her using them on
John, and began to realize just what five-star, fully
paid up jealousy feels like.

Not nice, I can tell you.

Frida was sitting on an ancient leather pouffe
Dorothy had used for putting her feet up. 'If you
and Sally want coffee, I need more cups.'

'I'll get them,' Jacko said. Still limping slightly, he
went out.

'*Such* a nasty accident, poor man,' Nina said, once
he'd gone. 'I heard all about it, of course, via Rosie.

160

Thank you.' This was smiled sweetly at Frida, who'd just handed her a mug.

'I gather some old auntie left you half this house,' she went on. 'I hear you're selling in the spring?'

Rosie had been busy. 'Yes, that's when the market traditionally picks up.'

I began to think she'd just come for a good old nose, after all. She obviously hadn't a clue about John, and Suzanne might not even have mentioned Stuart. Nina would probably have forgotten him, anyway. He'd meant nothing to her, except as another conquest. As she cast a shrewdly appraising eye at original plaster mouldings on the ceiling, I could see her thinking, 'Seven hundred grand or so, less fees and death duties and divide by two – still not bad for the likes of Harriet Grey.'

I have to say the room didn't look too bad with only table lamps and the firelight. Square and high-ceilinged, it had a massive bay window curtained in ancient maroon velvet, which at least kept the draughts out. The sofas and armchairs were ancient chintzy stuff that had once been 'good' and had looked a lot better after someone from Kleen-o-Brite had done the honours. The floor was polished wood, mainly covered with a faded old oriental carpet, which was probably still valuable. The fireplace was the original, of the type specialist burglars nick to order for the dodgy loaded.

Jacko limped back with the cups. 'Does it still hurt?'

Nina asked, all concerned sympathy as he reseated himself beside her.

'No, he just wants sympathy,' Sally said.

Frida said, 'Sally! How can you say that? His leg is still stiff, poor Jacko.'

'Yes, but I'm playing it for all I can get,' he grinned.

Nina gave the kind of tinkly laugh I remembered all too well, and bestowed on him the kind of smile that had always gone with it. I'd seen her do it at parties in my teens, when flirting with some boy I'd have loved to flirt with, if I hadn't thought he'd ask where my paper bag was. She'd look almost like a sweet, innocent little girl who could, however, turn extremely naughty if anyone fancied a game of doctors and nurses after tea.

You'd think it'd make the average grown-up male puke, but she somehow did it subtly and the formula still seemed to be working. I wouldn't have thought she'd try it on Jacko, though. He wouldn't be her type. He wasn't flash enough. He never even pretended to be sophisticated. Maybe it was sheer habit with her. She'd feed on the admiration.

On the other hand, because he was just Jacko, I often forgot that although he'd never stop traffic, he was passably nice-looking. And if he'd had a worst enemy, even he'd have had to admit there was something about Jacko. He was a lot less scruffy tonight, too. Now his plaster was off, he was wearing khakis and a newish green sweatshirt, but together they'd probably cost about a tenth of what she was wearing.

And if she was flirting, he was lapping it up. It made me livid to see him fall for it, but that was blokes for you. I imagined John lapping it up in exactly the same way and instantly my stomach was full of green snakes again, writhing. Why hadn't he pushed a bit, damn him? Why *had*n't he said the odd night out wouldn't hurt? Wasn't I worth making an effort for?

Nina was giving another tinkly laugh. 'Goodness, I was nearly forgetting what I came for.' Taking an envelope from what was probably a Prada bag, she got up and handed it to me. 'The invitation – do hope you can come.'

Thinking, oh shit, I opened it and thought, thank God, instead. 'I'm terribly sorry – it would have been lovely – but I've just accepted another invitation for next Sunday lunchtime.'

Jacko shot me an accusing *liar!* look. 'Who from?'

'Sophy and her bloke. My old boss at the agency,' I explained to Nina. 'She's gone into head-hunting now – I haven't seen her for a couple of months.'

'Oh, well . . .' Nina gave a regretful little smile. 'Another time, then.'

'Yes,' I smiled, loathing my own hypocrisy.

But Nina was eyeing the plaster mouldings again. 'As a matter of fact, someone at work's looking for a house like this. She doesn't want to pay for someone else's idea of tasteful improvements, and have to rip them all out. Of course, there really *would* be an awful lot of work on this, but maybe I could put you in touch with her. Might save you all that estate-agent hassle, never mind the fees,' she added with a kind little smile.

And with a bit of luck I'd be so grateful to avoid all that hassle, I'd let it go for rather less than a shrewd agency would have got. 'Thanks, I'll bear it in mind.'

As Tom was getting restless, Sally yanked up her jumper and fed him.

Just for an instant Nina looked startled, as if she'd heard that in the distant past breasts had another function apart from man-bait, but had never quite believed it. Maybe she realized I'd noticed, because almost immediately she said, '*Sweet* little baby,' as if to cover up.

'Yes, isn't he?' Sally said, with a complacent smile.

Widdles chose that moment to wake up. Still lying on his side, he gave everybody his usual contemptuous stare before sitting up. As if to say, 'And this is what I think of you lot . . .' he began licking his bottom.

'About time too,' Sally said. 'And do it properly please – save me attacking you again with a baby wipe.'

Jacko said, 'Sal, do you have to?' as if he'd never dream of speaking about anything so gross.

'Sorry.' With a sweet smile at Nina she went on,

164

'I spend so much time attacking crappy bottoms these days, I quite forget it's not a fit subject for the drawing room. How's your boyfriend, by the way? Rosie said you had a fantastically yummy boyfriend with a helicopter.'

Nina gave an almost awkward little laugh. 'Oh, it's not *his* – just a corporate thing, you know. But yes, he is pretty "yummy",' she added, managing to indicate quote marks to show she wouldn't normally use such a word.

'Jacko has a plane,' Frida said. 'His own one.'

'Really?' Nina was all wide-eyed again, but at Jacko, not Frida.

'It's only half mine,' he said, almost apologetically. 'Just a little Piper – fifty-fifty with the old man. Dead handy for nipping to Blackpool for a night out, though.'

Nina produced a silver-bells peal. 'Isn't he a hoot?'

Frida said, 'When I come and see you in Liverpool, will you take me for a fly in it?'

'Of course, my angel. Just pick a day when there isn't four hundred feet of cloud cover, will you?'

'You wouldn't catch me in it,' Sally retorted. 'I used to go out with an airline pilot once. He said weekend pilots were all lethally overconfident and skipped their checks.'

'I'd never take you anyway,' he replied. 'You'd be a right back-seat driver, all "Slow down a bit, can't you?" and "Watch that UFO, dickhead!"'

Nina gave another silver-bells peal.

Then Sally said, in that innocent tone, 'I hear you're going skiing at Christmas, Nina. Austria, was it?'

'Oh, no, *Asp*en. In the States,' she added, as if we wouldn't know.

'Gosh,' said Sally, wide-eyed. 'Isn't that the really smart place where all those *Hello!* types go?'

While I tried not to laugh, Nina did a good job of trying not to preen. 'Well, I suppose it *is* pretty exclusive. Of course, John would have loved to come, but he feels obliged to do the family thing.'

'What a shame,' Sally said, deadpan.

'I must go,' Frida announced.

Jacko watched as she rose in a lithe, fluid movement to her feet. 'Where are you off to in those leathers?'

She was dressed for going out, in slinky black leather trousers, but her hair was still wrapped in a towel. 'Tramp,' she said. 'Cecilia met someone who can get us in. Costs shitloads but what the hell. I must go and dry my pig's-dinner hair.'

Jacko watched her fluid-leather exit. So did Nina, with an expression I would not describe as entirely benign.

'Clubbing,' Jacko sighed. 'God, she makes me feel old. I can get over-excited just watching the Teletubbies these days.'

Nina let out another tinkling peal. By the time she left, half an hour later, I was beginning to wonder

how many more I could have stood without slapping her.

When I saw her to the door, Jacko came, too. He
pecked her on the cheek, and said, 'See you, pet.
Take care.'

She gave him her best little-sweetie smile. 'Bye bye
– it was *love*ly to meet you.'

Once we'd watched her broomstick zoom off, I
turned to Jacko. 'If you even *think* of saying it, I'll
thump you.'

'What?' he said, all hurt.

'You know what. "I don't know what you were on
about, I thought she was really nice." And before you
say God, I can be really nasty, I'll tell you something
about Nina. She nicked a bloke of mine, years ago.
Someone I liked as much as you liked Michaela. She
didn't really want him – she only nicked him to prove
she could do it.'

He looked as if someone had just told him Liverpool
had been relegated to the fourth division. 'Why didn't
you tell me?'

'Because she did it so cleverly I only just found
out.'

Leaving him to un-daze himself, I took the cups to
the kitchen, where Sally joined me once she'd put
Tom back in his cot. 'I thought she was a friend of
Frida's!' she said. 'I nearly had a fit!'

'*You* nearly had a fit?' I put the dishwasher on. 'I
thought she must be on to me, but it was just a good

167

old nose, like I originally thought. Checking out the house.'

'Maybe she came to check out Jacko, too.'

'Why would she want to check him out?'

'Because the other night I told Rosie he was loaded,' she said, a trifle sheepishly. 'Or that he's been half running his old man's empire – it's much the same thing. I mean, he looks so scruffy all the time and acts such a dickhead, so when she asked if he had a job to go back to I couldn't resist telling her, just to see her face.'

And Rosie, of course, had passed on every detail of William 'Jacko' Jacques, of Jacques Loadsamoney Enterprises.

'No wonder she was practically flirting with him,' I snorted. 'Did you see him lapping it up like an idiot?'

'Given that he fancies just about everybody, he was bound to fancy her,' Sally pointed out. 'I'd love to say she's nothing special, but it wouldn't be true.'

I didn't need telling.

'Who was Michaela?' she asked.

'A consuming passion, years ago. Still, she cured him of all-consuming passions – all he's had since is multiple passing fancies. It was a nightmare when she dumped him. He hardly came out of his room for days and we all knew it was because he didn't want anyone to realize he'd been crying.' Just before his finals, too, which was one reason he'd only got a

168

third. Attending only about fourteen lectures in three years was the other.

Even Sally looked touched. 'Poor old Ape-Face,' she said, and a second later he came in.

'I wish you'd told me she'd nicked your bloke,' he said, still sounding hurt. 'I didn't think she was that great, anyway. That laugh of hers'd get right up my nose in five minutes.'

'Jacko,' I said, 'I love you.'

On the Thursday night I came home to find that Santa's little elves had called. There was a huge holly wreath on the front door. A round ball of greenery and mistletoe hung from a velvet ribbon in the hall. An evergreen garland was twisting up the banisters.

The sitting-room door was open. Another fire blazed in the grate. And in the corner of the sitting room, nearly brushing the ten-foot ceiling, was a massive Christmas tree. I stood and gaped like a four-year-old.

'Great, isn't it?' Jacko enthused. 'I got it this morning. We've only just finished.' It was draped in dozens of tiny coloured lights and decorations in every style and colour you could think of.

'Sal thinks it's not *Homes and Gardens* enough,' he went on. 'Wanted me to do it all arty-farty white.'

'I didn't!' Sally said defensively. 'It was only a suggestion.'

'She thinks it's naff,' he went on blithely.

'I don't!'

'Yes, you do, Stretch Marks. I think it's great, anyway.'

'*I* think it is beautiful,' said Frida, planting a kiss on his cheek.

'Thank you, my angel.' He gave her a smacking kiss back.

'It's lovely,' I said, shooting a Look at Sally. She was turning into such a nit-picking wet blanket lately. '*Every*thing looks lovely.'

'I *do* think it's lovely,' she protested. 'My mother would never have a real tree, because of all the needles on the carpet.'

'I am going to make some *glogg*,' Frida announced.

'I'll help you,' Jacko said. 'And then we can all get Swedishly rat-arsed by the fire.'

Once they'd gone I said to Sally, 'Did you have to throw cold water on it? Why do you always have to have a go at him?'

'I never said it was naff! He took it the wrong way on purpose!' She huffed off, leaving me by the fire with Widdles, who approved highly of this novel heating system.

Jacko and Frida came back with mugs of hot *glogg*, which had raisins and God alone knew what alcohol in it, and was lethally moreish. Sally came back, having evidently made up her mind to be nice. By now the room smelt like a whole pine forest – I could almost have got drunk on the scent. Jacko

170

had bought a corny Christmas CD, too, with stuff like 'Last Christmas I gave you my heart' on it, and we sang along and got merrily festive by the fire. After the second round of *glogg*, Jacko said, 'There's only one more thing that tree needs.'

'You're not putting anything else on it?' Sally demanded. 'You've already spent a bomb!'

'Not *on* it, Sal – *under* it. Presents!'

As we eventually staggered up to bed, Sally said to me, 'I hope to God he's not been spending a bomb on presents, too. I wish we'd all set a limit of a tenner or something. I just can't afford any more just now and I'll feel awful if everybody else does.'

'Sally, he won't care if you only spend a fiver. He's not going to compare costs.'

'That's not the point! I hope you haven't spent bombs either – I'll kill you.'

With Widdles snuggled beside me, I lay under my duvet, trying to work out whether it was the *glogg*, or whether I actually was feeling marginally more content than I had for the past couple of weeks. Helen, at least, had kindly taken herself off the 'urgent preoccupation' list, having phoned that afternoon. She and Oliver were spending Christmas in Saffron Walden with her sister, who had a son much the same age. Lawrence and the twins were going to his mother, who adored the twins as they were so like her only son. Francesca was going to friends of her own,

but there was no question of her and Lawrence split-
ting up. Did I know she'd moved in next door already?

Yes, I'd gathered as much, from the Renault that
had appeared over the past few days. Helen had
finally seen Lawrence at her solicitor's office, and
while the atmosphere had been sub-zero he'd made
neither scenes nor threats. She'd sounded so relatively calm, I began to think she'd done the right
thing after all, and even if she hadn't, it wasn't
my fault.

Then I thought about Christmas, instead. Dear old
Jacko. Might have known he'd go right over the top
in the tree department. He was just a big kid at
heart, and so was Sally, though she wasn't half so
upfront about it. I'd do stockings for both of them,
with daft little presents and a satsuma in the bottom.
Widdles was getting a stocking, too, ready-stuffed by
Santa Tesco.

In fact, I was going for the whole corny bit, including a box of spectacularly tacky crackers. We'd watch
the usual festive stuff on the television and play daft
games of Twister. In short, the kid in me was looking
forward to the whole thing more than I had for years.
So naturally it followed that only days later, Harriet's
Perfect Christmas started falling apart.

It began with a call from Jacko's mother that lasted
twenty minutes and left him more exasperated than
I'd ever seen him.

172

'I *told* them,' he said, in up-to-here tones. 'If they'd kept their noses out she'd have got fed up with him by now.'

It was Tara. There had been a huge row over Lee. Parental feet had been firmly put down. He was a Bad Influence and distracting her from her A levels. All right, they couldn't stop her seeing him, but he was absolutely forbidden to come to the house any more, and if she brought him in while they were out there'd be massive trouble.

And after saying, 'O*K*, don't go on,' with sufficient sulks to fool them, she'd disappeared while they were at a Rotary dinner, taking a few clothes, all her make-up, and her building society cashcard. As her allowance had just been paid into her account, they knew she had at least three hundred pounds to play with. She'd left a note saying she was eighteen, she could do as she liked. School sucked, it was a waste of time, she loved Lee and was going with him into the wide blue yonder, which was nowhere near Liverpool, by the way, so they needn't bother looking for her. She would phone eventually, just so they knew she wasn't dead, and it served them right for being control freaks.

All this had happened three days previously. Jacko's folks hadn't dared tell him at first, thinking he'd say 'I told you so' (which he had). However, Tara still hadn't phoned and they were frantic. She'd be living in some filthy squat, getting her tongue and nipples pierced by back-street practitioners and dying of infection while Lee was too stoned to notice. She'd be doing heroin, catching HIV, getting pregnant, getting arrested. Lee would sell her to some pimp for the price of a fix.

'They want me go home, in case she calls,' he said. 'They think she might listen to me – that's a joke, for a start. She'll be home soon enough once she's out of money and misses her own bathroom. She's never had to rough it, not even for a day.'

'Hasn't she got a mobile?' I asked. 'They could phone her on that.'

'It's dead,' he said. 'She forgot to take her charger. They're having visions of her dead in a gutter – every time the doorbell rings they think it's the Old Bill coming to tell them.'

'She's probably having a ball,' I said.

'Try telling them that. I'd better go, though, before the old man's blood pressure goes through the roof and the old lady overdoses on Prozac.'

'Exert your famous chill factor,' I said. 'Instil a sense of proportion.'

'I could murder her, though,' he went on. 'She must know they'll be out of their minds. They've spoilt her rotten, you know. It's probably the first time in her life they've ever put their feet down.'

I tried not to care that my perfect Christmas was going down the pan; it just wouldn't be the same without Jacko. 'When will you go?'

174

'I said the day after tomorrow. I've got a physio appointment tomorrow afternoon.' He gave a ghost of his usual grin. 'The physiotherapist's a cracker – I've got to give her a Christmas kiss before I never see her again.'

Once he'd disappeared to the DD for beer and sympathy, Sally said, 'I dare say they have spoilt her rotten, but I bet they spoilt him rotten, too.'

'I don't think they did,' I said. 'When I first knew him he didn't have much more money than the rest of us. He did have a car, but it was a beat-up old thing. And his old man made him work for his pocket money – he had to go and polish the cars in the showrooms. He only told me that not so long ago. He was a bit sick because Tara's never had a job. At least, she went lifeguarding at the swimming pool for two whole Saturdays, but they made her mop the floors and it was too much like hard work.'

'Brat,' Sally said, with feeling.

Frida left on the morning of the twenty-second, saying if anyone fancied a proper, wintry New Year in Stockholm, with snow and more *glogg*, they were more than welcome. Jacko was leaving on the twenty-third. And on the evening of the twenty-second, Sally had a phone call from her un-proper aunt that threw her into an orgy of guilt.

'It's Mum and Dad,' she despaired. 'She said they're terribly upset that I'm not going home – Mum's been crying, apparently. They think *I* think they're ashamed of me.'

'Well, you do,' I pointed out.

'Yes, but they'd never put it like that, even to themselves. They'd say "disappointed", if they had to. Apparently the neighbours have been asking why I'm not bringing Tom home for his first Christmas, and Mum thinks *they* think she doesn't want us, and she's feeling awful.'

Knowing what was coming, I kept quiet.

'And I know they were a pain at first, but I can't help wondering how I'd feel if Tom didn't want to come home,' she went on. 'I mean, you do see things differently, somehow.'

To save her asking, I answered first. 'Look, don't feel bad if you want to go. I honestly don't mind a bit – I'll go to Mum's after all – she could probably do with a hand.'

She looked positively relieved. 'Are you sure? I'd truly much rather stay here, but I think I'd feel bad.'

I phoned Euston and booked her a ticket on my credit card, but when Jacko came home an hour later he was put out. 'I could have given you a lift! Chester's virtually on the way!'

'You weren't here to ask,' she said. 'Anyway, you've got no baby seat. It's too late now, I'm going to phone Mum and then I'm going to start packing.'

\*      \*      \*

Since there was little doing in the office, except Sandie telling us exactly what she was going to do to her boyfriend if he bought her tacky red lace knickers, I took the following morning off to drive Sally to the station.

Jacko left first. He and Sally had called a truce by then; she'd even let him open the twenty-third window on the Advent calendar. 'You needn't think you're getting rid of me for good, though,' he said. 'If you feel like tarting yourselves up for a wild night out, I'll come back for New Year.'

'Are you kidding?' Sally demanded. 'What sort of a wild night can I have with no babysitter?'

'We could get one. From an agency or something.'

'It'd cost a bomb. I hate New Year's Eve, anyway.'

'Since when?' I gaped.

'Since ages. It depresses me. You go out with massive expectations, all hyped up, and it's nearly always a let-down.'

'God, you're a right little ray of sunshine, aren't you?' Jacko said. 'Let me spark you up with my famous magic touch.' From his pocket he produced a mangled bit of mistletoe.

She received his kiss with reasonable grace. 'Happy Christmas, Ape-Face. Be good.'

'Happy Christmas, pet. Try not to murder your folks – I'll probably be murdering mine and I don't want you sharing my headlines in the papers.'

Then it was my turn. 'Good luck,' I said. 'If Tara shows up, give her a good slap for me.'

'I'll probably be murdering her, too. Come and visit me when I end up in Broadmoor. Smuggle me a couple of beers in your bra.'

He then kissed Tom, perched on Sally's hip. 'Bye, mate. Smile a lot at the wrinklies and say hi to Father Christmas for me.'

Although he'd have left after Christmas anyway, I hated seeing him go. After several weeks he'd begun to feel like a permanent fixture. He'd be down for the odd weekend, but it wouldn't be the same.

After we'd waved him off the house already felt empty. While Sally was collecting her things I went into the sitting room. It felt chill and forlorn, with cold ashes in the grate. Even the tree looked dejected, all its glory about to be wasted on thin air and Widdles. However, there were things under it that had not been there an hour before. When Sally came down, I showed her.

'Oh, my God,' she said. 'What the hell has he done?'

There were identical, normal-sized presents for me and Sally, and a huge one for Tom. The card read, 'It might be a bit big for you just now, mate, but at least you won't need a licence. Love, Jacko.'

'You can hardly take it on the train,' I said. 'Are you going to open it now?'

'I suppose so,' she said fretfully. 'Jesus, I wish he

hadn't done this . . .' She ripped the paper off, to reveal a blue, toddler-sized Thomas the Tank Engine. It was dual purpose: push along with the handle, or sit on and ride, according to your toddler-whim. There was even a lift-up seat like a mini-boot, for putting your teddy in.

Sally stared. 'For God's sake, it's miles too big for him!'

I was hurt on poor Jacko's behalf. 'He'll grow into it in no time! He'll love it!'

'He shouldn't have done it! And what the hell's he got me?' Picking up the present, she stared at it. It was rectangular and floppy, indicating clothing. 'God, I hope it's not some horrible tacky nightie . . .'

'Don't be such a cow! Poor Jacko – I wish he hadn't got you anything!'

'So do I!' She started ripping the paper.

'You can't open it now!'

'Why the hell not?'

'It's not Christmas!'

'Oh, for heaven's sake . . .' Impatiently she tore the rest of the paper off.

'Well, thanks a lot,' I said. 'He's got me exactly the same – you've spoilt my surprise now.'

'He won't have got you the same colour!' From its neat folds, she was shaking out a soft, fine-knit sweater in palest pink.

She was already checking the label. 'It's *cash*mere! Bloody cashmere! I could kill him!'

I was really getting worked up now. 'If you dare say anything mean to him when he comes back, I'll kill *you!*'

I could have kicked myself the second it was out. Already her eyes were wet with leaks. 'Why did he do it?' she choked, through miserable tears. 'He knows I can't reciprocate! All I got him was that stupid fart pot and a paperback!'

Feeling awful, I tried to comfort her. 'He'll love the fart pot! I bet nobody else'll get him one!' In case you're wondering, the fart pot was a tub of green goo you stuck your fingers into. It made wet-fart noises, and Jacko was something of a connoisseur in that department.

Sally was not comforted. 'It was only one ninety-nine! And the book was only three ninety-nine – how much did this sweater cost, for God's sake?'

'Sally, he won't care! He's the last person to give a toss!'

'He still shouldn't have done it! Doesn't he realize how bad it makes me feel?'

Hearing her distress, Tom started crying. Tearfully grabbing him from me, she ran upstairs for the last of her things, leaving me worn out with the let-down of it all. Widdles wandered in and sat in front of the fireplace, mewing, as if he could suddenly make that lovely warm red stuff appear. It worked with kitchen cupboards; he only had to yowl and one of those dopey humans would magic cod'n'liver out.

180

I hated leaving him, but two days of dry food wouldn't hurt. I hadn't phoned Mum yet, but I'd go down late on Christmas Eve and be back by Boxing Day evening.

Sally was still fretful on the way to the station. 'Whether she's been upset or not, I just know Mum'll be having a go before I've been there an hour. I'll get tensed up just waiting for her to do it.'

*Happy Christmas, ho ho ho.*

Still, she was passably cheerful by the time I waved her off, which was more than you could say for me once I got home via an afternoon at work. The house was horribly quiet. The Christmas tree looked even more dejected, as if it were thinking it might as well die now and have done with it.

I didn't get round to phoning Mum till seven thirty and barely got a hello in before she launched into a hurried monologue: 'I'm up to my elbows in stuffing – we've got people tonight as well so I'm trying to get on top of everything – Bill's very good of course, but he's been entertaining the children – all five of them now, would you believe – Juliet phoned last night to say their central heating boiler had packed up and nobody can come to fix it until after Christmas so of course the house is freezing.'

Juliet was Bill's daughter, who had two kids.

'So she asked if they could come too, and we could hardly say no,' she went on. 'The children'll have to sleep end to end, though I'm sure they won't mind –

Juliet and Mike'll have to share that single bed in the little room but it's just too bad – unless they toss with Roger and Gail for the sofa bed – thank heaven we bought it – somebody would have been sleeping on the floor otherwise. I do hope the turkey's going to be big enough with four extra – I didn't get such a big one this year because we only end up throwing half of it away. And goodness knows how we're all going to fit round the dining table – Bill invited the Parkers last week as well – Oh Lord – hang on – something's boiling over –'

It was just as well; those ten seconds gave me time to think.

'Wretched cranberries,' she said, half panting as she got back to the phone. 'I really don't know why I bother making cranberry sauce except that it's so much nicer. I've got sticky red goo all over the hob now, but that's the least of my worries. By the way, did you know it's far better to cook your turkey upside down till half an hour before the end? You just turn it over to brown it, and do take it out of the oven a good half-hour before serving – it carves better like that.'

'Yes, I'll do that,' I said brightly. 'Have you got that special brandy butter recipe, by the way? That's why I was ringing, actually.'

'Oh, Lord, I haven't made brandy butter for *years*. I should go to M&S if I were you, and don't leave it till the last minute – they always sell out of everything. I'm sorry, darling, but I really must dash – I've got soufflés

182

in the oven and half the village in the sitting room – I'll phone on Christmas Day, all right?'

Of course there were people I could have phoned, but I'd neglected a lot of my old friends since Sally had come to live with me and besides, I didn't want people feeling sorry for me. In any case, every single I knew was either going to family (most of them moaning that it was going to give them rectal ache) or opting out and heading for the sun. Or to the ski slopes, like Witch Nina. Virtually every couple I knew was either doing likewise, or planning a cosy Christmas *à deux*, in which case they could do without gooseberries. Ridiculously I began to think it was Witch Nina's malevolent fault that my perfect Christmas had fallen apart. Like her Narnia counterpart, she was making it always winter and never Christmas.

I phoned the organic butcher first thing on Christmas Eve to cancel the turkey, but he said sorry love, he couldn't guarantee he'd sell it – why didn't I just sling it in the freezer?

Because I only had a titchy one, that's why. Still, I collected it and stared at the purply-white carcass, wishing it hadn't died in vain.

I didn't tell anyone at work that my Christmas was down the pan. After packing up at twelve thirty, we went for drinks. Lesley got plastered and said her mother-in-law was coming and she and her husband invariably rowed when the old hag showed up. Plus mother-in-law gave her a horrible frumpy nightie every year, which she knew for a fact was usually one she'd had from someone else the previous Christmas and stuck at the back of the wardrobe, saying, 'Well, it'll do for Lesley.'

Sandie got pissed and said actually she didn't mind if Dave got her tacky lace knickers after all, we should just see what she'd got him from Ann Summers.

Jess got pinkly tiddly and said a widower from her Italian class had invited her round for dinner, and even asked whether she'd fancy one of those culture tours to Florence and Siena in the spring, when it wouldn't be too hot. 'He's called George,' she confided. 'Really *awfully* nice – he helped me with my homework last week. I was getting in a terrible muddle with my verbs.'

It was coming to something when even Jess had a better social life than me.

When I got home I put Capital on, to cheer myself up, but by around seven thirty it was only making me feel that everyone in the entire universe was out partying, except for me. I knew they weren't, I knew there were thousands of people eating M&S dinners for one right this minute who were lonely all year, but that was how it felt. I thought of Jacko, probably out somewhere cheerfully noisy with a crowd of friends. I thought of Mum and Bill's packed house, stuffed with food and drink and people, and wondered why on earth I hadn't told her. I could have slept on a sofa, and even those kids were probably bearable if you had enough of Bill's punch.

And then I thought of the Witch of Narnia, who'd made my perfect Christmas fall apart. Skiing. Probably skiing right now, given the time difference. Or sitting in a chic little café with that Silicon Valley billionaire, sipping *vin chaud* in snowy sunshine. The Witch of Aspen, ha ha.

*Of* Aspen.

*In* Aspen . . .

The thought didn't exactly hit me, it sneaked up when I wasn't looking.

*Phone him.*

*What, now?*

*Why not?*

*He's still seeing her.*

*Not just now, he isn't. What do you care, anyway?*

*He'll be busy.*

*He might not.*

*He's probably gone to his folks already.*

*Then he might be glad of some light relief.*

Before another twenty seconds had elapsed I was pinging his number, my heartbeat going haywire.

Brrrr . . . Brrrr . . . Brrrr . . .

*He's not going to answer, is he?*

Brrrr . . . Brrrr . . .

*Yes, but what if he does?*

Br . . .

I jabbed 'off' in mid-ring and would like to make

it perfectly clear that this was not due to any onset of sudden, irrational panic in case he answered, after all. It was Christmas Eve, for God's sake. I could hardly say, 'Hi, John, fancy going for a pizza?' In fact, I could imagine the conversation exactly.

'Oh, hi, John, it's Harriet.'

'*Who*? Hang on, I can't hear . . .' (Pause while he moved away from sounds of riotous revelry, loud music, champagne corks popping, etc.)

'That's better. Sorry, who is it?'

'Harriet.'

(Pause for memory search followed by mental 'oh shit'.) 'Oh, *Harriet*! Hi, how's it going?'

'Oh, not bad.' (No, scrub that.) 'Pretty good, actually.' (Said with bright vivacity, as if about to do something brilliant, e.g. wild party.) 'Just thought I'd call and say good luck with your tribal warfare.'

'Oh, right. Thanks. Hang on a tick . . .' (Pause for throatily sexy female voice to yell, 'John! Get your gorgeous butt over here – it's our turn to do "Summer Lovin'" on the karaoke.')

(Aside from phone:) 'I'm on my way, Sugar . . .' (Back into phone:) 'Look, sorry, Harriet, but I'm a bit tied up just now . . .'

'Yes, I gather. So am I – just off out – whoops! There's my taxi – bye bye then.'

I shoved my phone back in my bag. 'This is what you call getting desperate,' I said to Widdles, who was curled up on the sofa beside me, but actually awake for once. 'It's a pathetic human condition you wouldn't know about.'

He gave a massive yawn.

'While the cat's away, he's hardly going to be sorting out his stamp collection, is he?' I said. 'After all, he had no qualms about playing, even when the cat was only a couple of miles down the road.'

Widdles gave his left front paw a thoughtful lick before recurling himself into a tabby ball.

'I'm going to go really mad, now,' I told him. 'I'm going to make some cheese on toast and a cup of tea.'

I went to bed at ten, with Widdles and one of Dorothy's collection of ancient Regency romances. Except for the creaks an old house makes at night, it was so horribly quiet, I'd even have welcomed a ghost to natter to. We could have had a nice cosy chat about what it was like to be laced into your stays.

Still, Dorothy's book soon took my mind off it. I'd never have thought she'd be into this sort of thing, which just goes to show you should never judge by appearances. Had she secretly dreamed of a lusty Sir Tarquin, known all over for his skill at both swordplay and love? *'I can never marry you,' wept little Dorothea, tears tumbling from her china-blue eyes. 'For I am fated to grow old and arthritic in Putney and moan about the Government. O, pray unhand me, sir! Have the goodness to remove your hand from my placket fastener!'*

Poor old thing. By page ten I was beginning to

fancy lusty Sir Tarquin myself, but when my phone rang I was still so desperate for human contact, I almost broke my neck tripping over a chair to get to my bag.

It was Jacko, bless him. 'Hi, pet – how was your drive to darkest Devon?'

I wasn't going to tell him there hadn't been one. He'd feel bad and invite me straight up there. I might even have gone, if I could have faced a four-hour drive. 'Not bad – how was yours?'

'Diabolical. Still, I've calmed the wrinklies down a bit. She still hasn't phoned, though. And even if she does, I don't know how I'm going to speak to her without having a massive go. And then she'll hang up and we'll be back to square one. You'll never believe what the old man's suggesting now – telling her he'll give her a new car if she comes home! She hasn't even passed her test, for God's sake!'

After we'd talked for a couple more minutes I switched the light off and put my phone on the bedside table. And just as I'd drifted into sleep, it rang again.

# Seven

'Hello?' I said dozily.

'That was quick,' the voice said. 'I thought you might have your rubber gloves on and be doing unspeakable things to turkeys.'

I was still groping for my brains. 'Er, sorry, who is it?' Even as I said it, though, a massive flying jelly hit me in the guts.

'John. John Mackenzie.'

My voice had gone. They really should do something about those jellies.

'You weren't asleep, were you?' he added.

*Help. Think. Say something intelligent.* 'Erm, no, not really, just sort of nodding . . .'

'I think you called me, earlier,' he said. 'Only there was a hell of a racket and my phone was in my jacket pocket, and by the time I got to it . . .'

Partying, as per my imaginings. I was nearly stupid enough to come out with a lie he'd never believe for an instant, e.g. 'Oh, sorry, I was trying to call someone else only I was so pissed I dialled the wrong number.'

But my brain kicked in just in time. 'Well, it didn't matter. It was only going to be a quickie, to say good luck with your tribal warfare.'

'Let's hope I don't need it. Plying the old man with enough single malt might help. At least he won't be able to shoot straight if the old biddies drive him beyond endurance.'

I think I laughed, while simultaneously checking the clock. Was that all it was? Only 10.47?

'If you weren't attacking turkeys, I'd have thought you'd be out partying,' he went on.

From the sounds of it, he still was. Hearing raucous chatter in the background, I had to keep my end up. 'I *was*! From lunchtime! Twelve thirty, to be precise. So by the time I rolled in half an hour ago, I just fell into bed.'

'Just as well, if you're cooking tomorrow. Don't head cooks have to be up at the crack, shoving the stuffed sacrifice in the oven?'

'Not now, I don't. I'm not cooking, after all.'

'Eating out, instead?'

'No, they've all gone home.'

'Sorry?'

'Gone home. Last-minute changes of plan.'

'So you're all on your own?'

'Well, yes, except for Widdles.'

'Not tomorrow too?'

God, was I sounding plaintive? 'Yes, but to be honest, I'm really looking forward to the P&Q. Nothing to do all day long but eat, drink, and watch all the corny old films I like.'

'Think of me, then,' he said wryly. 'You need a

United Nations peacekeeping force at our dining table. Maybe it's the carving that gets the old man going. All that ritual knife-sharpening . . .'

From the mixed voices in the background, one suddenly stood out. 'John, we're about to go – are you coming?'

Female, wouldn't you know it.

'Yes, hang on . . .' To me he said, 'Look, I have to go. Enjoy your P&Q tomorrow.'

'Will do. Enjoy your non-P&Q. I hope there won't be too much blood on the carpet.'

He laughed. 'Goodnight, then.'

'Goodnight.'

I lay back on the pillow, my eyes suddenly pricking with miserable tears. 'Bastard,' I said to Widdles, who was looking put out at all the disturbance. 'Why did he have to phone back at all, if he was only going to get me all worked up for nothing?'

Unable to get back to sleep, I returned to the lusty Sir Tarquin. He had secret designs on Lavinia, who thought him a philandering rake, up to his immaculately tied neckcloth in gaming hells, loose females and so on. Still, if she'd called his mobile while he was quaffing Buck's Fizz from loose-female slippers, he'd have done more than just check the number and call her back. He'd have driven at breakneck speed in his phaeton, whatever that was, and broken the door down, tossing devoted old retainers aside en route.

'Useless bugger,' I said to Widdles. 'I don't know why I bothered. His loose females can have him.'

He woke me at ten to eight, by patting my cheek with his paw.

'Go to sleep,' I mumbled, turning over.

He came round the other side of the pillow, rubbed his nose against mine, like an Eskimo kiss. This meant, OK, ten minutes, but after that I'm going to get seriously worked up about breakfast. He then curled himself into the mog-shaped space between my chin and my shoulder, and started purring like a traction engine, in anticipation of food.

I was just nodding off again when Widdles took himself fatly to the door, where he sat and produced his best Open Sesame yowl.

'OK, *OK*.' Dragging on my dressing gown, I went via the bathroom to the sitting room, where I drew the curtains and switched the Christmas tree lights on. In the kitchen Widdles was already yowling up at the cupboard. I spooned Succulent White Fish and Prawns in Delicious Jelly into his dish. 'I bought it specially, as a treat,' I told him. 'So you'd better love it.'

I switched on Capital, put some coffee on, and ate an apfelstrudel yoghurt, by which time Widdles was yowling for more. At least I thought he was, until I checked his dish. He'd merely licked off every vestige of Delicious Jelly, while leaving the Succulent White Fish and Prawns intact. 'You fussy little beast!'

I scolded. 'There are millions of starving cats in the Third World!' Still, I gave him the rest anyway; it was Christmas, after all.

Knowing I'd slob all day in my dressing gown otherwise, I went straight up for a bath, as I couldn't face that dribbly shower. There were advantages to being on your own; at least the hot water wouldn't run out. I then dragged on jog bottoms and a sweatshirt and went down to open my presents.

Despite the tree, the sitting room didn't feel very festive. Unless those curtains were drawn Nature's air conditioning was always finding its way through Edwardian window frames. Which meant I'd either have to lay a fire or turn on that useless fan heater, which only felt warm if it was actually blowing on you.

I opened Jacko's present first. As I'd thought, it was just like Sally's, except that mine was scarlet. It wasn't a colour I wore often, but I tried it on and studied the effect in the ancient gilt mirror over the fireplace.

Why didn't I wear scarlet often? It suited me brilliantly. In fact, it looked pretty damn good altogether. Classy, elegant and expensive, just like every other garment I possessed, ha ha.

*Thank you, dear old Jacko, kiss kiss.*

Next I opened my mother's. Another roll-neck sweater, but a chunky, dark grey mohair mix this time, with one fat cable down the front. She'd added a note, too. 'It's M&S men's, but I thought it was your type of thing. Receipt enclosed, feel free to change it.'

Well, I wouldn't. I rather liked it. She'd added some pink grapefruit Body Shop stuff, too, and a bestseller.

*Thank you, Mum, kiss kiss, hope those kids aren't driving you mad.*

Sally's, next, which gave me heart failure at first. A couple of months back I'd seen a scarf in a magazine: Kenzo or something, price £179. I'd said, 'I wouldn't mind that, if it was ten quid instead.'

She'd put in a note. 'Old Dorothy's knitting needles came in useful after all. I've made a few bums but I don't think they're too obvious.'

Somehow she'd reproduced it: broad, irregular stripes in gloriously clashing shades of red, shocking pink and purple. It must have been a metre long. My eyes misted to think how many hours she must have spent while I was at work, or even at night, in her room. I hadn't had a clue. I didn't even know she *could* knit.

I put it on and went back to the mirror. One of the reds matched Jacko's sweater exactly.

The card on the last parcel read, 'Lots of love and dribbly kisses from Tom XXX. PS. Mummy bought it for me – I was too embarrassed.'

It was a pair of knickers from La Senza: satiny, girly ones in cream.

I sat in a sea of paper, suddenly miserable as sin. It was no fun just *opening* presents; you needed the donors there to kiss and say thank you to. You had to dish them out, too, and see people's faces, even if they weren't as ecstatic as you'd hoped. Still, there was always Widdles. He was asleep on the kitchen sofa but I took him his stocking anyway.

I picked him up, just to wake him up, and put him on my lap. 'Look! Lots of pussy treats!' I offered a couple of Fishy Favourites.

He sniffed disdainfully and turned away.

'How about these, then? Lovely Seafood Nibbles?'

Again he sniffed disdainfully, got off my lap, and recurled himself into the sleep which had been so rudely interrupted.

*Oh, sod you, then.*

I poured myself a massive Baileys, knocked it back in two goes and poured another. Might as well get pissed. Might as well get completely pissed, rat-arsed and bollocksed. Might as well start now, although it was only ten past ten. Might as well cook that turkey, too. At least the lovely roasty smell might make me feel a bit Christmassy – nothing else was going to. Just as I was looking for the cookery book with roasting times, the doorbell rang.

I was half expecting carol singers; the local kids made a cottage industry of it. They never actually sang a carol; they just chanted 'We wish you a Merry Christmas . . .' and stood there with their cheeky little hands out. I invariably gave them a pound, just for their nerve.

The chap on the step was a mite big for a carol singer.

'Hi,' he said. 'I just called to say Happy P&Q.'

'John!'

He wore a casual, bluey-grey jacket and a little smile. 'And sorry for waking you up last night.' He gave a nod in the vague direction of parked cars. 'I'm on my way to the tribe, but I made a minor detour.'

Still in shock, my brain had been in better working order. 'Well, that was nice, but you needn't have bothered. I wasn't really asleep, just sort of nodding . . .'

'You sounded pretty asleep to me.'

*Get with it, Harriet. An appropriate lie, please.* 'All right, I was flat out. That's what comes of partying from lunchtime till nine o'clock.'

'I know the feeling,' he said. 'Although I didn't start till three-ish.'

I suddenly realized that his spark had lost maybe ten per cent of its edge. He was showered and shaved and all that, but his face indicated serious partying. 'And finished about three-ish, I bet. If you don't mind my saying so, you look just a bit rough.'

'I feel just a bit rough. You wouldn't have a coffee, would you? I found an empty packet when I got up. I'm afraid I uttered a foul curse or two.'

Even at ninety per cent spark level he was still pretty effective, especially when he chucked in that lethal little smile. 'I expect so. Come in.'

'Thanks.' En route to the kitchen, he glanced

through the sitting-room door. 'That's one hell of a tree.'

'Lovely, isn't it? Jacko did it.'

By now, of course, flutters that had been temporarily displaced by shock were getting going again. However, I had a stern word with them. From now on they would be required to behave in a circumspect manner. They would do a feasibility study before taking off with all wings flapping. If he was warming up an old possibility while the cat was away, or had just thought I'd make a convenient pit-stop . . .

The kitchen was less of a tip than usual, no maternity bras strewn on the sofa for once. 'Take a seat,' I said, nodding at it. 'That's Widdles, but I won't formally introduce you. He's not very keen on men, so don't take offence if he goes off in a huff.'

A creaky squeak told me he'd sat. Somehow I hadn't thought he would.

I'd expected him to stand against the worktop right beside me, which would have made it harder to remain circumspect from a flutter point of view. As it was, it was easy to be calm and collected while spooning Rich Roast into the filter. 'How far have you got to go, to the tribe?'

'West Sussex – only about an hour's drive. Do the bells still work?' he added, evidently noticing the glass case on the wall.

'Oh, yes. Jacko was very tempted when he was just out of hospital, but Sally would have thumped him.'

'How's the junk going?'

As I'd hardly touched it since Sally had come, I had to lie. 'A nightmare. I've been to the tip at least fourteen times and about ten times to the charity shop. But the trouble is, it *isn't* all junk, so I have to go through it with a sieve.'

While the coffee was filtering I collected mugs and milk, as if he were just any common-or-garden bloke. I felt quite pleased with my casual demeanour.

'I don't smell any turkey,' he said.

Rich Roast was wafting nicely, though. 'I might shove it in later. Widdles will appreciate it. How do you like your coffee? Milk?'

'Just a splash. No sugar.'

This was when I heard that sofa creak again. 'To tell the truth,' he said, coming up to the worktop after all, 'I didn't just come to say sorry for waking you up.'

Something in my stomach gave a violent lurch. Only about a foot away, he was leaning against the worktop, arms folded, his eyes on me. Traces of whatever shaving stuff he used were wafting into my olfactory thingies, sending deprived hormones suddenly rampant. I'm afraid I even had fleeting visions of kitchen-table quickies.

But you'd never have known. 'I gathered that,' I said, avoiding his eye by the neat technique of putting a jar of Marmite back in the cupboard. 'You came for a coffee. Probably a piece of toast, too.'

'Make it a bacon sandwich and you're on.'

For a second I really thought he meant it. I turned to him with a piquant retort all ready, which was exactly what he intended.

'But I didn't come for that, either. I thought you sounded a bit down last night. A bit hacked off at being on your own.'

This was when I realized my hormones had been galloping ahead of reality. At the same time it was so unexpected, I had no trouble looking taken aback. 'God, no.' I even added an airy little laugh. 'To tell you the truth, I'm really looking forward to the peace.'

Since the coffee was now ready, I could turn away from him to pour it. 'Sally and Jacko have been squabbling like a pair of nine-year-olds lately. And I actually had a bath this morning without the hot water running out. Jacko's a devil for running the tank dry. There you go,' I added, handing him a mug.

But that was when my bluff ran out. There was something so weakeningly nice-bloke-ish about the way he was looking at me, I couldn't help it. 'Well, I was a bit,' I confessed. 'I was really looking forward to it and suddenly, *phut*, it was all gone. Still, I'm glad Sally's gone home. I think she'd have felt bad afterwards if she hadn't.'

'Why didn't you go to your mother's, after all?'

'I was going to, but she was already overflowing with unexpected hordes, panicking about where to put everybody – you know what they're like. So I just didn't tell her.'

'You could come with me. To my war-zone Christmas dinner.'

It took me a moment to locate my voice. 'You're not serious?'

'As serious as I'll ever be after a heavy night.'

Which evidently wasn't saying much. 'Look, it's very kind of you, but I couldn't possibly.'

'No,' he said, half perching on the counter as he took a sip of coffee. 'I must have been off my head to suggest it. Put it down to caffeine deprivation first thing. Mind you, I've probably exaggerated the scarier aspects, if that's what's worrying you.'

It wasn't. 'They don't know me from Eve!'

'So?'

Wasn't it obvious? 'Won't your mother have a fit if you turn up with a total stranger?'

'She'll probably be relieved. The old man's far more likely to behave himself with a total stranger.'

This was a point I hadn't thought of. 'OK, but aren't you staying over?'

He shook his head. 'I've got some work to catch up on tomorrow. At least, that's the noble intention. I might end up catching up on some sleep, instead.'

'Yes, but it still seems an awful cheek.'

'I don't see why. I'll give my mother a ring, if you like.'

Masses of things were racing through my head. I thought of being on my own all day, and the next, falling asleep over films I'd seen before. I thought of

200

hitting the Baileys and the gin, picking at a twelve-pound turkey, talking to Widdles like a nutter. And last, but far from least, I thought of Nina, deliberately setting out to steal Stuart when she didn't even want him . . .

'It's really very kind of you, but I couldn't.' I said it firmly, looking away as I put the milk back in the fridge.

'Can't say I blame you,' he said. 'I'd run a mile, too.'

Well, that did it. 'Actually, I'd love to come,' I confessed, turning back to him. 'I only said I wouldn't to be polite. I can't think why – it's not very polite to turn down invitations just to be polite, is it?'

He suppressed what might have been a lethal smile if he'd let it out.

'But ring your mother first,' I went on. 'And if she says, "Oh, *please*, I'll have to hoover the stairs," you will tell me?'

'She won't.' Taking a mobile from his jacket pocket, he pushed buttons rapidly.

It was answered almost immediately. 'Hi, it's me,' he said. There was a short pause. 'Of course I'm coming!'

Was that telling, I wondered?

'Look, would you mind if I brought a friend?' he went on. 'She's unexpectedly on her own.' There was another pause. 'Harriet,' he said. After a further pause he added, 'No, just a friend.'

Well, he had to say that, didn't he?

Another pause. 'Yes, I've told her all that.' Giving me a brief up-and-down check that ended with a little wink, he went on, 'Yes, I think she's bomb-proof.' (Pause.) 'I don't know – I'll ask.' To me he said, 'Are you nervous of boisterous, slobbering hounds?'

I was trying not to laugh. 'No, I like them.'

'She likes them,' he said into the phone. After a longer pause, he said, 'Yes, I told her you'd say that. She thought you might throw a fit and think you had to hoover the stairs.' After another short pause, during which he was laughing silently, he turned to me. 'She says there is rather a lot of dog hair on the stairs, so please try not to notice.'

Thank God for normal people.

Into the phone he said, 'All right, we're on our way. Bye bye.'

Shoving the phone back in his pocket, he looked at me. 'Ready?'

Was he kidding? I looked down at my jog bottoms. 'Can you give me two minutes? I do mean two,' I added, seeing a flash of obviously educated cynicism.

'There's no mad panic. Have ten, if you want.'

I charged upstairs, thanking God I'd already had that bath. My hair was more *au naturel* than I cared for, but there was no time for hot brushes. I yanked off the joggers, yanked on a black skirt but left Jacko's sweater. Not only was it Christmas-coloured, it was also clean and not lying at the bottom of a bone-dry

202

heap of ironing. I pulled on my long black boots; I might have worn shoes, but the only clean tights I could find had a little ladder at the ankle.

Since there was no time for major facial renovations either, I just added lipgloss and mascara, a squirt of CK1 and charged down again.

'Christ, that was quick!' he said, evidently impressed.

'I did say "two".' All I had to do now was leave lunch and afternoon tea for Widdles and grab a jacket. On an impulse I also grabbed Widdles's Fishy Favourites; the slobbering hound surely wouldn't turn his nose up.

He'd parked a little down the road. It was a dark green Saab convertible, newish, with lovely leather seats. I've got a bit of a thing about leather car seats. I don't know why, as I don't care for leather sofas. Maybe it's that quietly expensive smell they give off when the heater's on.

Half a mile down the road, of course, I was doing some belated thinking. On the one hand, I wasn't naïve enough to think he'd merely felt sorry for me, although he probably had. On the other, I wasn't sure what else was in his head.

I don't think I'd ever encountered a man so impossible to make out. One minute he was pure nice bloke – look at the way he'd checked on Tom, for a start. But he was beginning to remind me of someone I'd known years ago, who'd tangled with a friend of mine. After he'd failed again to call for days on end Lisa would be fuming, saying that was *it*, she'd *had* it, if the bastard ever dared show his face again she was going to disembowel him. Yet when he did she'd be melting in seconds, making him a fry-up and saying, no, it was OK, honestly, she knew he'd been busy, and before the frying pan had gone cold they'd be in bed. And afterwards she'd say helplessly, 'Yes, I know, but the thing is, he can be really really *nice* . . .'

The *x* factor, she'd called it.

The Helicopter factor was what I was beginning to call it. And a damn sight better than the *Teletubbies Christmas Special* and a Marmite sandwich.

He stopped for petrol half a mile down the road. While he was filling up, I picked a couple of bunches of narcissi out of a bucket on the forecourt. They were lovely, sweet-smelling, making you realize spring wasn't far away. 'For your mother,' I said, as he joined me in the queue. 'I don't like to go empty-handed, especially on Christmas Day.'

'It's really not necessary but I dare say she'll appreciate it.'

We headed south in typical English-Christmas weather, i.e. cloudy, mild, and wondering whether a spot of rain mightn't be a good idea. I couldn't help wishing for proper Christmas weather: snowy and crisp, the trees prettily frosted. This in turn made me think of ski slopes, brilliant blue sky, and you know who.

I don't know whether it was all that Baileys on a

virtually empty stomach, but suddenly I thought of her skis turning into a broomstick and zooming off, her tinkly cackles echoing over the mountain. I thought of her making it always winter and never Christmas in America, land of 'Deck the halls . . .' and fat Santas going *ho ho ho*. I thought of the White House sending up Stealth fighters to blast her off her broomstick. I even thought of Superman being called in, to rid the world of this Threat To Civilization As We Know It.

And I'm afraid to say I laughed. Not silently enough, either, because John glanced across at me. 'Something funny?'

'Just something daft on the radio.'

After a moment he said, 'What made your friends decide to desert you at the last minute?'

'It wasn't their choice.' After telling him a little about Sally's 'proper' parents and even more proper neighbours, I got on to Jacko, terminally indulged Tara and the Lee ructions.

'They should let her get on with it,' he said, a good deal more drily than I'd expected. 'I'm only surprised my sister never did anything like that. I suppose I shouldn't say it, but she can still be a bit of a pain.'

'How old is she?'

'Twenty-two, but still acting fourteen and a half now and then. She dropped out of college, went au-pairing, didn't like that, dropped back into college, dropped out again, went to be a chalet girl, didn't like that either, generally titted about for years.'

'Sounds a bit like me,' I said.

'For God's sake, she's nothing like you. You were paying your way. She's actually in her first year of a Media Studies degree now. I swear she only picked it to brown the old man off. She might as well have said she was doing a combined BA in Political Correctness and Woolly Lefty Liberalism. He's just a tad old-fashioned,' he added wryly. 'If you want to see an interesting display of red turning to puce and facial veins popping, just say you think it'd be a jolly good idea if that nice Mr Blair allowed gays to marry in church.'

I laughed. 'I get the message. We keep off politics.'

'You might – Lucy won't. She winds the old man up on purpose.'

'Well, it's better than those nightmare family dinners where people just say, "I think I might cut the grass later," and "Did you pay the gas bill?"'

He laughed, but I couldn't altogether join in. 'I was speaking from bitter experience,' I confessed. 'I sat through some awful meals like that when my folks were about to split up. There would be these hideous, tense silences, punctuated by trite remarks that were supposed to sound normal, for my benefit. My father would say, "This is a nice piece of pork," and my mother would say, "Yes, but it's not as good as we used to get from Owens." It made me want to scream.'

It had all come to a head that summer after my

first year at university. They'd taken separate holidays the previous year, which should have warned me. At the time I was distraught over Stuart, Dad had been in Greece, pottering around Marathon and Salamis. Mum had gone to Minorca in June, with a friend. At the time I'd told myself it was just because they liked different types of holiday. Dad liked ruins and museums; Mum liked flaking out on a beach with a Jilly Cooper. She liked sitting in crowded harbour cafés, having a drink and a laugh. Dad liked sitting quietly on his balcony, reading the *History of the Peloponnesian War* in the original.

Mum had been sitting in just such a harbour café with her friend Gina when a man had said, 'Do you mind if I take this chair?' He'd sat at an adjacent table with a couple of friends, and that, as they say, was it. Bill's wife had died three years previously so she wasn't breaking anything up there, but she'd agonized over Dad.

She'd told me on the thirtieth of June, almost exactly a year after first meeting Bill. She'd been trying to work up to it, having told Dad ten days previously, which was why we'd had all that hideous Silent Sauce with meals. I'd cried for Dad. He'd looked so lost and bemused, but it would never have occurred to him to be angry, even though Mum had met Bill a few times when she was supposed to be on shopping trips or at a health farm, getting some of her fat off.

However, after a few months Dad had realized it

was for the best. I think he might even have been relieved, once he'd got used to the idea and sussed out how to work the microwave. Nobody would ever say again, 'David, *must* you wear that awful old jumper?' He could spend months of evenings learning Middle Egyptian for his trip to the Upper Nile, without anybody saying, 'Don't tell me you've forgotten we're going to the Tuckers' tonight?'

Looking back, I understood Mum's almost constant irritability, but it had been awful to live with at the time. I was glad they were friends again, but I still often wondered what had brought two such incompatible people together.

Only recently Mum had said to me, 'He's a lovely man, really, but he should have been an academic. He should have been sitting in a study in one of those tweed jackets with leather patches at the elbows, taking twenty years to write a book on Roman coins.'

John said, 'I guess it's harder when you're an only child. When my parents were going through a bad patch, throwing things or not speaking, my sister and I used to retreat to the garden shed and work out ways to get ourselves adopted.'

As I laughed he went on, 'That was my other sister. I was only about ten – Anna was a year younger. She's in Sydney now, hitched, and about to produce her first sprog. When we'd grown up a bit we worked out that Lucy must have dated back to a serious making-up session in that bad patch. The folks never really rowed since – obviously terrified of the consequences.' He shot me a dry little glance. 'But maybe I shouldn't have told you that. My mother'd kill me.'

'Don't worry,' I soothed. 'I'm hardly going to say, "Oh, hello, Lucy – I've heard all about the circumstances of your conception."'

'She'd only say, "Well, it doesn't take rocket science to work *that* one out – Dad got carried away. I was a mistake." She used to throw that at them all the time,' he went on. 'Wailing, "You didn't *want* me – I was a mis*take* . . ." I have to hand it to her,' he said, with a grin. 'It used to work particularly well when she was after a pony or a school ski trip.'

This took me right back, almost with the pain of longing I'd felt at the time. 'God, I wanted a pony. *Wish for a Pony* was my bible.'

'And you didn't get one?'

'No such luck. My mother said I'd get fed up with it – she'd end up traipsing across fields herself with buckets of pony nuts.'

'That's more or less what happened with Lucy's, once she discovered boys. He got so fat from lack of exercise the old man put his foot down, said the poor little bugger'd die of obesity, and found him another home. Are you warm enough?' he added.

'Fine,' I said, rather surprised. 'Aren't you?'

'Yes, I'm fine.'

'But I've got still got this scarf on,' I went on, unwinding it. 'Turn the heating up, if you want.'

'No, I'm fine. Really,' he added more firmly, as if I were about to push it.

Well, if he said so. What man ever wanted heating turned up, after all? 'Christ, it's like an oven in here,' was the usual term.

Neither of us spoke for a bit, so naturally I started thinking again. I thought of that night in the cab, vibes swirling like mist. I dare say it made a difference that it was daytime, he was hungover and we were heading for a family do, but any vibes were behaving so disappointingly discreetly they might not have bothered. He wasn't casting me any lingering little glances. He'd hardly eyed my thighs, of which a fair extent was visible. He hadn't made one remark that held any hint of anything.

To be honest, it was a bit of a let-down.

To cheer myself up, I imagined him dumping Nina right after she'd come out of Heathrow Terminal Four with bags of duty-frees and a ski-tan. I imagined him saying, 'Look, I'm sorry, but . . .' I imagined her throwing a fit, whacking him over the head with a half-litre bottle of Giorgio. Which was maybe why he was putting it off, if indeed he was ready to do the deed. Too afraid of a scene. Most blokes would do anything to avoid tears and scenes. Or maybe he was being devious, trying to get her so browned off that she'd dump *him*. I'd known blokes resort to such tactics: deliberately forget it was Valentine's Day or say her mum looked like a bit of an old slapper.

I was dying to somehow bring up Nina, or make up

a friend who'd gone to Aspen, so *he* might bring her up. But I couldn't bring myself to do it, in case he said, 'Oh, she's ancient history,' and I knew it was a smootharse lie.

On the other hand, *would* it be a lie? What if he'd done the deed already and Nina hadn't liked to admit it even to Suzanne? After all, to someone like Nina this might be a humiliation you'd keep quiet as long as possible.

As the soft cushions of the South Downs came closer and the sky brightened to milky pale blue, I realized there was something I should have done already. 'Do you mind if I make a pre-emptive phone call? If my mother tries the house phone and finds no-one answering, she'll think we're all dead from a gas leak.'

'Go ahead.'

It was Mum herself who answered, after only three rings. After I'd said Happy Christmas and thank you for the lovely presents, it was her turn. 'We haven't opened ours yet – we're saving them till after dinner, though goodness knows what time that'll hit the table. The children are all crotchety already – they didn't sleep very well with all the excitement. Bill waited till one o'clock to do their stockings – he'd borrowed a Father Christmas outfit, just in case – and can you believe that little devil Robert was still awake and said, "Is that you, Grandpa?" So Bill put on a heavy Scottish accent and growled, "Whisht ye bairns awee the mauldy nicht," or something, and Robert got back under the duvet, quick as a flash. And this morning he said, "How can Father Christmas read people's letters if he can't even speak English?" Six! I ask you.' Here she paused for breath. 'Are you having a nice day, darling?'

'Lovely,' I said brightly. 'I don't know what time our dinner's going to hit the table either, but I don't think anyone's too bothered.'

Out of the corner of my eye I saw John quietly laughing and tried not to follow suit.

'You're not in the car, are you?' she asked. 'I can hear a sort of engine noise.'

She had ears like a guard dog. 'I am, actually – I've just nipped out with Jacko to get lemons for the gin and tonics. I knew I'd forget something.'

'At least you *can* nip out – there won't be anything open for miles around here. Have you heard from your father lately, by the way?'

'I had a card. He said he'd be spending Christmas in Cyprus.'

'Yes, but did he say who *with*? I had a letter the other day – I forgot to tell you. He said he's met an "extremely nice woman" and they're spending Christmas together!' She sounded almost affronted by the idea.

'Well, that's lovely for him, isn't it?'

'Yes, but I'm wondering what *sort* of woman. Her name's Kathy, apparently!'

'So what's she supposed to be called? Agatha?' (My mother was called Pat, in case you're wondering.)

'Of course not, but I just don't see your father as a "Kathy" type. I'm a bit worried, actually. He said she adores Cyprus and now he's talking about buying a house there! I can't help thinking she's seen him coming.'

'For heaven's sake, Mum, he's not stupid!'

'He can be, darling. Clever people can be unbelievably stupid, believe me, especially men of a certain age when a certain type of woman starts flattering them. If she's found out he's got some money – there's half of Dorothy's house, after all, never mind his own, and all his investments . . .'

'He was a solicitor, for heaven's sake! He's not going to be taken in!'

'Yes, but it sounds as if this Kathy's exerting an undue influence. He said he might go skiing with her in the Troodos mountains! *Skiing!* He was always the most unathletic man alive – he'll crash into a tree and kill himself. What if she's got him to change his will?'

'Mum, I'm sure she's done nothing of the sort. And there's no earthly reason why he shouldn't go skiing – last time I went there were masses of fifties and sixties on the nursery slopes. He might even enjoy it.'

'Well, I'm not so sure about that. Bill thinks it's all a bit suspect, too. Your father said he might pop home for a week or two soon, anyway. Has he sorted out a power of attorney yet, for you to sell the house?'

'Of course!'

'He still shouldn't leave you to do it all on your own. House sales can be a massive headache, believe you me. Anyway, maybe he'll bring this Kathy and you can tell me whether she looks the type to see him coming. I must go, darling, I haven't even done the potatoes yet.'

I pressed 'end call'. 'Well, that was good for a laugh on Christmas morning. My mother thinks some scheming gold-digger's got her painted claws into my father. Thinks she's planning to get him killed on a ski slope in Cyprus.'

After I'd given the gist he said, 'You don't sound so entirely certain it's good for a laugh.'

On reflection, I wasn't. 'He probably *is* susceptible. I don't think there's been anyone on the scene for years.' The only one I knew of was a neighbour, a few years back. She'd been lonely after losing her husband and I had a feeling any kind of 'relationship' had consisted of companionable theatre trips and 'I've made far too much beef casserole – would you like to come and help me eat it?' She'd since remarried and left the area, anyway.

And there was no denying that Mum knew Dad better than anyone; she'd probably read a good deal between the lines of his letter. I began to imagine a rather younger woman thinking 'Silly old fool', getting him to buy her presents and fund trips. I even thought of him taking Viagra to keep up with her; he must be terribly out of practice, after all. I had a horrible, disloyal feeling that he mightn't have been the world's greatest lover in the first place.

Looking back, Mum had been impatient and irritable with him for years, though usually it had been just under the surface. With mature hindsight, I wondered whether it had less to do with failure to put shelves up, than with perennial sexual frustration.

I thought back to how lost and rejected he'd looked, like a lanky old dog taken to the rescue home because his owners had become fed up with him and got a puppy, instead. I thought of him looking like that again and couldn't bear it.

In fact it was partly because of Dad that I'd stopped working abroad. He'd had a minor heart attack: so minor he hadn't even realized what it was until he'd gone to the doctor, but it had put the wind up me when a neighbour had phoned me in Athens to say he was in hospital, having tests. I'd been spending at least ten months of the year away, and even when I was back I was all over the place, seeing old friends. Mum and Bill had been in Bali at the time, and I'd had a horrible vision of getting another phone call one day to say he'd been found dead by the microwave, with his dinner for one all dried up inside it. I'd thought that if I were working at home for a few months at a time, at least I'd see him more frequently.

As it turned out I'd seen him most often at Dorothy's, on the Sundays when Dad had come up to tidy the garden and take her out for the statutory roast.

Those lunches had been hard going for poor old Dad on his own, as Dorothy had invariably complained in a very loud voice that the food was too hot/cold/overcooked/undercooked/tough/sloppy, they didn't know how to make pastry any more, and why did that waitress wear such a short skirt with legs like that? Two of you could see the funny side, and as Dad had said, one of her pleasures in life was having something to moan about. She'd invariably been a lot perkier when she'd got home, and said it was all very nice – burp – that cauliflower was repeating on her, a small port and brandy might settle her stomach, David, look in the sideboard, will you?

I realized John had turned off the main road. 'It's not far now. Only a few more miles.'

We were in South Downs country now; the cushions rolled gently on all sides, some ploughed, some grassland dotted with sheep, even the odd early lamb. He drove through one of those villages that have probably been there since long before the Domesday Book or even the Saxons: clustered higgledy-piggledy round a church with a square Norman tower and a pub.

The lane wound on like a meandering river, past long-gone obstacles and gently rolling fields of sheep. Or maybe there never were any obstacles. Maybe it was a case of the rolling English drunkard making the rolling English road, like the poet said. You could imagine the Ancient Brits staggering home after four pints of mead, wondering whether 'er indoors would have given their pottage to the pig. You could imagine some Roman commander saying, 'Right, the first thing we'll do is build some proper bloody roads. See to it, Marcus Antonius: two straight lanes to Chichester by the Ides of March or you're lion's meat.'

He turned at a T-junction into a road leading through woods where I guessed there'd be a riot of bluebells come the spring. We'd just rounded a bend when a mud-splashed Land Rover coming in the other direction hooted and braked sharply.

'It's the old man,' John said, braking likewise as the Land Rover pulled up twenty yards further down. Reversing back, he stopped opposite the other vehicle and they both wound their windows down.

I saw a man with hair turning from red to grey, a beard to match, and a shaggy Dulux dog on the passenger seat.

'Flora's gone walkabout,' he barked. (The man, not the dog.) 'I'm taking the clockwise route – take the anti-clockwise, will you? She can't have gone far. Morning, Harriet – get weaving, John, chop chop – though with a bit of luck the old trout might have got herself run over already.'

# EIGHT

As Mackenzie senior shot off, Mackenzie junior shot me a look of comic resignation, fifty-fifty with apology. 'Well, I did warn you.'

I was doing my best not to laugh. 'Are we talking batty old aunts here?'

'Yep.' Putting the car into gear, he moved off. 'She must be getting worse. Looks like we're in for a remake of *National Lampoon's Christmas Vacation.*'

'I loved that. But I hope we won't meet your old man coming the other way with a mangled old dear on the roof rack.'

'He doesn't mean it.' He bore left around another bend that struck me as positively lethal to a wandery old aunt. There were no pavements, of course.

'Actually, that's not true; he does half mean it,' he went on. 'Another subject to keep clear of is compulsory euthanasia of the senile. He says, "If I ever lose my marbles, I hope someone'll bloody well push me down the stairs," and my mother says, "If you say that one more time, I will." And Lucy says, "What d'you mean, *if*?"'

I uttered a laugh which came out so much like a snort, I began to see the virtues of silver-bells peals.

After we'd gone another couple of minutes, however, his phone rang in his pocket.

The call lasted all of three seconds. 'Panic over,' he said, shoving it back. 'The old man's found her.'

He stopped, reversed into the muddy entrance to a field and headed back the way we'd come, except that he turned off again, down a lane you'd miss if you weren't looking. On the left were fields, on the right, about a hundred metres down, was one of those houses my mother had always fancied until she and Bill found their Devon longhouse. 'Perfect,' she'd have said. 'Plenty of space, but not big enough that you're rattling in it.'

It was lovely mellow old brick, double-fronted, probably Georgian, set well back in what looked like square miles of garden, compared with Dorothy's semi-detached patch, but was probably about half an acre. There was a curving, irregular front lawn and no actual drive, just a gravelled sweep leading to the front of the house, with outbuildings at the side.

There were several parked cars, including the Land Rover. Having just pipped us, Mackenzie senior was helping a very elderly lady out of the Land Rover. As John was parking alongside, the front door opened.

I saw at once where John had got his looks, though his mother might have been a copy with the colour toned down. She was altogether paler, with lighter hair that had no grey, and an expression of anxiety mixed with relief.

We got out to a cacophony of 'Flora, where have you *been?*' followed immediately by 'Harriet, how nice –' At the same time his father was saying, 'I should have locked the bloody doors,' and the Dulux dog, now imprisoned in the back of the Land Rover, was frantically barking to be let out.

In the next instant John's father released him, and a woofing mass of grey and white fur came at me like a Scud missile. I wouldn't normally bother, but since turbo-charged claws wouldn't do Jacko's cashmere much good I fielded him, catching his front paws in my hands in what I hoped was not an ungracious fashion.

Almost before he'd hit me, however, there was another cacophony of 'Angus, for heaven's sake!' from John's mother, 'Horace, get *down*!' from his father, and a sharper 'Down!' from John.

'It's fine, really.' I grinned at Horace, who was grinning at me in a matey, lollopy-tongued fashion and trying to get close enough to lick my face.

One thing about dogs, they do break the ice.

'I'm so sorry, he's only two and still terribly naughty,' John's mother said. 'I do hope his feet aren't filthy.'

Since Horace was quite a weight, I let him go, and John instantly took my right wrist and inspected my palm. 'Let's hope it's just mud,' he said drily. 'You don't want to know what else that animal gets into.'

'John, for heaven's sake take her in to wash her hands,' said his mother, in a harassed voice.

'Get her a large gin,' grunted his father. 'She's going to need it.'

The object of the trout hunt, meanwhile, was looking worried. 'Margaret, I can't seem to find my bag.' Suddenly aware of me, she peered at me suspiciously. 'Who's that girl? She hasn't taken my bag, has she?'

'It's in the *house*, Flora. You left it in the house,' Mrs Mackenzie soothed, while Mr M. muttered, 'Christ on a bicycle . . .'

Taking my elbow, John led me inside. 'I accept full responsibility,' he said. 'It's entirely my fault for exaggerating the scary bits. At this rate we'll have the domestic violence unit round before you can say, "Wash your mud off in here."' He opened a door off the hall.

'Thank you.' I shut the door behind me and tried to crack up quietly.

After that it was so relatively civilized for a bit, I thought all the real fun was over. John was still there when I came out, waiting to escort me into the drinks-and-chat hum. It was a large, light room, overlooking a garden I could see would be idyllic in the summer, a field stretching beyond with a couple of horses. There was a log fire and a discreet, six-foot Christmas tree in the corner. Nothing was new, but although there were lots of antiques, nothing was of the opulent variety.

After proper introductions, I was asked to call his folks Angus and Margaret. I explained why I was unexpectedly solo and we did the usual 'And what do you do?' bit. Angus was a vet, but semi-retired; he did farm animals. Margaret had been a registrar of Births, Deaths and Marriages, but had given it up because of Flora; she missed the weddings, but not the deaths. Neither Lucy nor the other aunt had appeared yet; Margaret had said Lucy was only just up and would probably be on the phone till lunchtime. Beatrice, her own aunt, did a lot of 'meditating' in her room, which usually meant lying on the bed with a book.

There must have been a dozen friends in for drinks, of much the type I'd have expected. A JP, a female vet from Angus's practice, a farmer and a retired couple who kept a yacht at Chichester and asked John when he was going to get back behind a rudder. John had once done a lot of sailing, I gathered. Beatrice then appeared, rather grand and portly in some flowing caftan thing in black and purple and nearly as much make-up as Barbara Cartland.

'Kept you quiet, hasn't he?' she boomed, looking me up and down.

'She's just a friend, Beatrice,' said Margaret hastily.

Beatrice said something that sounded very much like *hrrmph*. 'I'm beginning to wonder about you,' she said darkly to John. 'Thirty-two and losing your grip already?'

John shot me a little wink. 'Beatrice still has a

222

king-size grip. When she's drunk enough she might tell you about a certain sixty-five-year-old at her t'ai chi class.'

'He's sixty-eight,' she retorted, but evidently enjoyed this indication that she was by no means past it. 'And I'm never going to get drunk at this rate. If you're in charge of the bar, John, I'll have a large whisky. And no—'

'—bloody soda,' he supplied. 'Beatrice, I wouldn't dare.'

I suppose I was half laughing as he went, and Beatrice took it amiss. 'I wasn't always a fat old bag,' she said, in a terse boom. 'I was a hell-raiser. Walked on aeroplane wings. Went through two husbands before my twenty-fifth birthday. They've got no stamina these days. They should bring back cod liver oil.'

Just as I was wondering what on earth to say to that, her attention was diverted. 'Margaret, that dog's slobbering in the nuts!'

Quietly hoovering up assorted nibbles from a bowl on a side table, Horace was told to behave himself and I had a minute to myself. Of course I'd been dreading someone saying, 'How's the lovely Nina, then?' but nobody had, and just as well. Throwing up on the carpet would have been highly embarrassing. John evidently kept his love life to himself, but that was normal enough. Who wanted family saying, 'Is it serious?' Beatrice's crack about losing his grip

223

would indicate that he hadn't mentioned anyone in ages.

After the last guests had left, I sat on a sofa with Margaret. John was standing by the French windows, talking to his father. Flora sat by the fire, constantly fingering her bag with a worried expression. She hadn't cast me any more suspicious glances. On being told I was a friend of John's she'd given me a vague, sweet smile and said, goodness, wasn't I tall.

'She used to come and stay a lot when the children were small,' Margaret confided. 'She loved children, poor old thing. She was marvellous when I was going mad with two toddlers – John could be a little devil and Anna copied everything, of course. Horace! Lie down, you're being a pest.'

I'd been stroking his head for five minutes; if I stopped for more than two seconds he put a huge paw politely on my knee. 'He's fine,' I assured her.

'He'll ladder your tights!'

'They're laddered already,' I confessed, and she laughed. I told her about Widdles, and she said they'd had a cat, too, but Angus had recently had to put her down because of age-related kidney trouble.

Once she said it, I noticed claw damage on the sofas, which had gently faded covers in a William Morris print. The armchair Flora was sitting in looked antique, the old-gold velvet also showing signs of animal abuse, but to me all this only made an already lovely room more relaxed and welcoming. I couldn't help thinking of Sally's parents' house and wondering how she was getting on. I should have rung her.

I'd driven her up when Tom was two months old. It had put me in mind of Hyacinth Bucket's house: everything gleaming and immaculate but somehow sterile, and I don't mean in the hygiene sense, although any germs unfortunate enough to get trodden in would probably have committed mass suicide on the spot. You certainly wouldn't have dreamt of putting your feet up on the sofa.

Lucy eventually appeared. Slim, about Sally's height, she had long, dark red hair, almost chestnut, and was dressed in baggy grey trousers and a top that might have been lying on her bedroom floor for a week. As as a former slob who'd only reformed from necessity, I recognized a kindred spirit.

'Lucy, you might have made a bit of an effort,' Margaret tutted. 'It's Christmas Day.'

'So?' She gave me an enquiring but friendly enough smile. 'Has he got it in for you or something?'

'Sorry?'

'Bringing you here. He hardly ever brings anyone, especially not girlfriends. Thinks they'll take one look at his genetic base and get put off.'

'Lucy, do stop it,' Margaret tutted.

John had just come back from topping up glasses. 'About time too,' he said to Lucy. 'I was about to come and haul you out of your pit.'

'No, you weren't. You were hoping I'd stay there

and not embarrass you.' There was a kiss, however, of the reasonably affectionate variety. 'Where's my present, then?' she asked.

'In my wallet,' he said. 'So if you want it, behave yourself.'

Margaret said, 'She's doing Media Studies, you know. In London.'

Angus gave a bristly snort. 'Media studies, women's studies – the academic world's gone mad.'

John said, 'Dad, give it a rest, will you?'

Lucy said, 'I could have done Women's Studies, Pa. In fact I *am* doing a Women's Studies module. I'm using you as a case study of traditional patriarchal attitudes that all stem from a primitive fear and loathing of female sexuality.'

Margaret said, 'Lucy, *please.*'

'You should use Freud,' Beatrice boomed. 'All that rubbish about penis envy – personally I always thought the male organ the most singularly unattractive of God's creations. Looks like the neck thing they give you with the turkey giblets to boil up for gravy.'

'Well, we're not having a turkey,' Margaret said.

'We're having beef,' Angus said briskly. 'Can't beat good Scotch beef. Food of the gods. Turkeys are vastly overrated. Buggers to carve, too – all that piddling about with a bit of breast and and a bit of leg . . .'

Horace, meanwhile, was nosing at my bag; evidently he could smell Widdles's Fishy Favourites.

'It'll be your boots, next,' Lucy said. 'I'm only

surprised he hasn't tried to have it off with them already. The only legs in this house he doesn't fancy are Auntie Flora's, but I suppose even Horace has standards.'

'Lucy!' barked Angus. 'Grow up!'

The entertainment continued over lunch.

The dining room was much the same style as the sitting room: faded 'good' that reminded me of Dorothy's stuff, except that Dorothy's stuff had been badly neglected and this hadn't. The table was an oak gateleg that must have been generations old, with generations of knocks and bashes, but glowing with generations of elbow grease and beeswax. In the centre was a lovely arrangement of greenery I guessed had been garnered from the garden, rather than the local florist's.

After goujons of sole for starters, Angus got stuck into carving a massive joint of sirloin, and Lucy got stuck into wind-ups. She was on my right, John sat more or less opposite me, next to Flora.

'What happened to that Natasha girl?' she asked, in demurely mischievous tones that reminded me of Sally when she got going.

A tiny frown creased his forehead. 'That was months ago.'

Lucy turned to me. 'He brought her to a cousin's wedding. TV presenter or something. Mummy said she was common.'

'Lucy!' Margaret remonstrated. 'I didn't!'

'You did. You thought it, anyway. You said it was irritating, the way she wouldn't say her t's.'

'Well, it was, a bit,' Margaret said defensively.

'What you don't realize, mother, is that you have to talk Estuary on yoof TV,' Lucy said. 'Even if you've been to Cheltenham Ladies' College.'

'Lucy, get your elbows off the table!' Angus rapped, passing some delicately carved beef to Flora.

For a while there was relative peace as we devoured delicious rare beef, parsnip purée, roast potatoes and tiny Brussels sprouts. I was starving, and needed to mop up Baileys and gin, as well as the mellow old red Bordeaux Angus was dishing out. After the beef came a traditional flaming pudding and an orange soufflé.

John abstained from both, which made Margaret's brow crease with maternal concern. 'What's the matter? I thought you loved Christmas pudding!'

'I'm just full,' he soothed.

'You should be relieved he's not stuffing himself,' Lucy said. 'Last time he came you said he was getting a bit of a tummy.'

'Lucy! I didn't!'

'Yes, you did. You said, "I think John's getting a bit of a tummy."'

'Well, maybe I did,' she said defensively. 'But only because there never used to be an ounce on him.'

'Not enough exercise,' Angus barked. 'He ought to take up rugby again. Used to be a damn good scrum half.'

228

'I don't have time to train,' he said, with a trace of exasperation.

Lucy turned to me. 'Where did you meet him, anyway? Not on one of his boys' nights out at Lapdance Heaven, I take it?'

John's brow furrowed sharply. 'Lucy, do you want your present or not?'

'How much is it?' she said sweetly.

'Nothing, the way you're going.'

He said it so tersely, even Lucy looked taken aback.

'She really can be very silly,' Margaret said, as if Lucy were six. 'And it's none of your business anyway,' she added pointedly to Lucy, and changed the subject.

John had taken me aback, though, too. If not quite chilled out à la Jacko, I'd expected him to be mellow, at least. I began to think he must have a morning-after head. He was much quieter than I'd expected, and while there was plenty of eye contact across the table, it seemed disappointingly devoid of undertones. It was more of the *how are you bearing up?* variety.

Inevitably, I suppose, the conversation got round to politics, starting with foxhunting. Angus, perhaps not surprisingly for someone who had to put down mauled lambs, was in favour, Lucy and Beatrice violently opposed. I kept well out of it, as there were enough combatants already, and John did the same.

Having done with foxes, Angus moved on to other

vermin, aka young offenders who trash cars ad lib without ever getting locked up.

'Pa belongs to the hang 'em and flog 'em school of political philosophy,' Lucy said. 'Thinks the country's going to the devil.'

'They say the devil's back on earth,' said Flora. 'I saw a programme about it. That's why we've got all these awful wars and things.'

'We always had awful wars and things,' John soothed. 'Only they weren't all over the six o'clock news every night.'

'They give me nightmares,' she said. 'All those poor little children. And *Crimewatch*. I do like that Nick Ross on *Crimewatch*. He always says not to have nightmares, but I still do.'

She could sound so relatively lucid, you wouldn't suspect a thing.

'Then why do you watch it?' Lucy asked.

'Because I like Nick Ross, dear. I think he's got a nice face. I like that Nick Berry on *Heartbeat*, too.'

'He hasn't been on for ages,' Lucy said.

'He had a nice face, though. Nicks often have nice faces, I always think. Look at Father Christmas. He's Saint Nicholas, isn't he?'

'And the devil's Old Nick,' Angus said briskly. 'So that's your neat little theory gone for a burton. Still, if he was on *Heartbeat* I dare say you'd say he had a nice face, too.'

'Don't be silly, Angus,' Flora said, with dignity. To

John she added, 'I'm knitting squares, you know. I've done nearly a whole blanket to send out to that awful place where all the refugees are.'

'Well done,' he said, and patted her hand. It seemed somehow pathetic on the white cloth, with papery, transparent skin and joints that looked arthritic.

'Thank you, dear.' Across the table she said to me, 'He was a lovely baby, you know. I used to look after him sometimes. I used to sing "Golden slumbers kiss your eyes," and knit him little jumpers with mittens to match. There's a picture somewhere. Blue and white it was, Fair Isle, with a little hat, too. Blue for a boy.'

Under her breath Lucy said, 'Oh, my God . . .'

But Flora hadn't finished with me. 'I'll knit yours a little jumper when it's born. No sense starting till I know what colour to get. When's it due again? You're not showing yet, are you?'

'Flora, dear, that's *Anna*,' said Margaret hastily. 'In Australia, remember? John isn't married.'

'Isn't he? Dear me, I do get so muddled lately . . .'

She looked suddenly so worried, I felt awful for wanting to laugh before. It was as if she'd just realized there was something wrong with her, but couldn't quite work out what it was.

'Never mind.' John slipped an arm around her and gave her a squeeze. 'You can knit me a jumper when you've finished your blanket. And a hat. I might grab a week's skiing in February and I've lost my old one.'

I added a couple of Nice Bloke points here; in fact I thought, 'Aah, how sweet,' and went a bit gooey and sentimental. I found no grounds for adding any other points, though. In fact, the only undertones I sensed were increasing irritation with Lucy and general 'let me out of here' stuff.

Once we'd sat over coffee and fruit, chocolates and more coffee, it was nearly five o'clock. Margaret refused help in the kitchen, saying it was all going in the dishwasher. Beatrice disappeared upstairs, Lucy likewise to ring her boyfriend, and Flora was put in a smaller sitting room to watch *The Sound of Music* on the video. Margaret said *The Sound of Music* was a marvellous babysitter – she didn't know what she'd do without it. Angus said it drove him to the bottle, you could hear the appalling sugar two rooms away, he was going to take Horace for a walk.

John said to me, 'Do you fancy a walk, too?'

I did. Having had seconds of almost everything, not just to be polite, I felt uncomfortably full and disgusting.

In the utility room where John pulled on wellies there must have been scores of assorted scarves, hats and waxed jackets hanging on hooks. As always in rural houses where mud is a fact of life, there were assorted spare wellies, too, but none of them fitted me. They never do, when you take size eights.

The sky had cleared so there was moonlight, which was just as well on the route Angus took.

It led through woods, where carpets of dead leaves at least cushioned the mud. Angus strode briskly, with Horace charging off after foxy smells. My skirt was not cut for brisk striding, however, and since my heeled boots weren't ideal footwear, either, I had a job to keep up.

Whatever John's reason for not bringing Nina, I thought, he was right. She'd want a much more impressive country house, with at least nine bedrooms and a lodge. I couldn't see batty old aunts going down a bomb, either. Not unless they were titled, in which case they could be as batty as they liked. '. . . and his *other* aunt, Lady Flora, was com*plete*ly ga-ga but terribly sweet . . .'

After a few minutes John said, 'There's no need to bust a gut – let the old man charge on if he wants.'

He was walking very close, the sleeve of his jacket almost brushing mine. A little further on he said, 'I have to hand it to you. You bore it all with remarkable aplomb.'

'It was a nightmare,' I retorted. 'I don't know when I've suffered such excruciating discomfort, trying not to crack up.'

He gave a half-hearted little laugh. 'You can be rude if you want. The old man's out of earshot.'

I was about to duck under an overhanging branch, but he held it out of the way, instead. 'I thought he was remarkably restrained,' I said.

'He was. You exerted a civilizing influence.'

'But I do see what you meant about Lucy.'

'You probably made her worse,' he reflected. 'She likes an audience to play to.'

A little wind was blowing up, stirring the leaves on the path. 'It was funny, though.'

'She could do with her backside tanned,' he said drily. 'That'd give her something to bitch about in her Women's Studies module.'

'I thought elder brothers were supposed to be dotingly indulgent,' I said, tongue in cheek. 'You're destroying my tender illusions.'

'I am bloody indulgent. Who d'you think she came to when she'd spent a whole term's allowance in her first three weeks? The old man would have gone ballistic.'

'I should think so. Why didn't she just get an overdraft like—'

My heel had caught in a root; I stumbled badly and would have gone inelegantly flying if he hadn't caught me.

Having done a magnificent save, he just held my arm. 'Are you all right?'

The moonlight was filtering through bare branches, a little cloud scudding across its pale face. 'More or less,' I said unsteadily, thinking I should have done it on purpose. His face was in shadow, but suddenly I was acutely aware of his warmth. From somewhere in the leafy undergrowth came the scream of an animal, or a nocturnal bird. It sounded eerie, almost primeval. 'What was that?' I asked.

'Probably a rabbit getting hard luck from a fox.'

I shivered. Suddenly the whole place felt primeval. There was no artificial light. There was no traffic noise. There was nothing but night, and nature getting on with her bloody business. I knew it was stupid, but I was getting the creeps. I thought of aptly named Grimm fairy tales, evil things lurking in forests, and the pagan spirits that were once supposed to haunt the woods.

At least, part of me was uneasy. The other part knew the main road was only a mile away, where people would be belting along with Britney Spears blasting out, telling their kids to stop squabbling in the back. Part of me wanted to be scared. Part of me wanted to do the pathetic girly bit, admit I was getting the creeps, have him say 'There, there', and put his arm around me.

But he said, 'Come on, it's getting cold.' Letting my arm go, he gave me a brisk pat on the back, instead.

I'd never have done the girly bit anyway, but I didn't quite care for that pat. It had a 'Come on, chop chop', feel to it, as if he were trying to get a sluggish horse moving.

And once I'd started moving, I realized I wasn't exactly 'all right'. My ankle was slightly tender; nothing desperate, but I felt it. However, I certainly wasn't going to say so, now he'd started treating me like a domestic animal. He might think I wanted him to carry me, God forbid.

Once in the mood for mental bitching, I soon found something else to bitch about. Why should it be all right to inflict his lunatic family on me, but not on Nina? Did he think her too delicate to take the strain? And how dare he call me 'bomb-proof', earlier? It was positively insulting. Nina would have told him about her ankle, you could bet, and he'd have scooped her up before you could say 'sucker', feeling all big and strong and macho.

'I thought we'd hit the road in about an hour,' he said. 'After the secondary rituals of cups of tea and presents.'

It would still be only around half past six. 'Won't your mother be upset if you shoot off so early?'

'Probably, but I can't hang around until nine o'clock, stuffing ham and pickled onions.'

I could bet she'd cooked a ham specially, made mince pies and a Christmas cake, and he was just going to disappear. 'That's not very nice. She's probably gone to a lot of trouble.'

'It's too bad. I've eaten far too much already.'

'It's Christmas, for heaven's sake!'

'I know!' His tone changed immediately, however. 'Look, to be honest, I'm a bit knackered.'

'Not to mention hungover.'

'OK, that too.' Saying this abruptly, he resumed a fast walk back.

Misery, I thought crossly, trying to keep up in a tight skirt. He hadn't exactly made much of an effort all afternoon, except with Flora.

We arrived back to the predicted cups of tea and dishing out of presents. To my acute embarrassment, Lucy gave me a beautifully wrapped little gift containing Belgian chocolates. Knowing they'd probably been scurrying around saying, 'For heaven's sake, have we got anything to give her?' I thanked God I'd taken those narcissi. I thanked them as nicely as I could, hoping they didn't realize I knew they'd been scurrying around.

As we took tea things back to the kitchen, John announced that we had to hit the road.

As I'd feared, his mother's face fell. 'I've got some lovely ham! Aren't you staying for supper?'

'Mum, I've eaten far too much already.'

'Yes, but it's Christmas!' Instead of pushing it, however, she covered her disappointment with a bright smile. 'But I dare say Harriet has to get back. I'm sure she's endured quite enough of this clan for one day.'

'It's not, that, really.' I hated her to think we were leaving on my account, as if I'd said to him, 'For God's sake, when can we go?' On an impulse I regretted almost at once, I added, 'John's feeling rather tired.'

'Well, I might have known,' she tutted. 'He works far too hard.'

He shot me an exasperated glance. With a trace of irritation he said, 'No harder than anybody else.'

'No wonder you've been so quiet,' she went on.

At this point, Angus entered the kitchen.

'You'll get run down, working all the time,' Margaret went on to John. 'And there's this horrible fluey thing doing the rounds.'

'We could do with a good dose of flu here,' Angus snorted. 'Best thing for Flora by a long shot. Nature's euthanasia, flu.'

'Angus!'

'For God's sake, Margaret, she's well past her sell-by date.'

'Angus!' To me she said apologetically, 'He doesn't mean it – he's really very fond of her, but he can't bear to see her like this. She'd hate it herself if she knew.'

It was another twenty minutes before we actually left, and even as we drove away I knew John was browned off with me. I knew a browned-off man when I saw one. I could tell from the way he put the car aggressively into gear and reversed more sharply than necessary.

I thought a pre-emptive strike was in order. 'I'm sorry, but I had to say it. She thought it was me, wanting to get away.'

'No, she didn't.'

'She did. She thought I'd had enough.'

He changed up sharply. 'Well, hadn't you?'

238

'I wasn't in any hurry! I certainly didn't want her thinking you were leaving early on my account.'

'She wouldn't have thought that.'

'She would! I'd have felt awful.'

For a couple of miles he uttered not a word, and I felt increasingly cross and upset. If he was shattered, he should have said so. It would have been grossly unfair, letting her infer that *I* wanted to get away. I'd been fed, watered and entertained all day, and what about those chocolates? If he was going to sulk like a baby all the way home, I'd start to wish I'd stayed with Widdles. In fact, I began to be glad he was sulking. It was a perfect reason to go off him, even if I'd needed another.

Nina should be quite enough. What on earth was I doing in a car with a pathetic, sulky bloke who'd ever fancied Nina? Even if he was going off her, fancying her in the first place was enough of a contraindication. Any bloke I fancied should possess the insight and discrimination to see right through her. I was just starting to compile a list of Perfectly Valid Reasons For Going Off John when he slowed down and pulled into the side of the road.

'Won't be a tick,' he said shortly.

Well, there was another reason to add to the list. Why did blokes who'd only just left entirely adequate facilities at home have to stop to pee up against trees? Did their primitive instincts urge them to plant their scent all over the place, like a dog, or did they think a blast of fresh air strengthened their equipment? Or maybe it was merely puerile stuff. Jacko had once told me he loved peeing out of doors, given sufficient space. He'd take aim at some particular target (as in darts) and see if he could score a direct hit.

I'm ashamed to say I glanced over my shoulder, to see whether John was into grass-verge target practice.

He hadn't even got his dart out.

Grabbing tissues from my bag, I almost ran from the car.

'Harriet, get back in the car,' he said tersely.

'You've just been sick!'

Instantly he threw up again, all over the grass verge.

As he stood there, trembling with cold and aftershock, I passed him a tissue. 'Are you all right?' I asked, like an idiot.

'Brilliant.' He wiped his mouth. 'Will you please get back in the bloody car?' He then threw up again, retching painfully, but nothing much came out.

'Shit,' he said shakily.

'At least you missed your shoes.' I passed him another tissue. 'Couldn't you have got this out of the way last night?'

'Harriet, it's nothing to do with last night. I didn't even drink that much.'

'You said you were hungover!'

'No, I didn't. You did.'

240

Light was dawning fast, particularly in relation to quietness and refused Christmas puddings. 'Were you feeling ill all afternoon?'

'I don't know . . . I wasn't feeling great over lunch – I guess I felt a bit rough this morning, but I didn't think it was anything.'

Full of compunction now, I said, 'Do you think you're going to be sick again?'

He shook his head.

As we headed back for the car, I said, 'Are you sure you're all right to drive?'

'When I'm not, I'll tell you.'

Once we were back on the road, more things were making sense. 'Why didn't you tell your mother you were feeling rough, instead of pretending you were just shattered?'

'How could I? First, she'd worry, second, I couldn't face the fussing. I just wanted to get home and hit the sack.'

In the distance I saw the lights of a petrol station. 'If you pull in, I'll nip out and get you a bottle of water. You'll feel better if you rinse your mouth out.'

He pulled in, and I was in and out in thirty seconds.

A hundred yards up the road he stopped again, took the bottle and got out of the car. From the window I watched him rinse two or three times and get shot of the rinsings. More things were suddenly making sense. When he got back in I said, 'Were you feeling cold in the car on the way down?'

'No!' But then he added much less sharply, 'Well, a bit, maybe. I thought the heater was playing up.'

'You've probably got this bug.'

'I never get bugs,' he said, pulling away. 'I never even get colds.'

'Well, you've got something. Do you think you've got a temperature?'

'Christ knows. I feel more cold than anything.' He turned the heating up.

I'd only had a fluey thing once, but I remembered. 'Achey and shivery all over?'

'For crying out loud, Harriet, what is this? If you really want to know, I feel like non-specific shit all over.'

I didn't ask any more *A–Z of Family Health* questions. Firstly it would irritate him to death, secondly I didn't need to. 'Non-specific shit' was a pretty good indicator. Definitely the bug, or one of them. Maybe there was a whole family doing the rounds.

'Whatever it is, I'll sweat it out tomorrow with a game of squash,' he went on.

Might have known he'd react like this. On the other hand, the most unlikely blokes could be appalling babies, wittering about their stomachs or their sinuses, wishing their mummies were there to give them a good rub with Vick and make that special eggy pudding they only ever made when they were sick.

Then you had type B, who'd go to work even if he was dying of plague, and say it was nothing, putrid

242

pustules all over your body never killed anyone, a hot whisky and lemon'd soon sort him out.

Or a game of squash.

Definitely type B.

More than once over the next few miles I saw him shake his head briefly but rapidly, in the way people do when they feel themselves nodding off. 'John, if you're falling asleep, please let me drive.'

'You'll be over the limit. I don't want you losing your licence on my account. And I'm not falling asleep.'

I would be over the limit, if only just. However, a minor argument might keep him awake. 'You were then. I'd rather lose my licence than end up in a body bag when you crash across the central reservation.'

'Harriet, I am not – falling – asleep! All right?'

Not now, he wasn't.

He put the news on, which probably helped keep him alert, too. Since he was obviously feeling too rough to talk, though, I kept quiet.

My Going-Off-John list was looking a bit sick now. Nearly as sick as him. The only remaining contraindication was Nina, though she was more than enough. I wondered when she was coming back. I had a vague feeling she'd left around the twenty-third, which meant probably not until just before New Year. He'd be over it by then, and just as well. I couldn't see her charging over with hot-water bottles and Lem-Sip.

Now and then I glanced across at him. His face looked whitish-grey, but so did mine, probably, in that light.

It seemed a quicker journey than on the way down. As he finally turned into Dorothy's road I said, 'How are you feeling?'

'Pretty bloody rough,' he said wearily, pulling into the kerb.

I was amazed that he'd admitted it. If a hard-core type B said he was feeling pretty bloody rough, he must be feeling really ill. 'Have you got any paracetamol at home?'

'Probably not.'

'I should have. There might even be some of Sally's industrial-strength flu stuff. Do you want to come in for a minute while I find them?'

I'd expected a short 'No, I'll be fine,' as hard-core type Bs usually scorn such things, thinking them fit only for wimps. In fact I saw him hesitate, but then he said, 'I guess they're worth a try.'

I'd left the heating on high for Widdles, so at least the kitchen felt moderately warm. I said, 'Take a seat, then, while I find them,' and he sat heavily on the sofa, where Widdles was curled up, as he probably had been all day. He raised his head in an affronted fashion, to see who was invading his throne.

If I were a more organized type of person I'd have known at once where to put my hand on a packet of Panadol: in a particular pocket of my bag, for example, or the front left-hand corner of my bedside drawer, or the top shelf of the bathroom cupboard. As it was I spent half a minute rummaging through sideboard drawers, where every type of junk lurked but what I wanted. Saying, 'Won't be a tick,' I charged upstairs, where I rummaged more, but I eventually found a packet gathering dust on an ancient chest of drawers in Jacko's room. There were actually six left, too.

I charged down again, about to say, 'Here you go,' but it died in my throat.

Slumped against the back of the sofa, he was asleep. As least, he looked as if he was. 'John?' I said quietly.

No reply.

He looked awful. His face was pale, a sheen of sweat on his brow. I put a hand to his forehead; it felt cold and clammy. Gently I slipped a hand inside his jacket. His shirt felt damp and chill.

I thought for a moment of bringing a duvet down, just covering him and leaving him there, but instead I shook him gently. 'John . . .'

He opened his eyes.

'I don't think you should go home on your own – you're really not well.'

Still half asleep, looking grey and groggy, he made an effort to collect himself. 'I'm fine. Really.'

'You're not fine at all – why don't you stay the night?'

'Christ, Harriet, I'm not quite dead on my feet yet . . .'

As he started to get up, I had a Cunning Thought. 'All right, but why don't you just take some Panadol and go to bed for a while? At least you might feel a bit better when you wake up.'

He hesitated, but I knew the magic word 'bed' had done it. 'I wouldn't mind,' he confessed.

'I'll wake you up in a couple of hours.' I took him to my room, as it was reasonably tidy and the sheets were more or less clean. It was chilly, though, so the first thing I did was light the archaic but extraordinarily efficient gas fire. From the way he was already taking his shoes off, I knew he was longing with desperation for bed. I fetched him a glass of water and gave him two Panadol.

'Thanks,' he said, knocking them back.

'There's a spare toothbrush somewhere – would you like one? Your mouth must be feeling horrible.'

'That'd be great, thank you.'

I unearthed one of those airline freebies from a drawer and handed it to him. There was an old-fashioned washbasin in the bedroom but he might need something more. 'The bathroom's just across the landing.'

'Thanks.' He was taking his jacket off; I didn't wait to see him do ditto with his trousers.

Widdles was still on the kitchen sofa when I went down, but he deigned to come and greet me, rubbing up against my legs with an, 'Anything to eat?' mew. Widdles had a whole repertoire of mews: there was the Open Sesame mew, the 'Hi, I'm back' mew, and the 'Hurry up, woman, I'm starving' mew.

Since he'd eaten the Succulent White Fish and Prawns at last, I gave him some Duck'n'Rabbit in Delicious Gravy, and wondered about making hot honey and lemon for John. Since there actually were both lemons and honey I did so, adding some cold water to cool it down.

I went up again and tapped on the door.

Since there was no reply, I pushed it open. Already the gas fire had taken the chill off the room. The fireclay glowed hot and cheerful.

I tiptoed over to the bed. He was tucked almost completely under my green checked duvet cover; I could barely see his face. His jacket, trousers and shirt were slung over a chair. The shirt was still damp and chill, so I hung it over my cheval mirror, near the fire.

Having followed me up, thinking it was bedtime already, Widdles wandered in. I glanced at my watch. It was still only twenty past eight. This meant waking him at say, half past ten. I turned the fire right down and tiptoed out.

'Only I'm not going to wake him,' I whispered to Widdles, shutting the door behind us. 'What's the point? Just so he can get dressed again, drive home and get into another bed? He said he needed to catch up on some sleep, anyway.'

Funnily enough, prissy big sister was back in my head as I went downstairs. 'You can't fool me. You just want to keep him here. Play Florence Nightingale and wipe his sweaty, fevered brow.'

'So? He's sick!'

'Yes, but you'd never feel like wiping sweaty fevered blokes if you didn't fancy them rotten.'

'I looked after Jacko, didn't I?'

'He wasn't sweaty and fevered and Sally did most of it anyway – you were at work. I bet you're hoping John'll be so sweaty and fevered and weak tomorrow you'll have to give him a cooling sponge down.'

Honestly. As if any such thing would ever have entered my head.

# NINE

Before I was two minutes older, bursting to tell her, I phoned Sally. But I had to wait while she went to the upstairs phone, because the other was in the sitting room and the Horrible Harcourts from next door but one were round for sherry and nibbles.

During the telling she went from sheer *What*? to old-Sally mischief. 'Looks like Father Christmas brought your Helicopter after all,' she giggled.

'Yes, but he's still got strings attached.'

'Maybe you should come clean. About Nina, I mean.'

'How can I? I'd have to tell him I was hiding from her like some pathetic invertebrate.'

'And how she made you feel like a bog-roll dinosaur.'

'Exactly. And then he'll think I need a shrink, which I probably do.'

'He might just tell you he's got shot of her already.'

'No chance. I'm sure I'd have heard. I'm hoping he's just putting it off. Too nice to dump her.'

'Yes, and it could be the old CBA syndrome.'

This meant 'can't-be-arsed'. It also meant Sally was back in cynical mode.

'When it comes to the point, CBA kicks in,' she went

on. 'They think, oh, well, she's not a bad shag, I really can't be arsed with all the aggro.'

This was cheering me up no end.

'Keep me posted, anyway,' she went on. 'I shall expect detailed daily bulletins – I need something to perk me up.'

'How's it going?' I asked.

'Better than I thought. Tom's not whinged much, and Mum's doing her damnedest not to say, "If you pick him up every time he cries . . ."' She paused, but when she spoke again I heard a telltale wobble in her voice. 'I've been feeling really bad, actually. They've decorated the little spare room like a nursery – bought a lovely new cot and everything. Apparently they did it weeks ago, assuming I'd be bringing him home. And you'll never believe what wallpaper they used.'

'Not Thomas the Tank Engine?'

'Hole in one. So between them and Jacko, I've been feeling like mountains of really smelly nappies.'

'You can talk – how do you think I felt when I saw that scarf? When did you do it? Half the night, every night?'

'Well, sometimes. I was doing quite a bit during the day, but Jacko said at the rate I messed up, Tom's first words would be "Oh, big fat hairy *bollocks*."'

At least it looked as if fences were being mended. After hanging up I poured myself a Baileys, put the fan heater on, and kept the Christmas tree company, watching half a corny old film.

At five past eleven I went up to check the patient. I tiptoed in and across to the bed, where the covers were all over the place. He lay on his back, the duvet pushed halfway down his chest, which I will fully admit to inspecting. Nice. Firm and well-muscled, with just enough fuzz to indicate abundant male hormones without making him a gorilla. He shifted restlessly as I replaced the duvet, but I didn't try to wake him. I turned the fire off; the room was very hot.

I woke at ten past seven, in Sally's bed. Sally's room was next to mine, and except for Widdles snoring under the duvet, it was horribly quiet. I lay for a minute or two wondering whether I should go and check in case he'd actually died of some rampant, flesh-eating plague. However, eventually I heard giveaway creaks.

Dragging on a dressing gown over a Snoopy nightshirt I'd had for ten years, I went and tapped on his door. 'John?'

'Harriet?'

I went in. Clad only in a pair of white boxers, he was sitting on the side of the bed with the bemused look of a man who's woken up in someone else's bed and can't quite remember how it came about. 'Weren't you supposed to wake me?'

'I tried,' I lied, belting the dressing gown, which was actually a shortish thing in subdued tartan, belonging to Jacko. 'You were out for the count. How are you feeling?'

'I don't know . . . All right, I guess.' Evidently still

half asleep, he looked around. His hair was damp and dishevelled, his face flushed. 'Where are my clothes?'

I indicated the chair and the cheval mirror. 'You don't look very all right to me. Get back into bed for a bit – I'll put the fire on.' Apart from the fact that it had only just come on, Dorothy's central heating was what they called 'background' and my bedroom window functioned like another of those Edwardian air conditioners.

'Where did you sleep?' he asked, as if it had just hit him.

'In Sally's bed.'

'Well, I'm sorry to have deprived you of your own, but you should have woken me. Given me a good whack on the head or something.' With the duvet turned back, his left hand was resting on the bottom sheet, and suddenly he lifted it. 'Christ, it's damp. I've been sweating in your sheets all night. Sorry.'

'They weren't exactly pristine anyway,' I said, but I might as well not have bothered.

Briskly, he stood up. 'Look, it's high time I was out of here.' He went to the chair, started pulling on his trousers. Yes, I was checking out his other bits, which all matched his chest. It would have been a horrible let-down if his legs had turned out skinny and white, or even hairless. You can never tell.

'God knows what I was thinking of,' he went on, in a mutter.

'You were sick! You looked awful!'

252

'Yes, and I still feel bloody awful, and I'm going to pass it on to you.'

'If you're going to pass it, you'll have done it already. I never catch things, anyway.'

'Neither do I,' he said shortly, zipping his trousers. 'This thing's picked the wrong host.' He reached for his shirt. 'I'll sweat it out on the squash court. That'll teach the little bastard to choose its living quarters with a bit more . . .'

Not only did his voice suddenly seem to die on him, he actually swayed, only a fraction, but enough to make him reach for the mantelpiece to steady himself.

I was there in an instant, holding his arm. 'For God's sake, go back to bed!'

'I'm fine!' As if to prove it he let go of the mantelpiece, but anyone could see he was unsteady. He looked shocked, as if he couldn't believe it had happened.

'You're not fine at all! You nearly fell over!'

Even for a type B, he was impressive. 'For crying out loud, Harriet, stop fussing. I just need something to eat. A piece of toast or something.'

From experience, I knew type Bs needed careful handling. 'All right, if you'll get back in bed to eat it.'

Already buttoning his shirt, he stopped. With an exasperated expression he held his hands up, in that warding-off-evil fashion. 'I'll be fine, OK? Run along and stick a piece of toast on, like a good girl.'

I knew he was saying it on purpose to infuriate and

253

therefore get rid of me, but that didn't stop me. 'Get it yourself!'

I banged out and flounced downstairs, where Widdles instantly started yowling at the cupboards. 'Oh, shut up,' I said irritably. 'Bloody males – you're all the same.'

However, I gave him some more duck'n'rabbit, put some coffee on and grabbed a mango-flavoured yoghurt from the fridge. Five minutes after finishing it, it occurred to me that John should have been down by now. How long did it take to put shoes and socks on, for heaven's sake? God, what if he'd fallen, after all? What if he'd bashed his head on the corner of a chest of drawers and fractured his skull?

I ran upstairs two at a time.

My room had once been Dorothy's and there was still an old armchair near the fire. With his socks on but no shoes, he was sitting back in it, his eyes closed.

They soon opened, however.

'Get weaving, John, chop chop,' I said, with more than a trace of acid. 'You're supposed to be off to the squash court to sweat that little bastard out. Only pathetic people get sick, don't they? If they were bloody-minded enough, like you, and didn't give *in* to it, the entire NHS would be out of a job.'

He produced a smile so faint, it wouldn't even have made a self-respecting ghost. 'You can talk about bloody-minded. The other night, for a start, when I paid the bill.'

'That was stroppy,' I said. 'And by no means my best

performance, I can tell you.' Taking matches from the mantelpiece I lit the fire. 'To save arguments, can we agree now that you're hardly fit to get down the stairs, let alone drive home?'

'OK, I'll go back to bed for a bit. Sweat some more in your sheets.'

'Not yet, you won't. I'll change them first.'

That was entirely the wrong thing to say; it galvanized him. 'Harriet, if you're going to start changing sheets on my account, I'm out of here now.'

'You can't. I've hidden your car keys.' They were actually exactly where he'd left them, on the kitchen table.

He sat back, half closing his eyes. 'Great,' he said weakly. 'Imprisoned, now. Held captive by a stroppy, fearsome woman in a man's dressing gown.' He opened his eyes again. 'You haven't got cellars, have you? Fitted out with implements of torture?'

There *were* cellars, full of the junk of ages. 'Yes, but only for my paying customers,' I said sweetly.

With another sick-ghost smile he started to rise from the chair.

'Stay put, will you? Until I've changed those sheets.'

'Harriet, I'm going for a pee. Feel free to come and watch,' he added, with wraith-like sarcasm. 'Make sure I don't make a run for it through the window.'

He'd have a job. He moved gingerly, as if every joint, muscle and cubic centimetre of brain were aching. I was beginning to revise my type B diagnosis. I suspected type C instead: the man who had never been ill before in his entire life, had thought people were grossly exaggerating when they said they felt like death, and couldn't believe it was happening to him.

I stripped off sheets, listening for sounds of skulls crashing onto lavatory pans, but all I heard was a flush. While he was gone, however, I thought maybe I *had* gone a bit OTT. Also I was uncomfortably aware that I was not acting from purely saintly motives.

When he came back, still as gingerly as a fresh green root, I said, 'Look, if you're really desperate to get home, I'll drive you. I can always get a taxi back.'

'*Now* she says it.' He flopped down into that chair by the fire.

'Well?' I straightened up, my arms full of sheets.

He shook his head. 'I don't think I've even got the energy for being chauffeured across London.'

'Where *do* you live, anyway?'

'Half a mile the other side of Tower Bridge.'

'What, on the river?'

'Yes.'

Very nice too, I thought, but something else was occurring to me. 'Would you have stayed at your folks' last night, if not for me?'

His hesitation was answer enough.

'You would, wouldn't you? Only you had to get me home.'

'All right,' he said, almost irritably. 'I might, just.'

I felt so bad, I had to go the other way. 'You should

have left me here with Widdles,' I said crossly, picking up a stray pillowcase. 'Instead of which you practically force me to be an extra on a black comedy film set, and then force me to take in sweaty, infectious bodies. I've got a good mind to charge you for the laundry.'

But he made no reply. When I looked up, his eyes were closed again. I went over, put a hand to his forehead. I'd expected him to push me away, but he didn't. He wasn't cold and clammy any more, either. You could have fried a burger on his forehead.

'You're burning up!' Dropping the sheets, I grabbed another couple of Panadol and thrust them at him with a glass of water. 'Get these down, now.'

He didn't argue.

I remade the bed at top speed before ransacking Jacko's room for one of those pairs of pyjamas his mother had bought him for hospital. He'd left them behind, saying I could take them to the charity shop. One was still in its wrapping; probably a size too small, but better than nothing.

When I gave them to him he actually winced. 'I haven't worn pyjamas since I was at school.'

'I don't care. They're warm and they'll mop up any more sweat. Put them on and get back into bed.'

'Are you always this bossy?' he asked faintly.

'This is nothing, I can tell you.'

As I made for the door, that dead-on-its-feet sarcasm followed me. 'Well, hallelujah. I thought you were going to stay and boss me into my nice warm jamas.'

'I think you're just about capable,' I retorted. 'I'll go and get you some nice warm fluids.'

I went downstairs, thinking that if he'd been a common-or-garden bloke in such a dire state, or a mere friend, I might have stayed and helped. Offered to help, anyway, and probably been told shortly that he wasn't quite dead yet, thanks very much.

Or maybe not. Even when half dead your average bloke enjoyed getting his kit off with a female audience. Better still, having his kit *got* off by a female, as long as it wasn't his mother.

But I wasn't going to put him to the test.

Since there was nothing much else to offer in the warm fluid department, I made some more hot honey and lemon and took it up with a jug of water on a tray.

He was back in bed, nearly asleep again.

Call me daft, but suddenly I really felt like doing the Florence Nightingale bit. Despite the unshaven chin and generally grotty appearance (or perhaps because of them) he looked oddly vulnerable. 'I've brought you some honey and lemon,' I said. 'You ought to get some fluids down.'

He struggled to a half sitting position. 'If you say so, nurse.'

I sat on the end of the bed while he drank it. 'I hadn't hidden your car keys,' I confessed.

'I thought not. But I was glad you said you had. Saved me the effort of arguing any further.'

I couldn't believe he'd admitted it.

'Do you still want that toast?' I asked. 'Or anything else to eat?'

He shook his head and winced, as if the movement had set off internal throbbing.

'You've never had anything like this before, have you?' I asked.

Much more gingerly, he shook his head again. 'Even my eyes are aching. I used to think people who said they had flu were lazy malingering bastards. Most of them, anyway.'

'Well, some are,' I had to concede. 'Some people have only got to sneeze and they're convinced they're dying.'

He finished the honey and lemon. 'I'm sure you've got better things to do than play nurse.'

Funnily enough, I couldn't think of anything. 'Masses. But I still owe you at least fifteen quid, remember? Never mind that suit.'

'I'd forgotten that. But now you've brought it up, there's one little thing you could do for me.'

'Yes?'

'I feel sweaty and gross,' he said. 'You couldn't manage a bed-bath, could you? I think I'd sleep better.'

Heaven help me. 'Well, erm, I've never given any-one an actual *bed*-bath before . . .'

Too late, I realized I'd been had. Even in that state, an ember of his spark was glinting.

'I was kidding.' He actually started laughing, which turned rapidly to a racking cough, as if he were on forty fags a day.

'That sounds positively terminal to me,' I said tartly. 'Don't expect the kiss of life, will you?'

He quickly got it under control, however. 'No, Nurse Fearsome. But would you do me a little favour on your way out?'

'What?'

'Pass me my mobile – it's in my jacket pocket. I need to check my messages and make a couple of calls.'

After a shower, I decided to roast the turkey before it went off. After ramming ready-made stuffing up its backside with rather more force than necessary, I found from the 'poultry' section of the *Clueless Cooks' Book* that I should be stuffing the other end, 'pulling the flap of skin firmly over to tuck underneath'. After which I should, 'truss neatly with a trussing needle and string.'

'Fuck it,' I said to Widdles, who was sitting on the table, watching the operation with interest. Was this a genetically modified sparrow, or what? He tried batting a wing to see if it flapped.

'What normal person has trussing needles lying about?' I demanded. 'Mind you, if John's phoning the Witch of Aspen, I'd like to bloody well truss him up. "*How are you, my little sweet?*" I'd like to stuff something up his backside, I can tell you. A six-inch suppository might wipe that grin off his face. And if she's phoning *him*, in my bed, I'll have to fumigate it.'

I shoved the untrussed turkey in the oven, poured myself a large glass of wine, and phoned Sally.

'He can't be that sick if he's making cracks about bed-baths,' she said.

'He is. He just couldn't resist winding me up.'

'Typical bloke,' she said scathingly. 'I'm beginning to revise my opinion. It's almost Jacko stuff.'

'He never asked you to give him a bed-bath, did he?'

'He wouldn't have dared – I'd have thumped him.'

More than likely.

'So how long d'you think you'll be playing nurse?' she went on.

'I can't imagine him staying beyond tomorrow morning. You weren't thinking of coming back just yet, were you? I'd hate to think of him passing it on to Tom.'

'I said I'd stay until just before New Year, so let's hope the sweetness and light lasts that long. I think Mum's beginning to crack. This morning she said, "I hope you're going to give him *proper* food, not just those lazy-mother jars."'

'What did you say?'

'Nothing. Don't know how long I can keep that up, though.'

\* \* \*

I checked John an hour later, but he was out for the count. Then I checked the turkey, which was wafting Christmassy pongs through the house. I wondered about putting some potatoes in, too; the smell was making me positively ravenous. Maybe even John would fancy some after sleeping half the day – he'd had nothing since his mother's mince pies yesterday afternoon.

The doorbell rang while I was in the middle of peeling muddy potatoes. On opening the door in my rubber gloves I was hit by a) a temperature that had plummeted since yesterday, and b) Helen on the step.

'I thought you were in Saffron Walden!' I gaped.

'I was, but I came to pick up a few of my things while Lawrence is out of the way. Are you busy?' she added, eyeing the potato peeler still in my hand.

'Not exactly. I'm cooking the turkey for me and Widdles.'

Her eyes widened. 'Where are the others?'

'Come in and I'll tell you.'

Over coffee for her and a glass of wine for me at the kitchen table I gave her the gist of Harriet's Revised Christmas. Having kept quiet about John before I didn't like to come out with it now, so I just told her I'd gone home with a friend who'd felt rough on the way back and was sleeping it off upstairs.

She accepted it without a murmur, making me think her mind was half elsewhere. She looked strained, as if she'd had several sleepless nights on the trot. I nearly said, 'Not having second thoughts, are you?' but swallowed it in case she said 'Yes', and burst into tears. I didn't think I could handle it. 'How's Olly?' I asked, instead.

She gave a little sigh. 'Worried about *me*, bless him. Still, he's having a good time with Laura's boy – they were out partying on Christmas Eve and last night. He asked me to pick up a few of his things, too; CDs and winter clothes he hadn't taken.'

'Have you been in already?' I asked.

She nodded. 'It was weird, seeing her stuff hanging in the wardrobe. She'd cleared what was left of mine into the spare room. Or Lawrence had. Probably it was Lawrence.'

She spoke almost mechanically, but I was convinced it was a cover. I felt sure she was on the point of bursting into tears after all, saying she'd made a terrible mistake. 'Have you spoken to Lawrence again?'

She nodded. 'Just briefly. He's going to try to get the twins into boarding school for next September. He wanted them to go anyway, but we didn't apply before. We rowed about it. He said it would do them good. He said I spoilt them.'

She was still speaking in a curiously detached way. 'And I suppose I did. I suppose he was right. They won't care, anyway, as long as they're together.'

'Have you spoken to them over Christmas?' I asked.

'Not for long. Lawrence had bought them the latest

PlayStation; they couldn't drag themselves away from that for long. They couldn't be bothered to talk to Olly for more than ten seconds, either. He still hasn't spoken to Lawrence. He won't. Lawrence thinks it's me, poisoning Olly against him.'

I just didn't know what to say, but the silence was filled by a jolly London Live weatherman telling us to expect overnight frosts, so make sure you've got your windscreen de-icer, folks.

'He wanted Olly to go to boarding school, too, but I fought him,' she went on. 'Olly hated the thought of going away. I suppose I spoilt him, too, but it was only because I loved him. Spoiling didn't *spoil* Olly, if you know what I mean. He never treated me with that sort of dismissive indifference, like the twins. Not that they could help it. They copied it from Lawrence.'

She produced a wan little smile. 'So you needn't worry that I'm agonizing over having done the wrong thing. I'm not. Not about that, anyway.'

I picked this up at once. 'What do you mean?'

An odd look crossed her face, like a kid who's been up to no good and is about to get found out. At the same time, there was a hint of *but I don't care.* 'I've done something incredibly stupid,' she said. 'I still can't believe I did it.'

'You haven't trashed Lawrence's suits?'

She shook her head. 'Worse.'

'Not *Francesca's* suits?'

She shook her head again. 'I think I'm pregnant.'

'What?' I gaped. 'But I thought you and Lawrence –'

'It wasn't Lawrence.'

*'What?'*

'I knew you'd look like that,' she said, with a despairing sigh. 'As if you thought I didn't have it in me.'

I was too shell-shocked to utter a syllable.

'Lawrence would never think I'd have it in me, either,' she went on. 'I suppose *I* didn't think I had it in me, come to that.'

I found my voice. 'Who was it?'

'A man on a train.'

*'What?'*

She looked almost offended. 'We didn't *do* it on the train! We did it later. In a hotel room.'

I think I'd have been less shocked if she'd told me she'd joined some New Age travellers. I mean, you just didn't associate Helen with shenanigans. 'What hotel room? What *train*, for God's sake?'

'The Eurostar, to Brussels.'

'When?' I gaped.

'That weekend Lawrence took the boys to Euro-Disney.'

'You said you were going to your sister's!'

'I was. But I was so low and miserable, I suddenly thought, why shouldn't I have a break, too? I picked Brussels but it could have been anywhere – I just didn't care.'

God help us. At this rate Widdles would be telling

me he'd like a tossed green salad for dinner. I topped up my glass. 'Go on.'

'And there he was.' Cradling the coffee mug in her hands, she went on, 'Just across the aisle. He was working, but after a while he asked if he could borrow my *Telegraph*. At first I just thought he wanted to read the paper – but after a few minutes I realized it was an excuse to talk to me. *Me!* The boring wife and mother who's only good for picking up socks and chauffeuring!'

I could have shaken her. 'Helen, *why* do you say things like that?'

'Because it's how Lawrence sees me! It's how the twins see me! I'm invisible!'

It was no use arguing. It was probably true.

'And there he was, talking to me as if I were a *person*,' she went on. 'We talked all the way there. And gradually it dawned on me that he was attracted to me. Nobody's looked at me like that in ages. But I could see him looking at my wedding ring, so I told him I was separated.'

'Well, you were.'

'Yes, but I said *legally* separated. And I told him masses more lies. I didn't want him thinking I was just a housewifey bore, washing football kit and going to Sainsbury's. I told him I only had Olly. I told him I was running a catering business of my own. I even gave it a name: Cooking to Go. I said it right off the top of my head, but he believed me. I said I was taking a break in Brussels because I'd been working so hard, and he believed that, too. He said he had a meeting in the afternoon, he was going back that night, but why didn't I meet him for dinner?'

Who needed the *EastEnders Christmas Special* when you had this? 'And one thing led to another?'

She nodded. 'I suppose I'd had a lot to drink, but I still knew what I was doing. I *wanted* to do it.'

Well, I knew the feeling.

'I didn't even have to ask him up to my room,' she went on. 'He knew. I think we both knew even before the coffee arrived that it was going to happen.'

What could you say? 'Was it lovely?'

She gave a reminiscent little sigh. 'I swear, if I'd ever realized it could be like that, I'd have done it before.'

Except for the consequences, I swear I was getting jealous. 'And then he buggered off and got the train back?'

'No, he stayed the night. He left first thing in the morning. He asked for my phone number.'

Something in her tone told me we were getting to the cold-light-of-day bit. 'But he hasn't rung?'

'I don't know. I gave him the wrong number.'

I gaped at her. 'Why?'

'I don't know!' Sighing, she ran a despairing hand through her hair. 'Well, I do. When we woke in the morning he'd overslept – he had to rush for the train – and suddenly I wondered what the hell I'd done. My knickers were lying on the floor – I couldn't believe I'd done it. He was frantically shaving and getting dressed – he only asked for my number just before he left, and I thought of one of the boys answering the phone – they use mine so often – and I panicked. I just gave him the first number I could think of.'

Honestly, shaking was too good for her.

'But he gave me his number, too,' she said.

Now she told me. 'So have you phoned him?'

'How can I? I'd told him all those lies, and now this . . . I told him it was safe! I thought it *was* safe!'

She gave another despairing sigh. 'I can't believe I was so stupid. I stopped taking precautions months ago but it took me ages to get the twins – we were trying for nearly two years! They said it might be secondary infertility. I never, ever thought I'd get pregnant. It sounds so stupid saying it now, like those girls who think you can't get pregnant if you do it standing up.'

I suppose I gave a gallows-type little laugh.

She gave a wan smile. 'Maybe it's the "the last fling of the ovary". It's supposed to hit you in your late thirties. Kids itself you're eighteen again for a couple of years, before it starts going downhill.'

'Maybe it's a case of intense orgasm triggering spontaneous ovulation. I'm sure I've read about that somewhere.'

'That wouldn't surprise me. It felt like something exploding.'

Having wandered over from his day-throne on the sofa, Widdles jumped onto her lap.

'He doesn't get any thinner,' she said, stroking him.

Never mind Widdles; we were talking *Brief Encounter* here. 'You weren't kidding, then, when you told Jacko you'd have a fling with the first man who asked you. You'd already flung.'

She looked up. 'I still can't believe I did it. If anyone had asked me, three months ago, whether I'd ever go off and have sex with a man I'd just met on a train . . . But I don't regret it,' she added, with a touch of defiance. 'At least I found out what I've been missing. It was the always the same old thing with Lawrence: *me, me, me* . . . I suppose I thought that was just how men *were*. I'd never had sex with anyone else before I met him. Mind you, it was slightly better then. He used to make some kind of effort.'

I fully admit it was not a noble reaction, but I couldn't wait to tell Sally. Sensing that more was coming, I kept quiet. Obviously it was offload-the-baggage time; I was beginning to feel like a paid-up counsellor.

'When I think how besotted I was . . .' she went on. 'I even liked ironing his shirts, for heaven's sake. Which is why he married me, I suppose. I did wonders for his ego, not that it needed much boosting. That's why he couldn't handle it when Olly came along and I had someone else to adore.'

By now the turkey was spitting so merrily in the oven, there was smoke seeping out of the door. It was just tough, though. Counsellors don't say, 'Can you hang on a tick while I turn the oven down?'

'Not that he ever actually did anything, but I knew he was jealous,' she went on. 'It wasn't till the twins that I realized how Olly had missed out. He was entirely different with them. He *enjoyed* them and they adored him. Mind you, I think he had someone else adoring him by then. I swear he was having an affair around the time they were born. I never actually found out, but I sensed it. I was far too enormous to have sex with, after all. Like the dome of St Paul's.'

Suddenly she looked over her shoulder. 'Maybe you should turn the oven down – it's spitting fat like mad. You should put some foil over that turkey.'

I suppose the cook bit becomes automatic after so long. Even when you're talking wild flings, part of your brain's on domestic autopilot. 'I forgot to buy any,' I said, but turned the oven down anyway.

'Weren't you doing some potatoes when I arrived?' she asked. 'Look, if you've got masses to do . . .'

'I haven't! I'm only cooking it so it won't go off.'

'If you're thinking of your friend upstairs, I'd do some mashed potatoes,' she said. 'Mashed are more palatable when you're not well. Mash them with butter and hot milk.'

'Helen, will you stop talking about bloody potatoes? How can I be thinking about mashed potatoes when you've just told me you think you're pregnant? Haven't you done a test?'

270

'I don't need to. I'm late, and I'm hardly ever late.' She paused. 'But I don't want to. If I do a test I'll know for certain.'

I must have been utterly thick, but it was only then that I realized how her mind was working. I stared at her. 'You want this baby, don't you?'

She didn't even have to nod.

She left half an hour later, leaving me to reflect again on the monumental power of hormones. Or maybe it was more basic; she just wanted someone to love her, to have her as the centre of their universe, as even the twins must have done when they were little. Tom had probably played a part, too. She'd said, when he was a few weeks old, 'They're so lovely when they're tiny – it's almost enough to make me broody again.' I could still see her face: nostalgic, almost wistful.

She didn't care about Lawrence going all outraged and hypocritically pompous when he found out, or even using it as an excuse for cutting down whatever money he'd be obliged to shell out. But she couldn't face telling the boys she was having a baby by some man she'd met on a train. Most especially she couldn't face telling Olly.

After seeing her off I returned to the kitchen and poured myself another glass of wine. 'At least I can't say I've had a boring Christmas,' I told Widdles. 'All I need now is to find John dying of some *X Files* plague, with parasitic aliens eating their way out of his guts.'

When I checked him five minutes later, he was out of bed. 'What on earth are you doing?' I gaped.

'I need some fresh air.' Minus his pyjama top, he was trying to get the sash window open. This was not easy at the best of times, on account of forty-three layers of paint and an antiquated mechanism.

Suddenly giving in, it shot right up and a blast of freezing air rushed in.

Charging over, I yanked it down again. I was hardly a hyper-cautious type but I had a feeling that sudden sub-zero blasts on naked, feverish torsos would not do much good. 'You'll catch your death!'

'I'm suffocating! It's like an oven in here!' He shoved the window up again and another Siberian blast tore in.

'OK, *OK*!' It *had* felt like an oven as I'd come in; even on low, that fire was unbelievably efficient. 'I'll turn the fire off, all right?'

'I've already turned it off.'

Only just: the clay was still glowing. I pulled the window down again, leaving a few inches open at the bottom. 'Then go back to bed, for heaven's sake, before you get pneumonia.'

'I'm not going back to bed!'

For a moment I thought he was about to say he was off home, but he went on in more moderate tones, 'I need a shower first. I feel disgusting.'

I could tell without touching him that he was still feverish. He looked hot and dry as Sahara sand. His pillow-rubbed hair might have graced a hedgehog at the adolescent punk stage and his stubble was increasingly impressive. 'You look pretty disgusting, too,' I agreed, reasoning that this would go down better than old-woman fussing. 'But I'd better warn you that our shower's as Jurassic as the rest of the plumbing.'

'I don't care. I feel like something festering on a tip.'

I drew the curtains back across the window. 'Have a bath, then.'

When I turned around he was sitting on the end of the bed, as if the effort of yanking windows and arguing had suddenly exhausted him.

'But have something to eat first,' I went on. 'You've had nothing since yesterday afternoon, and you threw up what you did have. If you're feeling weak, it's no wonder.'

He made an exasperated, up-to-here noise that almost made me want to slap him.

'Is this some stupid macho thing or what?' I demanded. '*Every*body feels weak when they've got some vicious bug and they haven't eaten for nearly twenty-four hours! It's not weak to admit it!'

'Do you have to shout?' he winced. 'Your bedside manner leaves a good deal to be desired.'

'Don't push your luck.' Fully expecting him to jerk irritably away, I put a hand to his forehead. He didn't jerk away, however, and it was just as Sahara-ish as I'd thought. I pressed another couple of Panadol out of their bubbles. 'Here, get these down and I'll make you something to eat. What do you fancy?'

'Eggs Benedict. With a side order of Caesar salad and some freshly squeezed guava juice. You did ask,' he added, seeing my face. 'Cornflakes'll do.'

I'd have liked to see this piss-take as a sign that he was on the mend, but had a feeling it was just in character. 'I haven't got any cornflakes. There's some of Sally's economy muesli.'

He shook his head. 'I could force some scrambled eggs down, if it's not too much like hard work.'

At least it wasn't Mummy's special eggy pudding for the not-vewy-well lickle soldier. 'I could just about manage that.'

'But I need that bath first.' He ran a hand over his chin. 'And a shave, if I can borrow a razor.'

'You can borrow mine. I'll find you a towel.'

Trying to walk in a relatively robust fashion and not quite succeeding, he went to the door. I could hear the bath already running as I unearthed a clean king-size towel from the airing cupboard, and grabbed Jacko's dressing gown from Sally's room.

I tapped on the bathroom door and when he opened it a cloud of steam hit me. 'There are some razor blades in the cupboard,' I said, handing over the towel. 'You'll probably need a new one.'

'More than likely. I never used a woman's razor yet that could actually cut anything first time.'

Naturally this made me wonder how many dozens

of impromptu sleepovers he'd enjoyed, and stirred a green pang in my stomach. 'There's some of Jacko's shower gel, too,' I said, with a trace of tartness. 'That stuff that's guaranteed to make all men irresistible.'

'That'd be wasted on me just now. I wouldn't have the energy to test it.'

Suddenly I had misgivings. 'Don't fill it too full, all right? And not too hot either – I don't want you passing out and drowning on me.'

'Look, if you want to stay and supervise the operation, feel free,' he said, in tones so dry, a little more effort would have desiccated them completely. 'I'm not coy.'

'No, thanks,' I said tartly. 'I'm going down to watch *Pet Rescue Christmas Special* and burn some scrambled eggs.'

Knowing how long blokes can take over a bath and shave, I gave him forty minutes. As it happened there were half a dozen oranges, so I squeezed three for vitamin C. I'd done two eggs, scrambled more or less reasonably, on wholewheat toast. I'd wondered whether to cut the crusts off, but this struck me as OTT, as if I were cunningly trying to impress a bloke I fancied rotten. I mean, absolutely *nothing* like that was anywhere near my mind.

I took it all up on a tray, and tapped at the door. 'John?'

As there was no reply, I entered and went instantly ballistic. He was asleep, lying face down on the duvet, naked except for a towel that was coming adrift. He'd opened that window wide again; the room felt like a freezer. I put the tray down, livid enough to slap him. In fact, I did slap him. Since that coming-adrift towel was revealing most of one olive buttock, I slapped it, hard.

'Jesus!' Starting violently, he jerked to a sitting position. In the process his towel came further adrift, revealing glimpses of a respectable-looking dart and etceteras. I was almost too mad to look, however, which just goes to show how mad I was.

'Are you actually *trying* to give yourself pneumonia?' I demanded furiously, yanking the window closed. 'It's like Siberia in here! You've got virtually nothing on!'

He was already adjusting the towel. 'For crying out loud, Harriet, I just—'

'I *know* what you did! You lay in a too-hot bath for far too long, came back feeling like a boiled lobster, and thought you'd cool off! Haven't you got *any* brains, for God's sake?'

My words echoed around me.

Too late, I was wishing I'd saved my breath. The only effect was to bring back more than a glimmer of his temporarily indisposed spark. 'I'm beginning to see what your "paying customers" are paying for,' he said, with an edge of wry amusement that almost made me want to slap him again. 'Not that I'm into that kind of thing, of course.'

276

'Oh, for God's sake . . .' It was grossly unfair, sparking like this when he'd only just been exposing buttocks and darts. Irritably I retrieved his pyjamas from where he'd slung them on the chair and chucked them at him. 'Put those on and get back into bed. I'll have to put the fire on again now.'

This allowed me to keep my back to him while he was making himself decent, but I had to pretend a few matches were failing to strike. Having done that, I went and drew the curtains.

When I finally turned back to him, he was sitting up in bed, buttoned into Jacko's pyjamas and wearing an expression I had a horrible feeling was a feeble attempt to suppress laughter.

'At least you don't look quite so disgusting now,' I said, in grudging tones. 'Which is more than you can say for your scrambled eggs. They'll be stone cold.'

I plonked the tray on his duvet-covered lap. '*Bon appétit.* If you throw up again, please try to make it to the bathroom first.'

He looked down at the tray. 'Is that fresh juice?'

'That depends what you call fresh. The oranges probably came off the tree months ago. I'll leave you to it, then.'

I'd intended to do just that, but as I turned to go, he caught my wrist. 'Harriet . . .'

Something in his tone made my heart turn over. '*Now* what?' I said, like Snow White's Grumpy.

'Sorry if I've been an awkward, ungracious bastard.'

As if that weren't enough in my suddenly wobbly state, his grip tightened on my wrist. Pulling me down, he brushed my cheek with his lips. 'Thank you.'

I think I avoided audible wobbles. 'Don't mention it,' I said briskly, and cleared off downstairs, where I could wobble in private over yet another glass of wine. The strength in his grip had amazed me; what on earth would he manage when he was fit? And he'd used Jacko's irresistible gel after all, not that he'd needed to. I could still smell it warm on his skin.

Never mind his voice, gently husky, though maybe that was down to a sore throat, too. Between them, all these were enough to make a girl go as pink and gooey as something out of a corny old film. *'Oh, John,' she whispered, melting submissively in his arms. 'Oh, John, take me. Take me now before that beastly doorbell goes again . . .'*

Because it just had. 'Shit,' I said to Widdles. 'I can't even have a pink fantasy in peace. Who the hell's ringing doorbells at this time on Boxing Day?'

I thought it was one of those tea towel vendors, at first. The girl on the step was scruffy and unkempt, with a bag slung over her shoulder.

But then I saw her face. Grubby, wary and defiant, all at once.

The picture of Runaway Love.

# TEN

'Tara!' I gaped. 'If you're looking for Jacko, he's not here!'

'I know! Do you think I'd have come otherwise? I phoned home yesterday,' she added, in answer to the question I was about to ask. 'Can I come in, or what? I need somewhere to stay for a couple of nights.'

I was still taking it in. 'If you like. Where's Lee?'

'In Leicester. Look, just hang on while I tell my friends it's OK . . .'

She shot off to a car parked a couple of spaces down and was back in thirty seconds.

Once she was inside, I bit back fifty nosy questions about what the hell was going on. She looked positively dirty. Her hair needed washing. Her combats looked as if they'd been through a *Soldier, Soldier* exercise and there were exhausted circles under her eyes. However, I guessed from her defensive body language, as I took her through to the kitchen, that any big sister-ish questioning would make her clam right up.

'I thought William was supposed to be staying here for Christmas,' she said, dumping her bag on the floor.

Some instinct made me play it down. 'He was, but your mum and dad were a bit upset about you not being there, so he thought he'd go home after all. Take a seat,' I added brightly, indicating the sofa. 'Like a coffee?'

'OK.'

I'd met her several times over the years, on the odd visit to Jacko's. She must have been about eleven the first time, and nice enough. At thirteen or so she'd been getting lippy, making cheeky remarks. The last time I saw her was immediately after Jacko's accident. She'd come down with her parents while he was still in a bad way and his mother had been terrified of brain damage. Tara had said flippantly that his brain was damaged already; her mother had been dreadfully upset and screamed at her to shut up, she was a little bitch.

Now, her mother wasn't the type to scream any such thing, but she'd been out of her mind with worry. And I'd felt awful, because I'd known Tara had only said it as a cover because she was worried, too. Later her mother had realized as much, felt bad and said so, but Tara had retreated into a defensive, clammed-up shell.

From what I gathered, she hadn't come out of it since. Unlike Jacko, she had very little accent. His mother had once told me that his accent had become a lot more marked in his early teens, when he'd developed his Scouse-comic act. She'd told me that she'd privately thought it was a defence mechanism. She had an idea he'd gone through a phase of being bullied at school over his reddish hair but by the time he was fifteen or so he'd always had plenty of friends, so it must have been short-lived.

Tara's hair wasn't remotely red. Around five foot seven and very attractive, she had long hair of a natural corn gold, rather than Sally's platinum. She had hazel eyes, like Jacko's, but darker brows and lashes. You couldn't see much of a figure under the shapeless stuff she had on, but she was very slim.

While I was filling the kettle she said, 'I only phoned home to let them know I was OK, but Mum started going on and on, and then William took over and had a go at me and I hung up.'

Well done, 'William'. 'I wouldn't have thought you'd remember where I lived.'

'I didn't have to.' From the little bag still slung over her shoulder she retrieved two grubby envelopes, obviously Christmas cards, addressed to William Jacques, with his home address crossed out and mine added. 'Mum asked me to stick them in the post a couple of weeks ago, but I forgot.'

Having done much the same more than once, I said nothing.

I passed her a coffee and from the way she took it I guessed it was some time since she'd had anything of the sort. There were dirty-looking smudges around her eyes, exactly the mess you get from crying. It must have been hours ago, as her eyes weren't red, but I'd have put money on it. 'Lee's in Leicester, then? Will he be joining you?'

'He's playing a couple of gigs.'

'I'd have thought you'd want to stay and watch.'

She replied with a wary defensiveness that gave her away, if she'd only had the wit to realize it. 'Look, I got fed up with him, OK? He was only an excuse – I'd have left anyway.'

He'd slung her out, then. Or something had happened to make her walk out. Either way, it had been far from the Runaway Love she'd imagined, but she'd die rather than lose face by admitting it. 'I know the feeling,' I said. 'I nearly left home more than once, I can tell you. Thought about it, anyway.'

She was stroking Widdles, who was curled up on the sofa and didn't even have the courtesy to wake up. 'You work in an employment agency, don't you? I thought you could get me a job.'

I should have seen it coming. 'What sort of job?'

'*Any* job! I thought maybe I could stay here for a bit, too,' she went on. 'William's not coming back, is he?'

At last we were getting to it. 'He might be back for New Year.'

Her face fell. 'Then I'll go somewhere else. He'll only have a massive go at me – I can't stand it.'

Feeling my way, I said casually, 'Now you're here, it might be an idea to give your folks a call – just let them know where you are.'

282

'Are you kidding? They'd only be on at me again.'
Sudden suspicion dawned. 'You won't tell them I'm
here, will you?'

I suppose I hesitated.

'*Please!* They'd be down here in five minutes! Promise you won't tell them?'

'All right, I promise!'

'It's none of their business where I am, anyway,'
she went on, in warily defensive tones. 'I was eighteen
three weeks ago – I don't have to tell them anything.
I let them know I was OK, didn't I?'

'Yes, you did.' After debating a moment I went on,
'What about the friends who dropped you off? Don't
you want to stay with them?'

'They haven't got room,' she said flatly.

Well, OK.

'But you can get me a job, can't you?' she went
on.

I sat at the table, wondering what on earth to say.
'Have you got any experience of anything?'

'I can type! I've done some of my essays on the
computer.'

I got the picture. 'If you're talking two-finger stuff,
it's not enough. And to be honest, hardly anyone
I deal with is going to take on someone with no
experience.'

The defiant mask came back as if it had never
slipped. 'Forget it – I'll find something myself – it
can't be *that* difficult to get a job in London.'

'Oh, no. There are masses of jobs.' She could probably walk into something unskilled tomorrow. Earning anything like enough to support herself was another matter. 'Look, I've got a turkey in the oven – it's just about ready. Would you like some?'

She gave a not-bothered shrug. 'I wouldn't mind.'

So gracious.

She watched me turn it over, splash fat and juices everywhere and curse.

'Where's the one with the baby?'

'Sally went home too. She thought her parents might be upset if she didn't.'

'Were you here all by yourself yesterday, then?'

After telling her briefly about Mum's hordes and my 'friend' upstairs, I thought he might still be peckish; two scrambled eggs wasn't much in twenty-four hours. 'I'll nip up and see if he fancies any turkey.'

When I tapped on the door he called, 'Come in,' in a just-dozing voice.

I sat on the end of the bed. 'How are you feeling?'

'On a scale of one to ten, about three better than I felt this morning. Maybe I steamed the little bastard out in that bath.' He started raising himself to a sitting position. 'But I still feel as if someone's taken half my stuffing out. It knackered me just going for a pee half an hour ago.'

I said, 'I shoved that turkey in the oven earlier –

it's just about ready. Would you like a bit with some mashed potato?'

'I could murder some.'

Definitely feeling better, which amazed me, considering his earlier state. Either it was down to a cast-iron constitution, or sheer bloody-mindedness was playing a part, after all.

I told him about Tara's arrival, ending, 'She's asked me to get her a job and made me promise not to tell her folks she's here.'

'But you're going to do exactly that?'

'Of course I am, having sworn I wouldn't. But I'll have to talk to her first, make her see I don't have much option.'

'Do it now. Pass the buck back where it belongs. It's what she wants you to do, or she'd never have come here in the first place.'

'Maybe she just didn't have anywhere else to go. At that age nearly all your friends are still living at home – their folks'd be on the phone to your folks in two seconds.'

'Harriet, call them. It's what she wants, believe me. She won't crawl home admitting they were right – she wants them to do the running.'

It annoyed me a good deal that I hadn't thought of this myself. 'For someone who's never laid eyes on her, you seem to have it all well sussed!'

'You forget Lucy.' He started a fit of coughing but quickly overcame it. 'She used to create havoc, have the folks tearing their hair. It's called attention-seeking,' he declared, as if this were a novel concept.

'She'll be trouble,' he added. 'I can smell it from here. Get on the phone now, while she can't hear. If her folks are anything like mine were, they'll be in the car inside fifteen minutes.'

They probably would. 'I'll have to talk to her first. I promised.'

'Harriet, promises are like speed limits – made to be broken.'

Then he started another fit of coughing, so I went to the bathroom cupboard for half a sticky bottle of Benylin. He'd stopped coughing by then, but I told him to have a good swig anyway.

Having swigged, he lay back on the pillows, exhausted. It was very unsettling. I was overwhelmed with a sudden desire to do caring-nursey things, e.g. tuck the covers round him, plump up his pillows, lay a hand on his forehead to check fever levels. In fact, any excuse to get up close and personal.

But I fought the impulse womanfully. 'Back to the turkey and Tara, then,' I said briskly.

'Send her up here,' he said darkly. 'I'll sort her out.'

I knew it was rhetorical, but I replied nevertheless. 'I need a diplomat, not a half-knackered bulldozer. Anyway, I wouldn't want her catching your bug. One awkward patient's more than enough.'

'I know. I'll be out of here tomorrow.'

His sudden, softer tone melted me instantly. 'Look, it's fine.'

'Harriet, I can't stay here.' Pausing just long enough for me to melt a bit further, he added, 'Any more brutal whacks on the arse and I'll have a relapse.'

'You asked for it,' I retorted. 'And any relapses will not be nursed by me – I've got to go to work tomorrow. There won't be much doing but some-one's got to be there and everybody else was tied up.'

Halfway to the door, I thought of his shirt, stiffly starched with the residue of evaporated sweat, and nothing else to put on tomorrow. Since there was stuff to shove in the machine anyway, I gathered it up, with his socks and boxers. 'I'll add these to your laundry bill,' I said. 'At this rate, I'm going to be quids in.'

Tara was nearly asleep on the sofa when I went down, but she roused instantly, looking almost guilty, as if I'd caught her up to no good.

After peeling an extra couple of potatoes for John, I set about manhandling the turkey out of the oven and making gravy. I was actually quite pleased with the bird. Apart from the fact that its untrussed legs and wings were all over the place, various extrem-ities were burnt and most of the breast skin had stuck to the bottom of the pan, it didn't look too bad at all.

I did some frozen peas as well, for want of anything

else, and when I finally put a plateful in front of her, Tara fell on it like Jacko used to when he'd just come back from water polo.

I said, 'Look, I've got to go to work tomorrow and John's probably going home in the morning but he's still not very well – could you make him some breakfast? Scrambled eggs or something?'

She nodded, her mouth full. When it was half empty she said, 'Is he your bloke?'

'No, just a friend.'

She digested this over another mouthful. 'Have you *got* a bloke?'

'Not at the moment.'

'Why not?'

'I'm getting picky. I can't be bothered with blokes unless they score eleven out of ten on my picky scale. All right?'

Over another couple of mouthfuls she gave me a rather searching look. 'Mum was thinking William might fancy you,' she said.

I could almost have laughed. 'What on earth made her think that? Jacko and I have only ever been mates.'

'That's what I told her.' Stuffing a massive piece of roast potato in her mouth, she added, 'I said you'd have to be desperate.'

She was as bad as Sally. 'Oh, come on! That's not very nice!'

She shrugged. 'She thought it might be a reason

288

why he hadn't come home, anyway. Dad's been really pissed off. He relies on him more than he admits.'

'He was just recovering and enjoying some slobbing. Mind you, he does have a bit of a thing about Frida —'

'The Swedish one?'

'And his physio at the hospital. He doesn't usually limit himself to one passing fancy at a time, in case you hadn't noticed.'

'He never has more than passing fancies,' she snorted. 'Dad reckons all those EU grain mountains are William's wild oats.'

While she ate, I had a job not to laugh again, thinking of me and Jacko as an item. I had slept with him once, but that was all it was. Sleeping. And only because I happened to have a double bed.

I'd only known him about three months. It had happened on a cold December night in that grotty student house. Sometime in the small hours, Jacko and mates had thought it would be a laugh to make missiles out of condoms filled with water and bomb each other all over the house. Not long after I'd gone to bed (to avoid the bombs) there had been a tap at the door. 'Can I come and cuddle up, pet? My bed's like a swimming pool.'

'Go and cuddle up with Guy!' I'd retorted. (Guy had the only other double.)

'He told me to sod off,' he'd said pathetically. 'Said he'd feel like a poof.'

So I'd said, 'Oh, all right, then . . .' and he'd slid in beside me. We'd talked for a bit; it had actually felt quite cosy and companionable until I was nodding off at last, when there had been a hopeful whisper in my ear. 'S'pose there's no chance of a shag?'

'For God's sake, go to *sleep*!' I'd given him a furious elbow in the ribs, too.

'Ow!' He'd then turned over with a hurt 'I only asked to be polite.'

Perversely, that had made me even crosser. Although I'd never remotely fancied him, I'd been a bit put out at the time that Jacko seemed to fancy just about everyone but me. At first I'd put it down to my underendowment in the bra department, but had soon realized my mistake. Fried eggs, grapefruit, pumpkins: Jacko wasn't fussy. If it liked a laugh and there was half an ounce of chemistry, it scored a ten on the Jacko scale.

But the only chemistry between me and Jacko had been the 'friends' variety. And although he could dickhead for England, Jacko had been a good friend. Even better than some of my girlfriends – at least we'd never fancied the same people.

Back to Tara, though. After devouring seconds she asked if she could have a bath, so I showed her up by way of Jacko's room, where she'd be sleeping. His sheets were still on, and if you'd applied a Geiger-counter thing to detect traces of farts it would probably have exploded, but she obviously wasn't expecting TV-ad sheets, smelling of verdant summer meadows, tra la.

Feeling like a bed-and-breakfast landlady, I went down and mashed John's potatoes. I hacked him off a couple of slices of breast, added a delicate portion of mash, peas and gravy, and took it up with more orange juice.

He was awake, listening to the London Live news.

'There you go,' I said, depositing the tray on his lap. 'Not exactly *Masterchef*, but probably edible.'

He sniffed appreciatively, as if even the smell was perking him up. 'It looks great. How's the runaway?'

'In the bath.' I hadn't intended to, but I sat on the bed. 'I wish she'd run somewhere else, to be honest. I've already had one major drama today.' I hadn't intended to do this either, but I told him about Helen.

'Is she the one you had to get back to after we went for drinks?' he asked, after I'd given him rather more than the basics.

I was surprised he remembered. 'Yes, and I came home to find she'd done the deed, after I'd more or less put the idea into her head. Still, at least I'm not remotely responsible for a pregnancy.'

'You're not responsible for runaways, either. Get on that phone and pass the buck back where it belongs.'

'I will. Only I've got to talk to her first.' It was much more tempting to stay and talk to him. For a few minutes the relationship had seemed more like a heart-to-heart between friends, everything else temporarily tucked under the duvet. He'd been listening in a sympathetic fashion, just throwing in the odd shrewd comment.

However, I left him to eat in peace. Since Tara was still in the bathroom as I passed the door, I went downstairs rehearsing convincing arguments about parents worrying themselves into heart attacks or other dire conditions.

But by the time I'd loaded the dishwasher and vaguely tidied up, I became aware that everything had gone ominously quiet. I went back up to find that she'd crashed out already. So had John, when I went to collect his tray.

Downstairs again, cross with both of them, I phoned Sally.

She was stunned to hear about Helen, of course. 'Maybe she subconsciously just wanted another baby,' she said. 'To give her a purpose again. Kids are all she's ever done, after all.'

'Imagine Lawrence's face when she tells him! He'll probably be affronted that she could even want anybody else.'

Then I got on to Tara.

'Brat,' Sally said eventually, with feeling. 'She just went to bed without even saying goodnight or thank you for the dinner?'

'Yes, and now I've got to phone her folks, after

swearing blind I wouldn't. Still, John might be right. Maybe she just wants them to do the running.'

'If I were them, I'd let her get on with it.'

'I can't see them doing that, but it's not a bad idea. If I found her a really crappy job paying peanuts, I bet she'd never stick it a week.'

In the event I phoned Jacko on his mobile, and his main reaction was apology that I'd been landed with her. However, the folks would be profoundly relieved that Lee was history and she wasn't sleeping in some heroin-infested squat. He'd call them (he was in some pub, of course) and get back to me.

When he eventually did, it wasn't quite what I'd expected. Yes, they were overwhelmingly relieved, but turbocharging straight down might not be wise. First, if she refused to come home they could hardly force her to, and there'd only be another row. Second, if she *was* expecting me to blab and them to do the running, it might not be a bad idea to let her think they weren't going to. Let her sweat a bit. So they hated asking, please feel free to say no, but if I wouldn't mind terribly having her for just a couple of days . . .

'OK,' I said to Jacko. 'It's not as if there isn't room.'

'Thanks, pet. Don't so much as make a coffee for her, though, will you? She's used to the old lady waiting on her hand and foot.'

No, there'd definitely be no more 'waiting', I

thought. I might even tell her there were no free lunches in this house, she could clean Widdles' litter tray, for starters.

Since they were both still asleep, I didn't see either of them before I left in the morning. I scrawled a note for Tara: 'Help yourself to anything and please feed and water John if he's still feeling rough. Tell him his clothes are in the airing cupboard. Back around six.'

Underneath I added, 'If you're bored, the kitchen floor could do with a wash.' I was pleased with that. Neat, I thought.

I needn't have bothered going to work at all. The phone only rang twice, and one of those was Lesley, saying she wished she'd come in instead, mother-in-law had said her fridge needed cleaning out, tut tut, did she know there were eggs dated 17th November at the back, and was she really going to allow the children to help themselves to After Eights whenever they liked? And what's more . . .

By the time she hung up, I realized I'd been doodling all over my pad. I'd written *John Mackenzie* a dozen times in various styles from italic to old-fashioned loopy, drawn a little stick man in bed and a little stick witch on a broomstick, going, *'Aagh!'* as Superman zoomed in.

My artwork pleased me so much, I added a further scene. I drew Superman hurling the Witch into space, where she'd be fated to orbit Planet Zog on her broomstick for evermore. Underneath I wrote *Serve you right, too.*

Then I wrote *Get a life, Harriet,* tore the page out and chucked it in the bin.

At twelve fifteen I phoned John's mobile. He answered after four rings and any rumours that I was going fluttery just waiting to hear his voice are a malicious slander.

'John Mackenzie,' he said.

'It's Harriet,' I said. 'How are you feeling?'

There was a minute pause. 'Oh, hello, Graham. How's it going?'

It took me only half a second to catch on. 'Tara's with you, I take it?'

'Not so bad, thanks.'

'Is she talking?'

'I might have to get back to you on that one, but it's possible. Look, can I call you later? I'm a bit tied up just now.'

I was bursting with curiosity until he called back about an hour later.

'Sorry about that, but she was in the middle of a tearful flood about Lee. Plus she'd just been saying you'd probably told her folks she was here already, she should never have come.'

'I have told them. Where is she, anyway?'

'Just nipped to the shops. For shampoo or something. The flood went on for quite a while after

295

you phoned. Look, I've sworn not to tell you any of this, but she walked out on Lee. He'd taken her to some scruffy house in Leicester, where half a dozen of his friends were living. At least two of them were women he obviously knew very well – older than Tara and much harder nuts, from what I gather. They looked at her as if she were some pathetic little kid, she said. Sniggered behind her back, that sort of thing. She felt uncomfortable from the word go.'

I could just imagine it.

'She soon sussed out that one of them had been more than just mates with Lee,' he went on. 'She made it very obvious and Lee wasn't complaining. Nothing happened till the other night, though. She said she "woke up" – reading between the lines she'd been stoned – but she found Lee on the verge of having a pretty good time with this woman. So she threw a fit, and the woman just laughed at her, and Lee told her to chill out.'

I felt for her. I really did. 'Poor Tara.'

'Yes,' he said. 'So that was the last of her naïve little illusions down the pan. She packed her stuff and walked out.' He paused. 'I gather she told you some friends dropped her off?'

'Didn't they?'

'She hitched. She's got hardly any money left. Some elderly couple made a detour and brought her to the door.'

Another detail explained, then. 'After that little lot, you'd think she'd be dying to go home.'

'Well, she isn't.' He paused again. 'Look, I got the impression that it's not just losing face she can't stomach — something else has been going on that she won't talk about.'

This was possible. 'I suppose it's nothing to do with school? She might be being bullied.'

'Why would anyone bully her?'

'They don't need much of a reason! She's pretty and her parents have got money. Jealousy'd be quite enough for some girls, I can tell you.'

'Well, whatever it is, she's not saying,' he said. 'Maybe you should ask her brother — see if he's got any pointers.'

'You've changed your tune, haven't you? What happened to last night's dire threats of sorting her out? How did you get her to come out with all this?'

'I didn't "get" her. She made me some scrambled eggs and we started talking. I said I gathered she'd just left home, and it all started flooding out. Not quite all, perhaps, but a few hundred gallons.'

Belatedly I asked, 'After all that, how are you feeling?'

'A damn sight better, thanks. I'll see you later — I won't leave until you're back.'

For the rest of the afternoon I wondered what 'something else' might be. Maybe she was in minor trouble with the police and was dreading her parents finding out. If she'd nicked an eyeshadow just for the hell of it, she certainly wouldn't be the first.

When I got home they were sitting at the kitchen table, over empty plates. 'Been busy?' John asked, as if we hadn't spoken.

'There was sod all going on. I might as well not have bothered.'

'I made him a baked potato with some cold turkey and salad,' Tara said. 'We'd have waited for you, but we were starving.'

'That's OK,' I said brightly, and went to put the kettle on.

'I washed the kitchen floor,' she added.

'Yes, I can see that. Thanks a lot.'

'And I made John some scrambled eggs, earlier,' Tara went on, as if I'd demanded an account of how she'd justified being here all day. 'I didn't think they looked very nice, but he ate them anyway.'

'They were ambrosial,' he soothed.

I turned around. Tara looked like a different animal from last night. For a start, she was clean. She wore a soft grey fleece top and her hair hung in a rippling, corn-silk mass. She wore no make-up, smudged or otherwise, and if she'd been crying it couldn't have been for long. Her face bore no sign of it.

'I hope you don't mind, but I borrowed your

hairdryer,' she said, still slightly defensively, as if I were the enemy in disguise. 'And I put all my clothes in the wash – they were minging.'

'No, that's fine. And thanks for looking after John. I take it you're feeling better?' I added, to him.

'About seven points up on yesterday. Tara's been great – I couldn't have had better service at five hundred quid a night in the London Clinic.'

She didn't exactly smirk, but she looked decidedly pleased with herself, and shot him a little glance, as if to check that he wasn't just saying it.

'At least she didn't yell at me,' he went on, in mock-hurt tones. 'I tell you, Tara, if your average NHS nurse were like Harriet, the hospitals would be half empty overnight. People would be too bloody terrified to get sick.'

She looked at me, her eyes widening. 'You didn't yell at him, did you?'

'You should have heard her,' he said, shaking his head. 'Like a harridan on speed.'

'You asked for it!' I retorted. 'Lying in sub-arctic blasts with virtually nothing on . . .'

Turning back to the worktop to make my tea, I heard Tara quietly giggling, and suddenly felt acutely hurt that he was making jokes at my expense. I almost wished he'd revert to last night's hard man, sharply sorting her out.

'But she had some justification,' he went on. 'I was probably the world's most awkward patient.'

She giggled again, as if he'd winked at her as he said it.

I knew it was ridiculous, but suddenly I might have been fifteen again. Behind my back I felt a two's-company conspiracy, having a quiet snigger about Harriet. I hated myself for minding so childishly, but I couldn't help it. It had been obvious as soon as I'd entered the room that there was a certain rapport between them. If he'd been trying to gain her confidence he'd certainly succeeded. As far as she was concerned, I was in the enemy camp. It felt as if they were ganging up against me.

Telling myself for God's sake to get an adult grip, I joined them at the table.

After shooting John a glance, Tara turned to me. 'I suppose you've already told my mum and dad I'm here?'

From the way she said it, I knew there was no point lying. 'I'm sorry, Tara, but I had to. They've been out of their minds.'

She shot John a 'told you so' look.

'But you needn't worry that they'll be charging straight down,' I went on. 'They said there wasn't much point, as you'd probably refuse to come home and they couldn't very well force you.'

If this startled her, she covered it instantly. 'At least they've sussed that much out. And just as well, because even if they did come I wouldn't be here.

300

John said there's a flat I can stay in, till I get myself sorted.'

'It belongs to a friend of mine,' he explained, in answer to my *What the hell?* expression. 'He's in Abu Dhabi – won't be back for a bit.'

'So when they phone again, you can tell them that's where I am,' she went on, in a tone poised between defensiveness and triumph.

What *had* been going on here? 'Won't your friend mind?' I asked John, with a trace of acid.

'He won't know,' he soothed, and Tara stifled another giggle.

So much for 'sorting her out', I thought. 'And what do I tell your folks if they ask for an address?'

'You'll be able to tell them with perfect truth that you don't know,' Tara said. 'I'm not obliged to tell them anything. And John agrees with me absolutely,' she went on, giving him another glance. 'I'm eighteen, not a little kid.'

'She does have a point,' he said.

No wonder it had felt like a conspiracy. I couldn't believe John had stuck his oar in like this, without even asking me. 'Look, Tara, as far as I'm concerned you can do what you like.'

John glanced at his watch. 'We ought to be making a move. Tara, go up and get your things together.'

She went off like a lamb. Once the door had shut behind her, I said, 'What the hell are you up to?'

'I didn't have much choice!' Lowering his voice he

went on, 'Look, she'd made up her mind that you'd spilled the beans already and her old man'd be here by tomorrow morning. She'd have left by now if I hadn't offered.'

'Left for where? She's got nowhere to go!'

'Exactly. She asked me to lend her some money for a cheap bed and breakfast. God knows what sort of dive she might have ended up in.'

I was beginning to think a few nights in a really crummy dive would have done her the world of good.

'Look, do you think I need this?' he went on, evidently seeing only my exasperation. 'Believe me, I've got enough on at the moment. I will give you the address,' he added.

'Even though you evidently told her you wouldn't, no matter how I tried to wheedle it out of you?'

'I had to, didn't I? She was on the point of packing her things and taking off.'

He'd lied beautifully, then. So beautifully she'd believed him utterly. My stomach contracted, as I suddenly thought of what other beautifully believable lies he might have told. 'You're a pretty convincing liar, then.'

'You can talk,' he said, in drily amused tones. 'Little Miss, "Oh, dear, I've lost my purse . . ."'

'I thought I had!' I said it more tartly than I'd intended, because something else had just hit me. Even if Tara's parents didn't ask who this friend was, gaily dishing out flats like Smarties, Jacko certainly would. What the hell was I going to tell him? *'Remember Smootharse? Well, I know I told you he was just being nice, but I did see him again, even though he's still seeing Nina, and I went home with him for Christmas while Nina was conveniently in Aspen – I lied about going to Mum's, by the way – and he just happened to get the flu . . .'*

Suddenly I knew exactly what was meant by cans of worms. 'You should have kept out of it! It was none of your business!'

'Look, just what is the problem?' he said, beginning to sound exasperated. 'I'll talk to her folks, if you want. Or her brother.'

'No, it's fine,' I said hastily. 'I'll talk to them.'

Tara came back just then, with tension still hanging in the air and me looking decidedly browned off.

This appeared to worry her not at all, rather the reverse. 'I'm ready,' she said expectantly, dumping her bag on the floor.

'Right, let's hit the road,' John said, before patting his jacket pocket. 'I left my mobile upstairs. Run and get it, will you?'

Obediently she shot off again.

Once she'd gone, he said, 'Look, I felt sorry for her, if you want to know. She's just a kid.'

Not that much of a kid, I thought. She hadn't been playing Lego with Lee, had she?

'After a week I'll tell her she's got to go,' he went on. 'By then she might have got herself some slave-labour job and be thinking it's not so great after all.'

'*I* could have got her a slave-labour job! You might at least have asked me first!'

'OK, and what if she'd just taken off? Nobody would have a clue where she was!'

But Tara was coming back. 'I couldn't find it anywhere!'

'Then where the hell . . . ?' With a frown, he patted his jacket pocket again, before his eyes went to the sideboard. 'Over there – sorry. I'm still not a hundred per cent with it.' Pocketing the phone, he shot me a tiny wink that said he'd known it was there all along.

All right, it was only a convenient little lie, just so he could speak to me in private, but I was beginning to think he was too bloody good at this for comfort.

'Can I just make a quick call?' she asked. 'I want to phone my friend.'

'Go on, then.'

As she went off, out of earshot, he gazed down at me. 'You look seriously hacked off.'

I could hardly go into the Smootharse bit. 'I don't suppose it matters. I just hope she won't trash your friend's flat.'

'She'd better not. It's mine.'

I gaped at him.

'It seemed expedient,' he said, in apologetic tones.

304

'An Abu Dhabi friend liable to come back at, say, forty-eight hours' notice . . .'

'And it's just sitting there, empty?'

'Of course not – it's between lets. I was in a position to hang onto it when I moved,' he explained. 'The way property prices were going, I'd have been mad not to. But I'll have to tell the agency not to bring anyone round for a bit.'

Another lie. They were popping up like Kleenex from a box. I turned away from him to put the kettle on. I didn't want tea or anything else, it was just so I wouldn't have to look at him and wonder whether here was a fully paid-up Smootharse, after all.

He came closer, within a couple of feet of me. 'You are hacked off with me.'

'I'm not. I just wish she'd picked somewhere else to run to.'

'She will be somewhere else now.'

I still wasn't looking at him. 'I hope you can cope with her, that's all. Jacko says she can be a right arsey little madam.'

'I have years of experience with arsey little madams. Lucy was arsey from the word go. She used to whack me with her rattle.'

Of course he said it in that trying-not-to-laugh tone that melted me, and of course I had to look at him.

This was just what he'd intended. 'Harriet, thanks for everything,' he said.

'You're welcome. And thanks for Christmas.'

'I don't know about thanks. I wasn't very scintillating company.'

'Everybody else was. Especially Horace.'

'Yes, you scored a hit there.' As we heard Tara's feet in the hall, he added more crisply, 'I'll give you a call.'

Looking a lot perkier than she had last night, Tara handed back his mobile.

'Ready?' he asked.

As she looked up at him, nodding like an eager little puppy, I suddenly saw him through her eyes, and not my own. She saw an older man, not old enough to be remote, but properly grown-up. Relaxed, but with that indefinable aura of substance and *savoir faire*. A man who had flats at his disposal, who would never be stuck with hardly any money and nowhere to go. She'd have snorted in derision if I'd actually said it, but he was the eternal white knight, galloping up just as the dragon was about to have you for breakfast.

He picked up her bag. Well, that's what white knights do. They never expect you to carry them yourself.

We paused by the front door. 'Thanks again,' John said.

Now he was about to go, I was perverse enough to have misgivings about my misgivings. Feeling better or not, he still didn't look much more than eighty per cent. I wanted to say, 'Look after yourself,' and other nursey stuff, but strangled it at

306

the tonsil stage. 'Wait till you get the bill,' I said. 'Take care.'

'You, too.' Brushing his lips against my cheek, he added a little pat on my waist. 'I'll be in touch.'

Looking rather awkward, Tara said, 'Thanks for having me. And for the dinner and everything.'

'You're welcome.' I opened the door to a blast of cold air. Since Dorothy's house had only a token front garden, the car was merely yards from the front door. I watched John unlock the passenger door, and watched Tara get in, looking almost excited. Then he opened the driver's door and gave me a little parting wave. I watched the car disappear down the road, closed the front door and went back to the kitchen.

'I wish she'd never come,' I said to Widdles. 'Is there some massive sign out there I haven't noticed? *Please feel free to come and foul up Harriet's life a bit more – she can't do it fast enough herself*?'

He gave a huge yawn.

'Fat lot of use you are,' I said crossly. I spent the next half-hour picking at the turkey and scouring the Christmas TV guide for anything that might cheer me up, like *Men Behaving Badly*, ha ha.

Having put it off that long, I rang Tara's folks. I told her mother I'd had a friend staying over. While I was at work he'd somehow got her talking and this was the result. I asked what she thought the 'something else' John had mentioned might be, but she couldn't think of anything. Tara never told her anything anyway.

Eventually she went on, 'I'm praying she'll come to her senses before school starts, but I must say it was very kind of him to step in like that. I just hope she won't turn his flat into a pigsty in two minutes. You should have seen the state of her room after she left. Apple cores everywhere and at least three bowls with dried-on cereal like cement. And she smokes on the quiet, you know. I found a burn on the duvet cover. Is it good stuff in this place of his?'

'Probably, but I haven't been. It's his old flat,' I added hastily.

'Well, I just hope she won't damage anything,' she said, in resigned tones. 'She really is the end, giving all this trouble. But what a relief she's away from that Lee. He was most unsavoury, you know. I've got absolutely nothing against long hair, but you'd think he might wash it now and then.'

After she'd hung up, I thought a similar line might do for Jacko. Tara was staying at a flat belonging to an old friend I hadn't happened to mention. He'd believe me, and if he ever found out I'd tackle that when I came to it. I thought I'd get Sally's opinion, but when I tried her number it was engaged.

I was just about to try again when the phone rang. It was Rosie.

# Eleven

This was a wee bit spooky. Since I hadn't heard from her for a week, I'd been thinking of ringing her for the past forty-eight hours. But I hadn't actually done it. I couldn't bring myself to pretend I was just asking whether she'd had a lovely Christmas, while hoping there might be some little news items she'd forgotten to pass on.

Rosie was still back home, and bored. 'The most exciting thing in this house lately is Dad doing his Ali G impression, but we have to take the whole week as annual leave so I thought I might as well stay. Besides, I have to help Mum out of a dire personal crisis.'

'What crisis?'

'About fourteen boxes of Belgian chocolates. She's back to Weight Watchers next week. I've eaten so many I feel sick, but I have to keep eating them to take temptation out of her way. Did you get any exciting prezzies? I've ended up with a pair of those massive furry-dog slippers that make you walk funny, and some bath stuff that smells like strawberry puke. I just knew I'd be given some of those slippers. Before I came home I said to Suzanne, "I bet you I'll get some of those furry-dog slippers", and she said yes, or flannelette pyjamas with bunnies on, because it's a law of nature that people like us end up with furry slippers and pyjamas, whereas Other People whose names she wouldn't mention end up with colossally expensive earrings from Helicopters. She was a bit pissed off, as you may gather.'

This was another reason I hadn't rung her. In case any news items turned out to be ones I'd rather not hear. 'Typical. Not diamonds, I hope.'

'I don't know, but they were really nice. He gave them to her the night before she left. So much for her paranoid imaginings.'

My antennae pricked right up. 'What paranoid imaginings?'

'Oh, didn't I tell you? Well, maybe I didn't – I haven't spoken to you for a bit. She'd been getting in a bit of a tizz, thinking he was cooling off.'

'Not taking her home for Christmas, you mean?'

'Oh, it wasn't just *that*. He'd been *working late* – her italics. I mean, don't we all? But she'd got this idea he might have someone else on the go.'

I wasn't sure I wanted to hear this. How many times had he been 'working late'? And which dates, exactly?

'But Suzanne thinks she might well be right,' Rosie went on. 'She said colossally expensive earrings smelt of guilt offerings to her. She said all he'd have to do now was send some flowers to Aspen and she'd know for certain.'

'How horribly cynical of her,' I said lightly.

'Well, that's Suzanne for you. Mind you, she never quite took to Helicopter in the first place. Says she never trusts blokes with pulling power coming out of their ears. It's too easy for them, she says. Like picking up Mars bars in Tesco's.'

I gave a carefree little laugh I thought came off rather well. 'What a nasty, suspicious mind.'

'Yes, that's what I thought. He never made a proper move on you, did he? Not real Mars bar stuff. Still, maybe he thought it'd be too much like hard work to get your wrappings off.' She started tee-hee-ing helplessly at her own joke, and I produced another carefree little titter.

'But I wish someone'd give *me* colossally expensive guilt offerings,' she went on, in plaintive tones. 'At least they beat strawberry puke and furry-dog slippers.'

We nattered for another ten minutes until a 'call waiting' took my mind right off Mars bars.

It was Dad. He'd tried to phone on Christmas Day, but no-one had been answering. Maybe we'd all gone to walk our dinner off. (Dad, thank God, wasn't the type to think *'Gas leaks!'* and call the Fire Brigade.) I said yes, more than likely. Yes, I'd had a lovely Christmas – had he?

'Extremely nice, thank you, dear.' He then got to the point. 'I don't know whether Mummy told you, but I've met a very nice woman.'

'Well, that's lovely,' I said brightly. 'I heard you were thinking of going skiing.'

'As a matter of fact, we're in the mountains now.' He sounded positively tickled with himself. 'Kathy's quite the expert, she's rather younger than me, of course, but I've had a few goes and only fallen over half a dozen times. It's rather fun, isn't it? Kathy says I'll be off the nursery slopes in no time.'

I tried not to think of what Mum had said about susceptible old fools and flattery.

'She says we should maybe go to Val d'Isère later in the season,' he announced, in the same tickled-pink tones. 'She says I'm an awful lot more athletic than I look.'

I did try not to see the Viagra on the bedside table.

'But the reason I was ringing was to say I'll be back in the next week or two,' he went on. 'Haven't quite worked out the dates yet, but I'll let you know. Kathy'll be coming, of course; she wants to go and see her family in Basingstoke. I thought we could all have dinner together.'

'That'd be lovely,' I said. 'Will you be staying here?'

'Oh, no, dear, I wouldn't want to put you out. I'll book a hotel. I do hope you'll like her,' he added anxiously.

There's a technique to sounding bright over the phone. You force your mouth into what in low circles is called a split-arse grin, and believe me, mine was stretched ear to ear. (My mouth, I mean.) 'I'm sure I shall. How long will you be staying?'

'Oh, only a few days, then we'll be off to Egypt. Kathy's never been to Egypt; I'm looking forward to showing her the Valley of the Kings. We'll stay in Luxor a week or so, and then on to Aswan. Kathy's got a yen for the Old Cataract Hotel; it's rather famous, you know. Very scenic.'

I'd heard of it. I think I'd even seen it, on *Wish You Were Here* or something. 'Well, that'll be lovely,' I said, still split-arsing for England.

'I hope so. Kathy does love the sun. Actually, dear . . .' He paused. 'I wasn't going to say this just yet, but it's not *quite* going to be just an ordinary holiday.'

No flying jellies hit me; I'd seen it coming. Or rather heard it, in a voice you could only describe as besotted. Trying not to think of Mum going ape when she heard, I did a split-arse extreme enough to require surgery. 'Are you telling me it's going to be your honeymoon?'

'Well, yes,' he said, sounding half embarrassed but chuffed at the same time. 'I do hope it's not too much of a shock.'

'No, it's *lovely*! Have you told Mum?' I added, knowing full well he hadn't, or phone lines would have blown up by now.

'No, dear; I'm not going to tell her till after the

event. We haven't actually tied the knot yet – that'll be next week. I was going to ask you and a few others to come, but Kathy didn't want any fuss. I'd rather you didn't tell Mummy just yet; she'll only think I'm rushing into it like some infatuated old fool.'

'I'm sure she wouldn't,' I said, thinking he didn't know the half of it. 'How long *have* you known her, by the way?'

'About seven weeks,' he said, almost bashfully.

God help us.

'I know what Mummy thinks of me,' he went on, in wry tones I'd hardly ever heard him use. 'She thinks I'm a bit clueless about a lot of things and she's probably right, but I know I'm doing the right thing. I'm really very happy.'

I don't quite know why that changed anything, but it did. My eyes were suddenly misting, my throat pricking. 'I'm happy for you, too. I'm really looking forward to meeting her.'

After hanging up I was straight into another quandary. If Mum wasn't forewarned she'd have a fit. She'd screech 'David, you've done *what*?' as if he were sixteen, and not sixty-one. While debating whether to phone her I watched *The Simpsons*, but half an hour of Homer and Marge made me think that if they could make a go of it, there must be hope for Dad and Kathy. At least she presumably hadn't got blue hair.

When I eventually did phone Mum, her reaction

was entirely predictable. 'He's *what*?' she almost screeched. 'Heaven help us, I knew it.'

'Mum, calm down!' I gave a few more details.

'Heaven help us. Where are they getting married?'

'He didn't say.'

'It'll be in the British Consulate, I bet. I've got a good mind to—'

'Mum, will you shut up? I'm only telling you so you'll be prepared! If you dare say anything horrible I'll kill you! He sounds really happy!'

'Of course he does! God knows what she's been doing, flattering him and heaven knows what in bed – dear Lord –'

'For God's sake, does it matter, as long as he's happy?'

'Yes, but for how long? Why didn't she want anyone coming to the wedding? That's very telling if you ask me – she knows we'd get her measure fast enough. How old is she?'

'I don't know. Younger, anyway.'

'Well, I guessed as much. Thirty-seven if she's a day, I bet. Did he say which hotel he's staying at?'

'No.' And just as well. I wouldn't have put it past her to get on a plane and sort the scheming Jezebel out.

'And they're going to Egypt for their honeymoon? Not one of those Nile cruises, I hope. She might be planning on pushing him over the side.'

'Mum, for heaven's sake! They're going to Luxor,

and then to the Old Cataract Hotel at Aswan. Kathy's got a yen for it, apparently.'

'For goodness sake – that's not a very good omen, is it?'

'Mum, what are you on about?'

'They made that Agatha Christie film there! *Death on the Nile*! I'm getting a very bad feeling about this woman, I can tell you.'

This was becoming ridiculous. 'Mum, will you just stop it? You're working yourself up into a positive hate thing about this Kathy!'

'I can't help it. I'm sure he's making a terrible mistake.'

'So what if he is? It's his mistake, not yours! You're not responsible for him!'

'I *feel* responsible! I was married to him for twenty-two years!'

'Well, you're not bloody well married to him now, are you? You left him!'

'Harriet!'

Something in me was flipping, fast. 'For God's sake, can't you just be happy for him? He deserves to be happy – when was he ever properly happy with you?'

'Harriet! That was uncalled for! I'm only thinking of—'

'You think he's stupid – you always did! You were impatient with him for years – snappy and irritated – he couldn't do a thing right!'

'Harriet!'

'Don't "Harriet" me! You've been a damn sight different since Bill, that's for sure! I never saw you look like that with Dad, not once! I never saw you look *at* him like you look at Bill! Why the hell did you marry him in the first place?'

There was an awful silence. When she finally spoke, her voice was shaky, as if she were about to cry. 'I really don't think there's any point prolonging this conversation. I hope he'll be happy, believe me. I've wanted nothing else ever since we split up. I'm more fond of him than you'll ever know.'

And she hung up.

I went to bed thoroughly miserable, wondering what the hell else was going to happen. Steve appearing, asking if Sally was up for another quick shag?

Lying on a pillow that smelt of John didn't help either; no, of course I hadn't changed the sheets. It smelt of clean male hair and Jacko's irresistible shower gel, though it smelt a damn sight more irresistible mixed with John. Just to torture myself further, I wriggled down and sniffed the sheets, too.

Why had I let myself lose my rag with Mum like that? Why did she have to make me feel guilty for upsetting her, even if it was her own fault, which it bloody sodding well was? Couldn't Rosie have given a purely encouraging bulletin for once? Why did John have to plaster his tantalizing scent all over my sheets, forcing me to imagine he was still there, minus both bug and pyjamas? Why did this delicious fantasy, which was no more than I deserved after all the aggro I'd had lately, have to be wrecked by imagining the bastard with someone else, only not in my bed, of course?

And thanks to Mum's ridiculous conjectures, I had nightmares, too. In glorious Technicolor I dreamt *Death on the Nile II*. I saw Hercule Poirot and Captain Hastings investigating the suspicious death of one David Grey, newly married to Kathy. I saw them at the Aswan High Dam, right down to Poirot's waxed moustaches.

'Yes, a tragedy *véritable*, 'Astings, *mon ami*. But I employ ze little grey cells. They were standing 'ere, yes, taking ze photos. And suddenly, *pouf*, Mr Grey is over ze barrier, falling to 'is death. Zere are conveniently no witnesses.'

'Dash it all, Poirot, you're not saying it was the *wife*? Seemed like a jolly decent girl to me. Dashed pretty, too. Crying her eyes out, poor thing.'

'Ah yes, my good 'Astings, but reflect. I 'ave 'ere a communication from ze bank manager in Basingstoke, to say zat Mrs Grey 'ad ze overdraft *énorme* and 'e 'ad to cut up 'er credit cards. *Voilà.* We 'ave a motive, *non?*'

I suppose there's a minor silver lining to nightmares; at least there's that blissful relief when you wake up. The way things were going, I was fully expecting to wake again at seven with a sore throat and shivery aches, but I went to work feeling fine.

318

My phone rang while I was on the train home.

'Oh, hi,' said a bored voice. 'It's Tara.'

Having done an instant vertical take-off in case it was somebody else, my spirits crash-landed into a mangled wreck just out of Parson's Green station.

'John gave me your number,' she went on, with the *Neighbours* signature tune in the background. 'I just thought I'd say thanks for having me the other day. I think I've left a black bra in William's room, but I'll get John to pick it up if he's passing.'

Would she, indeed. 'What have you been up to?'

'Not a lot. It's a lovely flat. A sunbed and everything. I tried it earlier – I've got a little bit of colour already.'

She sounded as if she were lying on a sofa, examining her nails and flicking through a magazine at the same time. 'Have you looked for a job yet?'

'Give me a chance! I did buy an *Evening Standard*, though – there are millions of jobs. Has my mum been on to you again?'

'Yes, but she just said she hoped you wouldn't turn the flat into a pigsty.'

'That is just so typical. Look, I'd better go – John said he'd pop in about now.'

Did he, indeed.

'At least *he* treats me like an adult,' she went on. 'We had a long talk last night, about my long-term career plans.'

'What are your long-term career plans?'

'Nothing to do with History A level, anyway. I've got to go, I think I just heard a key in the door.'

Great.

Before I'd even got off the train, I had a horrible smell in my nose, worse than Rosie's strawberry puke. It smelt of Mars bars, aka bruised little plums called Tara, suddenly faced with white knights. It smelt of white knights whose 'sorting out' talk had melted away once faced with pretty girls in tears. Who might well have started out with purely knightly motives, but who were, under the shining armour, but mortal men.

By the time I got home the smell had grown so strong, I was seeing Tara prancing around in a thong, saying, 'How d'you like my tan?' Even worse, in tears again, saying she must be hideously ugly or Lee would never have fancied that slag. And mortal man would melt again, and say, 'Tara, you're as lovely as the rosy-fingered dawn, come, let me stroke your hair and dry your little tears – oh, what the fuck . . .'

And the more I told myself he wouldn't, no matter how flirty or provocative she became, the more I saw the mortal bloke under the armour. In his defence, I argued that if he'd had anything like that even subconsciously in mind, he'd have taken her to his own place. Then the prosecuting counsel argued that of course he wouldn't, not if he was going to have Nina or assorted Mars bars coming round. Would they want a younger model draped over the sofa, showing them up? M'lud, I rest my case.

I was so wound up, it took me an hour to notice that Widdles hadn't come to greet me. He wasn't even on his throne. I looked upstairs in case he was on my bed, or on a pile of ironing he thought would be vastly improved by three thousand cat hairs, but there was no sign of him. I opened the back door and called, even though it was raining and he hated getting wet, but he didn't come. Then I opened the front door and called, but he didn't come.

Beginning to be worried, I walked up the road, calling him and praying not to see a bedraggled tabby corpse in the gutter. For a cat he had reasonable road sense or he'd never have lasted this long, but he was getting old and slow, and the road was something of a rat run.

I checked well beyond his usual range, calling all the way, but the only cat I saw was sitting in number seventy-three's window. When I got back, hoping he'd have come back in through his cat flap, I found only a mog-shaped indent in the sofa, his empty dishes, and silence.

Unearthing a torch, I went back outside. In the rain I checked every front garden in case he'd been injured and crawled under a shrub. What if he'd died already? What if someone had phoned the council's dead-cat department, to have him taken away? With a horrible feeling I was wasting my time, I started phoning local vets, in case some kind person had taken him there.

After three vets I gave up, and that was when John called.

'I hope you're not in bed with my bug,' he said.

'I told you, I hardly ever get bugs.'

'I can imagine,' he said, in drily amused tones. 'Any bug hoping to breach your defences would need to be armed to the teeth. Kalashnikovs and Semtex, at the very least.'

Well, thanks a lot. More 'harridan' stuff was all I needed just now.

'Have you spoken to Tara's folks?' he went on.

'Of course. Her mother said it's very good of you, but she's worried she won't be back in time for school.'

'I'm not surprised. She told me she's got her mocks coming up and the mere thought makes her want to yak up. She was talking of modelling. If you ask me, she's got some cloud-cuckoo-land notion of walking into an agency and earning ten thousand a day within weeks.'

'She's not tall enough!'

'I wouldn't know about that. I said it was a tough business, and she got upset and asked if I was politely trying to say she wasn't pretty enough.'

Almost worse than my imaginings. 'To be honest, John, I couldn't care less at the moment if she wants to do exotic dancing with a python. She's a spoilt brat.'

'Maybe, but she's had a bit of a rough time.'

'*Rough*?' I said, incensed. 'Have you any idea what kind of home she's come from? She's got her own bathroom, for God's sake! There's a tennis court in the garden! And she's worried her parents sick and couldn't give a toss!'

'Harriet, I know all that, but she's just a kid.'

'Not that much of a kid!' Hearing myself doing the snapping-turtle bit again, I tried to calm down. 'Look, I'm sorry – I've had rather a bad day. While you're there, could you give me your folks' address, for a thank-you letter?'

Having dictated that, he said, 'Did Tara give you her mobile number?'

'No.'

'Then I'll pass it on, in case of emergencies.'

'I thought she'd left her charger at home. Has she got hold of another?'

'No, I bought her another mobile.'

'You *what*?' I couldn't believe this. 'Don't you realize mobiles are like oxygen? You should have made her do without!'

'For God's sake, Harriet, I need to be able to contact her – the phone in the flat's disconnected. It's just one of those pay-as-you-go things and I only gave her twenty-five-quids' worth of calls.'

After I'd scribbled the number he said, 'Unless

anything earth-shattering happens, I'll call you in a couple of days, all right?'

'All right.'

After hanging up, I realized I hadn't even asked how he was.

Not that I cared. Did he care that I'd had a bad day? Of course not, when he was so busy caring about poor little Tara. Harridan Harriet was fine for making scrambled eggs and squeezing oranges, mashing sodding potatoes and changing sweaty sheets, but she could look after herself.

Sod him.

For the fourteenth time, my eyes wandered to the cat flap. I'd have given anything to see Widdles ooze fatly through it, with his 'Hi, I'm back' mew. At least he loved me.

Or used to love me, if he wasn't dead.

By the time Jacko phoned, all I could see was a pathetic little corpse under a bush. He was so upset for me, saying he wished he was there to give me a cuddle, that I got a bit weepy. So by the time he got around to my 'friend' with the flat, it had turned into something of a secondary issue. In between sniffing into a tissue I said things like, 'I don't think you ever met him, I hadn't seen him for a bit . . .' while hating myself for lying.

After saying well, good luck to him, he was buggered if he'd lend Tara a flat, he got onto other matters. 'Got your tiara polished for New Year's Eve?'

'Jacko, you surely don't want to come down here? What about all your mates?'

'They'll only be getting hammered down the pub. If I don't come, I bet you and Sal'll just stay in with crappy telly, being boring.'

In fact I'd had two invitations, but one was from an old friend now living in Perth (Australia), the other was from a ditto living in the wilder reaches of Kent, which meant a two-hour drive and a sleeping bag on her floor. 'If you're thinking random agency babysitters, forget it. Sally'd never leave Tom with a total stranger. She hates New Year's Eve anyway, remember?'

But Jacko had a Cunning Plan for getting even misery-guts Stretch Marks out for a bit of a knees-up: the Drunken Dragon, in shifts. Him and me, me and Sal, him and Sal. And the other one would babysit.

I thought it might just work, but suddenly had cold feet in case John turned up or phoned, and cans of worms were opened. So I said I wouldn't bother, she was such a misery-guts lately she probably wouldn't even do that.

The doorbell rang just as I was going to bed.

There was a sixtyish woman in a rain hat on the step. I didn't recognize her, but her arms were full of Widdles. 'Is he yours?' she asked anxiously.

'Yes – where on earth was he? I've been looking everywhere!'

'In one of my armchairs, I'm afraid, at number

fifty-nine. I'm so sorry, I did try to send him home earlier, but it was raining and he just wouldn't go. He does pop round now and then – I often have little nibbles left from dinner parties. You naughty boy, I *told* you, didn't I?' she added to Widdles, in doting-scold tones. 'I *told* you your mummy would be worried!'

Unmoved, the faithless beast jumped like a ton of lard to the floor and waddled kitchenwards.

'Quite a weight, isn't he?' the woman said brightly. 'I asked my husband to bring him, but he's got a bad back.'

I changed the John sheets before I went to bed, and then wished I hadn't. I told myself I'd be very nice when he phoned again, sympathetic about Tara, so he wouldn't think I was a cow. I told myself I'd be sparkly and amusing and warm and fascinating. And then I thought no, I wouldn't, I'd be merely pleasant and polite in a coolish sort of way. Sod him. Sod him and bugger him and fuck him.

And then I thought about that, too.

The doorbell rang again at ten to eight. Expecting the postman with something that wouldn't go through the letterbox, I found a boy on the step, looking embarrassed. About fifteen, he lived a few doors down.

'My mum asked me to bring these round,' he said. 'They came yesterday but you were out, so they brought them to our house. I tried to bring them last night, but you weren't in.'

'I was looking for my cat,' I said, feeling suddenly sick. 'Thank you.'

I shut the door and looked down at an armful of spring. Scented narcissi, hyacinths, freesias – I could almost have got drunk on the scent. God help me, what must he have thought when I didn't even say thank you?

Assuming it *was* him – what if they were from Tara's folks, as a thank you for having her? With dithery hands I tore the little envelope open.

The card read simply,

*Thank you,*

*John*

Well, what was I to make of that? I hadn't expected a *'love'*, but would *'Thanks so much for everything'* have been more encouraging? Was simplicity somehow more eloquent? Or had he just dictated the first suitable phrase with his credit-card number?

You can tell the kind of pathetic wreck I was turning into, agonizing over three words on a florist's card. I agonized more over what to say to him, but when I eventually phoned he wasn't answering, so I left a message:

'John, it's Harriet. Thanks so much for the flowers, I only just got them, they'd taken them to a neighbour and I was out last night looking for Widdles, he'd gone walkabout like Flora. Sorry if I was a bit ratty last night, but I was worried about Widdles. Thanks again for the flowers, they're really lovely but you shouldn't have. Bye.'

He phoned back when I was on the train home. 'Glad they turned up, I was beginning to wonder.'

'You can blame Widdles. He's found someone who gives him nice little leftovers from dinner parties. How are you feeling?'

'About ninety per cent, thanks.' He paused. 'I was going to give you a call anyway. Tara's got an interview lined up, with some modelling agency.'

'*Already*? I'd have thought they'd all be closed over the holiday.'

'It's not till the second. She's fizzing with it.'

'Her mother'll have a fit. I spoke to her earlier – she already had one fit when I mentioned modelling. She's read articles about models living off cocaine and air. And both her folks are getting worked up about her not coming back in time for school. She's got a place at Manchester, but she needs two Bs and a C.'

'The only thing in her head at the moment is this interview. I said I'd meet her afterwards for something to eat.'

On the second? Four days away? 'Won't you be seeing her till then?'

'I thought I'd leave her to her own devices for a few days. She's already complaining of being bored: nothing to do and no-one to do it with. So I said a job'd soon fix that – nothing like a workplace for meeting people.'

I had to hand it to him. At the same time I was beginning to feel really bad about my mortal-bloke imaginings.

'If you feel like coming, I could make it a table for three,' he went on. 'You'll be able to give her folks a first-hand report. Whatever the agency tells her, I thought this might be a good time to bring my Abu Dhabi friend back. Landing at, say, seven ten on the sixth might be good.'

I was beginning to wonder how I could ever have had mortal-bloke thoughts at all. What sort of jealous, suspicious cow was I turning into? 'Then she'll ask if she can stay with you for a bit, I bet. What will you say to that, Mr Fixit?'

'I'll think of something. Will you come?'

Wild elephants wouldn't stop me. Already I was buzzing at the mere thought of seeing him again. 'I could probably make it. Where?'

'I'll give you a call tomorrow.'

'Tomorrow' was the day before New Year's Eve. He gave the name of a Mexican place Tara had chosen, because she thought it looked cool. Then, although I'd promised myself I'd do no such thing, I said, 'Doing anything exciting tomorrow night?'

'Possibly even dangerous,' he said. 'I made a wild promise a couple of months ago to dust off my

329

sporran and skean-dhu. I think there might be a few bets on as to whether I go for orthodox Highland freestyle underneath. I might have to get drunk enough to do the lambada, but don't tell anybody. How about you?'

'Oh, out raving,' I said brightly. 'I might even get drunk enough to do the Birdie dance, but don't tell anybody that, either.'

He chuckled. 'Happy New Year, then. Have fun.'

'You, too.'

Shit. Dress kilt. Black velvet jacket with silver buttons. That frilly white shirt that ought to look poncey but somehow just looked gorgeous. Ravening hordes of champagne-soaked, giggling women trying to see up his kilt to check out his freestyle accessories. A black-tie do arranged weeks ago, which probably meant Nina in a slinky dress with her tits out, or someone else ditto. Almost certainly Nina, though; she must be back by now. I was dying to ring Rosie, but couldn't bring myself to in case she said, 'Oh, it was just Nina getting paranoid. He's taking her by helicopter to some seriously posh New Year ball in a castle.'

Sally came back that same evening, and if not exactly ratty, was quiet and twitchy. I made the mistake of telling her about Jacko's Drunken Dragon plan, and she said, 'Why did you tell him I'd turn my nose up? I'm not *that* much of a misery!'

So I phoned Jacko, but he was in bed, feeling

'like shite'. When I related this to Sally she commented, 'I bet you're just hungover,' into the phone, and he retorted, 'A hangover's *normal* shite! This is *shite* shite!'

Another one down with flu, then.

Our New Year's Eve wasn't exactly a bundle of laughs. Sally made a Thai green curry that went wrong, but we ate it anyway and watched some *Ally McBeal* Sally had taped. We had a good old bitch about how unbelievably annoying she was, followed by an interesting discussion about whether people only watched it because she *was* so unbelievably annoying, and whether the producers had planned this all along, or had realized later and were making her more annoying on purpose, because it was so good for the ratings.

And all the while I was watching the clock for midnight, thinking of Big Ben and 'Auld Lang Syne', and John kissing Nina, or some other cow with a four-inch cleavage he'd been drooling into all night. How I was going to last until the second, I could not imagine.

The restaurant was in Leicester Square, which didn't surprise me. Leicester Square was exactly the sort of place you'd gravitate towards if you were eighteen and new to London. It was the sort of place you'd long to go to when you were on a school trip to Tate Britain or the British Museum. You'd love the neon, the noisy, cheerful buzz, the total lack of anything even pretending to be cultural. You'd love the crowds, the stalls full of tacky Union Jack souvenirs and the smell of fast food, especially after that sensible packed lunch your mother had provided as requested by Miss Whitton, Deputy Head of Art.

I arrived a few minutes early. The restaurant was cheerfully buzzing too, in a 'Mexican' way. It was all done in sand-coloured mock stone, with lots of ceramic tiles, huge terracotta pots, big fake plants and salsa music playing.

John was there already, in a dimly lit corner, on his own. He didn't look bad for a man who'd been prostrate with flu only days ago. I wouldn't have said he looked exactly bushy-tailed either, but only a head transplant from a warthog would have stopped my heart and stomach doing a drunken little *pas de deux* when I saw him.

Especially when he looked up with a little smile. Even more when he stood up and kissed me. All right, it was just a quick brushing of lips on cheek, but such morsels can be almost orgasmic when you're obsessed. I loved that fleeting roughness of his cheek. Ditto that tantalizing waft of shaving stuff, clean hair and shirt. Someone should bottle it, to aid the pathetic fantasies of obsessed wrecks like me.

'How's it going?' he asked.

'Oh, brilliant,' I said, in a sparkly, non-wreck fashion, sitting opposite him. 'Apart from the fact that

332

my father's about to marry this Kathy and my mother thinks she's planning to drown him in the Nile.'

He started laughing, but Tara had just arrived.

I saw at once that she was underwhelmed with joy to see me. She said, 'Hi, yes, he said you might be coming too,' in a tone that said . . . *and I suppose I'll just have to put up with it.*

'So how did it go?' John asked, as she sat next to him.

'Pretty good,' she said, perking up a bit. 'They said I had good potential but I'll need to get a portfolio done first.'

'Have they recommended a photographer?' I asked.

'No, but there are millions of photographers.'

'How much will that cost?' John asked.

She shrugged. 'About a hundred and fifty quid.'

John shot me a tiny, conspiratorial little wink that did possibly illegal things to my vital organs. Casually he said to Tara, 'How are you planning to get hold of a hundred and fifty quid, then?'

'A job, of course. I'll have to save up.'

He gave me another little glance, raising his eyebrows minutely, but just said, 'Shall we look at these menus?'

After we'd ordered (tortillas and fajitas, plus beer for him, Coke for her and a margarita for me), John turned to Tara. 'Have you done anything on the job front?'

'Give me a chance!'

'Well, you'd better get your skates on. My Abu Dhabi friend e-mailed me this morning. I'm afraid he's coming back on the eighth.'

I hadn't expected him to come out with it so quickly, nor so briskly. Her face lost about thirty per cent of its perk instantly, but regained most of it almost at once. 'I could stay with you for a bit.'

'I don't think so, sweetheart.'

'Why not?'

'I work a lot at home. You'd distract me.'

Far from deflating Tara, this only seemed to encourage her. 'I'd be very good,' she said, in tones that managed to be simultaneously demure and pertly flirty.

I realized that at least half my imaginings had been spot on. She'd worked him into some fantasy romantic hero who'd fallen for her instantly but wasn't admitting it because he'd feel like a dirty old man. However, by chapter ten his high-minded scruples would be overcome by his latent seething passion, plus her towel conveniently falling off just as he burst into the bathroom by mistake.

'Tara, it's just not on,' he said, a good deal more firmly.

All the sympathy I hadn't felt for her suddenly came upon me in a rush. If he'd intended to crush her, he'd certainly succeeded. Mortified, she looked down at her place mat. I could have sworn I even saw her eyes well up.

I felt for her. I really did.

A waiter brought our drinks. Once he'd gone John said in kinder tones, 'Tara, I'm not sure you've really thought this through. Have you any idea, first, of what it costs to live anywhere in London, and second, what you might expect to earn in the kind of job you're likely to get?'

'I'm not stupid,' she said, with a return of the defiance I'd seen that first night. 'I know it's not cheap.'

'It's horrifically expensive. You'll be hard pushed to find a shoebox to live in and eat, let alone save a hundred and fifty quid.'

'Other people manage,' she said.

'Most people your age are still living at home,' he said. 'Which is a bloody sight cheaper, even if you're paying your folks something. You'd save your hundred and fifty quid a lot faster if you went home.'

'I'm not – going – home!'

John wasn't even mildly taken aback; it was as if he'd been testing the water one last time. 'OK, OK,' he soothed.

'I could get a job in a hotel,' she said doggedly. 'A live-in job.'

This was where I stepped in. 'Tara, hardly any hotels have live-in jobs any more, not in London, anyway. Rates are so sky-high, they're hardly going to waste even titchy rooms on unskilled staff.'

'Then I'll find something else, OK?'

For a few minutes John and I talked inconsequential rubbish, while Tara sat silent. Eventually, though, she looked over her shoulder. 'Where's that *food*? I'm starving!'

'They're rushed off their feet,' I said, glad of a diversion. Not far away an irate waiter was saying in heated Spanish to another ditto that no, he was not doing table twenty-eight, he was up to his testicles.

'Maybe your folks will sub you that hundred and fifty,' John said, in tones that sounded like devious guile masquerading as innocence.

'I'm not asking *them*,' she said obstinately. 'I'll get it myself.'

The food arrived at last: colossal, American-style quantities on yard-wide plates. Tara got stuck into her fajitas as if she were about to go on a crash diet for a month. Which maybe she was. Maybe that agency had told her she didn't look anorexic enough.

I caught John's eye but he only raised his eyebrows in a way that could have meant anything, e.g. 'Nothing wrong with her appetite, then', or 'So far so good'.

Tara's eyes remained firmly on her food, but I could have sworn I saw her eyes welling again. She was keeping it back through sheer effort of will. Feeling for her more than I ever had, I said, 'You could come back to me for a bit.'

'No, thanks,' she said, as if I'd offered a nice cup of poison. 'I'll sort myself out.'

After what could barely have been ten minutes,

having shovelled most of her food down, she mumbled, 'I'm going to the loo,' grabbed her little rucksack, and departed.

Once she'd gone, John's eyes met mine across the table.

'She's upset,' I said. 'If you ask me, she was doing her damnedest not to cry.'

'Oh, shit,' he muttered, running a hand awkwardly over the back of his neck. 'I didn't want it to come to this.'

I realized then that he knew exactly what had been going through Tara's head.

'She'd somehow got the wrong idea,' he went on, in wryly apologetic tones. 'I've been trying to ignore the signs in a "tactful" manner, but maybe I've been too tactful.'

'It's not easy,' I said, wondering just what the signs had been. Very obvious body language, probably, that she fondly imagined was subtle.

'No, but I didn't want to be brutal.'

His eyes were suddenly so warm, so utterly nice-bloke-ish, I had to finish my margarita to fortify myself. 'You weren't exactly brutal.'

'That's how it came across. After Lee I think she's what they call emotionally bruised. She'd have latched onto just about anyone.'

I wasn't so sure about 'anyone'. 'You were sympathetic,' I pointed out. 'She was in what she saw as dire straits, and you helped her.'

'And as you said, I should have kept my nose out.'

'You were only trying to help.' I was getting so gooey by this point, I nearly put my hand across the table to take his.

'The balance of my mind was temporarily disturbed,' he said, looking me right in the eye.

'Probably,' I said lightly. 'Maybe you were under the influence of drugs. All that Panadol and industrial-strength cough stuff . . .'

'I was certainly under the influence of something.'

Something in the way he said it made my heart turn over. Suddenly my vibe sensors were back on red alert. 'Meaningful eye contact!' they were screaming. 'Undertones!'

But a millisecond later he was only eyeing my empty glass. 'Another margarita? Or something else?'

I glanced at the drinks list, and then wished I hadn't. Restaurants should be banned from putting things like 'Sloe Comfortable Screw' and 'Screaming Orgasm' on their cocktail menus when people like me are trying to cope with overdoses of flutters in a public place.

However, I managed to say, 'Yes, same again, please,' as if I weren't thinking a 'Sex on the Beach' would go down very nicely, too.

'Was that why you invited me along?' I went on, in semi-jokey tones. 'Because you needed a chaperone?'

His mouth quivered. 'How did you guess? I couldn't

possibly fend off an eighteen-year-old with half a litre of Coke inside her. I've led a very sheltered life.'

'Yes, I can tell,' I said, and his mouth quivered again, but he said nothing.

Maybe it was time for a change of subject. 'So where do we go from here?' I went on. 'Not that it's your problem. If she really won't go home or come back to me, I suppose her folks might sub her for a bit and I can pretend it's from me. She didn't seem quite as excited as I'd have thought over the modelling, though. Maybe they told her she was but one of thousands, all thinking they're the next Jodie Kidd. If they'd been really positive, she'd have been bubbling with it.'

'That's what I thought. And she'd have asked me to sub her that hundred and fifty.'

'She still might, once I'm out of the way.'

'Possibly, but I bet you she won't.'

More and more I was thinking this must be right. 'She'd never have admitted they'd turned her down, would she? Maybe they told her she'd only get minor stuff, catalogues and so on.'

'Maybe.'

After a moment he added, 'So how's the junk-sorting going?'

I'd forgotten the junk. 'I haven't done much lately,' I said, which was a joke, as I hadn't touched it for weeks. 'I've had other things on my mind.'

'I can imagine.' Again he looked me in the eye, and again my heart and stomach did a drunken little salsa together. 'Like your friend next door, and your old man's not-so-blushing bride.'

'Not to mention Tara,' I said lightly, but my eyes were probably saying *Not to mention you*. After one and a half margaritas they tend to say what the hell they like.

Or maybe not. Almost immediately he was nodding at my plate. 'If you're not going to eat the rest of that tortilla, pass it over.'

Entirely typical, wasn't it? My stomach doing Latin American dancing, his merely thinking of food. There was probably a whole section to that effect in *Women Are From Venus, Men Are Basically Just Greedy Buggers*.

After a few reflective chews, however, he stopped. And as our eyes converged again, I knew exactly what he was going to say.

'Maybe you'd better go and check on Tara. She's being a hell of a long time.'

'I'm not sure she'll want me checking. She's probably been having a little weep and trying to get rid of the evidence.'

'Now you're really making me feel bad.'

'Look, I'll go. I'll pretend I was going anyway.'

I hurried to the *Señoras*, which of course was in the furthest opposite corner from where we were sitting. There were three cubicles, a queue of six, and a couple of girls standing at the mirrors. I stood hesitantly a moment, before calling 'Tara?'

There was no reply.

'Tara, are you all right?'

Again there was no reply. A girl in the queue said, 'Someone's been in there for ages.' She nodded towards the furthest cubicle. 'Hope it's not some-one ill.'

Or crying her eyes out in private.

Feeling suddenly awful, I tapped on the door. 'Tara? Are you all right?'

'Do you mind?' said an irate voice. 'God, you can't even be egg-bound in peace any more.'

'Sorry,' I said, while the queue cracked up. Almost immediately, the doors of the other two cubicles opened.

Neither woman was Tara. Thinking I'd somehow missed her en route, I went back.

John raised an eyebrow. 'Repairing her make-up?'

'She's not there!'

His expression sharpened. 'She must be!'

'She isn't!' I gaped around the restaurant, just in case she'd somehow got into conversation with somebody, but I knew I was wasting my time.

My eyes swivelled back to John, who was already on his feet.

'Oh, Christ,' he said. 'She's done a runner. I'll get the bill.'

# TWELVE

But it was I who grabbed a passing waiter. I told him in Spanish that we had an *emergencia*; if he brought our bill in two seconds I'd give him a massive tip.

'We must be bloody stupid,' John muttered, as we waited.

He took the words right out of my head. She'd still had her jacket on. She'd had her bag over her shoulder. She'd shovelled that food down as if she wasn't expecting another square meal for days. 'She'll be heading back to the flat, first, to get her things.'

'Obviously.'

The waiter came back in a miraculous thirty seconds. I thrust various notes at him, thirteen quid over the odds, and John didn't argue.

'Have you got wheels?' I asked, as we exited.

'No, and just as well; the traffic'll be a bitch. It'll be quicker on the underground.' As we hurried through the crowds in cold, mist-like drizzle, he glanced at his watch. 'She can't have got much of a start. We should catch her.'

'Where the hell can she be thinking of going?' I asked, as we passed a scruffy bundle of humanity huddled in a doorway.

'God knows.'

We shouldered our way through dithering crowds at the barrier and reached the escalator, pushing past tourists who didn't understand Stand on the Right signs.

He said nothing as we hurried through tunnels to the trains, but I knew he was thinking much the same as me. He was thinking of just what type of person a naïve girl with hardly any money, who thought she knew it all, might meet, wandering on her own with a backpack. Of her disappearing into this vast city, with all its seedy little holes where a girl might hide. Then I thought of the really dark, vice-ridden holes she might fall into, and wondered what on earth I was going to tell her parents. Then I cursed myself for saying she could stay in the first place. She wasn't my responsibility, for God's sake.

Still less was she John's. As we waited on the platform in more heaving crowds I said, 'I'm sorry I landed you with all this.'

'You didn't land me. I didn't have to get involved.'

But he had. And now, like me, he felt responsible. Like me, he was imagining her falling into vice-ridden holes. When he was busy and had just been ill, and could do without it. *I* could do without it. I was twenty-nine, not a middle-aged parent. I had an adolescent father to worry about.

A noisy rush announced that the train was coming.

'Look, in the circumstances, maybe I should go on my own,' he said suddenly. 'If I'd handled the situation better, she wouldn't have gone.'

'It's not your fault!'

'All right, but I'll deal with it myself. Go home,' he added, as the train whooshed out of the tunnel. 'I'll call you later.'

As I'd expected, Sally had little sympathy. 'Attention-seeking,' she remarked acidly. 'She knew he'd go after her, didn't she? And he did. Without you, which was exactly what she wanted.'

'Yes, but I did feel sorry for her. She was really upset.'

'Oh, stuff her. He'll have found her back at the flat, I bet, and she'll be putting the tears on again and secretly smiling like a little Cheshire cat.'

I wasn't so sure. I was even less sure when nine o'clock came, and ten, and he still hadn't phoned.

Eventually, at ten past eleven, he did.

He sounded raggedly up to here. 'I found her two hundred yards down the road from the flat, heading for the main road with her stuff.'

'And?'

'I asked where the hell she was going, and she told me to piss off, what the hell did I care?'

'Jesus. Then what?'

'I said suit yourself, then, I'd had enough.'

'No, you didn't.'

'No, but I felt like it. I'd run from the station in the rain and found the flat empty.'

'Where on earth was she going?'

'She was planning to hitch to Colchester. Some ex-schoolfriend moved there a year ago. She didn't even know what road to take.'

'What did you do?'

'Told her to phone the friend first. And when she did, the friend said she couldn't have her anyway, there wasn't room. Eventually I got her back to the flat and square one. I told her I'd sort something out, but Christ knows what.'

'You sound exhausted,' I said.

'I am.'

'It'll be aftershocks. Flu does that to you.'

'Yes, I'm finding that out the hard way. Look, I'll call you tomorrow – I've got to hit the hay.'

'If he's just had the flu, he can do without all that,' Lesley said firmly, next morning.

This was a paraphrase of what I'd just been saying. I'd told them the gist, while not going into detail about John.

'I'd have her back with me for a bit, but I know she won't come,' I said.

Oddly enough, it was Sandie who came up with a possibility. Her sister's friend Rachel had a room spare, because Rachel's supposed friend and sharer Jo had gone off to Cardiff, taking both Rachel's best pink snakeskin boots and her boyfriend, Dan. It was a pretty grotty house in a pretty grotty area, the burglars were regulars by now, practically said 'Hi' and made themselves cups of tea, but it was really cheap.

I seized on this like a lifeline. Just before leaving the office I even managed to phone Rachel, and got the address.

I phoned Tara as soon as I got home.

'Thanks, but John's found me somewhere to live,' she said, in her former bored tones. 'And a job thrown in.'

I was gobsmacked. 'Already?'

'He's got a friend who manages some flash country club in Wiltshire or somewhere,' she went on. 'I can live in. It's got a health club and gym and everything. He's going to take me down on Saturday.'

It was no earthly use pushing Rachel's grotty house now, but I was mad that he'd sorted it when I'd been trying to sort it, to save him the trouble. Biting back everything I wanted to say, I forced a smile into my voice. 'Brilliant. What exactly will you be doing?'

'Whatever,' she said, with a shrug in her voice. 'Bar, waitress stuff . . .'

With no experience? I thought. In a smart country club? 'I hope you'll at least tell your folks where you're going.'

'I will! It's a seriously flash place, you know. They get stacks of celebrities. Even film crews on shoots.'

Suddenly her voice held a thread of excitement and

it didn't take a genius to figure out why. She saw her-self waitressing, in a short black skirt. She saw herself serving some Merchant Ivory director, currently shooting a costume drama in the quaint English countryside. She saw him eyeing her up as she dished out his pan-fried monkfish, saying, 'Honey, you're wasted here. How would you like a part in my movie? Gwyneth Paltrow's just gone sick.'

She bounced back, I'd say that for her. 'Well, good luck,' I said brightly. 'Mind you don't slosh hot soup in any celebrity laps.'

John phoned forty minutes later.

'Yes, I heard,' I said, as he started to tell me. 'Why the hell didn't you phone me first? *I'd* found her somewhere to stay – a nice grotty place with hot and cold running burglars – perfect for making her miss her own en suite bathroom. Why a flash country club, anyway? Wouldn't a crummy dive in Paddington have been more appropriate?'

'I don't know anyone who manages crummy dives in Paddington!'

Well, of course not. 'Never mind film crews! You know what's going through her head already, don't you? She's going to be "discovered". She's going to end up in Hollywood, sticking two fingers up at everybody.'

'She won't last a week,' he said.

'Are you kidding? She's seeing wall to wall *Hello!* types and Leonardo DiCaprio popping in for—'

'Harriet, I know what she's seeing. Will you give me credit for a little intelligence?'

A little intelligence was precisely what I'd just been lacking. Mentally whacking myself on the forehead I went, *Dhuurr!* 'You've built it right up, haven't you? So it'll be a massive let-down?'

'Not exactly. It is pretty flash and they do get the odd celebrity, but she won't get anywhere near them.'

I was catching on fast. The kitchen, probably. Scraping plates into bins and other scullery-maid stuff. 'You're a pretty devious so-and-so, aren't you?'

'Now and then. If it's going to get a result. If it doesn't, I go to plan B.'

'And what's that?'

'Trying again,' he said. 'Or giving up, depending on the stakes.'

I tried not to think of other applications for this strategy. 'And does this friend of yours actually need any unskilled staff at the moment?'

'Of course not. It's back to low season.'

A favour between friends, then. 'And you've agreed to pay her wages, I suppose? How much?'

When he didn't answer immediately I went on, 'John, I can't have you shelling out!'

'I can shell peanuts. Pretty miserable peanuts at that.'

'That's not the point! Let me pay it.'

'All right, we'll split it. I haven't got the energy for arguments.'

348

Since he was still probably suffering from post-bug fatigue, this made me feel bad. 'I know she won't be thrilled at the idea, but I could drive Tara down.'

'No, I said I'd take her, but thanks for the offer.'

'How far is it?'

'A couple of hours.'

Each way. Not exactly a killer, but more than enough.

'But I was going to ask you to come along for the ride,' he went on.

My heart did another vertical take-off. It was getting quite good at them lately. 'More chaperone stuff?'

'No, I think I hit that one on the head. I thought you could keep me awake on the way back. I have to go away on the Sunday morning, so I'll probably be knackered after catching up with the work I should have been doing last night.'

This was a dampener, but not enough for a crash landing.

'So can you make it?' he asked.

'I should think so. I can't have you falling asleep on the way back. You might splat a poor little hedgehog. I'd never forgive myself.'

'Hedgehogs are hibernating,' he tutted. 'But I might splat a poor little bunny. I've been known to splat bunnies even when I'm awake.'

'Not on purpose, I hope.'

'Harriet, do I strike you as a malicious bunny-splatterer?'

'No, just checking. I could drive, if you like. Then you could put your seat back and snore all the way home.'

'You never know, I just might. I'll pick you up about three, all right?'

I wasn't looking forward to passing on this latest development, but Mrs Jacques had already heard from Tara herself. 'I just hope she'll come to her senses before school starts,' she said, in resigned tones. 'But I'm beginning to doubt it.'

'Are you sure there's nothing else?' I asked. 'Apart from not wanting to lose face over Lee, I mean?'

'I really can't think of anything. I have a feeling she did fall out with someone at school – I think it might even have been over Lee – but I can't think it's that.'

'It's possible.' Even worse than having your parents say 'I told you so' was some ex-friend crowing that your grand passion had gone sour. On the other hand, Tara didn't strike me as the type to be crowed over.

'I did try to talk to her,' she went on. 'It was so good of your friend to get her that phone, by the way – do please tell him we'll settle up soon – but she only went all cross and prickly again. I'm beginning to think she'd rather go anywhere than come home. Anyone would think Dick and I were a pair of Victorian ogres.'

Half an hour after she'd hung up, Frida was on the phone. 'D'you want picking up from the airport?' I asked, as she was due back the next day.

'I cancelled my ticket. I had a big fight with Erik. He said if you go back that's it, finish. So I said OK, go and boil your big fat head.'

'But you're staying anyway?'

'Of course.' Her voice took on a mischievous note. 'He went to the travel agent. Two weeks in Jamaica. So I think I love him again, because he is paying. I'll come for a weekend soon, though, to see you all and get my stuff. Maybe I'll bring Erik, too. If he has enough Aquavit he will let you feel his muscles.'

Somehow I'd half expected it, but I was still deflated. 'Jacko, Frida – this house is going to feel horribly empty,' I said to Sally.

'Don't tell me. I'm almost missing Ape-Face already. I've only got you to bitch at now, and you don't even nick my squirty cream.'

Straight after getting home on Friday evening I decamped to the bathroom and indulged in what magazines laughingly call 'pampering yourself'. Personally I call it sheer hard work: face mask, manicure, pedicure, exfoliating everything and stinking out the bathroom with hair remover. All this was purely because I was long overdue for such treatments, of course: nothing to do with the fact that I was going to be spending two hours alone with John the following day.

Rosie turned up around half seven, just as I was descending the stairs in Jacko's tartan dressing gown and a green face. 'Flease, don't nake ne laugh,' I said, through a faceful of rapidly drying Mud and Cucumber. 'I'll crack it.'

'Got a hot date?' she grinned, doing her best not to crack her own face.

'I uish.' I took her into the sitting room, which was warm for once. Sick of sitting in the kitchen like a pair of below-stairs domestics, Sally and I had raked out the ashes like another pair of below-stairs domestics and got a fire going.

I charged upstairs and washed my Mud and Cucumber off. When I came down, Rosie was sitting on the sofa, with Tom on her lap.

'So what have you been up to?' I asked.

'Not a lot, apart from work,' she said, in between cootchy-cooing at Tom. 'Mind you, I'm making some really good commission. What did you get from Father Christmas, then?' (This was to Tom, in a voice half an octave higher.)

'Too much,' Sally said. 'I think I might flog some of it. Or swop it for a high chair.'

'You can't! She can't, can she, mean old Mummy?' Then she turned to me. 'Suzanne's friend's come back early from India. She got some awful bug or something. Had to be on a drip. She's with her folks for now, recuperating, but she's going to want her room back so I've got to find somewhere else sharpish.'

'There's always here,' I said.

'I know, thanks a lot. But I guess I should find something more permanent if you're selling soon, or I'll only be putting it off. Have you looked at any flats yet?'

I'd told her I'd probably be buying. 'Not yet.'

'You should get a garden flat. Great for barbies in the summer. And for Tom to play in, of course.'

Sally made an *Oh, Lord* face. 'Rosie, I won't be living with Harriet.'

'Won't you?' She looked startled. 'Why not?'

'Because I'm going home. To do a PGCE.'

I was dumbfounded. 'Since when?' I gaped.

'I've been thinking about it for ages,' she said, almost defensively. 'I discussed it with Mum and Dad over Christmas.'

'Teacher training?' Rosie asked. 'Won't that take years?'

'*One* year. I've already got a degree.'

I still couldn't take it in. 'You always said you'd never teach!'

'Harriet, what the hell else have I been doing for the past seven years?'

'Yes, but that's adults! *Motivated* adults! You always said you could never hack kids!'

'I know, but I wouldn't mind little kids. Tom's going to be a little kid soon, isn't he? I'm bound to understand them better. And it'll fit with school holidays and all that. Don't look at me like that,' she added. 'My mind's made up.'

'Your mother'll drive you mad!' I said.

'I'll just have to put up with it. They offered to have me; they weren't obliged to. Mum even offered to do some of the babysitting.'

'You could do a PGCE here!'

'I couldn't possibly afford it. Even with a grant, how could I do a full-time course and pay baby-minders and rent and everything? I'm doing it for Tom, not me,' she went on doggedly. 'I didn't give him a very brilliant start, but I'm damned if he's going to suffer for it.'

From bitter experience I knew that once Sally had made her mind up, you might as well ask the sun whether setting in the east mightn't make a nice change.

'At least I'll know what I'm talking about when I go to Tom's parents' evenings,' she went on. 'He'll be at school before you know it. I've got to think of him.'

I knew she was right. I knew it was the sensible, practical course, but somehow it depressed me to think of Sally being sensible and practical. It felt too much like growing up, a thing we'd both been putting off for ever if it meant permanent jobs and mortgages.

Suddenly I felt bereft. Jacko, Frida, Sally . . . 'When will you go?'

'At Easter. I'm committed to these adult classes till then. I've already spoken to a college near home,' she went on. 'I've left it a bit late, but they're going to contact me about an interview.'

And she hadn't even told me. 'You'll be a horrible teacher,' I said, trying to make a wan joke of it. 'All the poor little kids'll be scared of you. You'll make them all sit in the naughty corner.'

'I shall be Miss Perfect,' she said. 'And they'll all love me, the little buggers, or they won't get any gold stars.'

I spent the next hour in a sort of shell-shocked daze, while Sally and Rosie did most of the nattering. In fact I left them to natter while I went and made some pasta with tomato sauce and mozzarella, as Rosie hadn't eaten either. We washed this down with robust Tesco's red and were getting stuck into some chocolate-chip Häagen-Dazs, when Rosie suddenly said, 'Gosh, I nearly forgot!'

'What?' I said.

'Helicopter dumped Nina!'

My heart did a perfect backflip. 'Oh, really?' I said casually, avoiding Sally's eye. 'When was that, then?'

'Just after she got back from Aspen, but Suzanne only found out the other day. She said she felt a bit sorry for her, actually. Up to here with her too, though. Nina's really convinced he's got someone else now. She was ranting and raving, apparently, demanding to know who it was. He said there wasn't anyone, how many times did he have to say it, but she's not buying it. Suzanne said she can't accept that any bloke can just go off her. There has to be some poisonous slag of a Jezebel, enticing him away with her fiendish wiles. Takes one to suspect one, that's what I say. I bet she's done it enough times.'

'Well, maybe there is a Jezebel,' Sally said deadpan.

'Yes, that's what Suzanne said afterwards. I mean, he'd hardly *tell* her – she'd go round and stick dog pooh through the poor girl's letterbox or something. Mind you, I wasn't supposed to tell anybody any of this,' Rosie went on. 'Suzanne'd kill me. The official line is that she dumped *him*. The other way around doesn't suit Nina's image.'

That figured.

It was half eleven before Rosie left. Once the door had shut behind her Sally said, 'Well, hallelujah. All hail to the queen of the jungle telegraph.'

'I felt as if my numbers had come up on the lottery,' I confessed. 'Did it show?'

'Not unless you were looking for it.' She gave me one of her shrewd-and-searching looks. 'It's not just buzz, is it? You really like him.'

That depended on how you defined 'like'. If you counted total obsession, besottedness and almost thinking it might be nice to iron his shirts, I suppose 'like' might do. Not that I mentioned shirts to Sally; I just nodded.

She made her *I knew it* face. 'I knew it. I could tell.'

'I feel a bit bad now,' I confessed. 'Sometimes I'd look at him and think, yes, you're a smootharse *extraordinaire*, and all the time he was only telling the truth when he said it wasn't going anywhere with Nina.'

'Well, he took his time about it. How were you to know, anyway? The jungle's thick underfoot with two-timing reptiles, and I should know. Three- and four-timing, too. And I hate to do the cold shower bit, but how do you know he hasn't got a couple of hot options open?'

'He hasn't. I'm sure.' I was, now.

'Just watch yourself, that's all. I'd hate you to get hurt.' Less grudgingly she added, 'Still, enjoy your little pink cloud. At least you can dream of him tonight with a clear conscience.'

I had a nice little fantasy shaping up already. The car would break down on the way back and he'd ask whether I could take my tights off for an emergency fan belt. So I'd have to take my trousers off first – I'd better make sure I was wearing trousers – and it wouldn't work anyway, because it wouldn't be the fan belt after all, but the turbo-compressor-manifold thing, and he'd phone the RAC, who'd say they couldn't come for at least four hours, so could we just sit tight and hang on . . .

A pretty piquant start, you have to admit.

'Why the hell didn't you tell me about this PGCE?' I said, as we went back to the dying fire.

'I was going to, but I knew you'd only say I was mad.'

'I wouldn't!'

'You just did!'

'Only because it was such a shock!' I paused. 'And the thought of you turning into a proper, grown-up alien.'

'Harriet, I'm nearly twenty-nine. I'm a mother, for God's sake. It's about time I grew up.' She was sitting on the end of the sofa, looking into the fire. 'Tom's only got me. If I don't do my best for him . . .'

There was suddenly a crack in her voice. She looked at me, her eyes misting. 'What if something happened to me?'

I was appalled. 'Nothing's going to happen to you!'

'It might! If it did, would you have him?'

I couldn't believe she was saying this.

'Harriet, I need to know,' she went on, almost desperately. 'I know you love him, I haven't got any brothers or sisters, and Mum and Dad are too old and pernickety – they'd never cope. What if he got taken into care?'

Suddenly I realized that this must have been on her mind for ages. 'Of course I'd have him! But nothing's going to happen to you!'

'It might! OK, I know it's not likely, but people get run over and murdered every day.'

She was suddenly calmer, though, as if it were a massive weight off her mind. I was about to say, 'You've written Steve off, haven't you?' but bit it back. I already knew the answer.

*    *    *

358

John arrived twenty minutes late the following afternoon and I let Sally answer the door. It would have been cruel not to; she was dying to check him out.

Lurking in the kitchen, inspecting the kind of make-up that's supposed to look as if you're not wearing any, I listened to 'Hello, you must be Sally,' and so on. I then sauntered through the hall as if I hadn't been bursting with anticipation all day, checking four times that I had a toothbrush for pre-snog situations.

I'd known it'd feel different, seeing him this time, but I hadn't realized just how different. It was as if I'd been looking at him through cynic-coloured glasses, and had now found the rosy ones. In fact it was a job not to charge straight at him, throw my arms around his neck and cry, 'Oh, thank you, thank you, for doing it at last.'

But it can't have shown, as he was disappointingly businesslike. 'Sorry, we're running a bit late,' he said, with a glance at his watch. He added a lopsided little smile, though, which was better than nothing.

I gave him one back. 'That's OK. I'm not in any rush.'

He gave me a brief up and down glance. If you're interested, I was wearing new grey flannel trousers of the smart-casual type, short black boots, and a black roll-neck sweater of the casual-casual type. No jewellery, nothing that looked remotely tarted up.

I was giving him a once-over, too. He'd pinched my colour scheme. In fact, he was wearing exactly the same as he'd been wearing that first day: black polo shirt, dark grey jacket and lighter trousers. It seemed oddly apt, as if we were starting again. Back to 'Go', with ladders, but no snakes.

All he said was, 'Ready?'

'Yep. See you later,' I added to Sally, who was behaving perfectly, as if he were just any common-or-garden bloke. She didn't even give me a conspiratorial *See what you mean!* look, but that was probably because I'd said I'd kill her if she did. Such looks are apt to be caught by the wrong person.

Evidently someone was having a party; he'd had to park about ten houses down. It had gone really cold again. We walked past cars with ice on their windscreens, which was unusual at this time of day.

On the way, I told him what Tara's mother had said. 'If it *was* over Lee, it's possible that she can't face the crowing.'

'It can't be that. She's got a fair old mouth on her; she'd give as good as she got.'

We couldn't discuss it any further, as we'd reached the car. Tara was in the front seat, trying not to look put out that I was coming along.

'Are you all excited?' I asked, as he headed for the main road.

'Not particularly,' she said, with a shrug in her voice.

Probably more apprehensive, I thought. A new environment, jobs she'd never done . . . Her hair was up, twisted into a scrunchie with wispy bits hanging out. It made her look older, probably by design.

'Bloody miserable weather,' John grunted, switching on the wipers as a few drops of rain started to fall.

'The weathermen have forecast snow,' I said.

'Expect a heatwave, then. I should have had my air conditioner serviced.'

'Where are you off to tomorrow?' I asked.

'Sofia.'

'Where on earth's that?' Tara asked.

'Bulgaria. I take it you weren't doing A level Geography?'

'No, thanks. English and History and Economics were horrible enough.'

'What time's your flight?' I asked him.

'Twelve-ish.'

'Why didn't you book it for Monday morning?'

'I have a meeting first thing on Monday. Next question?'

It was a while before anybody spoke again, but once we'd hit the M3 Tara said, 'Is there an indoor pool at this place?'

'Probably,' he said. 'Why?'

'I could do pool duty,' she said. 'I'm a qualified lifeguard. I've got experience.'

Recalling what Jacko had said about her two whole days, I had to admire her nerve.

'And I've never done bar or restaurant stuff,' she went on.

'I wouldn't worry about that,' he said. 'I doubt you'll be seeing much of bars or restaurants.'

'Then what will I be doing?'

'Whatever unskilled staff do in hotels,' he said casually. 'Making beds, kitchen stuff . . .'

'*Kitchen* stuff?' She sounded horrified.

He gave a little shrug. 'With no track record you can't expect to walk into a place like that and pick and choose. We're not talking McDonald's here.'

In the appalled silence that followed, I realized just how devious a devil he could be. Having let her think there was going to be some element of glamour, he was letting her down hard.

'But you don't have to go,' he went on. 'We can head back now and I'll tell them you've got the flu.'

'But then I'll have to find another job,' she said, in a subdued voice. 'And somewhere to live.'

'That's the downside, I guess.' He paused. 'Well? Shall I do a U-turn?'

'No,' she said quickly. 'I don't mind working in kitchens.'

After another five minutes' silence, I said, 'Which way are you going?'

'M3, A303,' he said. 'After that I'll have to consult my directions.'

'Haven't you been before?'

'No. Gisela hasn't been there long.'

'*Geez*ler?' Tara echoed. 'What sort of a name's that?'

'G-I-S-E-L-A,' he spelt. 'She's Swiss.'

There was a taken-aback silence. 'You mean *she's* the manager?'

'Yes.'

'I thought it was a bloke!'

'Really, Tara,' he tutted. 'For a kid your age, that was a very sexist assumption.'

'I didn't mean that! I just assumed your *friend* was a bloke!'

So had I; I don't quite know why. But I realized at once that this had skewed Tara's ideas drastically. She'd been imagining someone like John, someone vaguely indulgent to a pretty eighteen-year-old.

'What's she like?' she asked, in a voice that said she already suspected the answer.

'A pretty tough cookie,' he said, in matter-of-fact tones. 'But I don't suppose you'll be seeing much of Gisela. You'll be under her underlings. Or her under-underlings.'

Almost smelling apprehension coming off Tara, I felt for her more than I ever had. Any new job was scary. Even a job that seemed like the most hideous reaches of hell on your first day could seem quite a laugh by the end of the week, but she wouldn't know that because she'd never really had one.

The traffic was relatively light; we were soon heading south in the dusk, the fields either side lightly frosted. John and I talked about general things; Tara sat in silence. We left the M3 and turned south-west, passing right by Stonehenge, just visible and looking creepy in the wintry dark. By contrast the inside of the car was luxurious, leather-scented warmth, but the atmosphere was something else.

Apprehension was still coming off Tara like mist. Tension was also coming off John, partly, I guessed, because he sensed her state of mind and felt bad for misleading her. Then again, I guessed he was having misgivings in case she'd be having a ball by this time next week and Gisela would be on the phone, saying this wasn't the deal. He'd said it would be a week at the outside, was she supposed to sack her, or what?

I'd been hoping for another kind of tension. Something like I'd once experienced with Stuart, funnily enough, when I'd just started seeing him. We'd planned to go to some party, but his folks had insisted that he stay in and look after his little brother. They were going out and the babysitter wouldn't come any more. Once I'd been there an hour, I'd understood why. Daniel was about ten and a little sod. He'd thrown jelly around the kitchen, demanded to see my 'bosoms' and refused to go to bed until past midnight. Both Stuart's and my hormones had been seething with frustration, the air thick with *'once he's out of the way . . .'*

If there was anything of the sort here, my antennae had yet to pick it up. All I was picking up from John was the odd muttered curse as someone came the other way with undipped lights. Having turned onto a minor road he cursed again as we approached about the third rural crossroads.

'Which road are we looking for?' I asked.

'The right one,' he said shortly.

'Which one's that?'

'I'll know it when I see it.'

I got the picture. 'You mean you can't remember?'

'I mean I'll know it when I see it.'

Bloke-speak for 'I haven't a clue.' 'Why don't you give me the directions? You have *got* the directions?'

'Of course,' he said, even more shortly.

'Pass them over, then.'

'I can't, unless you want me to take my head off.'

I counted to ten. 'You mean you didn't write them down?'

'Only in my head.'

What was it with men and directions? 'And now you can't remember them?'

'I will,' he said, in terse tones. 'Once I get my bearings.'

'How can you get your bearings if you've never been before?' Tara demanded.

'Instinct and unerring judgement,' he said. 'And a few bloody road signs might be good.'

I counted to twenty. 'Have you got a road atlas in the car?'

'No.'

365

Typical. 'Then let's go back to that pub we passed a couple of miles back and ask.'

'Look, I'll get us there,' he said, in that dogged tone men invariably use when they won't admit they're lost.

Tara gave an eyes-to-heaven tut. 'You're just like my dad.'

'Thank you, Tara,' he said drily.

'Well, you *are*,' she retorted. 'My mum always says, "Are you sure you know the way, because if you don't say now before we go," and my dad says, "Yes, stop fussing." And then he drives round in circles for ages, and Mum says, "For heaven's sake let's stop and ask," but Dad never will, because he's got this stupid macho thing about always having to know the way everywhere. So they always end up half an hour late and not speaking, and Mum says that's it, she's driving next time, but she never does.'

'Well, thank you for that,' he said, in the tense, polite tones phone-in hosts use when someone's just been telling the nation that Maggie Thatcher's actually Boadicea, or whatever. 'And that's enough from you in the back,' he added, over his shoulder.

I'd never thought Tara would have it in her to make me laugh, but life is full of surprises. 'I didn't say a word!'

'No, but you do a good snort.'

I probably had, trying not to crack up. 'May I make a suggestion?' I said. 'I don't mind asking the way, so

366

why don't you let me drive? You could pretend you're foreign, if you like.'

This produced a snort from Tara.

'Thanks, but I don't think that'll be necessary,' John said. And to give him credit, he sounded as if he were at least thinking about cracking his face.

'I don't see why not,' Tara retorted. 'She's going to drive on the way back, isn't she? So at least she'll know the way. You said she was only coming to drive on the way back, so you could sleep all the way home.'

Great, I thought. Brilliant.

'I'm not so sure about that any more,' he said. 'If I start snoring she'll probably wallop me. She walloped me when I was sick, you know. She's got a very callous streak.'

Tara turned to me, shocked. 'You didn't, did you?'

'He was trying to give himself pneumonia,' I said. 'I had enough to cope with without him dying on me.'

'See what I mean?' John said. 'A cold, hard-hearted woman.'

'Now you're just taking the piss,' Tara said crossly.

As she retreated into a clammed-up huff, John gave an exasperated little 'tut', but not on her account. 'Bloody thing,' he muttered, adjusting his rear-view mirror. 'It's got a mind of its own. The Old Bill could have been on my tail for miles.'

I looked up to see him still adjusting. And as he skewed it, I realized exactly what he was up to. As our lines of vision converged for a second, he shot me a tiny, conspiratorial wink.

This was quite enough to warm me up nicely for the next few miles, I can tell you. In fact, I was well into a thorough reworking of that breakdown fantasy when he said, 'Ah! I think we have lift-off.'

You could say that. In my head he'd just been saying, 'I think it's the fan belt – would you mind taking your tights off?' Whereupon I'd found that my trouser zip was unfortunately *completely* stuck, whereupon he'd had a go and found he couldn't shift it, either. So I'd said, 'Now what? I can't very well rip them off!' Whereupon he'd said, 'No, but I can. So if you'd like to brace yourself for some brute force and ignorance . . .'

I kept this spicy little version going as he turned left down a road that could have been on Mars for all I cared.

About ten minutes later we passed a sign to the Haddon Hall Hotel and Country Club, and suddenly, round a bend, there it was. Set in lawns, lit up in all its glory. It was the kind of house the nineteenth Earl of Muchacre might have built in 1683, after his countess had put her foot down. She didn't care if the castle had been in his family since William the Conqueror, it was freezing cold, nobody who was anybody lived in castles any more. She wanted a flash new place with forty bedrooms and an orangery. She'd heard of a rather good little chap called Jones. Inigo Jones or something. So the earl had torn down the castle, whacked up the house, and two hundred and fifty years later the twenty-third earl had had to flog it to pay death duties.

Even before we reached the car park, I could see it was the kind of place where one night would cost the same as a cheapie week in Greece. 'What d'you think?' I said to Tara.

She shrugged. 'It's like a place I stayed at with Mum and Dad. They played golf all the time. It was dead boring.'

It was freezing as we walked from the car park, but inside it looked and felt like the sort of place I'd choose if anyone offered me a stately home. No gilt or grandeur, just supreme comfort with unobtrusive minions to peel your grapes. Clusters of squashy chintz armchairs were grouped near a huge fireplace, where half a forest was burning. There was the tinkling of teacups, and the hum of quiet, civilized conversation. As we headed for reception I saw discreet signs to the Pool and Fitness Suite, the Trellis restaurant, the ballroom.

'Is Gisela Koch around?' John asked at the desk. 'John Mackenzie – she's expecting me.'

'Oh, yes,' the girl smiled. 'One moment.'

We were shown into an office near reception and if I'd had a smile on, it might have frozen. Around thirty-three or -four, Gisela reminded me most horribly of Nina: little and dark with sleek hair. Her eyes swept over you in an assessing instant. Her manner was spiky and staccato, like the peckier kind of bird. 'John, good to see you,' she said briskly, before he could get a word in. Her voice was like her manner, staccato, with more than a slight accent. To me she said, 'And you are – ?'

'Harriet. How do you do?'

'Hello. And you must be Tara.' Her eyes darted over her rapidly. 'You may as well start now – they are short in housekeeping. Two are sick with flu, or say they are. It is very convenient, flu, when they have been partying. Someone will take you to the staff block – it's behind the tennis courts – and then to Sue, who looks after housekeeping. We can sort out your paperwork tomorrow.'

After another assessing sweep, she looked into her face. 'Any questions?'

If Tara was fazed, it showed only a moment. 'Erm, I was wondering whether you needed anyone at the pool,' she said. 'I'm a qualified lifeguard.'

Gisela's eyes swept over her again. 'I have pool attendants. In any case, you would not be right.'

Tara was not so easily put down. 'Why not?'

'My dear,' she said, with the edge of sarcasm I associated with a certain type of teacher, 'most of my pool customers are middle-aged women with money, cellulite, and not enough to do. They don't want someone like you showing them up. They like big brown muscles to feed their fantasies.'

I was dumbfounded; Tara wasn't. 'Are you telling me you never hire female lifeguards?'

'Not if I can help it.'

'That's sex discrimination!'

'No, my dear, it's business. I give my customers what they want.'

She picked up a phone on her desk. 'Michelle, Tara Jacques is coming. Please ask Maria to show her to her room, and take her to Sue.'

She then looked at Tara. 'If you go back to the office behind the front desk, Maria will see you there.'

My heart went out to Tara. She had the air of a condemned prisoner who's only just realized it isn't a bad dream. 'Good luck,' I said, and meant it.

John patted her shoulder. 'I'll give you a call in a day or two.'

'OK. Thanks.' Without even looking at either of us, she picked up her bag and exited.

The door shut behind her. Gisela glanced at John. 'Well?' she said. 'Too nasty? Not nasty enough?'

I was shattered. Her whole demeanour had changed. She suddenly had the mischievous look of someone who'd be a really good laugh.

She was human, after all. Warm and attractive and human.

I wasn't quite sure I liked it.

# THIRTEEN

I felt even more uncertain when I saw the way John's demeanour had suddenly changed, too. He was quietly cracking up. 'Christ, Gisela – you nearly had even me messing my pants.'

She laughed a rich, throaty laugh, and went up and kissed him. 'Poor girl,' she said. 'But don't worry, nobody will eat her.'

Then she turned to me. 'You are her sister?'

I pinned on one of those hideous, bright smiles you reserve for such occasions. 'No, she's a friend's sister. It's a long story – John was in the wrong place at the wrong time.'

She motioned us to sit down. There were two easy chairs near the desk, which she perched on, showing elegant legs. 'In fact, Sue will be glad of extra hands,' she said. 'We have a conference starting tomorrow night and more will be sick, I'm sure. Most live out, so we have to believe them when they say they are dying. There will be plenty for her to do,' she added, to me. 'After three days she will be very expert in cleaning toilets.'

'I don't suppose she's ever cleaned a toilet in her life,' I said.

'She will learn. It is very good for kids to work, I think. They get real very fast.'

Then she turned to John. 'It's been too long,' she said, in playfully accusing tones. 'And then you only call me because you want something. I think I will go in a big sulk.' But she smiled and added at once, 'I know, you have been up to your backside. Well, me too. I didn't call you, either.'

Ever felt like a gooseberry? I didn't need blatant hints. After what was a pretty hefty favour, she'd probably like to catch up with him alone. 'I'll go and have a wander around,' I said, rising to my feet. 'I'd like to see it properly while I'm here.'

'Help yourself.' Gisela gave me a friendly smile. 'I can find someone to show you, if you like.'

'No, it's fine.'

John didn't object, either. He even looked as if he'd been hoping I'd do exactly this, damn him. 'Don't get lost,' he said, glancing at his watch. 'I thought we'd hit the road in about half an hour.'

'Fine,' I said brightly.

So much for stuck zips, then. Well, it served me right for getting carried away. Had they had a thing going, or what? An old flame? Even if she was an ancient ember, you didn't have to blow very hard to turn old embers into flames. Half an hour should certainly do it.

Thinking I'd definitely wallop him if he started snoring on the way back, I wandered around acres of lounge area. There was another fire, as big as the first, and huge flower arrangements all over the place. It all smelt of flowers and discreet money. There was hardly anyone there, just the odd couple catching up with the papers, or on the tail end of afternoon tea.

I nearly ordered some myself. Tea and sandwiches would at least kill half an hour, but although I'd felt peckish on the way down, my appetite had suddenly vanished. In any case, it was past afternoon-tea time. It was coming up to Happy Hour, not that they'd have such a thing in a place like this.

I strolled over to the Trellis restaurant, all beauti-fully laid up for dinner, and checked the menu displayed by the door. Starters at seventeen pounds fifty, surprise surprise. Seafood *crêpes*, too. In normal circumstances I'd be salivating just at the thought.

For something to do, I went in search of the Pool and Fitness Suite. There was a desk there, and a pile of fluffy towels, but nobody at it. So I followed the chlorine smell to a lovely big pool with only three people in it. Two were men, the third was a woman in a one-piece and goggles, making heavy weather of a front crawl. At the side of the pool stood a barefoot set of brown muscles in shorts and T-shirt. As she reached the far end he called, 'That was great, but you're working too hard. Don't take your head so far out of the water.'

The accent was pure Oz, the physique pure Bondi. I was beginning to understand Gisela's strategy. For swimming lessons with such as him, many a woman would be tempted to pretend she could barely doggy paddle.

Heading back to the lounge area, I found a squashy armchair near the fire and a colour supplement. This would at least take my mind off any rekindling of embers. Maybe she was merely plying him with coffee and sandwiches; she'd surely offer something. But if so, wouldn't she have offered it to me, too? Trying not to think of what else she might be offering, I concentrated on that colour supplement. It was full of food and cookery, e.g. 'A perfect Sunday roast with a difference', followed by, 'Stuff the calories for once: sticky winter puds to die for'.

Suddenly I was starving after all, though it probably had something to do with that indoor-pool smell still hanging in my nostrils. After years of after-school swimming clubs I still associated chlorine smells with being ravenous. Stuff it, I would order something to eat. Tea and sandwiches would take my mind off embers. Strawberry gateau and blueberry muffins, too. And a couple of poached eggs on toast, dammit. Past tea-time or not, it wouldn't matter. In a place like this you could order Weetabix with squirty cream at two in the morning, if that was what you fancied. Nobody would bat an eyelid.

I looked around for someone to order from and saw John, heading briskly from Gisela's office.

'Ready to go?' he asked.

It was a relief to see no visible smirks, or any other signs that might indicate urgent 'other business' transacted across desks. 'More or less, but I was just thinking about ordering some tea.'

'If you're hungry we can stop at the services,' he said crisply. 'Grab a sandwich or something.'

About to object, I bit it back. He didn't want to hang about. He probably had things to do before tomorrow.

It was bitterly cold outside. 'So much for your heatwave,' I said, as we got back in the car. There was a film of ice on his windscreen already. 'Have you got any de-icer?'

'No, but the heater'll soon get rid of it.'

We sat for a minute waiting for it to melt. 'I have to hand it to Tara,' he said. 'She's got balls. Arguing the toss like that about lifeguards.'

'Especially as she only lifeguarded for two days in her life.'

Having explained that I went on, 'Talking of lifeguards, I checked out the pool and found some of those big brown muscles. About twenty-six, I should think. Australian. Prime latching-on material, if she's thinking about latching.'

The ice was melting fast. As he turned the wipers on to whoosh it away, John shot me a wry little glance. 'Well, it seemed like a good idea at the time.'

'It probably still is,' I conceded. 'Even if she ends up staying six months. Gisela was right: work makes you get real. And I think Tara could do with some getting-real time.' I paused. 'I felt sorry for her, though. I think it had only just hit her, what she was letting herself in for.'

'How d'you think I felt?' he said, turning into the road. 'Like when I once took the dog to the kennels. He thought he was heading for one of those mega-walks you have to drive to.'

'Aah. Poor old Horace.'

'It wasn't Horace. It was Marmaduke, now buried in the garden. The old man planted a tree on top but it died. He said it was probably Marmaduke's ghost peeing on it.'

I laughed rather louder than I intended, partly to cover a rumble in my stomach. Visions of seafood *crêpes* were suddenly filling my head. Why hadn't I had some proper lunch, instead of just a yoghurt and a banana?

Because I'd been too buzzy to think about food, that's why.

Five miles down the road I began to wonder why I'd been buzzing at all. For all the vibes I was picking up, I might have been Horace sitting there. It was a criminal waste now that I was right beside him, bathed in warm leather scents and a whisper of whatever stuff he'd used for shaving.

Not that vibes were the only thing on my mind; the state of my stomach came a good second. Gisela might at least have offered some sandwiches. What sort of hotel manager let friends go away unfed? 'Where did you meet her?' I asked. 'Gisela, I mean.'

'At a conference, years ago. She was managing the conference centre.'

'In Switzerland?'

'Glasgow. She's been around a fair bit since then. St Lucia, Washington, Cape Town . . .'

I really wasn't in the mood for hearing about Gisela's jolly travels. 'I thought she might have offered us a sandwich or something,' I said, as another empty-pang seized my stomach.

'She did, but I said we should hit the road.'

'You might have asked me first,' I said, a tad irritably. 'I'm starving, and it's miles to the services. I hate service-station sandwiches anyway. They always taste of yucky synthetic mayonnaise.'

'We might pass a pub,' he said. 'Grab a plough-man's or a baked potato or something.'

'Let's find one, then. That one we passed on the way, where you wouldn't stop and ask. The Royal Oak or something. It wasn't far.'

Until then I hadn't been paying attention to where we were going. For a start it was pitch dark; second, I tend not to when someone else is driving. Now, however, I peered out into black Wiltshire night. 'Is this the way we came? It doesn't look very familiar.'

'Gisela gave me another set of directions,' he said. 'Quicker than even the last lot should have been if I hadn't cocked up.'

I wasn't so sure about that. Instead of turning into a major road, the route he was taking seemed to be getting ever more minor. 'Are you sure? It looks to me as if we're getting buried in the country.'

'Don't worry,' he soothed, in a way I could imagine Tara's father trying to soothe her mother. I'd never had this macho-dad stuff. Dad had always been perfectly happy for Mum to wield the road map. I could hear her saying, 'Next left and right at the roundabout – David! Watch that van!'

'Have you written these directions in your head as well?' I asked, trying not to see *déjà vu*, and nothing to eat until ten o'clock.

'Don't fret,' he soothed. 'It's all under control.'

I fought an increasing desire to thump him. Men who tell me not to fret in that tone invariably bring out my violent side.

'I thought you wanted me to drive, anyway,' I said.

'I'll get you something to eat first. There's bound to be some baked-potato joint soon. Then I can lie back and snore with a clear conscience.'

'You'd better not.'

'You can talk,' he said. 'I can hear your stomach from here.'

'What the hell do you expect? Why didn't you let me order some tea?'

'Tea's a waste of time. Itsy-bitsy little cucumber sandwiches – a baked potato's proper food. With chilli. Put hair on your chest.'

Great. Hairy fried eggs were all I needed. However, the mere thought of a king-size baked potato heaped with chilli or beans and cheese was making me desperate, and salvation was at hand. 'That looks like a pub, coming up on the left,' I said. 'Quick, pull in.'

He slowed down. 'Doesn't look very brilliant,' he pronounced, speeding up again right past a sign I could have sworn said BAR FOOD.

'Why didn't you stop?' I could really have thumped him now. 'It did *food*! Not every pub does food on a Saturday night!'

'Calm down! We'll find somewhere else.'

God, he was impossible. In fact he was fast turning into the most infuriating man I'd ever encountered. I sat fuming, my stomach doing empty-pangs every three seconds. 'And it's snowing now,' I said crossly, as a couple of little flakes hit the screen. 'I knew it was going to snow.'

'It won't come to anything.'

'I bet it will. We'll get buried in a drift down some bumpkin lane and die of hypothermia.' I was too hungry even to see the possibilities of getting buried down lanes, which goes to show how famished I was.

He made no reply, which was just as well. Anything he'd said then would probably have sent my thump-urge through the roof.

A minute later he slowed down past a sign that

said *The Hen and Peacock, next left, half a mile.* He turned to me and raised an eyebrow. 'Shall we give it a go?'

'We could,' I said acidly. 'But it might be simpler to nick a couple of frozen turnips from a field.'

He turned down the kind of rural road you tend to find blocked with sheep in the daytime. But at least the Hen and Peacock looked promising. Set back from the verge, it was one of those quaint old places you see on postcards: rambling, with crookedy timbers and funny little windows. There was a fair-sized car park, too, two-thirds full, which was a good sign. And when we finally made it to the entrance I saw a sign showing a couple of stars, awarded by the Pub Grub guide.

Even better. Feeling more mellow already, I pushed the door open. It was a larger than usual saloon bar, with comfortable seating, lots of blackened oak beams and a fire. Through one of those low timbered doorways was the restaurant area, with maybe a dozen tables. 'It looks pretty full,' I said dubiously, as we stood on the threshold and lovely foody smells wafted out.

'No harm trying,' he said, as a white-shirted boy came up.

'Have you got a table?' I asked.

'Er, have you booked?'

Bugger it, I thought.

'Yes,' John said. 'Mackenzie. Table for two.'

'Oh, yes, sir. This way.'

I turned disbelieving eyes on Mackenzie.

'Gotcha,' he said, doing his damnedest not to laugh.

It's a weird fact of life that in the space of fifteen minutes you can go from wanting to thump somebody to wanting to kiss them. When you've been wanting to kiss them for weeks previously the effect is naturally multiplied by forty-seven and you think about having their babies, too.

But I settled for laughing. 'Bastard,' I added in a whisper, as we followed the boy to our table. Next to a curtained little window it was cosy and secluded, because of high-backed two-seater wooden benches that made you feel separate from everybody else. They were nicely padded, though, both seats and backs. We sat opposite each other, the boy lit a candle, dished out menus and departed.

'Gisela recommended it,' he said, before I asked.

In that case I forgave him for wanting me out of the way. 'Wasn't she offended that you didn't suggest eating in the Trellis?'

'She said not to bother, her head chef's down with flu.'

As long as the Hen and Peacock chef wasn't. Already checking the starters, I almost started salivating. 'Coquille St Jacques! God, I *love* coquille St Jacques – I haven't had it in ages . . .'

The boy came back for drinks orders. 'I'll drive the

rest of the way,' I offered. 'I'm sure you could do with a couple of glasses of something.'

He shook his head. 'I'd stick to one anyway. I need a clear head tomorrow.'

Accompanied by a large glass of house white for me and a beer for him, we ordered. On a seafood kick, I added linguini with mussels and prawns to my coquille; he went for some fishy pâté thing and local venison. After that came the really heady bit: conversation and delicious, candlelit eye contact, while that wine shot straight to my head.

Not that my head could be described as entirely clear anyway; it was stuffed to the gunwales with fluffy little pink clouds. Why had I ever doubted him? Not that I ever really had, of course. It had been perfectly obvious from the start that he'd been smitten from day one. All that stuff about Mars bars and CBA syndrome was just dreadful cynicism from people with no romance or poetry in their souls. I should have known better than to listen to them, poor things. In fact I felt sorry for them, for being so sour and world-weary that they had to look for maggots in peaches. It was about time I had a peach, after all. A peach who'd planned all along to bring me somewhere special for a lovely dinner, fill me with food and wine before we got back into those lovely leather seats and drove home . . .

Just before the starters arrived he drew back slightly, put his head on one side with a quirky little smile. 'There's something different about you tonight.'

*You sussed that out, then. My brakes are off at last.* 'Just a couple of early nights,' I said lightly.

'Is that it? I thought you might have done your hair differently.' His mouth gave a little quiver as he said it, so I wasn't quite sure whether he meant it, or was sending his entire gender up and had already sussed out the brake situation, even if he didn't know why.

I thought for a moment of coming clean at last, telling him the story of the bog-roll dinosaur, but our starters had just arrived and I began talking rubbish about trying to make salmon pâté with Widdles trying to help. Still, it would keep. Now was not the time, anyway. Live for the moment. Food, wine, and him. Gisela's judgement was spot on. The food was the type that shouldn't be hard to find without taking out a bank loan but usually is: fresh, perfectly cooked, and served in a warm, relaxed atmosphere.

By the time the main course was cleared away I was in that delicious state that only comes from alcohol, lovely food, your brakes off and reciprocal vibes so heady you could drown in them. He was leaning forward, resting on his forearms. I had my elbows on the table, resting my chin on my hand as we talked light nonsense. It wasn't just candlelight putting a glint in those greeny-blue eyes. For the first time I noticed tiny brown flecks around his irises, but since I couldn't drool into his eyes non-stop, now and then I looked at his mouth, instead. Mobile and quivery, it excited the headiest anticipation I'd ever felt. He had lovely white teeth, too. 'All the better for nibbling your bottom with,' as Sally used to say before she went off men.

As we were looking at pudding menus, I became aware of conversation at the table behind John. A forty-five-ish couple, obviously regulars, were talking to the waiter while he topped up their coffee. 'I told him,' the woman was saying. 'Those people at the Met Office aren't all idiots.'

'It won't be much,' the man scoffed.

'Can I have that in writing? Just look at it!'

Realizing what they were on about, I drew back the little curtain and glanced outside. 'Look,' I said to John. 'It's really snowing now.' Large flakes were falling softly, the ground already white.

'If it carries on like this, our lane'll be blocked,' the woman said, in half-joking tones. 'We got snowed in back in eighty-three. Drifts. We'll wake up in the morning and not be able to open the front door.'

'We won't get three inches,' the man scoffed. 'It's global warming we've got, not global freezing.'

'He hopes,' the woman said to the waiter. 'He doesn't want to have to shovel it.'

The boy was half laughing. 'You could always stay here. Two rooms upstairs going begging.'

'No chance,' the man said. 'We've got two geriatric dogs and a geriatric mother. They'll all be doing puddles on the floor.'

John and I were both chuckling quietly. As our eyes

met across the table he shot me a little wink that made my insides turn to warm goo.

Nodding at the window, he said, 'Maybe you were right about bumpkin-lane drifts. I hope you've got your thermals on.'

I was actually christening those La Senza knickers Tom had given me. After all that hard-labour exfoliating, they'd seemed only appropriate. 'You could keep the engine on,' I pointed out. 'And the heater blasting.'

'Profligate waste of fossil fuel,' he tutted. 'The heater wouldn't do you much good anyway. Not while you're outside, pushing.'

I stifled a cackle. 'I'll push if you shovel.'

'No chance. I'll be inside, directing operations.'

'Wimp!' I threw my napkin at him, he ducked, and it landed on the back of the man's head, behind him.

'Sorry,' John said apologetically, retrieving it. 'My friend's getting violent.'

'We'd better push off, then,' the man replied, in genial tones. 'Before she starts with plates and glasses.'

They left shortly afterwards, and half an hour after that John asked for the bill.

'You've done the driving,' I said. 'Let me get it.'

'No,' he said firmly, and I didn't argue.

'Mind how you go,' the waiter said, as we left. 'Roads'll be on the slippy side.'

We stepped out into a hushed winter wonderland. The ground was carpeted white. The trees and shrubs were softly iced, every leaf laden. An old-fashioned street lamp stood near the door, its light making every tiny crystal sparkle like diamonds on white velvet. It was still snowing but not as hard. The flakes were drifting down in a gentle hush.

I had to stop and take it in. 'Don't you just love it? I haven't seen snow since I last went skiing, and that was two years ago.'

'Brings out the kid in you,' he agreed.

'Makes me think of Father Christmas.'

'Makes me think of sledging.'

'And snowmen.'

As we approached the car park at the side, where maybe a dozen cars wore two-inch snowy coats, I thought of snowballs, too. Walking just behind him, I scooped up a handful and moulded it rapidly. 'John?' I called sweetly.

It was a brilliant shot, she said modestly. I slung it while he was still turning and his reactions weren't quite fast enough. He ducked but it hit him on the side of his neck, disintegrating on contact, half of it going down the collar of his shirt.

'Right,' he said, in mock-mad tones. 'This is war.'

I don't recall much about the next couple of minutes, except that we might have been back in the playground. There was ducking and darting behind cars and rapid rearming from snowy bonnets. But I remember my taunt of 'Rubbish!' as he missed me by a whisker. I remember him saying, 'Right, I'm playing dirty now . . .' I remember running for cover, finding myself cornered and shrieking as he grabbed me from behind. I remember him saying, 'Do you surrender?' and shrieking, 'Never!' I remember pretending to fight as he held me in a powerful one-armed grip, seeing his other hand scoop up a handful of snow from a nearby bonnet.

Most of all, I remember yelling, 'OK, *OK*!' just as he was about to stuff it down my neck. I remember the exact moment when I stopped pretending to fight, his grip relaxing as I turned around. There were snowflakes on his hair. I looked at him, and he looked at me, and suddenly neither of us were laughing any more. In a rough-soft voice he said, 'Do you surrender?'

What a question.

In the next few minutes I recall thinking that if I died right now, it'd be a brilliant way to go. I felt my heart rate rise as he gazed down at me, brushed a snowflake from my cheek. I remember exactly how it felt: the quivering electricity in his fingertips.

Apart from that, there was no pussyfooting about with tentative nibbles.

We came together like two irresistible forces held apart for too long. To be frank, it was the kind of kiss that used to make poor old Dorothy go all embarrassed and say she was going to write to the

BBC about all the smut and filth on the television. We devoured each other as if our lives depended on it, holding each other with frantic desperation, breast to chest, hip to hip, thigh to thigh.

I don't know when I'd ever felt such an instant explosion of desire. It welled up in me like a hot volcano, unstoppable. And I felt the same in him: not just in his mouth and arms, but elsewhere. Well, you tend to when you're pressed up tight in the hip and thigh area.

I suppose it was a couple of minutes before we came up for air. I was trembling, my heart going like horses' hoofs at Kempton Park.

He drew back a fraction, looked down at me. 'That'll teach you to play dirty.'

There was laughter in his voice, but only ten per cent. The rest was the rough echoes of his own volcano. And I thought, now what?

Ten yards away a car was passing tentatively down the lane, snowflakes fluttering in its headlights. Half turning away from him, I watched it go. To fill the silence I said lightly, 'The waiter was right about the roads. I hope you've had a session at the skidpan.'

'Afraid not,' he mused, his breath warm on my hair. 'I can never remember whether you're supposed to drive into a skid or out of it.'

About to say *liar*, I stopped. Suddenly I knew exactly where he was heading. Having steadied slightly, my heart rate shot back into overdrive. 'In that case, maybe I'll stay here,' I said, in supposed-to-be-casual tones. 'I don't want to end up in a ditch.'

'But it's all right if I do, is that what you're saying?'

It took some doing, I can tell you, carrying on a daft conversation like this with hidden agendas swirling around like hot mist. 'I suppose I might feel a bit bad,' I conceded. 'When they're digging you out tomorrow morning, half dead from hypothermia, while I've been snuggled up nice and warm all night.'

I was still half turned away from him. It seemed easier like that. I mean, I wasn't the type to come straight out with it, e.g., *'Can we just stop messing about and get a room?'*

Neither was he, evidently. His arms came around me, locking together just under my breasts. 'Now you've really put the wind up me. Given the treacherous state of the roads, do you think I should risk it?'

'Maybe not,' I said unsteadily. 'Perhaps we should do the sensible, prudent thing.'

'I think it might be wise.' As he brushed his lips against my hair, I felt a tiny vibration of suppressed laughter. 'Shall we go back inside?'

God knows why, but as we walked back into the Hen and Peacock I felt it surely showed, like LCD displays on our foreheads, *Just popped back for a shag'*. But nobody gave us knowing looks. When we went up to the bar and John asked the landlord whether we might have a room, he just said very wise, sir, the roads'd be terrible, the council were always caught on the hop. If they had the grit wagons out by midnight, he'd be surprised. Would we mind waiting ten minutes while he checked with Annie, though? She might not have got fresh sheets on after the last lot. She liked to put them on nice and warm from the airing cupboard. Would we care for a nightcap while we waited?

I can't even remember what we talked about, sitting by the fire with a couple of cognacs. Tara, I suppose, and whether the snow would have turned to slush by morning, while wondering how the hell Annie could take so long with those sheets.

Eventually the landlord called that we could go up, second on the left at the top of the stairs. Annie was still there, smoothing a candlewick bedspread, telling us anxiously that she was sorry the bathroom was a bit old-fashioned, in fact everything was a bit old-fashioned but they were having the rooms refurbished in the spring. As I went over to the window, trying to pretend I was only interested in winter wonderlands, she went on to tell us we could have breakfast any time after seven, just give her a shout. Sorry there wasn't a telly, it was on the blink, but the clock-radio did work. Oh, Lord, she'd forgotten the bits and pieces for the tea and coffee tray – if we'd just wait a minute . . .

John said, no, everything was fine, thank you. I smiled nicely and said thanks very much, and she

looked relieved and said, well, goodnight, then, sleep
well – oh, Lord, she'd forgotten to check the bedside
light – it had been playing up – click – yes, it was
working, thank heaven – well, goodnight, then.

And she shut the door.

From opposite sides of a small double bed, draped
in pink candlewick, John and I looked at each other.
Quite frankly I'm surprised neither of us died on the
spot from spontaneous combustion. The invisible line
between our eyes crackled with half a million volts.

'I thought she'd never go,' he said.

# FOURTEEN

Alas for Annie's nice smooth candlewick.

There was a lot of unseemly haste, I'm afraid, as garments were flung aside with reckless abandon, and much of it was from me. I dare say I was behaving like a desperate old slapper but it had been so long, a caveman quickie would have gone down fine. Still, as it didn't say in the old *Girl Guides' Handbook*, when a man not only has an expert knowledge of erogenous zones and how to operate them, but also possesses the equipment and stamina for a really efficient ravishing, a girl should count herself lucky and enjoy it.

By the time he thought I'd suffered enough, I don't know how I didn't scream my head off. Instead I think I made the kind of noises that used to cause Dorothy to switch to the snooker on BBC2. Right afterwards he followed suit, and all I heard for a bit after that was the mutual thumping of hearts.

We were still conjoined, as it were, when he rolled onto his side. I like that. I don't care for prompt withdrawal once business is transacted, as if you were a bloody cash machine. As we lay entwined, still drifting back to planet Earth, I gave him an intimate little squeeze.

He planted a damp kiss on my forehead. 'Was that a "hi" or a wake-up call?'

'Just a "hi". I don't expect miracles.'

He followed the kiss with another. 'Give me half an hour.'

That was a laugh. I could tell from his sleepy murmur that he was drifting off already, not that I minded. I mean, I'm not greedy. I don't expect a repeat performance inside a few hours, especially not a performance like that. Some cuddle-up talk would have been nice, though. I might even have got round to Nina-confessions, but I'd have ended up talking to myself.

'Speaking of wake-up calls . . .' Rousing himself briefly, he reached across to the alarm. He set it for six thirty, which made me wince, but twelve o'clock flights meant ten thirty check-ins and he had to get home, shower, change and pack . . .

Sliding back under the covers, he wrapped his arms around me. 'I'm falling asleep already,' he murmured. 'Lousy manners, but it's all your fault for knackering me so mercilessly.'

'It's all right. Go to sleep.'

Moments later, he had done so. I lay for a while, wondering when I'd last felt so warmly replete, so like the moggy who'd got the cream. There was a lot to be said for abstention if it was like this when you stopped abstaining. If you'd offered me a lottery jackpot just then, and an empty bed, I'd have told you to stuff it. Millions could never buy this catlike contentment, with the man you fancied most in the universe cuddled up beside you.

Certain he was asleep, I ran my fingers down over his chest and stomach. I hadn't had time to appreciate them properly before. I don't know why his mother had said rude things about 'a bit of a tummy'. Perhaps it wasn't quite reinforced concrete, but who wanted to snuggle up to building works?

I suppose I drifted off soon afterwards. The next thing I knew was suddenly finding myself awake in the dark. First I wondered where the hell I was, and when I remembered I thought I must be dreaming. Then I knew why I'd woken up: I needed the loo. For a moment I wondered whether this was still a dream, of the hideous childhood kind where you dream you're dying for the loo, dream you're going with a vengeance, and then wake up in a swimming pool. However, after running a reassuring hand over his chest, I thought I was safe.

He was still sleeping like the dead. Easing myself from his arm, I crept to the bathroom. Annie was right, it was old-fashioned. There was a little dark patch of mould on the wall, too. Suspecting that the old-fashioned flush would make a racket and wake him up, I left it. I crept back to the bedroom; the clock said 4:53. Still starkers, I tiptoed over to the window, drew the curtain aside. There was condensation on the pane, which didn't surprise me after all the steam we must have made, so I eased the sash half open.

The room faced onto the garden. It had stopped snowing. There must have been security lights on as it was all lit up, sparkling white and silent. Except for a few pawprints, the snow on the lawn was pristine. Then I saw what had alerted the security lights. From under a hedge to the side, a fox padded across the lawn. Probably from instinct, it looked up. Unfazed, it gazed at me for several seconds. 'Hi,' I whispered. 'How's it going?'

'I hope you're not fraternizing with burglars,' said a voice behind me.

'I thought you were asleep!' Turning around, I saw him propped on an elbow, watching me.

'I was.'

With the snowy light from outside, I could see him well enough, even down to the sleepy little half-smile. 'There's a fox in the garden,' I explained. Then I felt daft for talking to it, and slightly self-conscious to be scrutinized in my full-frontal glory. Yes, I know we were hardly strangers, but I'm always slightly self-conscious at first about my fried eggs. I have no such qualms about my rear elevation, however, so I turned back to the garden, where the fox was sniffing around a wooden bench. 'It's lovely outside,' I said. 'Come and look.'

'I've got a lovely view from here, thank you.'

All right, it was corny, but I liked it.

'I thought you had a thing about open windows and naked bodies,' he went on, in lazily teasing tones. 'I still have nightmares about Nurse Fearsome beating the shit out of me.'

'You were sick – I'm not. And it's boiling in here.' It was, too. Maybe Annie was worried about that damp patch and her guests growing mould in the night.

'Come back to bed,' he said.

'In a minute. I'm watching the fox.' He was still there, moving silently in the snow.

I heard the bed creak as he got out, and the soft pad of his feet on the floor. He came to stand right behind me, his arms stealing around my waist.

'Shut that window,' he said firmly.

'Certainly not. It'll all be melted by morning.'

'You're getting cold.'

I was, a bit. 'No, I'm not.'

'You are.' He ran his hands down for an exploratory stroke. 'You've got goose pimples on your bottom.'

After all that exfoliating, too. 'I have not!'

'Yes, you have.' Then he traced a lazy, upward curve to my fried eggs. 'Dear me, what have we here?' he tutted. 'A pair of frozen raspberries?'

Suppressing a violent giggle, I felt the stirrings of another volcano.

Particularly when he went on, in softly wicked tones, 'I'd better warm them up before they get frostbite.'

*Well, if you insist . . .*

During the next twenty seconds, as he applied delicate first aid, I felt as if the bones had been filleted right out of my legs. I did shut the window, though, with hands suddenly afflicted with DTs, but we didn't go back to bed. We stayed there, steaming up the glass as he continued his first aid, nuzzling my shoulder, while behind me I felt firm evidence that I hadn't knackered him quite as much as he'd made out.

There was an armchair by the window, with a back at just the right height. I will say no more, except that I got my caveman quickie after all. And believe me, no Cavewoman Slapper of the Year ever enjoyed it more.

I don't remember much about the aftermath, except that I murmured, 'You'll be fit for nothing tomorrow,' as we cuddled up again under the covers.

He chuckled quietly. 'A couple of Shredded Wheat'll soon sort me out,' he said, and dropped a kiss on my hair.

And that was it: I was gone.

At some point I had a daft dream. I dreamt he was telling me it was time to get up, I had homework to do, but I held onto him, asked him to stay five more minutes, my German homework wasn't due in till Tuesday, and hadn't I left school anyway? And he kissed me and said OK, Sleeping Beauty, dream on.

When I awoke it was light. I sat up in a panic, saw

8:47 on the clock and an empty pillow beside me. I called 'John!' and raced to the bathroom, but it was as empty as the bed.

Dazed, I went back to the bedroom and saw a note on the old-fashioned dressing table.

'You were flat out – I didn't like to wake you. A taxi is coming at 9.45 to take you home. Annie will bring up breakfast at 9.15 if you haven't woken up by then. I'll call you from Sofia. John.'

God help me. Was it only half a dream, then? Had I really been wittering about German homework?

But there was a PS, too. 'Two things were lovely last night, but one of them was lovelier. And it doesn't melt by morning.'

German homework notwithstanding, this was possibly the best start to a Sunday morning I'd ever had. All right, I'd much rather he'd yanked me out of bed, but I couldn't complain, except that I wouldn't see him for days. I tried calling him, but only got his voicemail, which didn't altogether surprise me. He'd probably still be driving home.

Naturally I called Sally next. Her 'Hello?' sounded tired and listless, but half a minute livened her up. 'I thought you must have gone back to his place, you old slag,' she said. 'Was it nice?'

'About fifteen out of ten,' I confessed. 'But I expect that was partly due to my long abstention.'

'Thank God you got your act together – I couldn't

have stood the agony much longer. Did you come clean about Nina?'

'Not yet,' I admitted.

'Otherwise engaged, I suppose. Look, I'll see you later – Tom's about to fall off the sofa.'

After a quick shower, the downside of unscheduled stopovers came home to me. No deodorant, moisturizer or clean knickers, but at least I had that pre-snog toothbrush. I went downstairs, where Annie offered her full English breakfast with local dry-cured bacon and free-range eggs. I wouldn't normally have wanted it, but she seemed so anxious to please I couldn't turn it down. She disappeared before I could ask for the bill, so I went and found the landlord, polishing glasses.

He said morning, dear, no, it was all right, the gentleman had seen to it. This was much what I'd expected, but made me feel vaguely like a kept woman. Did he know how much the taxi was going to cost? He said not to worry, dear, the gentleman had seen to that, too – the Hen and Peacock had an arrangement with old Frank up the road.

I'm happy to say that feeling like a fully paid-up kept woman didn't stop me enjoying Annie's breakfast. Maybe it was true about sex sharpening your other appetites. Frank turned up just as I was finishing my second cup of coffee, a jovial man of sixty-five or so who told me he'd started the cab fifteen years ago after he was made redundant. It was still a nice little

400

earner; he got a lot of business from the Hen and Peacock. The snow hadn't come to much after all, had it? Already melting by the time he'd got up.

The sun was out when we left, the trees dripping already, but there was still enough white to make a passably pretty Christmas card. At least John wouldn't have had a treacherous journey. I tried him again but his phone was still off. Well, you had to switch them off on planes anyway. They interfered with navigation systems. He'd probably done it before he forgot.

His note was tucked away in my bag. I'd have got it out and re-read it all the way home but Frank was right beside me. The mere thought was like warm honey, though. How lovely of him not to drag me from my nice warm bed. How sweetly considerate. How wonderfully nice-bloke-ish.

As we got closer to London the snow disappeared altogether but only because there hadn't been any in the first place. The sun had retreated behind cloud, and Frank told me that he'd heard the weather forecast. A cold front was heading for the south-east, we might even get some snow in London.

We hardly ever did, but I wished we would. Snow brightened that dreary, winter-city grey. I'd rather have sunny cold than rain any day, even serious, ear-biting cold. With a personal warm front like I possessed just now, I could handle even blizzards.

By the time Frank dropped me off we were old mates, so after his bonhomie Sally came as a bit of a dampener. She wanted all the details, but not with the delicious, conspiratorial wickedness the old Sally would have enjoyed.

'Trust you to fire the first shot,' she said, when I told her about the snowball. 'A come-and-get-me tactic if ever there was one.'

Her less than fizzy tone rather took the edge off the telling. I decided then and there not to mention the armchair bit. You have to be in the right frame of mind for appreciating the finer points of really lovely smut and filth, and she hadn't been in the right frame of mind for months. I wasn't even going to show her his note, but she said, 'Go on, then. Let's see it.'

She read it with no great rush of enthusiasm. 'Yes, lovely. But I'm beginning to wonder if he isn't just a bit too good to be true.'

About to have a go at her on the subject of miserable cows, etc., I bit it back. If I were her, I don't suppose I'd be fizzing on my behalf, either. She'd had precious little to perk *her* up lately. Maybe she could do with a change of scene. 'Fancy taking Tom to the park?'

'No, thanks,' she yawned. 'It's miserable out and I'm getting hungry. Not that there's much in the fridge.'

'I could go to the deli,' I offered. 'Get some ciabatta and fresh pasta.'

Her face brightened. The only thing that ever

brightened it these days was food. 'Brilliant. We've got some sauce Napolitana.'

So I wound her rainbow scarf around my neck and headed for the deli. Suddenly bursting with energy and goodwill to the entire human race, I walked fast, the cold air putting a zing in my blood.

Just about to go into the deli, I almost collided with Rosie, coming out.

Which is where I think I began this whole saga. If you remember, Rosie was on her way to see us but she'd stopped at the deli for some of their speciality pasta and tomato salad. And the reason she was coming to see us was to pass on the latest bit of gossip: Nina had put a private dick onto John. So I sort of confessed, if you remember, and she said Nina was going to kill me, and we ended up in the Drunken Dragon.

I treated her to drinks. I owed it to her.

'I can't believe you didn't tell me,' she said for the fourth time, over a glass of Pinot Noir.

She sounded so hurt, I felt really bad.

'I suppose you thought I'd tell Suzanne,' she went on. 'Well, I can't altogether blame you, but I'm not quite that much of a mouth.'

'I didn't even tell Jacko,' I pointed out. 'He doesn't have a clue, either.'

This seemed to mollify her. 'I wonder if this dick realizes John's away till Thursday? He might be watching his flat for nothing. Are you sure nobody was tailing you on Saturday?'

I'd been thinking of that ever since she'd told me. 'I'm sure we'd have noticed.' Would we, though? Would anybody, when it's the last thing in their mind?

'You're safe till he gets back, then. But you'll have to tell him.'

How could I, until I came clean about Nina? 'Maybe she'll get fed up and call her spy off. It must be costing a fortune.'

'I bet she won't.'

'What the hell's the point, anyway? I could just about understand her having him spied on *before* he dumped her, but afterwards?'

'That's what I thought, but Suzanne said that's Nina for you. He said there was nobody else; she knew there must be. She's got to prove herself right. She's always *got* to be right. Especially when she's already got a fair idea who it might be.'

The 'dopey' blonde she'd had to introduce him to. I could bet she was nothing of the sort. 'Why does she think it's her?'

'God knows. Just a feeling. And the fact that she was flirting with him something rotten and they'd already met very briefly somewhere before. I bet she was only flirting with him to piss Nina off. Maybe she already had an idea she was going to sack her. In which case, I'd bloody well flirt with him, too.'

'She really is a bit twisted,' I said.

'Suzanne says it's part of the control-freak thing.

404

Like "refusing" to be dumped. I wouldn't be surprised if that's how she justifies having him tailed. So she can convince herself she was only getting the evidence to dump *him*.' She turned to me. 'What on earth will you do if he catches you? Shows Nina a shot of the pair of you together?'

Naturally I'd already thought of that. I'd been thinking of nothing else for the past twenty minutes. 'Then I'll go and see her.'

Rosie's face was suddenly horrified. 'If you tell her I told you about Stuart, Suzanne'll go mad! Nina'll kill *her*!'

'Rosie, calm down! I could say I found out ages ago. Bumped into a friend of Stuart's or something. In any case, Stuart's got sod all to do with it. I'd never have got involved just to get my own back. Nothing really happened till after John'd dumped her, remember?'

'Yes, but she's not going to see it like that, is she? She's going to think he dumped her for you.'

'It's just tough,' I said, draining my glass. 'Come on, Sally'll be wondering where on earth her lunch is.'

This latest news perked Sally up, at least. 'I wouldn't even wait for the photos,' she said, over the pasta Rosie stayed to share. 'I'd tell Nina now. Serve her right.'

After lunch I phoned Tara's mother, told her how it had gone. Angela Jacques sounded wearily resigned. 'I really can't see her making beds and dusting, but I dare say it'll do her good. I've given up hoping she'll be back in time for school any more. They go back on Tuesday, you know.'

'Will you ring her?' I asked. 'She's still got that pay-as-you-go.'

'I might, but even if she's answering she'll hardly talk to me. Maybe I'll leave it a bit. We've run after her far too much. It won't do any harm for her to think we're not tearing our hair out.'

John phoned a couple of hours later, and I tried not to sound as if I'd been dying to hear from him. 'You should have woken me,' I chided.

'I didn't have the heart. You were curled up like a warm puppy.'

It was enough to make me go gooey all over again. 'And you didn't have to pay the taxi.'

'I thought you might not have enough cash. You said before you don't often carry much.'

'I could have stopped and got some!' Not wanting to carp, however, I went on, 'How was your flight?'

'No delays, at least. I've got to get stuck into some work now. If I don't get my head round this project by tomorrow morning, I'm going to be about as much use as Horace.' He paused. 'I'm going to be really tied up for the next few days but if I don't catch you before, I'll ring you on Thursday night, all right?'

'All right.'

In a softer voice he said, 'I have to go. Take care.'

'You, too.'

No way could I possibly have mentioned the tail. That would have meant the whole Nina bit, and how on earth could I do that over the phone? Maybe I'd never have to tell him. If no evidence was forthcoming within a few days, Nina would surely give up and it would die the death. Of one thing at least, I was absolutely sure. However much of a mouth Rosie was, she'd never pass this on. Gossip she might be. Malicious mischief-maker she most certainly was not.

It started snowing that night. From the window I watched little flakes drift onto the pavement and thought I'd never feel quite the same about snow again. It was still there next morning, only about an inch, but enough to lighten the grey. The sky was still heavy, though. There was no sun, but I was positively overflowing with feel-good all day. So much so that Sandie said, 'Have you won the lottery or something?'

'It's my new vitamins,' I smiled sweetly. 'Vitamin J supplements. Highly recommended.'

'I've never heard of vitamin J,' Jess said. 'My Auntie Hazel swears by yeast tablets.'

At lunchtime I switched my mobile on and found a message from Helen: 'I have some news – I'll ring you later.'

Realizing that I hadn't given her a thought for days, I called her.

'I thought you'd like to know,' she said. 'I'm not pregnant after all. False alarm.'

If it had been me, I don't think I could have been more relieved.

'Felicity says it was probably stress,' she went on. 'And I am relieved really, but I can't help feeling a bit sad. That's probably my last chance gone.'

'It would have been crazy.'

'I know.' She paused. 'But I might just have another "baby" soon. I'm thinking of starting that catering business, after all. Felicity's got some friends who want a silver wedding party done on the fairly cheap. Only twenty people. She said why didn't I give it a go?'

This was the second best news I'd heard all month. 'Go for it, then. You're a brilliant cook.'

'No I'm not, but I'm competent. So maybe this will be my baby. Cooking to Go.'

'Brilliant. Have you phoned your demon lover yet?'

'No, but I'm thinking about it,' she said sheepishly.

'Then do it!'

I didn't hear from John that day, but on Tuesday he left a message. 'It's pretty hectic – I've been in meetings all day, and I'm about to go for dinner with assorted local bigwigs. I might not be back until Friday now, but I'll call on the Thursday night anyway. I've been trying to get Tara but she's not answering. If you get hold of her, say hi for me.' More softly he added, 'Take care. Bye.'

Later that evening Dad rang. He and Kathy were landing at Heathrow on Thursday afternoon and going straight to her sister in Basingstoke. They were coming to London on Saturday morning, though. I hadn't forgotten about Saturday night, had I?

I'd been thinking about it a good deal. I'd been thinking how sick I'd feel if John wanted to see me on Saturday night and I couldn't make it. Then I felt awful because I hadn't seen Dad in months.

'Of course not!' I said brightly. 'Would you like to stay here after all?'

'Oh, no, dear, I've booked a little hotel in the Cromwell Road. I'll bring Kathy to the house first, though, so you can get to know each other first. Have a nice chat. Would about six-ish be all right?'

'Yes, lovely.'

I just hoped it would be 'lovely'. What if she had that sugary manner that can go with narrowed, calculating eyes? What on earth would I tell Mum?

On Wednesday evening I tried phoning Tara but there was no reply till a quarter to ten. 'How's it going?' I asked brightly.

'OK, I suppose. Fine,' she added quickly.

'Have you made friends?'

'Not what I'd call friends. They're OK, but they all know each other. Most of them live out, anyway.'

I got the impression she was pathetically glad to talk

to anyone, but trying to pretend she wasn't. 'What's your room like?'

'OK.'

Can we have another adjective? I thought. 'Titchy, I expect.'

'Yes, but I wasn't expecting much else.'

'You should have seen the room I had when I worked at a hotel one summer. There were three of us sharing. We had to climb over each other's beds.'

'At least you had someone to talk to.'

If she'd actually said it, she must be feeling really lonely. Isolated.

Suddenly I thought I heard a muffled sob. It appalled me, but then I thought I'd imagined it, because she was going on, in a reasonably normal voice, 'What were you doing? In the hotel, I mean.'

'A bit of everything. Chambermaiding, waitressing, laying tables . . . It wasn't like Haddon Hall – it was just a three-star seaside place.'

'Did you know how to make beds? With sheets and blankets, I mean. I've only ever had a duvet.'

'I can't remember. I suppose so. They weren't that fussy.'

'They are here.' This time I knew wasn't imagining it; her voice was cracking. 'The under-housekeeper had such a go at me, she made me do them all again because I hadn't done the corners right . . .'

Feeling her fighting a river of tears, my heart went out to her.

'I mean, why didn't she show me first?' she went on, her voice trembling. 'How was I to know?'

I knew at once what sort of state she was in. So low, anything seemed like the end of the world. 'My mother calls them hospital corners. At least you'll know next time.'

She wasn't even fighting any more. She was dissolving.

Was this breaking point at last? Delicately, feeling my way, I said, 'Tara, you don't have to stay. Not if you really hate it.'

'I can't leave!' she sobbed. 'Two of them are off sick! What'll John say if I let his friend down?'

How could I tell her the truth? 'He won't care,' I soothed.

'He will! He'll think I'm pathetic!'

'He won't, not if you really hate it.' Was this the time for a gentle strike? 'You don't really want to make beds, do you? Let alone clean loos, be bossed about by under-housekeepers . . .'

There were more sobs, unmuffled, this time. 'Where would I go?'

If the iron wasn't hot now . . . 'Home,' I said. 'Home's not really so bad, is it? I know school can be a pain but you'll be finished in the summer, and you'll have such a laugh at university . . .'

'I can't go home,' she wept.

'Why not? If it's Lee, your mum and dad won't say anything, I'm sure.'

'It's not him! It was never just him – I can't –'

Terrified of mucking it up now, I hesitated. 'Then what is it?'

'You don't understand . . .' For a moment there was nothing but the sounds of rivers bursting their banks. 'Mum and Dad are going to kill me . . .'

I hung up twenty minutes later, feeling overwhelming relief. I almost wanted to laugh, too, but I'd have felt really bad.

I phoned Angela Jacques straight afterwards. Then, over a large glass of wine at the kitchen table, I filled Sally in.

'She hardly did any work last term. She had something like seven essays outstanding; the school were saying that if she didn't get up to date over the Christmas holidays they wouldn't let her sit her A levels. She meant to get on with it but there was so much, she just didn't know where to start.'

'Well, I know the feeling,' Sally said.

'Me too, but I don't think I ever got to seven. There was a parents' evening, but she didn't tell her folks because she knew her teachers would be having a massive go. So the school wrote to them. She knew they would, so she checked the mail every morning and grabbed the letter. It said she had no hope of even scraping her A levels at this rate, if she didn't change her attitude soon they'd prefer her to leave.'

'Well, they wouldn't want her mucking up their league table results.'

412

'Exactly. So having dug herself in this deep, she didn't know how to get out of it. She didn't dare tell her folks she'd opened that letter – they're paying massive fees and they'd have gone ape. So when Lee said he was off to Leicester it was like an escape route. She knew he didn't really want her to go, but she tagged along anyway.'

'So where have you left it?'

'Hang on, I haven't finished. That model agency she went to wasn't remotely pukka. It was some dodgy bloke with a camera, wanting her to get her kit off.'

'Oh, God,' Sally said. 'I've read about them. They're dead crafty; they even have a woman answering the phone, so it sounds on the level.'

'They did. The ad gave some pseudo-classy name like Dorchester Agency; it just said "Models wanted for well-paid photographic work." It never occurred to her that pukka agencies don't have to advertise. She hadn't a clue. She said it felt a bit dodgy even when she walked in, but she thought it was just nerves. It started off on the level, he took a few straight shots, but then he started asking her to take her top off. She said what for, and he said come on, love, she wasn't Claudia Schiffer, tops off was nothing. So then she realized he was working up to more than just tops and told him to get lost. But she felt sick afterwards, and such a fool for being taken in. She couldn't bring herself to admit she'd fallen for it.'

Thinking back to her welling eyes in that restaurant, I felt for her all over again. John's straight talk must have been the last straw.

'No wonder she didn't tell you,' Sally said.

'I wouldn't have told us, either.'

'So where *have* you left it?'

'Her folks are going down on Saturday, to stay the night. They're not telling her, of course, but they'll phone once they get there, and tell her they know what's been going on and it's all right, they're not going to kill her. So with a bit of luck she'll be so relieved she'll burst into tears, and they'll say they just happen to be there, so if she wants to grab her things . . .'

'I think I'd make her clean a few more loos,' Sally said.

'So would I, but we're not her folks.'

For the first time in ages, Sally wore a mischievous little smile. 'How many Brownie points does that make, then? You can phone John now and tell him smugly that you've sorted it.'

'Yes,' I said, glancing at my watch. 'But not now. It's one o'clock in the morning in Bulgaria.'

I phoned Jacko, though. He said Sally was right, they should let her sweat a bit longer, but thanks for sorting it, pet, he owed me one.

I almost told him about John but it was all far too complicated when I was dying for bed.

\*     \*     \*

414

I tried John at Bulgarian lunchtime on Thursday, but all I got was his voicemail. I left a message anyway, giving the gist about Tara. Next I phoned Gisela, filled her in, and said she might be missing a bedmaker by the end of the week. She said no problem, she was glad it was all sorted out.

I left work feeling like a diplomat who's just averted a Middle Eastern war. In fact, I felt quite smugly pleased with myself, especially as John was due to phone. I looked forward to him telling me how clever I was, how brilliant my people-skills were, how he'd known the second he laid eyes on me . . . etc. etc. If he'd managed to get the Thursday flight after all, he might even tell me all this in person. I sat on the train in a lovely warm buzz of anticipation, smiling at everyone, even some miserable old Victor Meldrew in a particularly poncey bow tie.

But then I got home.

I felt the atmosphere as soon as I opened the door: cold, crackling tension. 'Sally?' I called.

'In here.'

She was in the sitting room. It was chilly; there was no fire. She was standing with Tom on her hip, and she was not alone.

He stood apart from her. Tall. Good-looking. Light brown hair streaked with blond. But not quite so full of himself as before.

# FIFTEEN

'Oh,' I said. 'Hi, Steve.'

He had no time for the niceties. 'Were you in on this? Did you know she'd used me like some bloody sperm bank?'

Before I'd even drawn breath, Sally cut in like the avenging angel's sword. 'What the hell do you care? What was I to you but a quick, opportunistic shag?'

'I don't recall you complaining at the time!'

'No, and I'm not complaining now!' she flared. 'You could have been anybody vaguely passable! I just wanted a baby!'

I couldn't believe she was doing this. But before I could say anything she added, 'You weren't the only one, I can tell you!'

Heaven help me, I thought. What the hell was going on? Apart from wounded vanity coming off Steve in waves, I mean.

'How many?' he demanded, hands on his hips. 'I mean, I'd just like to know!'

To wounded vanity please add righteous affrontedness.

'It's none of your business!' Sally retorted.

416

I felt I had to do something, at least get her away for two seconds. 'Look, Sally—'

'Harriet, please keep out of this.' She shot me a look that said I'd be dead if I didn't. 'Steve was just going.'

'Like hell I am!' The waves were turning to bristles, but suddenly I realized that they were at least partly due to shock. 'You can't just tell me I might have fathered a child and then tell me to clear off!'

'Oh, can't I? Who says?'

God knows where this might have gone if Tom hadn't started whimpering. He invariably did when Sally was mad, poor little boy.

'He's getting upset,' she said, in more moderate but suddenly shaky tones that told me she was near to tears. 'Please, will you just go?'

There was a long, tense silence.

Steve was staring at Tom. 'He looks like me.'

'For God's sake, he doesn't look like anybody!'

'He does. I've seen pictures of myself at that age, haven't I?'

Sally was trying to calm Tom, shushing him, rocking him, kissing the top of his head. 'Steve, please, look what you're doing . . .'

'I want to know,' he said flatly. 'I want a blood test. I have a right to know.'

'You don't have the right to anything!' she burst out. 'You were bloody married!'

'It was on the rocks! She didn't even want kids!'

'And did you?'

'Not particularly, I'd hardly thought about it! Who the hell does?' From the way he was looking at Tom, anyone could see he was thinking about it now. 'I want a blood test. I'm entitled to it.' He turned to me. 'You tell her, will you?'

Then he turned back to Sally. 'All right, I'm going, but when I come back I want that test. I'll go to court if I have to.'

And he went. The front door banged behind him.

I looked at Sally. 'For God's sake, what the hell did you tell him that for?'

'I don't care!' she burst out. 'He just turns up after fifteen months, assuming I'll be over the moon – he's been back three weeks! Three *weeks*! Staying in bloody Northampton! How far's that, for God's sake? Sixty miles? And you know why he came? He's going skiing tomorrow – he thought he'd pop in and see me! Pop *in*! He thought he might get another quick shag and a bed for the night, nice and handy for Heathrow!'

And she burst into tears.

I suppose it was about two minutes later, while we were in the kitchen, with Sally still in floods and Tom coming out in sympathy, that my phone rang.

Perfect timing. 'John, I really can't talk now,' I said, nipping into the hall to speak to him away from Tom's wailing. 'Tom's father just turned up – it's all a bit of a nightmare – Sally's in a hell of a state. I'll call you later if I can – are you back home?'

418

'Yes, but don't worry – tomorrow'll do. And well done with Tara.'

'Thank God she's sorted,' I said, with feeling. 'I just wish I could sort Sally as easily. Look, I'm sorry, but I've got to go . . .'

Even before she'd calmed down a bit, I knew exactly why Sally had done it. When she was hurt, it was typical of her to flare up and say the first thing that came into her head. The way she eventually put it was this. He'd swanned in with a grin on his face, sublimely conscious of his own irresistibility. After months and months and months. After conveniently forgetting to tell her he had a wife in Singapore. She'd wanted to wipe that grin off his face. Make him think he wasn't so bloody irresistible, just marginally more attractive than artificial insemination. All right, she hadn't been conscious of the thought process, but your brain can speed up like mad when you're under stress.

He'd turned up only ten minutes before I'd got home. Having written him off, she'd been stunned. She'd had Tom on her hip as she'd answered the door, but it hadn't even occurred to him that he was hers. He'd told her he was off to Innsbruck the next day, he'd left his job in Singapore, by the way, he was looking for something else. He'd assumed she was babysitting. He'd said, 'Whose is the sprog?' as if Tom were some inanimate burden she was temporarily lumbered with.

That was when she'd said, 'He's mine.'

Of course he hadn't twigged, just looked vaguely

embarrassed and taken aback, as if she'd admitted to some weird, antisocial habit. Telling him had seemed impossible so she'd said sorry, but he'd better go, she was really busy.

But something must have given her away because, perversely, that was when he'd twigged. He'd looked at Sally and then at Tom; she'd seen his mind working back like a calculator. He'd said, 'For God's sake, don't tell me he's mine?'

That had cut her to the heart. Not for herself, but for poor little Tom. She'd retorted, 'I couldn't tell you, Steve. Probably not, but I couldn't give a toss who did the honours.'

And so it had gone on.

Eventually I said I understood why she'd done it, but she had to come clean when he came back. Sooner or later Tom was going to want to know who his daddy was. At least Steve hadn't taken fright and cleared off, had he?

She said OK, but it was just perverse macho stuff. If she'd told him straight off Tom was his, he'd have backed off at once. His vanity was wounded. He didn't like being told he was only one up from a turkey-baster when he'd fondly imagined he was irresistible.

I didn't remind her that she had found him irresistible once. There wasn't much point when she said doggedly that even if Tom didn't exist, she wouldn't be interested any more. Yes, OK, if and when he came back she'd come clean, but he probably wouldn't.

Once his wounded pride had healed, he'd think better of it. One way or the other, she really didn't care.

By the time we eventually got to bed, around midnight, I was getting seriously worried about Sally. She was listless, deflated, as if something had sucked all the life out of her, and I had a fair idea why. Somewhere she'd still had that little dream tucked away. If and when he'd turned up, her heart would have given a leap, and she'd have known it wasn't just lust and opportunity, after all. As it was, she'd been faced with a stranger she'd once had sex with on a faraway beach, with stars like diamonds on black velvet and silvery phosphorescence in the sea. On a doorstep in Putney he was just another bloke.

I slept badly, and I knew from up-and-down creaks that she wasn't doing much better. Around four o'clock I crept into her room and found her asleep, with Tom beside her and the cot pushed up to the bed to stop him falling out.

I didn't see her before I went to work. I felt like a rag, except for the thought of speaking to John, and the bright edge was even taken off that because I felt bad for having something to be happy about when Sally was so down.

He called shortly after one, just after I'd switched my mobile on. I went into the loo to speak to him; it was too cold outside and I didn't want every nosy ear in the office on stalks. Having done with Sally and Tara, we got onto other matters.

'How are you fixed for tomorrow night?' he asked.

Saturday. *Oh, bum.*

'I'm afraid I can't do tonight,' he went on. 'I've got a long-standing dinner thing – I had to back out of the last one – if I do it again feelings will be wounded.'

Swallowing my disappointment, I thought back to newly married Amanda, that night we'd had the drinks: *'You must come for supper . . .'* If not Amanda, someone else who planned everything meticulously and wouldn't want a last-minute extra when she'd bought one baby poussin and six quails' eggs per head.

'It's all right, I know what dinners are like – I wouldn't want to barge in anyway. Besides, I really ought to stay with Sally tonight – you'd think half a dozen vampires had been at her. But I can't do tomorrow night. My father's coming with his blushing bride. We're going out for dinner. I've got to check her out for Mum and take notes. How many horns she's got, and so on.'

He chuckled. 'You never know, her tail might not actually be forked. Good luck, anyway. I'll give you a call on Sunday morning. You're not tied up on Sunday, are you?'

'No.'

'Then I'll see you then.'

I couldn't wait.

When I got home Sally said, 'If you're staying in tonight because of me, forget it.'

422

'I'm not. He's got some dinner party tonight and I can't do tomorrow night because of Dad.'

'You could have invited him along for tomorrow night. If it's going to be a nightmare an extra body would dilute it.'

I would never have asked, even if I'd thought of it. First, it was far too soon to invite him to meet any family; second, I owed it to Dad to give him and Kathy my undivided attention.

It was around eight o'clock, just the time your average dinner party gets going, that certain aspects of meticulous planning occurred to me. Seating, for a start: *'Boy, girl, boy, girl, yes, I'll put John opposite Charlotte, those two are bound to hit it off . . .'*

Having got thus far, my imagination went a bit further. It came up with Amanda's other half sticking his oar in. *'You're not trying to get him off with Charlotte? She knackered Jerry Walters in ten days!'*

*'Miles, shut up. Did you get the ice?'*

*'Never mind ice. I know she's a friend of yours, but that Charlotte's a bloody raging nympho.'*

*'Oh, do be quiet, Miles. You're just jealous. And go and put another shirt on – that one clashes with the flowers.'*

To take my mind off Charlotte, I went to help Sally. After a fashion she'd come out of her listlessness. Like some sort of half-power robot she was getting organized, sorting out teaching materials. She was starting work soon with a class of assorted beginners, most of them refugees. We scoured magazines for

423

pictures to paste onto card, to get them talking. *What's this? It's a car, a pen, a bike. Have you got a car/pen/bike? Mohammed, ask Maria.*

After we'd ripped out six or so, she stared at them. 'What the hell are we doing? None of them have got bloody anything!'

'We could do kids,' I suggested. 'A baby, a little boy, a little girl . . .'

'Yes, great,' she said. 'And then what do I do if someone starts crying because their little kid got killed in the Kosovo shelling?'

I thought again of Charlotte when I went to bed, but by then my imagination was behaving itself. After the guests had left, Miles would say to Amanda, *'So much for getting her off with John, then, not that she didn't try. She asked him to take her home, you know. Said she had some fascinating Polynesian art to show him, ha ha.'*

*'Oh, do grow up. While we were in the kitchen he told me he's got someone, anyway. Harriet somebody. He thinks he's in –* Miles! *How many times have I told you not to put that silver in the dishwasher?'*

I slept very sweetly after that.

In the morning the heavy cloud had lifted at last. I looked out at cold, crisp sunshine and said to Sally, 'Let's get out of here. Right out, I mean. Why don't we go and have lunch in Brighton?'

'Brighton? Are you mad?'

'Oh, come on, it's only an hour's drive. We'll have

424

lunch in The Lanes and take Tom for a walk on the beach. He'll love it.'

I hadn't expected her to jump at it and she didn't, but she perked up a fraction. 'If you like. It'll be windy, though. I'll have to wrap Tom right up.'

Sally loved Brighton. She'd worked there one summer and had a ball. It was never the same in winter, but there were hanging baskets full of pansies and tubs of early spring flowers in The Lanes, and once you were out of the wind it was just warm enough to sit outside. We fed bits of bun to shrieking seagulls, tossing them in the air for them to catch. Tom was entranced. We bought him a helium balloon like a dolphin, tied it to his buggy and walked along the front eating chips. The salt wind freshened Sally's face, put a glow back in her cheeks.

We didn't mention Steve, or John, either. We talked about the old times, the laughs, the time we'd got completely pissed and gone waterskiing at two o'clock in the morning in our best clubbing gear, because some idiot had bet us five thousand pesetas we'd never do it.

We stayed later than I'd intended, so it was a rush when we got back. In Kathy's honour I tidied up, vacuumed and dusted, lit a fire in the sitting room, put tonics and wine in the fridge, and nibbles in little dishes. I went out for flowers from the petrol station, cleaned the bathroom and lit a sandalwood candle I'd had for ages.

By the time the doorbell went, at two minutes to six, I was sick with apprehension.

'Go on,' Sally said. 'It's only your wicked step-mother, not Nina with a carving knife.'

I opened the door with my split-arse smile glued on, and it fell straight off again. Was this the parent I'd last seen five months ago? What the hell had she done to him?

It wasn't just the tan. He'd filled out. He was even standing up straighter. He'd lost that almost apologetic, lanky stoop.

'This is Kathy,' he said, with loving pride.

With one glance I knew she was right for him. She looked almost as apprehensive as I'd felt, but was covering with a hesitant smile. I knew instantly that she'd been dreading this, dreading some bitch-daughter who'd hate her on sight.

During the next hour, over drinks and nibbles, I made notes for Mum. Fifty-three or four, which wasn't a guess, as she told me she'd taken early retirement last year at fifty-three. Quietly well dressed, in what Mum would call a Country Casuals way. Attractive, looking younger than her age (I was beginning to wonder whether Mum would go off her after all) with a quiet sense of humour. She'd been a history teacher (I could just hear Mum saying, 'Well, no wonder') and had three children, all grown-up. Her husband had left her when they were six, eight and eleven, yes, it had been a bit of a struggle ('Poor thing'). But they'd all turned out well: a doctor, a university lecturer, the youngest hadn't made his mind up yet and was waiting tables in Sydney on his postgraduation gap year.

Best of all, though I wouldn't tell Mum this in precisely the same way, now and then she looked at Dad in the way Mum sometimes looked at Bill. With that quick, serene, just-us happiness that only lovers use when they know they've hit the big one.

As for Dad, well, I could only think, 'He's in love.'

Bless him.

Dad had booked the River Room at the Savoy. We stopped to read the plaques on the wall when we came out, all about Geoffrey Chaucer having dinner there with John of Gaunt, and the Black Prince locking up some poor king of France there in the 1300s, when it was the Palais de Savoie. I wondered what he'd think about it now, with red buses trundling down the Strand and good ale costing the equivalent of forty oxen a pint.

I phoned Mum when I got back. She said thank God for that, and I went to bed thinking ditto, one major worry off the list. I just wished I could feel as happy about Sally. She was thinking the fun was over for ever; the Sally who'd gone waterskiing at two in the morning could never come back. She saw life stretching out as an endless sentence of grown-up, sensible behaviour, life insurance and Saturday mornings queuing at supermarket checkouts.

She needed something to look forward to.

'We'll go on holiday in the summer,' I said to her, over breakfast. 'Somewhere nice. You, me and Tom.'

She stared at me. 'What about your trip?'

'I haven't even thought about that for ages. I'm not sure I want to do that bit any more anyway, backpacking and staying in grotty hostels. We could go to Greece or somewhere. Think how Tom'd love the sea. And the pool.'

'He'd get burnt,' she said flatly. 'It'd be far too hot for him. Anyway, I wouldn't be able to afford it. And if you were thinking of paying, thank you very much, but no way.'

'God, you're so pig-headed!'

'I'm not! I just hate sponging!'

I had a good mind to book something anyway and tell her when it was too late to cancel. I wouldn't put it past her to be pig-headed even then, but she'd hate the thought of wasting the money. It wasn't noble self-sacrifice when I said I'd gone off the thought of my trip, either, although it hadn't quite dawned on me till then. I still had itchy feet – I knew they wouldn't stop itching till I was dead – but I didn't want to do the overgrown student bit any more. Above all, I didn't want to do it alone.

'Anyway, what about John?' she asked, a minute later. 'You might want to go away with him.'

Sometimes I thought Sally was telepathic.

'Wasn't he supposed to phone today?' she went on.

Already tingling with anticipation, I tried to look as if I wasn't. 'Yes, but he won't yet, will he? On Sunday morning?' It was barely half past nine.

When it actually rang, at twenty past eleven, I tried not to swoop on it like a gannet. 'Hello?'

'Harriet, it's me.'

'Oh, hi, Rosie,' I said, trying not to sound disappointed. 'How's it going?'

'OK. Well, not OK, actually. I had to ring you, I've just been talking to Suzanne. She was round at Nina's last night – I had to pretend I was coming out for the paper so I could ring you.'

'Don't tell me, she's going to pour primrose Dulux all over John's car. No, scrub that, she's already done it.'

'Harriet, she's got the photos. From the private dick.'

'Don't tell me he caught us last weekend?'

'No, that's why I had to tell you.'

It took a second for this to go in, and even then it didn't make sense. 'Rosie, I haven't even seen him since last weekend!'

'It's not you.'

One of those flying jellies hit me, but this time it was a killer. A cold green lump, right in the guts.

'I'm really sorry, but I thought you ought to know,' she went on. 'It was Thursday or Friday night, Suzanne said. There are at least four shots, and it's obviously not his granny.'

I felt sick.

'Harriet?'

'It's all right, I'm still here,' I said, trying to sound as if I wasn't about to throw up. Suddenly realizing something was wrong, Sally was making, 'What?' faces, but I held up a 'hang on' hand.

'Are you OK?' Rosie asked anxiously.

'More or less,' I lied.

'Are you sure? I thought you really liked him!'

My throat felt like cat litter. 'Look, it's not a massive big thing. OK, the other night was nice, but I don't have any claim on him.'

'Thank God for that. I'm not sure I'd be OK, though. I think I'd be in a bit of a state. Nina was in a right old state, according to Suzanne. She thought it was going to be dopey blonde, remember?'

As if I cared who it was.

'But it wasn't her at all. Still blonde, though. Looking up at him all sweetly adoring, Suzanne said.'

I clutched at straws. 'Could be just a friend.'

'Doesn't sound like it. Suzanne said they were pretty good shots. Zoomed-in close-ups. They were on their way from some bar to some restaurant.'

That jelly had turned into a cold green snake, winding itself round my guts. 'Was that it? Drinks and dinner?'

With a wince in her voice she said, 'They went back to his place.'

'For how long?'

'Well, the bloke waited outside till five o'clock in the morning. But that doesn't mean they actually *did* anything,' she added hastily.

Of course not. They played Beggar My Neighbour and had a nice glass of hot milk.

'You are upset, aren't you?' she went on anxiously. 'God, I knew you would be.'

'I'm not!' I even added a light little laugh. 'It's not as if I've been seeing him for six months.'

'Are you sure? I'd never have told you, but I thought you'd want to know you were off the hook. Nina's hook, I mean.' She paused. 'And to be honest, I thought you were quite keen, and *I'd* want to know. I know one night doesn't exactly constitute a relationship, but I'm not sure I'd like it.'

'Well, that's blokes for you, isn't it?' I said lightly. 'Always looking for the next bit of nectar to stick their proboscis in.'

'I suppose. At least you won't have Nina screaming on your doorstep.'

I thought she'd never get off the phone. When she eventually did, Sally said, 'For God's sake, *what*?'

It's weird how in the space of hours, roles can be reversed. Sally was now the comforter, the practical one with her life all sorted, while I felt like a lump of frozen sick.

She did her best, pointing at every reasonable explanation. 'He might have arranged to see her even before anything happened with you.'

'Yes, but couldn't he have stopped at dinner?'

'Look, just because people sleep under the same roof doesn't mean anything has to happen. Maybe she was just staying the night.'

'Yes, and maybe Jacko just signed up for a *passementerie* class.'

'What the hell's *passementerie*?'

'Tassel-making,' I said, like a numb mechanism. 'As in soft furnishings.' I'd never have known this either, only Jess had been to just such a class, so she could make nice tie-backs for her bedroom curtains.

'He told you he was going out on Friday night, didn't he?' she pointed out. 'You didn't exactly throw a fit then.'

'It was a dinner party! At least, that's what I thought he meant. A long-standing dinner "thing", he said.' Was that what he'd intended me to think? Or was it the truth? What if he'd seen Blonde on Thursday night? What if he'd met some rampant Charlotte on Friday night, too?

'Maybe it was a long-standing dinner *date*,' Sally said. 'An old friend who'd come up from the sticks. In which case, no wonder she stayed the night.'

The more she came up with reasonable explanations, the more I couldn't accept them. Every shred of suspicion I'd ever held about him was suddenly combining into a tidal wave. 'Working late', the ease with which he could lie . . . Had he told Nina he was working late when he'd been with me? Why had I blithely assumed I was the only one?

'Sally, Suzanne *saw* the photos. You can tell "old friend" stuff a mile off, and this was not "old friends".'

'OK, maybe it wasn't. Look, I'm not making excuses for him, but if you couldn't see him three nights in a row, you can hardly expect him to stay in watching the snooker. Unless he's signed some exclusive-rights contract you haven't told me about, you know you're overreacting.'

'I can't help it! He's not just some passing fancy I can take or leave!'

'Harriet, he's a *bloke*! That's what blokes do! You had one night with him, not a joint mortgage. You've got to get this in proportion.'

'You don't get it, do you? It meant something to me, the other night!'

'Of course it did! You'd let yourself get obsessed with him, and you hadn't had sex in ages!'

'It wasn't just sex!'

'Then you've got two choices. Either you put this out of your mind and take him as you find him, or you confront him. Tell him about Nina and her spy. At least it'll all be out in the open. Only he might say yes, he was seeing someone else the other night, so what? Do you want him thinking you're a jealous, possessive wreck?'

'I am a jealous wreck!'

'Then hide it!'

'I don't want to have to hide it. I can't handle a relationship like that – I'd never relax for a second. I'd be a mass of jealousy every time I wasn't with him. It's not just this, is it? He was seeing me behind Nina's back – maybe it serves me right.'

That was when my phone rang. It was still on the kitchen table, after Rosie's call. I stared at it, green snakes having babies in my stomach. 'I can't speak to him! I just can't, not yet . . .'

'I'll say you're in the bath.'

She picked it up. 'Yes, she's here,' she said, ignoring my frantic faces, and passed it over. 'It's Angela Jacques.'

Phew. I did my best to sound brightly normal. 'Hi, how did it go?'

They were in the car, on their way home. There had been a lot of tears, but everything was more or less sorted out. Tara was staying another week, she couldn't just walk out when so many were down with flu. She couldn't bear the thought of going back to that school; they'd discussed an A-level crammer for September. It was for the best, she could make a fresh start, though why on earth the silly girl hadn't come clean earlier was beyond them. They'd told her she wasn't going to doss until September, though. She'd have to get a job or do something else constructive, not lie on the sofa watching TV . . .

She went on for ages, and all the while I was

expecting a call waiting that would send my stomach into knots.

There was no call waiting. He phoned twenty minutes after she'd hung up, by which time I knew exactly how I was going to play it.

'How did it go with your old man and his blushing bride?' he asked.

'Oh, fine,' I said brightly. With a glued-on smile it was actually quite easy. 'She was nice. No tail, after all. Not so much as a horn anywhere. I was so relieved, I got a little bit pissed.'

'I hope you're not still in bed with a hangover.'

'No, not that pissed. I've been up for ages.'

'How about some lunch, then? If I come in, say, forty minutes?'

On the other end of that Nokia, I could almost see his face, expectant. Much more clearly, though, I could see his face that night in the snow as he'd brushed a snowflake from my cheek. I could see it in that pink-candlewick room, just after Annie had left. I saw it again as he'd gazed at me from the bed, telling me in lazy, wicked tones that he had a lovely view. Then I saw it as he'd been falling asleep, when I'd been thinking my cup was running over, life couldn't get much better than this.

And then I saw him doing it all over again, with someone else.

This was where the glued-on bit got harder. But it was the best way. Nice and bright and casual.

'Actually, John, I don't think I can make lunch. I'm a bit tied up, after all. I'm sorry, but something came up.'

In the tiny pause that followed, I knew he'd expected nothing like this. 'Dinner, then?'

'Probably not. I'm really sorry, but you know how it is.'

Keeping that smile glued on was harder by the second, but if I let it slip for an instant I knew I'd start dissolving, instead. Having just come back from changing Tom, Sally was gaping at me, which made it even worse.

'I thought I knew how it was,' he said. 'But I'm not so sure any more. Why don't you tell me?'

I put a puzzled note into my voice. 'What d'you mean?'

'Oh, Harriet, come on. We've been here before, haven't we? Off, on – hot, cold – is it just me, or do you have thermostat trouble with everybody?'

I couldn't keep this up much longer. 'Look, John, I think we might have got our wires crossed just a bit, and I dare say it's my fault. I probably got a little bit overheated last weekend, but you can blame it on the snowballs.'

'The snowballs,' he said, dry as Sahara dust. 'Was that it?'

'Well, not entirely – I suppose I got rather carried away.' I even managed to put in an apologetic note here. 'It was just a bit of fun, John. I'd love to have dinner with you – after all you've done I should be taking you to the Ivy – and I'm really sorry about today, but I can't help things coming up. I had Tara's mother on the phone earlier, by the way – she said thank you so much for everything and be sure to let them know how much they owe you. For her mobile and your petrol, and all that. Oh Lord, I still owe you for the hotel bill and my taxi fare, don't I?'

His reply was cool and sardonic. No melted chocolate at all. 'No, Harriet. Not this time. Have them on me.'

As he hung up, my glue was already dissolving. 'Bastard.' I slammed my phone on the table in tears. 'That'll teach you.'

Two minutes later I was blowing into the third soggy tissue. 'Sally, I *had* to. I had to make him think it meant sod all to me, too.'

'If you ask me, he's going to think the opposite. That it did mean something, but for some perverse reason of your own you're trying to make him think it didn't. He's just going to think you're screwed up.'

'Whose side are you on, anyway?'

'Yours! Anyway, you don't *know* it meant sod all to him.'

'It didn't mean much, did it? Not if he could go and do it with someone else inside a week. You're the one who said "don't get hurt", remember?'

'Well, you have, so it's a bit of a stable-door situation, isn't it? Anyway, I'm the last one you should listen to when it comes to relationships. Just look at me. A walking disaster area, with stretch marks.'

Something in her tone alerted me. Her eyes were welling up. 'Sally, what is it?'

She wiped them with her sleeve. 'Nothing.'

It obviously wasn't. Had I read her all wrong? 'It's not Steve, is it? You're not thinking of burnt boats?'

'It's not Steve! How many times do I have to tell you?' But she forced a smile. 'I'm just being daft. Catching it from you, probably. End of subject, OK?'

I lay awake for ages that night, thinking of burnt boats. If Sally had burnt a boat she really wanted, she'd never admit it. It was no use pressing her; I knew Sally too well. She'd just get mad and even more pig-headed.

Then I thought of my own burnt boat, of his cool, sardonic voice saying, 'Have them on me.' Where had the melted chocolate gone, once I wasn't melting? Could he turn it on and off like a tap? I thought of that night, of the snow, and cuddling up with him afterwards. I thought of how warm it had felt, how utterly right, as if every other man had been a mere rehearsal.

I thought of the postscript on his note, and my heart contracted painfully. Maybe it was second nature to him to write stuff like that. A few little words, to make you go all warm and gooey. Maybe he'd even meant them at the time. It wouldn't surprise me. It was all

438

part of his deadly appeal. I knew I'd done the right thing. How could I have ever handled a relationship with someone like that?

All the following day, I tried to put him out of my head. I told myself it was just as Sally had said: obsession and frustration combined. On Tuesday I managed not to think about him for about thirty-two per cent of the day, but when I arrived home that evening Sally got me going again. 'I've had a really horrible thought,' she said, the instant I was in the door. 'What if it was Tara?'

'*Tara?*'

'In the photos!'

'It couldn't be!'

'It might. What if he'd phoned her, and she'd had a day off, and he'd felt a bit sorry for her and said come up?'

'He'd have told me!'

'Harriet, you've hardly spoken to him, have you? He might not have got round to it. Rosie said she was blonde, didn't she?'

'Sally, it can't have been her. He'd never invite her up. She'd take it as encouragement.'

'OK, it was just a thought.'

But once she'd voiced it, I began to wonder whether she might just be right, which was a thought horrible enough to make me feel sick. What had Rosie said? Looking up at him, all sweet and adoring? Would that fit Tara, if he was being very nice to her again?

Treating her to an evening out because he felt sorry for her? I could see him doing it. *Poor kid* . . . She could have stayed the night before he put her on a train in the morning.

Purely to rule it out, I tried phoning Tara three times, but since she wasn't answering I left a message. Would she please phone me asap, it was very important.

By the following evening she still hadn't phoned back and wasn't answering, either. I didn't seriously think it could be her, but I was a churning wreck anyway. 'I'm going to see Nina,' I told Sally when I got home.

'You're not going to tell her?'

'I have to! This whole business is eating away at me like some horrible parasite. I have to get it out in the open.'

'Don't come running to me when she kills you. She might not even have the photos any more, anyway. She's probably torn them up.'

'I'm not going just to see the photos. I just have to get things straight. I can't bear this hole-and-corner stuff any more.'

'If you tell her you know about Stuart, you'll be dropping Suzanne and Rosie right in it.'

'I won't even mention them. I'll say I found out years ago. She might suspect as much. If she even remembers Stuart, that is.'

\*      \*      \*

440

As some serious psyching up was required, I didn't see Nina until the following evening. I didn't have to ask Rosie for her address, as I still had that invitation somewhere. Maybe I'd subconsciously kept it for this very purpose. I didn't phone first. When you're dropping bombshells, there's no harm in an element of surprise.

I went at around seven thirty, hardly expecting her to be in. Her flat was about two and half miles away, a conversion from one of those huge houses that used to have butlers and fourteen under-housemaids flirting with the footman.

There was an entryphone, of course. Feeling unbelievably calm, I pressed 9, waited half a minute and pressed it again.

'Yes?'

'Nina, it's Harriet. Have you got half an hour?'

'Harriet!' There was a taken-aback pause that sounded marginally flustered. 'I'm not really, well . . .'

'Nina, I have to see you. It's about John.'

*John?*' This taken-abackness was so different, I knew at once what she'd been thinking. Six letters, beginning with S. 'What on earth would you know about—'

'If you let me in, I'll tell you.'

After a momentary silence she said, 'Take the lift to the fourth floor. It's on the left.' Bzzzz . . .

Inside it was quietly upmarket, smelling faintly of polish. Her front door was substantial panelled wood and my first thought, when she opened it, was that

441

she'd shrunk. She was wearing a soft grey robe thing, like a long dress, of the type some people put on after a shower when they don't want to slob in a dressing gown but can't be bothered to get properly dressed. Her feet were bare, which was why she seemed to have shrunk. Her hair was wet, as if she'd just run a comb through it after a shower. Her face was devoid of make-up. She looked so different, her eyes so much less defined, I wondered whether she'd worn mascara even at school. She looked almost vulnerable, which is a word I thought I'd never use in the same breath as 'Nina'.

With heels on, I towered over her. And not for the first time since I'd grown into my feet, I felt the advantage of height.

Still at the door, she was eyeing me with guarded suspicion. 'What's this about John? I finished with him a couple of weeks ago, in case you didn't know.'

'No, you didn't. He finished with you.' As she opened her mouth for outraged denial, I went on, 'Nina, it's no use. I know what happened. I came to tell you I was seeing him, too.'

I don't think I'll ever forget her face. Take two parts of shock mixed with one of disbelief and you wouldn't be far wrong. She was too stunned even to add the splash of fury I'd expected.

'Can I come in?' I asked, before she got her voice back.

Wordlessly she showed me through. As Rosie had

said, it was all blond wood and uncluttered cream, with hardly a thing anywhere unless it was from a gallery. 'You can't have been seeing him,' she said in disbelieving tones, after I'd sat on a cream sofa without being asked. 'Where on earth would you have met him?'

I ignored the implication that someone like me just wouldn't meet someone like him during the normal social round. I don't think she even realized she was doing it. 'It was in the street, not long before Christmas.' It was amazing how calm you could be when the other person's just been squashed under your bombshell. 'You had just grabbed a cab – I was looking in a shop window. Suddenly he was there, talking to me. Nothing really happened,' I added quickly, seeing stirrings of outrage. 'Not until I knew he'd finished with you.'

She was steaming up nicely. 'I don't know how you've got the nerve to come and tell me this.'

'At least I waited till he'd dumped you,' I said. 'Which is more than you did with Stuart.'

I do recommend this tactic. Before your first bombshell's worn off, drop another. A dull flush suffused her face. She actually had the grace to look awkward, but I had to admire her for still looking me in the eye.

'I was wondering whether you ever found out about that,' she muttered. 'Who told you?'

'Does it matter? It was years ago. And before you ask, anything that happened with John had absolutely nothing to do with it.'

By now she was looking so much like someone wanting to crawl away and die, I almost felt sorry for her.

Almost. 'Why did you invite me to that lunch? Guilt?'

She gave an awkward little shrug. 'We were friends, weren't we?'

'I'll have to check my dictionary. I'm not sure my definition is quite the same as yours.'

Maybe I'd gone a bit far here. She wasn't quite squirming, but very nearly. 'I wouldn't mind a drink,' I said, in less acid tones. 'A glass of wine'll do.'

Worldlessly she got up, disappeared into the kitchen, and came back with two large glasses of something white that hadn't cost £2.99 at Tesco's. She had also recovered much of her composure. 'I gather Rosie's been busy.'

'Can we just leave Rosie out of it? Everything she told me was perfectly innocent. She hadn't a clue I'd been seeing him till the other day.'

Obviously about to argue, she bit it back. Her composure was returning fast; she looked almost in control again. 'I'm not making excuses, but has it ever occurred to you that Stuart must have been attracted to me, or he'd never have played along?'

It had. That only added salt to the wound, except that there wasn't really a wound any more, only a scar you could hardly see.

'He didn't need asking twice to come to Italy,' she

went on. 'He jumped at it. I never thought he would. It made it very awkward when Rob said he was coming after all.'

She was unbelievable, but I hadn't expected much else. 'I didn't come to talk ancient history,' I said, with an edge even I could hear. 'I came to talk about John, and the fact that whoever your spy caught him with wasn't the only one. God knows why, but I thought you might like to know you're not the only one who got hurt.'

She looked up at me. 'Did you sleep with him?'

I swallowed hard. 'Yes.'

After a tense silence she knocked back more of her wine. Looking down at her glass she said, 'I never felt sure of him, not even at first. There's something about him women just can't resist. He's got a way of looking at you as if you're the only woman in the world.'

As if I needed telling. My throat constricted painfully. For the first time I felt some real empathy with her.

'But I'm over him now,' she went on. 'I made myself get over him. You have to cut them out, like a tumour.' She looked up at me. 'Do you want to see the photos?'

'I wouldn't have thought you'd still have them.'

'I shouldn't still have them. I just didn't get round to throwing them out. I might even keep them, as a reminder not to get involved with anyone like him again.'

I couldn't say anything.

'After all, they cost enough,' she went on, with more than a trace of acid. 'Have you any idea what these private detectives charge?'

'I can guess.' This led to the next question I couldn't hold back. 'Why on earth did you do it? What was the point, when it was over?'

'I had to know,' she said flatly. 'I knew he was lying and I had to know. She's not even anything special. I can't imagine what on earth he could see in her, except that she's looking up at him as if he's the only man in the universe. Like some sweet, pre-feminist relic who'd iron his spreadsheets if he asked her.' She knocked back another mouthful of wine, put her glass down on a side table.

She disappeared for a moment, came back with a brown A4 envelope and handed it to me. 'There are six. He had a good camera, I'll say that for him.'

All taken at night, they were sharply focused black and white shots, about eight by ten. As I looked at the first, then the second and the third, my stomach felt as if it were being sucked into a vortex, like water down a sink.

Photo four showed only head and shoulders. They were evidently walking down the street, his arm close around her. She was smiling up at him, almost laughing in a shy way, as if he'd said something funny.

I'd known I'd feel sick. I just hadn't realized how sick.

# Sixteen

Whatever my face betrayed, Nina noticed. Suddenly sharp, she said, 'Don't tell me you know her?'

My voice came out dry and weird. 'It's not him.'

'What?'

Over my own voice echoing in my head I could hardly hear her: *It was just a bit of fun . . .* 'It's not John.'

'Of course it's John! What on earth are you talking about?'

'It isn't! It's nothing like him!'

Some flash of realization crossed her face.

'What?' I demanded.

Following realization came an after-rush of relief I didn't understand, either. 'Where, exactly, did you meet him?'

I told her, more or less.

'Well, I should have guessed,' she said, in almost matter-of-fact tones. 'That was *John*-John. Not *John*.'

Now I felt I really was going mad. But before I could say anything she went on, '*J-O-H-N*-John. As in John Mackenzie. As opposed to *J-O-N*-Jon. As in Jonathan King.'

It was her turn to drop a bombshell. 'You were seeing two of them? Both at once?'

'For God's sake, Harriet, don't we all sometimes?'

'You were mad about him! How can you see someone when you're mad about someone else?'

She looked from my face to my glass and back again. 'I think you could do with a top-up,' she said, in the kind-to-lesser-mortals tones I remembered from way back. 'So could I, come to that.'

While she was gone I stared at those photos, wondering what the hell I'd done and whether I'd ever stop feeling sick again.

She came back with the bottle, filled both our glasses, and sat down. 'All right, I'm not particularly proud of it,' she said, tucking her bare feet underneath her. 'But as I said, I never felt sure of him. I had a feeling almost from the first that it wasn't going to last. I had to have another iron or two in the fire.'

'An iron or *two*? How many were there?'

'A couple,' she shrugged.

Spinning through my head was all the warmed-up gossip Rosie had ever told me. I couldn't believe how stupid I'd been, except that it had all fitted at the time. 'You're not still seeing him? John Mackenzie, I mean?'

'God, no.'

'How long were you seeing him?'

'Not long.' She gave a little shrug. 'I only saw

him three times, maybe four – I really can't remember.' Suddenly her eyes narrowed, her expression sharpening like a lead pencil. 'You weren't thinking *he* finished it?'

My face evidently said it for me, because she gave an incredulous little laugh. 'He was quite sweet,' she added, in tones that suddenly made me want to slap her, 'but he really wasn't my type.'

My mouth was desiccated. 'I don't believe you.'

I'd expected a furious flash, as if I'd thrown down a gauntlet or whatever they did in the olden days when they wanted an excuse to run a sword through someone's guts.

I should have known better. In almost pitying tones she said, 'Ask him, then.'

Until then I'd thought my green snakes could not possibly get any worse. I don't know when I'd so desperately wanted someone to be lying, but known they weren't.

Twisting the honeyed knife, she went on, 'He was very keen, I can tell you. I didn't like hurting his feelings but it would never have done.'

Like a masochist I asked, 'What was wrong with him?'

She shrugged again. 'He just wasn't quite up to the mark.'

How I didn't slap her I'll never know. 'Was that the first time you saw him? At that restaurant?'

'Oh, no.'

'Did you sleep with him?'

'Of course not!' She looked as if the mere question defiled her. 'I only saw him three or four times – I don't dish myself out that easily.' After a pause she added kindly, 'I'm sure it would have been quite nice; it's not that I wasn't attracted to him, but it wouldn't have been fair to let him think it was going anywhere when it wasn't.'

He might do for me, in other words, but he wouldn't do for her. I remembered her once talking to me almost exactly like this in Home Economics, when I'd produced a reasonable cheese soufflé: 'Oh, well *done*, Harriet,' when she knew perfectly well hers was miles better, but it was amazing that mine had risen at all.

Unable to take any more, I rose to my feet. 'Thanks for the drink, but I think I'd better go.'

'Well, if you must . . .'

I don't know why I bragged about height advantage, earlier. On the way to the door she managed to make me feel like that bog-roll dinosaur all over again. In a subtle way her whole demeanour said *That was close at first, but it's game, set and match to me, I think.*

At the door she said sweetly, 'Do give my love to John when you see him.'

Slapping was too good for her. I wanted to ram her head down the loo and pour a bottle of Toilet Duck on top. That would have sorted her sodding silk curtain out. 'I'm not seeing him any more.'

'Really?' She raised delicate eyebrows. 'Not because you thought he was being a naughty boy with someone else, I hope?'

I made no reply, but she wasn't stupid.

'Just as well you came, then,' she said. 'If you've got any sense you'll get on the phone and sort it out. He might not be quite my cup of tea, but I've met thousands worse.'

I nearly stopped at an offie on the way home, for a mega-bottle of anything. I was beginning to see why people drank themselves to blissful oblivion. I'd happily have joined them, except that I never got to the blissful-oblivion stage, just to the feeling-yuck-and-throwing-up stage, your head spinning every time you close your eyes, puke-trips to the loo all night, and still feeling like death in the morning.

Sally said everything a friend should say, e.g. 'I *would* have shoved her head down the loo,' and 'Well, how were you to know? If it didn't occur to a cynic like me that she was seeing two at once . . .' This was followed by 'Come on, have some lasagne. It'll be all dried up.'

Since she'd actually slaved over it herself I tried, but it might have been cat litter. I said, 'I'm sorry, I'm just not hungry,' and poured myself another glass of wine, about the fourth since I'd got home.

Tom was still up. It was well past nine o'clock but

he was in a nocturnal phase. As he beamed at me from her lap, I grabbed him, gave him an extravagant, miserable cuddle. I needed someone to cuddle and Widdles was asleep on his sofa-throne. He never liked being picked up anyway.

'What did he look like?' Sally asked.

'Like any other good-looking bloke who looks nice enough, too. But nothing like John.'

An edge of exasperation came into her voice. 'Why the hell don't you just phone him?'

'How can I?' I asked miserably, over Tom's little head. 'I'd have to tell him everything – what kind of devious, screwed-up bitch will he think I am? First I pretended I didn't even know her, then I've told him to sod off twice, never mind telling him I just got carried away the other night . . . Carried away! He'll believe it, too. You should have seen me, trying to tear his trousers off like some starving rampant nympho . . .'

A ghost of Sally's old spark came to her eyes. 'Then he'll be glad if you come back for seconds, I bet. And thirds.'

'I can't.' Wretchedly I rained kisses on Tom's head, but he didn't seem to mind. 'I just can't face telling him all that, and having him look at me as if I need a shrink.'

'Even Nina said you should phone him, didn't she?' she went on. 'That's the one vaguely redeeming thing she said, if you ask me.'

It was, but to me that was just another point against Nina. 'I don't *want* her saying redeeming things! I want her to be a hundred per cent, twenty-four carat cow, so I can fantasize about Toilet Ducks with a clear conscience.'

After a minute Sally said, 'Are you sure it's just having to confess you can't handle? Nothing to do with him being one of Nina's rejects?'

'It's not that!' But I knew this wasn't quite true. 'All right, it galls me. It sickens me. I mean, how the hell could he possibly not be "up to the mark"? What mark, for heaven's sake?'

'God knows,' she shrugged. 'Except that it's just as well we don't all fancy the same people.'

'Yes, but if she didn't fancy him why would she see him more than once? I still can't believe it, but even I could see she was telling the truth.'

'Not fancying him should count in his favour,' she pointed out. 'I wouldn't have thought any bloke who'd appeal to her would ever appeal to you.'

'OK, but it still galls me.' I kept seeing her face: '"He was quite sweet, but . . ."' *Quite sweet*! I mean, how *dare* she?'

'Look, she was just trying to piss you off,' she said. 'And it looks as if she succeeded. Shouldn't you be ringing Rosie, before Suzanne gets it in the neck from Nina for blabbing, and Rosie gets it in the neck from Suzanne?'

I switched on my mobile and found a message from

Tara. Sorry she hadn't called back, but she'd lost her phone. Well, not exactly lost it, it had fallen down the side of her bed.

Not that it mattered now. I was dreading telling Rosie, but when I spoke to her she was more concerned for me. 'I feel really awful now,' she fretted. 'Only I never once imagined . . .'

'Neither did I. I'm just worried about you getting hell from Suzanne.'

'It's just tough,' she said philosophically. 'She wasn't supposed to tell me anything, was she? Anyway, I'll be moving out soon. Imagine Nina keeping irons in the fire like that! Honestly, she must be so cold-blooded. I wouldn't be surprised if Suzanne's glad of an excuse to row with her, anyway. She gets so sick of playing lady-in-waiting to the drama queen.'

'Yes, but if she does go off her head you can always move in here.'

'Thanks,' she said. 'You never know.'

Helen rang shortly afterwards. 'I phoned him,' she said. 'My demon lover from the train. I thought you'd like to know.'

About time too. 'And?'

'I've seen him twice.' Almost bashfully she added, 'I told him everything in the end, even the bit about thinking I was pregnant. He'd been upset when I didn't phone. He'd thought maybe I'd fibbed about being separated. He's a bit younger than me, only thirty-six, but it doesn't seem to bother him.'

454

I was so pleased for her, it almost took the edge off my own mess. 'How's everything else? Have you seen the twins?'

'Yes, last weekend. Lawrence dropped them off and I took them to Burger King and the cinema afterwards.'

The old, unloved note had come back to her voice, almost making me wish I'd never asked. 'And?'

'Nothing, really,' she sighed. 'I don't think they're even missing me. All they were concerned about was whether they could have double fries. Francesca won't have chips in the house.'

'Talking of chips, how's the cooking going?'

'I'll let you know after this party tomorrow night. I'm a bit nervous but I've been cooking and freezing for days. I'm having nightmares about dropping trays of canapés.'

'You'll be fine,' I soothed.

'At least the cooking and the bloke are taking her mind off those kids,' Sally said afterwards. 'She's obviously regretting it, but she'll never just call Lawrence and say she's changed her mind.'

She gave me a pointed look. 'Like you won't call John and say *you've* changed your mind. Don't come crying to me after you've taken two weeks to psych yourself up and then he's got somebody else. OK, I know you can't phone him now, you're half pissed.' She picked up the bottle; there was about an inch left at the bottom and most of it had gone down my throat, on top of what I'd had at Nina's. 'I wouldn't *want* you to phone him now. You need a clear head.'

A clear head was precisely what I didn't have next morning. It was partly the fact that I'd had white at Nina's and red at ours (because that was all we had) plus a large gin and a Cointreau once the red had run out. Mixtures never mixed well in my system, particularly on an empty stomach. I almost wished I could throw up, to get rid of it, but instead I woke up feeling like something decomposing behind the sofa after Widdles had dragged it in.

I should have taken a sickie, but I never took sickies. I went to work feeling dreadful, had a tuna and sweetcorn sandwich that made me throw up at last, and went home feeling double dreadful. Sally suggested some of Tom's baby rice with apple. I got about three tablespoons down, went to bed for a couple of hours and woke up at nine o'clock, looking and feeling like something that's been in a morgue for six weeks.

Sally said, 'For God's sake, will you please just *phone* him?'

'Like this? Just look at me! What if he came straight round?'

This was an unlikely scenario, but I couldn't risk it. I had rings under my eyes. My skin looked like wallpaper paste. I even had an incipient spot on my chin.

'He won't notice,' she scoffed. 'Have a shower. We could light a couple of candles and pretend all the bulbs have blown.'

Eventually I did phone him, at half past nine.

I got the answerphone. I tried at ten to ten and got it again.

My green snakes might never have gone away. 'He's out,' I said miserably to Sally. 'I might have known he would be. He's out with some non-screwed-up cow who doesn't look like something out of *Prisoner: Cell Block H.*'

'He's probably taken his booming auntie to see *HMS Pinafore*,' she soothed. 'Phone him tomorrow.'

I tried to ignore my snakes, but they wouldn't go away. In fact, they were turning into pythons. I saw him with nympho Charlotte after all, who was now an even more rampant nympho than I'd been the other night, telling him to turn his phone off, she didn't want interruptions while she tied him to the bedposts and shagged him senseless till dawn.

I sat watching rubbish television with Sally till half past ten. 'I miss Jacko,' I said forlornly. 'I wish Jacko were here.'

'Call him, then.'

So I did. He was actually at home, on his own. He hadn't even been out for a couple of pints.

'You're not sick again, are you?' I asked. It was Friday night, for God's sake.

'No, but I've had a lot to catch up with,' he sighed. 'I swear the old man's been piling it up on purpose. How's things?'

'Crap,' I said, and felt myself dissolving. 'Oh, Jacko, I wish you were here . . .'

I was on the phone for over an hour. I lay on my bed, telling him everything I'd never told him about John, everything that had happened since he'd left, all about Sally and Steve, and dissolving during much of it. 'I'm a daft cow,' I sniffed.

'Yes, but you always were a daft cow and I love you anyway. You'll feel better in the morning. Phone John then – I bet he's just having an early night. He's probably been crying into his beer non-stop.'

Then I passed him to Sally, who said, 'Hi, Ape-Face, why aren't you out on the piss?' She seemed perkier afterwards. I think she'd been missing all the squabbling.

I went to bed feeling better, woke up at eight and still felt better, until I looked in the mirror. My skin was still wallpaper paste, but I didn't notice that. You don't notice wallpaper paste when there's a huge red mountain on your chin.

I could have cried, but I cursed, instead. I touched it; it felt sore.

All thoughts of phoning John went out of the window. What if he came straight round? Yes, I know you can get brilliant concealers, I had one, but even the best of them don't last. They rub off on the pillow. You wake up after a lovely cuddly night, turn to the man of your dreams and smile sleepily – and all he can see is that colossal purple mountain on your chin.

It was going to go purple, I just knew it. I hadn't had a purple mountain in years, but once upon a time I used to get one regularly, every three months, always in much the same place. It was just typical sodding bloody sod's law that I was getting one now.

'You're run down,' Sally said, like someone's mother, which I suppose she was. 'You've done nothing but run round after other people for weeks. Take some vitamins.'

'Vitamins aren't going to do much good, are they?' I said miserably. 'How can I phone him when I look like this?'

'He won't notice. Put some concealer on.'

I tried putting hot compresses on my mountain, to hurry the process, but it only got worse. It had dug itself in for the duration. It leered at me evilly in the mirror, saying it wasn't going away for at least ten days, so there. It had a good mind to get a yellow head on it, turn septic and infect the whole lower half of my face.

It was a horrible day, too, drizzly and depressing. I dripped and fidgeted round the house, looking in the mirror every ten minutes and wondering why the hell modern science wasted time on stuff like the Internet when an instant zit blaster would do so much more for the human condition.

For want of anything else to do, I made an overdue assault on Dorothy's junk, much of which was in boxes in the two attic bedrooms, where I'd shoved it months earlier. Although I'd already got rid of masses, there was still enough to sink the Isle of Wight, but this was stuff that needed careful sorting. There were piles of books, some so old they might be valuable. There were letters, tied in dozens of bundles. There were photos, a whole battered old suitcase of them.

An hour after I'd started Sally brought me a coffee and since Tom was taking a pre-lunch siesta, she stayed.

'Have you seen this?' she demanded, holding up a fat, leather-bound volume entitled *The Englishwoman's Domestic Magazine*. 'Look!' She showed me a coloured fashion plate: a 'lady's morning toilet', dated Autumn, 1881. There was a pattern, too, for a 'baby's boot embroidered in silk'. It was pristine, unused.

'It must be worth a bomb!' she said. 'You should have it valued.'

I was going through the photos. Most were ancient, of people I dare say even Dad wouldn't have a clue about, but there were later ones, too. Even one of me, aged six or so. Then I found something else to show Sally.

'Aah,' she said. 'Your mum and dad?'

It was their wedding group, with old Dorothy looking sprightly enough at sixty-five or so. Mum was
wearing a traditional, frothy white dress: pretty, but
horribly dated. Dad wore a morning suit; they both
wore happy-ever-after smiles.

'Sad, isn't it?' Sally said, echoing my thoughts
exactly. 'Or poignant, perhaps. All those naïve expectations . . . Your mum was really pretty.'

'Still is,' I said.

'Mind you, your dad was quite nice-looking, too. I
wonder what went wrong?'

'Incompatibility,' I said. 'I often wonder how the
hell they hit it off enough to get hitched in the
first place.'

I soon found out.

As waking-up noises were wafting up the stairs from
Tom, Sally went to see to him while I got on with the
letters. In bundles according to the writer, some dated
back to the Twenties, but I couldn't throw any out
until Dad had seen them. Some, however, were much
more recent. I recognized the writing on one little
bundle: my grandmother, Dad's mother. The first
three were pretty mundane: the dreadful weather,
poor Muriel's sciatica, whoever Muriel was.

It was the fourth that caught my attention. '. . . I
can't pretend to be entirely pleased, but of course
there's no alternative. David seems perfectly happy,
anyway, and I was relieved to find Pat a nice enough
girl. They've arranged the wedding for 17th April

– couldn't get anything earlier except in a register office, which would not be very nice, but she'll be nearly five months gone – I hope to goodness she won't show. I need hardly tell you that no-one outside the immediate family knows; it'll be obvious soon enough, of course, but I'd rather not have any whispering at the wedding. Especially from Mona – you know what she's like . . .'

Something inside me went weird and frozen, until I read it again.

It didn't make sense.

I ran down to Sally, who was ladling puréed veggie casserole into Tom's mouth. 'Look at this!'

'That's it, then,' she said, once she'd read it. 'They "had" to get married, as they used to say. Because of you.'

'It wasn't *me*, dopey!' I was still in shock. 'They got married in April! I was born in January! Nearly two years after their wedding!'

I phoned Mum half an hour later.

'I've been going through some of Dorothy's letters,' I said, without preamble. 'Why didn't you tell me you were pregnant when you got married?'

There was an awful silence. 'Oh, dear heaven,' she said, in despairing tones.

It was a good forty minutes later when I finally hung up.

'Well, at least you know now,' Sally pointed out.

'She still should have told me.'

Of course, Mum had been in tears; it had been difficult getting much sense out of her at first, especially after we'd nearly had a row. She'd said she wasn't pregnant when she got married, and I'd said, 'Mum, *please*. If you dare lie to me now . . .'

She hadn't been pregnant, as it happened. She'd had a miscarriage a fortnight before the wedding, when she was nearly five months gone. It had been horrible, like going into labour except that you knew there wouldn't be a baby at the end of it. She'd hated even thinking about it afterwards, it had been so awful . . .

Eventually she'd got round to the rest. She'd met Dad when she was just getting over someone else, someone who'd treated her very badly. She'd been devastated and Dad had been like a safe haven after the storm. He'd been so kind . . . She'd thought she didn't want storms any more. She certainly hadn't married him just because of the pregnancy. They'd both been distraught over losing that baby. All she'd wanted, at the time, was to try again. She'd been 'happy enough' for years. That's exactly what she said; I thought it very telling.

It wasn't till I was about twelve that she'd become restless, suddenly craving more. She'd nearly had an affair, but couldn't bring herself to do it. She'd felt guilty, realizing she should never have married Dad, because safe havens just weren't enough any more. They'd grown further and further apart, they'd had different interests. But she'd never intended to leave him, not until she met Bill and found out just what she'd been missing. It had been agony, keeping him secret for a whole year. She'd hated hurting Dad, but he hadn't really been happy either, which was why she'd been so worried that he was doing the wrong thing with this Kathy. She wanted him to be happy more than anything, she felt she'd robbed him of something he should have had first time around.

I said to Sally, 'I can't bear to think of them staying together all those years because of me.'

'She didn't say that.'

'No, but they obviously did. They might have met the right people a whole lot earlier.'

'Or more wrong people. Let's face it, if we all only got involved with the right people, hardly anyone would ever get born.'

All this was still on my mind until around five o'clock, when we heard the front door open. 'Anyone home?' called a familiar voice.

'Jacko!'

'Thought I'd better come and cheer you up,' he grinned. 'Here. For my two favourite girls.' From behind his back he produced two identical bouquets of flowers.

'Oh, Jacko . . .' I was almost dissolving again, and even Sally wasn't as rude as usual.

'I missed you, Ape-Face,' she said, giving him a kiss. 'I won't say like what, but I missed you.'

It was quite a good evening, after that. We made a fire and a massive prawn curry (I had to go out for the prawns), and enjoyed a thoroughly cultured evening. That is to say, with crappy Saturday night television in the background, we played Monopoly with an ancient set of Dorothy's I'd just unearthed, with silver pieces. Sally and Jacko argued, of course. They both wanted the little silver doggie, Jacko said Sally was cheating and she said he couldn't have Mayfair, he'd lower the tone. She'd write to the Residents' Association and get him evicted.

After that things could only go downhill, culturally speaking. Jacko started a game we'd played as students, called Choose or Die. I think he had invented it, so needless to say it would have won first prize for puerility. We'd only ever played it after a really good night out, when everyone who hadn't passed out was up for anything.

What you did was this. You chose two of the most disgusting substances/activities you could think of and said to your victim, 'You have to eat (insert first disgusting substance) or (insert second). And you have to choose or die.'

The sole object of the game was to produce the loudest shrieks of disgusted laughter known to man. It follows that the substances that did the best drew largely on bodily waste, particularly of animals or ninety-five-year-olds; I'm sure you can imagine the activities.

After initial eyes-to-heaven stuff, Sally entered into the spirit of the thing. She cracked her face and came up with some moderately disgusting things herself. Jacko scoffed, said they were rubbish, and soon it turned into a battle between them to come up with positively the most disgusting things in the entire universe. It was me who sat like some sort of boring babysitter, wondering at their 'toilet yumour', as they call it across the pond. But then I was on the wagon and they weren't. The mere smell of alcohol still made me feel faintly yucky. I'd drunk nothing but tea, water, Ribena and Tesco's orange juice all day.

But if this was what a few glasses of wine and toilet yumour did for Sally, I was all for it. I hadn't seen her like this for ages. Her face was flushed with laughter, her eyes picking up the light from the fire.

Wanting an early night anyway, I left them to it and went to bed. I had a feeling early nights strengthened your resistance against purple mountains, but I took two supercharged vitamin Cs as well.

I was out like a light till seven fifteen. The first thing I did, naturally, was inspect my purple mountain in the dressing-table mirror. No worse, anyway. Possibly even a bit better. Nominally cheered, I went to the bathroom, padding softly so as not to wake Sally or Tom. Nothing would wake Jacko, he'd be hibernating under the covers till eleven. I still hadn't changed those sheets but he wouldn't care. Intending to retreat to bed for at least an hour, I crept back.

Sally's door was now ajar, Tom's early-morning gurglings wafting out. Then I heard, 'Well? Some of that leftover curry? Weetabix? I used to like a nice boiled egg with soldiers, me.'

I pushed the door open.

Wearing his tartan dressing gown, Jacko was lifting Tom out of his cot. 'Here's Auntie Harry,' he said to him. 'She was a bit of a boring old hag last night, but we'll pretend she wasn't.'

I looked from him to Sally's neatly made bed. 'Where is she?'

'Asleep,' he said.

'Don't tell me she crashed out on the sofa again?'

Jacko turned to Tom, perched in the crook of his left arm. 'Poor old Harry's a bit slow, isn't she?' he said to him. 'But she always was, first thing.'

Then he turned back to me.

A killer jelly hit me, but it bounced. I gaped at him, literally unable to take it in.

There was no hint of a smirk on his face, or even faint embarrassment. 'Why do you think I stayed here so long?' he asked.

I could not utter.

'I love her,' he said simply. 'I loved her from the word go.'

I was so stunned, I still couldn't get anything out. I waited for him to say, 'Only kidding,' grin and tell me I was dead easy to wind up at this time in the morning, but I waited in vain.

'I was asking Tom what he wanted for breakfast,' he went on, as if he hadn't just been launching airborne jellies. 'I heard him talking to himself, but I didn't want to wake Sally.'

I located some sort of voice. 'She usually gives him a bottle first thing. She's had to get him onto bottles, for when she goes to work. But he'll need his nappy changed first.'

'I thought he might. Like to give me a few pointers?'

Still stunned, I put the changing mat on the bed, handed him baby wipes. I watched as he laid Tom on it, saying, 'I'm not too bright at this, mate, so bear with me,' and saw Tom grinning back. I watched as he unpopped his sleepsuit competently enough, undid his nappy. He said to Tom, 'Boy, that's a corker. Like one of those ripe French cheeses, crawling off your plate.' I watched as he cleaned him up competently enough. Eventually, handing him a clean nappy, I said, 'Why on earth didn't you *tell* me?'

'I couldn't,' he said. 'I thought I might as well tell you I wanted Madonna. Which way up does this thing go?'

I showed him, and he managed the rest himself. With Tom back in his arm, he said, 'Could you give me a hand with his bottle?'

I followed him downstairs, wanting to ask fourteen thousand questions, but unable to get any of them out. I asked myself questions, instead. Had I been blind, or stupid, or both? What about Sally?

468

In a way, Jacko was carrying on as if nothing unusual had happened, but in another way he was different. An aura of placid, warm assurance hung about him, something I'd never quite seen in him before. After helping him with the bottle and feeding a yowling Widdles, I sat with Tom, while he made a cup of tea for Sally. Then he thought he'd add a piece of toast, and put it on a tray. While the bread was toasting he nodded at the box of snowdrops outside the kitchen window. 'Mind if I raid your little flowers?'

I said, 'No, pick some,' and he went out in bare feet, cut half a dozen and looked for an eggcup to put them in, until I remembered a tiny silver vase of Dorothy's. He put the snowdrops in that, buttered and cherry-jammed the toast, and inspected it all with satisfaction. 'Right, I'll take everything up.'

'You can't manage it all,' I said. 'Let me take Tom.'

'I'll manage.' So with Tom and his bottle in one arm and the tray in the other, he departed.

Once he'd gone, the thoughts I'd been refusing to think came to torment me. What if Sally had just got carried away? What if she'd just felt her urges coming back like a landslide? It was so easy to think of Jacko as a multi-fancying dickhead; hardly anyone realized how hard the real thing could hit him. And this was a hard hit, I just knew it. If we were in for Michaela all over again, I couldn't bear it. I couldn't bear it for him.

After two cups of coffee I knew I'd never get back to sleep, so I went for a shower, instead. I looked at Jacko's door, but it was closed and I heard nothing.

After the shower I went back to bed anyway, put Capital on, but I didn't sleep.

From the word go, he'd said. It had hardly been a laugh-a-minute 'go'. He'd first met her three days after that ClearBlue test, when he'd come down for a football match. Sally had been in no frame of mind even to notice he was there. He'd come again for the occasional weekend, but there had always been a reason. Liverpool playing West Ham, rugby at Twickenham, an old mate's stag night. I'd never thought it odd that he'd had something on every three weeks or so and needed a bed. I'd always been glad to see him. It was after a stag night that he'd had that accident, and I'd never wondered why he'd wanted to stay with us rather than go home. After all, it had only been sensible to stick with the consultant who'd patched him up. As for Frida . . .

A blind? A smokescreen? Or just Jacko being Jacko?

I went downstairs at five to nine and found the three of them in the kitchen. I don't quite know what it was, but something told me at once that my fears for Jacko were needless. Sally was sitting at the table, her hands wrapped round a mug. She wore the tartan dressing gown and a pink and sheepish grin. 'Hi,' she said.

470

I looked from her to Jacko. 'I've got a good mind to sue you two,' I said. 'I had to go back to bed to get over the shock.'

'Any excuse,' Jacko grinned. He was dressed, even down to his outdoor fleece. In his buggy, Tom was muffled up in his arctic all-in-one. Jacko shot me a wink, but it was Tom he spoke to. 'Right, mate, let's get out of here.' In a whisper he added, 'I think they want to talk about me.' He dropped a kiss on Sally's cheek. 'See you later.'

'Bye, Ape-Face,' she said. 'No speeding with that buggy.'

He opened the back door and pushed Tom out. Once the door had shut behind him Sally said, 'He's just popping up the road. We're nearly out of milk.'

Not for the first time that morning, I couldn't find any words that would do. Like Jacko, she looked subtly different. A pink, contented aura hung around her. 'Maybe you'll believe me now,' she said. 'About Steve, I mean.'

I found two words, at least. 'Since when?'

'I don't know . . .' She gave a helpless little shrug. 'Ages. I suppose it started dawning on me when he had his accident. And then when Frida came, and he started all that daft flirting, only I wasn't so sure it was just daft . . .'

I sat at the table. 'And last night it all just happened?'

'If you put it like that,' she said sheepishly. 'We were

still playing that stupid game and I was laughing my head off, but suddenly he was looking at me and I wasn't laughing any more. I just knew. And he said, "We can be just mates or I'll love you for ever. And you have to choose, or I'll die."'

Suddenly she wasn't sheepish any more. She was wiping a tear from her eye.

My throat constricted. 'Oh, Sally . . .'

'I couldn't believe it,' she went on. 'I mean, I knew he'd probably never have kicked me out of bed, but this . . . He kissed me. It's been so long, it was almost like the first kiss I ever had.'

I was a bit wet round the eyes now, I can tell you. 'But bed? I thought you couldn't face the thought.'

'That's just it. I thought I couldn't till then, but something started coming back. Only when it got to the point, I got cold feet. After all those stitches I couldn't imagine it not hurting. I felt almost as if I'd never done it before. I told him I didn't want to.'

I didn't say anything.

'And he said, "Never mind, we'll just have a cuddle." He was so sweet . . .' She wiped another tear away, her voice cracking.

The old Sally soon came back. 'But then I wanted to, after all,' she continued, with a wicked little grin. 'I'll tell you something, though. All that practice has paid off. He knows what he's about.'

We laughed, and suddenly things were normal

again. As normal as they'd ever be. After a minute I said, 'I still can't believe you didn't tell me.'

'I couldn't. I thought you might tell him and he'd start something just to be nice. It wasn't as if I exactly fancied him, either,' she said. 'I still felt as if something had died in that department. I just sort of *wanted* him, if you know what I mean.'

I didn't, quite, but then I'd never had forty-eight stitches.

'It was the bloody money factor, too,' she added. 'I couldn't bear anyone thinking it was just a bit too convenient, a broke single mother falling for a bloke with money. Already he's been talking about buying me a car,' she went on. 'This morning, in bed. Can you believe it?'

Knowing Jacko, all too well.

'I told him no way,' she declared. 'When I get one, I'll pay for it myself.'

Jacko was a long time getting that milk, but he did possess a certain amount of tact, when required. Eventually we got back to Steve.

She hadn't wanted him showing up, for various reasons. First, she'd thought he wouldn't want to know and she didn't want to *know* that he didn't want to know. She didn't want poor little Tom having a bloke like that for a father. Second, if he did want to know she'd feel she should get together with him, but knew she couldn't. It would really have been easier if he'd stayed away. If it hadn't been such a shock to see him there, she mightn't have reacted the way she did. Looking back, she'd been unfair to him. He'd said he would have phoned, if he'd had a number. He'd even said he'd been busy, having a pre-divorce clear-out of the marital home. So she shouldn't have told him he was one up from a turkey-baster, but it had all been too much, especially when she'd convinced herself he wasn't going to come at all.

Then we got back to Jacko. 'No wonder you were so ratty half the time,' I said. 'Thinking he was after Frida and Czech au pairs, and not telling a soul . . .'

She went all sheepish again. 'I did tell someone.'

'Who?'

'Rosie. She doesn't blab everything,' she added quickly, seeing my face. 'I told her that night she came round, when you were out. I wasn't going to, but she was going on about how sweet he was, and I just had to tell someone.'

Except for my mountain, I went through the rest of the day in a sort of rosy haze. After all, your two best friends in the world getting it together is something only the Emmas of this world dream about. If they even like each other you count yourself lucky. As for signs I might have missed, I couldn't see any. She might have been ratty anyway. As for her tears over his presents, she'd have been upset about those anyway. That was just Sally.

Jacko left around nine thirty. He had to be at work early and it was a long drive, but he was coming back

474

on Friday night. Once he'd gone Sally busied herself with preparations for starting work the following morning.

It was only then that the last of my rosy haze wore off. My mountain was subsiding, but I still wasn't sure I'd be anything like presentable tomorrow. Assuming I needed to be presentable, of course. What if he wasn't answering again? Even if he did answer, what was I going to say? *'John, I didn't mean what I said the other day . . .'* What if he said, with barely contained exasperation, *'Look, Harriet, I can't handle any more of this. Let's just leave it there, shall we?'*

I went to bed with a mass of nervous butterflies in my stomach, but at least they made a change from snakes. When I woke up they were still there, but my red mountain had subsided further. It was more of a pink hill.

Sally refused a lift to the childminder's. It was walking distance, she needed the exercise. I said good luck as she went off at a quarter to eight, had another coffee, and left the house at ten past.

I stepped outside to a mini-drama. It didn't look like a mini-drama at first, just Matt and Toby in their school uniform, dawdling out of their front gate. I hadn't even seen Francesca till then but she was standing by the car, looking harassed.

I don't know what I'd imagined: someone like Nina, I suppose, or even worse. But she looked just like any other reasonably smart and attractive woman on a Monday morning: wishing it was Friday, instead.

'Will you please hurry *up*?' she said, as Matt dropped something and picked it up with maddening slowness.

I hadn't even seen the boys since before Christmas. They were non-identical, but still alike. 'Hi,' I said.

'Hi,' they mumbled.

As Francesca registered me, I had to say something. 'Hello. I'm Harriet.'

'Hello.' She said it slightly awkwardly, which didn't surprise me. 'We're running late,' she added hurriedly. 'Lawrence is down with flu so I'm doing the school run. *Now* what?' she asked Toby. Having half got into the car, he got out again. 'I've forgotten my swimming things,' he muttered.

Something in her seemed to snap. 'Right, that's it. I *told* you to be ready – I'm late as it is.' She shut the door he'd just got out of, as the pair of them gaped at her from the pavement. 'I'm sorry, but you'll have to get the bus. When I said ready, I *meant* ready.'

She shot me an exasperated look. 'I'm sorry, but they've got to learn. I know their mother ran round after them like a slave, but I'm not prepared to.' And she got into the driver's seat and zoomed off.

Matt said crossly to Toby, 'Now look what you've done, dickhead! We'll be late now! The bus takes ages!'

I'd never felt much for either of them till then, but

once I saw Toby's face I felt awful. His lip was trembling as he went back into the house. He suddenly looked like a little kid whose world's just fallen apart. And I thought, they *are* kids. Only twelve.

I said to Matt, 'Look, I'll run you to school, if you like.'

He suddenly looked very young, too. 'You'll be late for work.'

I couldn't believe he'd even thought of it. 'Not much. It won't matter.'

Toby came back, stuffing a towel messily into a plastic bag. Matt said, 'Harriet's going to take us, dickhead. Get in, quick.'

The traffic was dreadful, as usual on a Monday morning. They sat in the back, not uttering, but after a few minutes I could have sworn I heard muffled sniffs. I looked in the mirror and saw Toby wiping his eyes on the sleeve of his blazer. Matt hissed, 'Shut – up!' but so quietly it was easy to pretend I hadn't heard.

While stopping at the fourth set of lights I said casually, 'Apart from this morning, how are you getting on with Francesca?'

'OK,' said Matt, in dull tones.

Toby said nothing, but I heard him sniffing. A hundred yards further on, though, he said in a wobbly voice, 'I wish Mummy would come back.'

Something in me dissolved. I'd never heard him call her Mummy before.

'Well, she won't, will she?' Matt said. To me he added, 'Dad says it's our fault she left. He said we treated her like a doormat.'

Bastard, I thought, changing viciously into third.

'I wouldn't treat her like a doormat if she came back,' Toby said tearfully. 'I'd make her cups of tea and tidy my room and everything.'

'Well, she won't,' Matt said doggedly, but some tiny timbre in his voice told me it was only a cover. He was just tougher than Toby. He refused to show how he felt.

On the point of saying, 'She might, if you asked her,' I bit it back.

When I dropped them off, Toby said, 'Thank you very much,' and Matt said, 'Thanks. I appreciate it,' in a trying-to-be-cool manner that might have made me laugh inside if their faces hadn't been so wan. 'Have a good day,' I smiled, and drove off.

I was late for work, of course, but it was just tough. It occurred to me as I walked in the door that I'd had enough of this place, anyway. Although I liked Lesley I couldn't take much more of her attitude to Solutions Software types who wanted bubbly long legs. I made a mental note to buy a paper later, scour the Appointments pages. One of those big recruitment companies, perhaps, who left data-entry and receptionist stuff to people like us.

Not that jobs were the main thing on my mind. At

478

lunchtime I phoned Helen. 'How did your party go?' I asked first.

'Quite well, actually,' she said, sounding almost bushy-tailed. 'Everybody loved my smoked salmon roulade. One of the guests even asked if I'd like to do her mother's eightieth birthday. I shall have to move out of Felicity's place, though, if I'm going to do it seriously. She's only got a little freezer and not much fridge space, either.'

I thought of her acres of Smallbone kitchen at home, of her cubic miles of fridge and freezer. 'I saw the twins this morning,' I said.

Her voice changed at once. 'How were they?'

I got off the phone ten minutes later feeling emotionally challenged, but knowing I'd done the right thing. What was the point of making points, of striking blows, if she was never going to be properly happy?

I told Jess and Sandie afterwards. They already knew the Helen saga. I didn't tell them everything, but I'd told them that.

'She was crying her eyes out,' I said. 'She's going to ring Lawrence and say she's going back.'

All afternoon I got steadily more sick with nerves over ringing John that evening, but it was easy to put it off. For a start, I had to ask Sally about her day. It hadn't gone badly. Quite a nice class, but as usual there were some who never stopped talking and others too shy to open their mouths. She'd had to phone the childminder three times to check on Tom, of course, she was in such a tizz in case he was crying himself sick, but the woman had soothed that he was fine; he'd cried a bit, but no more than the average.

Then she peered at my chin. 'I can hardly see your mountain any more. If you don't phone him tonight, I'll kill you. Jacko phoned earlier, too. He said to tell you if you don't get off your bum and do it, he'll make a Snowflake 1990 website with some pictures he's got.'

'He hasn't still got those?' I gaped.

'What pictures, anyway?' she demanded. 'He wouldn't tell me, the bugger.'

Blackmail, now. 'It was the Snowflake Christmas Ball. He bet me ten quid I wouldn't take my top off and dance on the table, and I was pissed and broke enough to do it. It wasn't just me!' I added. 'There were three of us, and the other two made me look like Titless Wonder of the year. I wanted to kill myself once I'd sobered up.'

After exploding she said, 'Now will you please get on that phone?'

I had another delay tactic ready: namely, Helen. So by the time we'd post-mortemed her as well, it was gone seven.

By then even I didn't want to put it off any more. I couldn't stand this sick tension any longer.

He answered after only three rings. 'Mackenzie,' he said crisply.

I felt as if I were about to cut my own leg off. It was going to be agony, but I had to do it or it'd kill me. 'John, it's me,' I said, like an idiot. 'Harriet, I mean. Please don't hang up – I really need to talk to—'

'Harriet, I'm sorry, but I can't do with any—'

'*Please*, just listen a minute! I know you're probably thinking I need a shrink and I can't blame you, but I didn't mean what I said the other day, *please* don't hang up – I know it sounds really stupid but there were all sorts of complications I didn't tell you – I knew Nina, you see – I know I should have told you before but I thought you'd think I was an idiot – Oh God, this is awful . . .'

After a pause for breath I went on in a gabbly rush, 'I really can't tell you over the phone, it's all so tortuously involved – you couldn't come round, could you – no, don't, I shouldn't even ask – I could come to you – I could come right this minute if you're not tied up . . .'

There was a short, agonizing silence.

'I'm afraid that's not going to be possible.'

# SEVENTEEN

That was it. The leg was off, I was about to die of agony and loss of blood, just let me crawl away and do it quickly. 'No, of course, not,' I gabbled. 'I'm really sorry for bothering—'

'Harriet—'

'No, it's all right, honestly, we'll leave it there, I knew I should never have phoned, it was very nice and all that, in fact it was lovely, but—'

'Harriet, will you listen to me? When I said it wasn't possible, I meant not possible. I'm in Prague.'

I hung up ten minutes later, in a jelly-splatted daze.

Sally was grinning all over her face. 'He told you to sod off, then.'

It *was* possible, after all. 'I can't believe it! I thought he was joking when he told me to come! Only he said I'd have to get my skates on, he wasn't sure what time the last flight leaves.'

'What about work, tomorrow?'

'Stuff work – everybody else takes sickies.' Suddenly I was in action-stations overdrive. 'Right, get moving, Harriet – could you call a taxi while I phone Heathrow – see if there's a flight I can make – God, where the hell did I put my passport – have a look in my bedside drawer, will you, and get those clean tights out of the airing cupboard – where the hell are the Yellow Pages – he said BA or Midland – you couldn't grab my pink jumper out of that pile in my room and give it a quick iron, could you – I've got to phone him back – God, I probably won't even have time for a shower!'

If I didn't make *The Guinness Book of Records* that night, I demand to know why. Checking airlines, fuming through recorded messages telling me to press one for reservations, slinging things in a bag, locating passport that should have been in bedside drawer but wasn't, phoning man of seventeenth-heaven dreams back to say I should be on the twenty-one fifteen with a bit of luck, frantic ablutions of underarms, no time for ditto of teeth but could do this on plane, momentary panic on realizing I had hardly any cash for taxi, cessation of panic as Sally pointed out possibility of stopping at hole in wall on way, further panic as taxi crawled in traffic – what if flight closed just as I got there?

Add to this charging like demented madwoman through terminal looking for right airline desk, cursing everyone in way, especially profoundly irritating old fart ahead of me at ticket desk, wittering on about non-availability of over-wing exit seat with leg-room, agonies while girl tapped keyboard with frown, assuming frown meant there was no seat after all, some loathsome bastard with corporate Platinum

Executive Club Card had pipped me to last seat, further panic over credit card, what if plastic fraudster had got hold of number and spent me over the limit? Subsequently rushing to shop with boarding card in teeth to buy deodorant as realized had forgotten to apply or pack any, abluted underarms therefore probably smelly again already, especially after charging like further demented madwoman to gate, as departure board flashed 'last call' . . .

Phew. It invariably happened. You break Olympic and possibly entire solar system records and find nine shuffling people ahead of you.

While I still could, I phoned man of seventeenth-heaven dreams. 'Just made it. I'm on.'

'I'll be there.'

'May I see your ticket, please?'

I gave the chap such a radiantly dopey smile, I wouldn't mind betting he radioed the captain: *'Ground to Yankee Foxtrot, possible nutter boarding, heading for 17D. Could be drunk or just loony – you'd better alert the cabin crew.'*

I boarded in a radiant, dopey daze. I didn't even curse those people who in normal circumstances I'd like to have taken out on the tarmac and shot, i.e. the ones who block the aisle for five minutes while they fussily stow fourteen pieces of hand baggage.

I love take-off. I love that bit as they turn onto the runway. I love the bit when they stop, rev their engines to screaming pitch and take the brakes off.

484

I love that G-force speed that rams you back into your seat.

There was no celestial blue to climb into, of course, no fluffy bouncy castle, but I didn't care. All the way I gazed down at the blanket of European night, cities dotted like gold fairy lights in the darkness, and felt sorry for everyone else in the entire universe, because they couldn't possibly be as happy as me.

He was there as I came out of customs. He wore a dark grey overcoat and a smile that made my heart turn over.

Like an idiot, I almost felt like crying. 'Are you sure you haven't changed your mind? Do you still want a lunatic, screwed-up prat like—'

I was hoping he'd shut me up like that. Mouth-to-mouth silencing is invariably the most effective, but it couldn't get over-steamy while we were in a public place.

Taking my arm, he whisked me to the exit. 'You could do with those thermals after all. It's brass-monkey stuff outside.'

It was, too. Sub-zero, diamond-frost stuff, sparkling wherever light shone.

There was snow, too: the real thing, not that poor relation that melts by morning.

He had a car waiting, with a driver who'd kept the heater on.

We sat close together in the back. As the driver moved off, he took my hand. It reminded me of that other night in the cab, except that so much had changed. Just like before, he gave it a minute caress with his thumb. 'Your hand's not cold now,' he said.

So then I knew he was thinking of that night, too, and how I'd gone cold on him, and how I'd done it again, only so much worse. 'That's because I got my thermostat fixed.' I hesitated, but had to ask. 'Did you think I was a complete bitch?'

It was a moment before he answered. 'I thought maybe you'd had some crushing experience that made you want to dish out exactly the same to the first likely-looking bastard who looked as if he needed his ego squashed.'

A bitch, then. I felt awful.

'Before that, I just thought you might have some-one else,' he went on. 'It seemed like a possible sudden attack of guilty conscience.'

Well, it was.

'I even thought it might be Tara's brother,' he went on. 'She said something to that effect. I thought you might be wavering between two options.'

'It was never me Jacko had designs on.' But I wasn't going into all that now. 'I thought it was you who had another option, that's all.'

It was another moment before he replied. 'Is Nina a friend of yours?'

I hadn't gone into detail over the phone, just the blurted-out basics. 'Not exactly. We were at school together. I hadn't seen her for years. I know it sounds pathetic, but that first day I met you I was hiding, praying she wouldn't see me.'

'Why?'

'She used to make me feel a mess. Badly put together. Like a Friday-night job, with bits falling off. And even then, in Covent Garden, she still did.'

In the dark taxi, his eyes were unfathomable. 'Go on.'

So I went. It was such a relief to get it out at last. I told him everything: Stuart, Rosie, and every garbled bit of gossip I'd misinterpreted so spectacularly. I told him about Jon, the private dick and going to see Nina and feeling sick.

Eventually I said, 'Had you any idea she was seeing someone else?'

'No, but it doesn't altogether surprise me.' After a pause he added, 'What did she say about me?'

Just as a nasty little green snake was about to worm its way back into my stomach, it evaporated. His mouth was definitely quivering. Only a bit, but it was. 'What?' I said.

'You first.' This time the quiver was more obvious. 'What did she say? She did say something, I take it?'

'Well . . .' I mean, how did you say it?

'Go on,' he said, squeezing my hand. 'I need to know. However much it hurts.'

I knew he was laughing now, if only on the inside.

And although my relief was profound, I didn't get it, whatever there was to get. 'John, *what?*'

'Hang on, we're here. We'll just drop your bag . . .'

The taxi pulled in at a hotel. John paid the driver and we went inside. It was one of those gracious old buildings that might have been a stinking rich merchant's house back in Mozart's day. It breathed atmosphere and quiet charm.

He left my bag at the desk. 'Have you eaten?'

'Yes, on the plane – what were you going to say?'

'Nothing. You have to tell me what she said first. I need to know,' he went on, in mock-anguished tones. 'But I need fortification before I hear the worst. The Old Town Square's only round the corner.'

I don't know when I'd been so dying for light to be shed, but I knew he was going to make me wait. After the hotel's warmth, it felt colder than ever outside. My coat was fine for London, but it didn't button right up. 'I should have brought a scarf,' I said, shivering slightly. 'I didn't think.'

He stopped, whipped out a scarf that was tucked inside his coat.

'No!' I protested, but he just told me to shut up and put it round my neck.

It was only a couple of minutes over cobbled streets to the Stare Mesto: the Old Town Square. On the way I told him I'd been before, a few years ago, but it had been summer, the square filled with people sitting at café tables and crowds milling round the medieval clock, where Death and Justice popped out on the half-hour, to be photographed by tourists.

It was not only midwinter now, but late. There were few people scurrying in the cold. We ended up in a typically Czech café bar, the type where you can get everything from apple dumplings to schnapps, with someone playing the violin. We went downstairs, to the even cosier cellar, and found a quiet little corner.

He ordered a beer; I ordered a coffee and a schnapps chaser. Schnapps reminded me of après-ski in Austria, hilarious evenings playing silly games in cellar bars, flirting with whichever gorgeous Klaus or Jurgen had been telling you all morning your parallel turns were rubbish.

But none of them had been a patch on the gorgeous John sitting with me now. After a mouthful of best Pilsner, he said, 'Right, my upper lip is stiffened. Massacre my self-esteem and tell me what she said.'

His mouth was barely quivering, but there was a wicked glint in his eyes. To be honest, I don't know how I didn't leap across the table and devour him right there. 'I'm afraid she said you weren't quite up to the mark,' I said plaintively. 'I'm dreadfully sorry.'

His mouth quivered a fraction more. 'Is that it?'

'Well, not quite. She said you were "quite sweet", but you'd never have done.'

'Dear me,' he tutted. 'I don't know how I'm ever going to get over this.'

I could contain myself no longer. 'John, if you don't tell me this minute –'

'All right, all right. I'm afraid I was a bit of a naughty boy.'

I was bursting to laugh. It was the combination of that lethally wicked glint and the mock-apologetic tones he used. 'Only a bit?'

'Well, more than a bit. You might say I was a thoroughly devious bastard. All right, all right,' he went on, seeing me about to burst. 'I met her at a wedding in Scotland. In fact I met her at check-in, on the way up. We sat together on the plane, shared a cab to the hotel, the whole bit. She joined me for breakfast the next morning; we were thrown together for the entire weekend.'

He paused. 'We were on the same plane home, so it was a repeat performance. She talked virtually all the way. And I listened, as you do. You talk back a bit. You take an interest. You try to look impressed when she starts name-dropping, scattering them like Lucy's budgie used to scatter his seed all over the kitchen. You smile.' He paused again. 'But the trouble is, you do it too bloody well.'

At last, I was beginning to get it.

'It had never occurred to her that I wasn't interested,' he went on. 'It occurred to me afterwards that it would never occur to her that anyone wouldn't be interested. She took it as read, more or less. So by the time I was yanking her bag off the carousel, she

490

was talking about lunch. And before we'd hit the taxi rank, she'd suggested a time and a place.'

'And you didn't like to say no?'

His eyebrows gave a wry little lift. 'It seemed slightly brutal.'

I hope no-one'll think I'm a cow for wishing he had.

'After that weekend, I already felt as if I'd been seeing her for a fortnight,' he went on. 'But I thought maybe it was my fault, for somehow giving her the wrong idea. By the end of that lunch, though, I knew I was going to have to be either brutal or devious.'

Devious, then. I still wished he'd told her to sod off, but there you go.

'I said dinner, this time,' he continued. 'I suggested a time and a place and said I'd pick her up.'

I waited, half expecting something on the lines of cheap, awful clothes, drunkenness and crude jokes, or loud belching in smart restaurants.

'I thought I had her sussed by then,' he went on. 'So I borrowed Lucy's car.'

Light was beginning to dawn. 'A beat-up old wreck?'

He shook his head. 'That would have been over-doing it. It's just a bog-standard Ford, getting on a bit, with ninety thousand on the clock and a few rattles.'

I suppose I'd never consciously worked it out, but he couldn't have dreamt up anything much better. Nina's main ambition, once, had been to have a boy-friend with a Ferrari. She'd once chucked someone for someone else, because he had a better car. The boy she chucked was nicer than the other, but she hadn't been able to resist the allure of 1250 cc of shiny new Golf, or whatever it was. I doubted that she'd changed very much. A moderately flash car would be even more essential than the requisite assortment of dangly bits.

'What did she say?'

'Nothing, at first. She just looked. But once we were moving, she said, "Is this your car?" I said oh, yes, I didn't believe in wasting money on fancy wheels when they only got nicked.'

'What did she say to that?'

'Nothing. And that was when I got the wind up and took it a bit further. Even before parking the car I started telling her I'd been suffering from stress. I was thinking of jacking my job in. I was even thinking of buying a smallholding in Wales and keeping goats.'

I nearly choked on my schnapps.

'I did wonder whether I'd gone a bit far here,' he went on, in wicked tones. 'But I must be a better fake than I give myself credit for. Even before we got out of the car I felt her freezing round the edges, but I didn't want to overdo it. I didn't mention it again till we were leaving the restaurant, but then I said I'd just had particulars of a couple of smallholdings. I said I was going down at the weekend to look at them, and I'd really love her to come along.'

By now I was giggling helplessly. 'You wicked, devious bastard . . .'

'Yes, I was pretty pleased with it myself,' he agreed. 'Particularly when it worked. She said brightly that she was actually tied up at the weekend – what a shame – but it was a lovely dinner, thanks a lot, maybe she'd give me a call sometime. Oh, and I really mustn't bother dropping her home – it was right out of my way – she'd take a cab. So I stood on a bloody freezing pavement for five minutes, finding her one.'

'I bet you paid her fare, too.'

'I did try,' he said, with a nobly heroic air that lasted only half a second. 'But not very hard.'

Once I was over the worst throes of laughter, he ordered me another schnapps. The first had gone down very well, sending liquid warmth to every extremity I possessed. Not that they needed much help.

'So that was your first official date, then,' I said. 'Just before we collided in front of old Wooden Wally.'

He nodded. 'And there I was, already formulating my Devious Plan even as her taxi shot off, and thinking I might go and take a proper look at Wally, as I'd noticed him a couple of hours earlier, when I saw this woman.'

Here he paused, shaking his head. 'She's been a sad trial to me, I can tell you.'

I was doing my best not to laugh. 'That'll teach you

to pick women up on pavements. Especially shameless trollops who pretend they've lost their purses so they can have a drink with you.'

'Disgraceful,' he tutted, but his eyes were glinting so wickedly I had to lean across the table and kiss him.

It was snowing softly as we eventually left the bar and walked across the Old Town Square. I told him about the witch and Planet Zog, and he laughed. I told him about the bog-roll dinosaur and he laughed some more, but differently. We stopped to look up at the twin gothic spires of the Tyn church, covered with new snowfall, and I said it was like fairyland, they reminded me of the Disneyland Castle, old Walt must have got his inspiration here. And he brushed a snowflake from my cheek and kissed me, and I knew exactly how old Walt's Cinderella felt when she found her prince. And then he said as we couldn't get much colder we might as well carry on to the Charles Bridge and do it properly. So pressed up together we walked to the bridge in the snow, and gazed down the river at all the bridges in the snowy lamplight, and back at the Old Town, all its fairyland roofs and spires white with new snow, and he said he'd never feel quite the same about snow again, and kissed me. Well, I kissed him too, naturally; I wouldn't want you to think I was standing there like some passive, dopey wimpette. But this time there was hardly anyone about, and even if

494

there had been we wouldn't have cared, so if any old Prague ghosts were shocked by twenty-first century lack of decorum, I apologize to them now.

By the time we arrived back at the hotel I was thoroughly warmed up, if you know what I mean. On the surface, however, I was still chilly. So as he put his key in the door I said, 'I might warm up in the shower. I didn't have time before I left.'

He closed the door behind us, tossed his key on the bed. 'Maybe I should join you. Foreign showers can be awkward little cusses – I could come and twiddle the knobs for you.'

Nothing of the kind had even occurred to me, of course. 'I think I can manage cussy foreign showers, but I am just a wee bit shattered. Some help in getting my clothes off wouldn't come amiss.'

For the umpteenth time since I'd met him, the wicked little candle that danced behind his eyes turned me to melting jelly. 'Your slightest wish is my command. Come here.'

I have to say, I've never had such wonderful room service in my life. Nor such an unbelievably thorough shower, bits I never even knew I had soaped to lazy perfection. I returned the favour, of course, and I think I can safely say that no lovely smut and filth was ever cleaner. It was just as well the bath had those non-slip things, though, otherwise he might have come a cropper hitching me up for the finale with my legs wrapped around him. I think I hung onto the shower curtain too, so I'm surprised I didn't yank the whole thing down.

Wrapped in fluffy towels we lay afterwards on the bed, talking delicious post-coital rubbish, laughing as we watched *Tom and Jerry* and eating chocolate from the minibar. Seeing the time, I said, 'Haven't you got to get up in the morning?' and he said, 'Yes, but I'll worry about that when I come to it.'

I don't know what time we eventually cuddled up between beautiful crisp sheets, but just as I was drifting off I felt a sleepy chuckle vibrate his chest.

'What?' I murmured.

'Nothing, my little bog-roll dinosaur. Go to sleep.'

I nearly was. 'This time, wake me up before you go.'

I sold the house in early April, to the second couple who came to look at it. I bought a lovely garden flat a couple of miles further into town. It had to be a garden flat for poor old Widdles; he might spend twenty-three and a half hours every day curled up on the sofa, but he needed his little constitutional. Besides, as Rosie had said, it was great for barbies in the summer. Rosie found a nice flat eventually and is out non-stop, but I still see her. She rarely sees Suzanne any more. It was a mite fraught after all the spilt gossip came out, but Suzanne had the grace to admit that she could hardly blame Rosie for passing on confidences when she'd done exactly the same herself.

I changed jobs around the same time as moving, so it was a hectic period. I went to one of the multinational recruitment companies, so my mother is very pleased that she'll be able to swank in her next Christmas letters to ex-neighbours at ex-home that I now have a really good job, which is mother-speak for 'earning at least as much as your wretched daughter, so suck on that.'

Tara did a computer-skills course for a month, went temping till July, and actually saved enough money to go to Greece with a friend. She started at that A-level crammer in September. Jacko said she's doing all right so far, but she'd better, because it's costing his folks a bomb. She phoned me, back in January, to say she was very sorry for giving me and John all that trouble. I had a feeling the call was partly prompted by her mother, but I wasn't complaining.

Helen has a little blue van with Cooking to Go painted on the side, and it goes quite a lot. Whenever I see her, which is not so often since I moved, she's up to her elbows in filo pastry or whatever, and has long since stopped running around after the twins, because she just doesn't have time. She didn't go back like a meek little worm, though. She told Lawrence she wasn't prepared to move out of her home. He might have paid for it all, but the thought and planning, the colour schemes, the renovations, everything that had gone to make it a lovely home, were down to her own creativity. She wasn't prepared to sacrifice it. If he and Francesca wanted something better than a doll's house, that was their problem. And Lawrence was so relieved she was going back, he barely argued.

She carried on seeing her man from the train for a couple of months (he was called Ian) but then he got transferred to Frankfurt and it sort of died the death. He did her a colossal service though, by making her realize just what she was capable of, and I don't mean hotel rooms. She recently mentioned some other chap, whom she met at some fortieth birthday party bash. He was called Philip, she said; he loved her Stilton-and-celery nibbles. As I said to Sally, no bloke she meets at these do's will ever be short of a chat-up line. He only has to say he loves her raspberry thingummies and he's away.

Exactly as planned, Sally went home to her folks at Easter. She stayed until mid-July, by which time it wasn't so much a case of them driving her crackers as Tom driving them. He was toddling by then, into everything, grabbing everything he could reach, and they had lots of those little tables with fragile knick-knacks all over them. (*No, I'm not putting them away, he has to learn what "no" means.*') As he was also constantly trying to climb everything both grandparents were constantly agitated in case he fell and fractured his skull. Then Grandmother was also constantly agitated about germs, getting cold, getting hot, sharp objects, dogs, cats (germs again), the unsuitable children he

498

might eventually meet at the wrong kind of school, woodlice going in his mouth, daisies ditto, the fact that he'd probably experiment with drugs when he was at university, and the fact that he wasn't yet potty-trained at thirteen months.

All of which had soon turned Sally into a nervous wreck, too.

So eventually, after Jacko had asked her forty-eight times to move in with him and save him coming to fetch her every weekend, and she'd said forty-eight times that she wouldn't until she was earning a proper salary, she did. It meant kissing goodbye to her place at that college, but she managed to get another through clearing at a college in Liverpool. She started at the end of September and is enjoying it so far. Jacko's like a proud parent every time she gets an A for her assignments, and Sally's relaxed again, because Jacko hasn't got any knick-knacks and even if he had he wouldn't care if Tom broke the lot. She still calls him Ape-Face now and then so I hope she won't forget herself and say, 'I take thee, Ape-Face,' when they get married next March, because I'm going to be best woman. It has to be in church because her mother said it wouldn't be a 'proper' wedding otherwise, and Sally said what the hell.

Steve did come back. It wasn't the cosiest of meetings at first, but they parted on reasonably civil terms. There was talk of finance and visiting but since he's got a job in Hong Kong now it's hardly going to be on a weekly basis, so I don't know how that's going to pan out. Tom adores Jacko, anyway. And as Sally says, it's the one who gallops round the kitchen at six thirty in the morning, giving 'horsey' shoulder rides, who counts.

Dad and Kathy bought their house in Cyprus, in a pretty little place called Pissouri. They're planning to spend half the year there and the other half back home. Both their UK houses are on the market; they're going to get something else that's 'theirs'. Dad's learning modern Greek now. Kathy said it was a hoot when he tried to talk to the locals in the ancient version, but they were terribly polite and nobody laughed.

I saw Nina again towards the end of September. It was a beautiful, breezy, golden day, around eleven on a Saturday morning. Off to see my mother, I'd just bought a bunch of flowers and a packet of Polos at a petrol station a couple of miles down the road when I saw her going in to pay.

'Harriet!' she said, looking taken aback.

'Nina! Hello again.'

There was a moment's awkwardness, but she broke it. 'Been somewhere nice?' she asked, looking me up and down.

I was wearing pink shorts, sandals, and a little white top. And the reason she asked was because I had a lovely golden tan, with sun-glints in my hair.

'Very nice, actually,' I said, holding my breeze-blown hair with one hand. 'Sailing round the British Virgin Islands.'

'Really?' she said, with a smile that had suddenly gone slightly tighter than it was already. 'I thought the weather in the Caribbean could be iffy at this time of year.'

'It can, but we were very lucky. It was gorgeous.'

The breeze was still blowing my hair. I was glad of this, because it allowed me to carry on holding it back with my left hand. I knew she'd notice and I don't mind admitting I wanted her to. Ninas always notice such things. Like a homing missile her eyes zoomed in on my finger. 'Are you engaged?' she asked, as if I'd just had a sex-change or something.

'Well, I suppose I am,' I admitted, holding my hand out for her inspection. 'I always thought getting engaged was a pathetic waste of time, but when you're moored in a perfect little harbour at sunset and someone suddenly produces something like this, you don't like to tell him to take it back to the shop.'

She gave another tight little smile. 'Very nice.'

I was almost expecting her to add, 'Is it real?' but she didn't go that far. It was a square-cut emerald, surrounded by diamonds that nearly knocked you out when the sun caught them.

'So who's the lucky man?' she went on, just as John came from paying for a tank of fuel.

'You've met him,' I said, but she'd already twigged.

I have to say he looked absolutely gorgeous. He was wearing shorts, too, and a half-open shirt. He was browner than me, and his eyes looked just like the Caribbean in those deeper-water bits, glinting bluey-green in the sun. Or greeny-blue, I can never make up my mind which. He looked like the more upmarket sort of pirate, a fact which had occurred to me while we'd been swimming off some gorgeous Treasure Island beach.

Anyway. He behaved with perfect aplomb. He said, 'Nina, good Lord!' in an entirely agreeable fashion, and shook her hand. 'How's it going?'

'Very well, thank you. And congratulations.'

'I'm taking him to meet my mother,' I said. 'I thought it was about time.'

'Yes, and we'd better get a move on,' he said. 'Lovely to see you, Nina. Take care. Hop in, Harriet.'

He opened the passenger door of the car, which was only about six feet from where I was standing with Nina. The hood was down and he'd had it cleaned the day before, so it was all nice and shiny dark green.

She didn't quite gape, because Ninas never do, but she got as near as dammit. 'Is that yours?' she said to John.

'I hope so,' he said, half laughing. 'Unless I nicked it in my sleep.' Suddenly he pretended to catch on. 'Oh, the other one, you mean. Well, I thought it was about time I got some respectable wheels. Harriet said she couldn't have that thing lowering the tone outside her new flat.'

She gave a silver-bells little peal, but the silver sounded definitely plated to me. And crappy old plate, at that. 'What about the goats?' she asked.

'*Goats?*' I gave him an askance look. 'What goats?'

'Oh, that,' he said wryly. 'It was just a bad patch. I had plans for a rustic idyll. I soon changed my mind when I went to look at a couple of rustic idylls. Nothing but mud and muck for miles.'

I looked at Nina, raising my eyes to heaven. 'Honestly. This is the first I've heard of it.'

'Well, you won't hear it again,' he said. 'Hop in – someone's waiting for that pump.'

So I hopped. I said, 'Bye bye then,' and smiled at her as we drove off in the sunny breeze.

For half a mile neither John nor I uttered a word. We didn't even look at each other. I didn't dare look at him because I knew we'd both crack up, and the traffic was too heavy to risk terminal cracking-up and possible loss of control.

Eventually, though, I said, 'Stop it.'

'Stop what?' he said, deadpan.

'Laughing. It's not very nice.'

'I know it's not very nice,' he said. 'That's why I'm not doing it.'

'Yes, you are,' I said, suppressing my own eruptions. 'I can always tell. You won't be laughing in a few hours, when my mother's showing you hundreds of photos of when I was two and seven and eleven, and making you wonder what the hell you're letting yourself in for.'

'I know what I'm letting myself in for, my little bog-roll dinosaur.'

Call me soppy, but it still made me go gooey every time he said that. It's amazing what can turn into a term of endearment, and as for that 'little' . . . I'd have killed him if he'd ever said it in public, of course, but it was strictly between us. I sometimes called him Tyrannosaurus, too, but only when he was about to devour me, so don't tell anybody.

At the lights he leaned over and kissed me. 'The sun, an open top and thou,' he said. 'What more could anyone ask?'

'How about a Polo?' I popped one in his mouth.

Except for lack of snow, it couldn't have been a lovelier day.